## "I SWEAR, SIMON, IF YOU PAINT A PICTURE OF ME FROM THE REAR I WILL NEVER FORGIVE YOU."

Simon gave Molly a smile and said, "I'd like to see your butt in those lacy La Perla panties. Even better would be to see your butt without any panties at all."

She scowled at him. "Those weren't my panties. And are you coming on to me?"

He chuckled. "Don't lie. Those were your panties. And maybe I am coming on to you. Because you're beautiful. One day I'd love to paint you..." He hesitated.

She finished his thought. "Naked? You want to paint me naked? Oh my God." She got up and stalked away toward her fishing gear.

"You'd be lovely. Backside and all..."

# Praise for Hope Ramsay's
# Heartwarming Series

### *Last Chance Book Club*

"4½ stars! [A] first-class romance, with compelling characters and a real sense of location—the town is practically a character on its own. This entry is sure to keep Ramsay's fan base growing."   —*RT Book Reviews*

"The ladies of the Last Chance Book Club keep the gossip flowing in this story graced with abundant Southern Charm and quirky, caring people. Another welcome chapter to Ramsay's engaging, funny, hope-filled series."
—*Library Journal*

"I love this story . . . Southern charm at its funniest."
—FreshFiction.com

"Last Chance is a place we've come to know as well as we know our own home towns. It's become real, filled with people who could be our aunts, uncles, cousins, friends, or the crazy cat-lady down the street. It's familiar, comfortable, welcoming."

—RubySlipperedSisterhood.com

"Hope Ramsay heats up romance to such a degree every reader will be looking for a nice, cool glass of sweet tea to cool off."
—The Reading Reviewer (MaryGramlich.blogspot.com)

## Last Chance Christmas

"4 stars! Ramsay's romance packs just enough heat in this holiday-inspired story, with lead characters who will induce both belly laughs and smiles. Her hero and heroine are in for rough times, but their heartache and longing had me longing right along with them."

—*RT Book Reviews*

"A captivating tale."

—RomRevToday.com

"Amazing...These lovely folks filled with Southern charm [and] gossip were such fun to get to know...This story spoke to me on so many levels about faith, strength, courage, and choices...If you're looking for a good Christmas story with a few angels, then *Last Chance Christmas* is a must read. For fans of Susan Wigg."

—TheSeasonforRomance.com

"Visiting Last Chance is always a joy, but Hope Ramsay has outdone herself this time. She took a difficult hero, a wounded heroine, familiar characters, added a little Christmas magic, and—Voila!—gave us a story sure to touch the Scroogiest of hearts...It draws us back to a painful time when tensions—and prejudices—ran deep, compels us to remember and forgive, and reminds us that healing, redemption, and love are the true gifts of Christmas."

—RubySlipperedSisterhood.com

*Last Chance Beauty Queen*

"4½ stars! Get ready for a story to remember when Ramsay spins this spirited contemporary tale. If the y'alls don't enchant you, the fast-paced, easy read will. The third installment in the Last Chance series is filled with characters that define eccentric, off the wall, and bonkers, but most of all they're enchantingly funny and heartwarmingly charming." —*RT Book Reviews*

"Hope Ramsay has penned an irresistible tale in *Last Chance Beauty Queen* with its unforgettable characters and laugh out loud scenes…Watch how an opposites-attract couple find their way to each other…and a possible future. Grab this today and get ready for a rollicking read." —RomRevToday.com

"A little Bridget Jones meets Sweet Home Alabama." —GrafWV.com

*Home at Last Chance*

"4 stars! Nicely told." —*RT Book Reviews*

"Entertaining…Readers will feel once again the warm 'Welcome to Last Chance' by the quirky Ladies' Auxiliary crew…Contemporary fans will enjoy the homespun regional race to the finish line." —GenreGoRoundReviews.blogspot.com

"An enjoyable ride that will capture interest and hold it to the very end."

—RomRevToday.blogspot.com

"Full of small town charm and southern hospitality... You will want to grab a copy of *Welcome to Last Chance* as well."

—TopRomanceNovels.com

## *Welcome to Last Chance*

"Ramsay's delicious contemporary debut introduces the town of Last Chance, SC, and its warmhearted inhabitants... [she] strikes an excellent balance between tension and humor as she spins a fine yarn."

—*Publishers Weekly* (starred review)

"[A] charming series, featuring quirky characters you won't soon forget."

—Barbara Freethy, *USA Today* bestselling author of *At Hidden Falls*

"Full of small-town charm and southern heat... humorous, heartwarming, and sexy. I couldn't put it down!"

—Robin Wells, author of *Still the One*

"A sweet confection... This first of a projected series about the Rhodes brothers offers up Southern hospitality with a bit of grit. Romance readers will be delighted."

—*Library Journal*

# ~LAST~
# CHANCE
## *Knit & Stitch*

## Also by Hope Ramsay

# ~LAST~ CHANCE
## Knit & Stitch

# HOPE RAMSAY

FOREVER

NEW YORK   BOSTON

Forever
Hachette Book Group
1290 Avenue of the Americas
New York, NY 10104

www.HachetteBookGroup.com

Printed in the United States of America

First Edition: November 2013
10 9 8 7 6 5 4

OPM

Forever is an imprint of Grand Central Publishing.
The Forever name and logo are trademarks of Hachette Book Group, Inc.

The Hachette Speakers Bureau provides a wide range of authors for speaking events. To find out more, go to www.hachettespeakersbureau.com or call (866) 376-6591.

The publisher is not responsible for websites (or their content) that are not owned by the publisher.

**ATTENTION CORPORATIONS AND ORGANIZATIONS:**
Most HACHETTE BOOK GROUP books are available at quantity discounts with bulk purchase for educational, business, or sales promotional use. For information, please call or write:
**Special Markets Department, Hachette Book Group**
**1290 Avenue of the Americas, New York, NY 10104**
**Telephone: 1-800-222-6747  Fax: 1-800-477-5925**

*For Mom, who loved to knit*

# Acknowledgments

Every author has a few people who make writing a book possible. I would like to give my deepest thanks to my knitting buddies Carla Kempert and Laura Graham Booth, who are relentless enablers of my yarn addiction and who were very helpful in coming up with a list of disasters that a toddler might unleash in a yarn shop. To my critique partner Robin Kaye, many thanks for a wonderful afternoon at Starbucks brainstorming this book's plot; I do not think I have laughed that hard in a long time. I'd like to give a nod to singer-songwriter David Wilcox for his inspirational song "Covert War," about the scars that marital strife can leave behind on children. And of course, Louisa May Alcott, for writing *Little Women* and inspiring me to want to be a writer like Jo March. As always, I could not get through writing a book without my dear husband, Bryan, my steady agent, Elaine English, and my talented editor, Alex Logan.

# ~LAST~
# CHANCE
## *Knit & Stitch*

# CHAPTER 1

Molly Canaday pulled the tow truck in front of the silver Hyundai Sonata. She killed the engine and used her side-view mirror to assess the stranded motorist.

He was not from around these parts.

For one thing, he was driving a rental car.

And for another, he was standing in the hot May sunshine wearing a black crew-necked shirt, gray dress pants, and a charcoal gray worsted sport jacket.

The sun lit up threads of gray in his dark, chin-length hair. He hadn't shaved today, but somehow the stubble looked carefully groomed.

This guy was seriously lost, like he'd made a wrong turn in Charleston and kept on driving.

She straightened her ball cap and hopped from the truck's cab. "Howdy," she said, putting out her hand for him to shake. "I'm Molly Canaday from Bill's Grease Pit. We're located in Last Chance, just down the road a ways. The rental agency sent your distress call to us. What seems to be the problem?"

Mr. I'm-so-cool-and-sexy regarded her hand, then let his gaze climb up to her battered Atlanta Braves hat, back down to her favorite Big and Rich T-shirt, ending with her baggy painter's pants. His mouth curled at the corners like a couple of ornate apostrophes. The smile was elegant and sexy, and might have impressed Molly if it hadn't also been a tiny bit smirk-like.

She forced a neutral customer-service expression to her face, even as she dropped her hand. She sure wanted to leave Mr. Urban Cool to burn up by the side of the road. Maybe walking the six miles into town in the blistering sun would help him lose that smirk.

He finally spoke in an accent that sounded like it came from nowhere. "Canaday, huh? Does Red Canaday still coach the Rebels football team?"

Whoa, this guy didn't look like your average football fan. Much less like anyone who would know anything about Davis High's football program. "Uh, yeah, he's my daddy." She studied his face, trying to place him. He had dark brown eyes and a sturdy, straight nose. He didn't look a lick like anyone Molly knew.

His steady stare sucked her in and left her feeling unsettled. If he knew about the Rebels, then he wasn't a stranger.

He wasn't lost.

"Nothing ever changes here, does it?" he said.

"Do I know you?"

Something flickered in his eyes. Was it kindness? It was there and gone in an instant. "You might remember me. I mean, I knew your father. But that was a long time ago, and you were little."

"Are you saying you're from around here?" No way.

"I'm Simon Wolfe. Charlotte and Ira's boy. I was a placekicker on the team a long time ago."

Oh. Wow. Talk about prodigal sons. She didn't really remember him. But she sure knew all about him. He had been a member of the 1990 dream team—the one that won the state championship. He was also the player who hadn't attended a single team reunion. The guy who left home, the guy who never came back, the guy who broke his daddy's heart.

And now his daddy was dead.

Two days ago, Ira Wolfe had keeled over right in the middle of his Ford dealership's showroom.

"I'm sorry for your loss," Molly said. Although Simon didn't look all that brokenhearted. In fact, he shrugged like a coldhearted idiot.

And he proved his cool nature a moment later when he said, "So Red Canaday's little girl grew up to become a mechanic. I guess that was totally predictable."

She clamped her back teeth together before she said something unlady-like. Not that she was much of a lady. Instead, she took a deep breath and tried to be *mindful* of her feelings, like Momma was always telling her to be. She sucked at being *mindful*, and she was not about to take up meditation the way Momma had.

"What seems to be the problem?" she asked in her sweetest voice, which admittedly was not very sweet. Sweet was definitely not her normal MO.

"I have no clue what's wrong with it. It stopped running," he said.

Boy, he might have been born in the South and even played football once. But he'd clearly lost his southern accent and attitude somewhere. Any local man worth his salt would have already popped the hood and taken a look. Local men would also have dozens of theories about what had gone wrong.

Not this guy. This guy spoke in short sentences, dressed like a *GQ* model, and didn't want to get dirty. Of course, he *had* been a placekicker on the team, and a good one, too. But placekickers avoided dirt. It was a well-known fact.

"Did it make any funny noises before it died?"

"Nope." He looked at his watch.

"I'm sorry. You have a wake to get to, don't you?" She didn't mention that she, also, had to get to Ira Wolfe's wake. She owed that man a great deal.

Simon turned his back on her. He walked a short distance away toward the edge of the road and put his hands on his hips. He studied the soybean fields like he was looking at some alien landscape.

"God, this place is like being nowhere at all." The words were spoken in a soft, low voice and not intended for Molly to hear. But she was just annoyed enough not to let him get away with them.

"Yeah, well, some of us like living here," she said, investing her words with all the civic pride she could muster.

She popped the hood and started poking around in the engine. "So, I take it you're not planning to stay very long." She aimed her flashlight down into the engine to check the fan belt.

"No, I have to get back to Paradise."

"Paradise? Really?" The fan belt looked okay.

"It's a place in California."

"Of course it is." He would live in a place called Paradise. She had a feeling he was about to discover that there could be hard times in Paradise, but far be it from her to be the bearer of bad news.

Instead she inspected the battery terminals and connections but didn't see anything obvious. There was probably a problem with the generator, or alternator, or maybe the voltage regulator.

She pulled her head out of the engine. "I'm going to have to tow it."

He checked his damn watch again. Boy, this guy was wound up tighter than a spring.

"Don't worry, I'll get you to the church on time. Or the funeral home, as the case might be."

Simon stifled the laugh that wanted to spring from his chest. It wasn't right to find Molly Canaday amusing on the day of his father's wake.

She helped him transfer his luggage from the Hyundai's trunk to the back of her truck. Then he stood back and watched while Coach Canaday's daughter hooked the Sonata up to a heavy chain and then winched it onto the truck's flatbed. The woman sure had a way with machinery.

Which didn't surprise him.

The last time Simon had seen Molly Canaday, she'd been a little kid in overalls, not much older than four, standing on the sidelines with Coach. She never missed a game. She never whined like other little kids. She never failed to inspire them all.

And Simon never attempted a field goal without first patting Molly's head. Her hair had been short and soft under his hands. It was longer now, but still dark and barely contained by her ball cap. He had the sudden desire to paint a portrait of her, with all that glorious hair undone and falling like a curly black waterfall to her shoulders.

"It's going to be tomorrow before we can figure out what's going on with the car. So I'll drop you by the funeral home. I'm sure Rob or Ryan Polk or one of their kids can give you a lift home from there. And you can use Ira's car. God knows he has a lot of them." Molly's words pulled him away from his suddenly wayward muse.

He climbed into the passenger's seat and checked his watch.

"So, I guess you're just counting the hours until you can leave again? Paradise is calling, huh?"

He kept his gaze fastened to the soybean fields that whizzed past as she pulled the truck onto the road and headed into town. He saw no point in responding to her question. She had summed up the truth. He needed to get back home and back to work, especially since the work hadn't been going well.

The fields gave way to houses with big yards, and then he caught his first glance of the Last Chance water tower—painted like a big, tiger-striped watermelon.

This scene was frozen in his memory. And yet, nothing was quite the same as he remembered it. A large commercial building with a big parking lot occupied what had once been cotton fields just north of town. A big sign at the gates of the facility said "deBracy Ltd." Not too far away, someone was developing a neighborhood of new single-family homes.

The Last Chance of his memory was gray and used-up and on its last legs. But in this town, bright awnings hung over the shop windows. In this town, pedestrians hurried about their business on the sidewalks. In this town, the movie theater was no longer an empty eyesore, but covered in a scaffold where workers were bringing it back to life. This town looked alive.

He wasn't prepared for the tight band that squeezed his lungs like a tourniquet, cutting off his oxygen. He refused to feel any nostalgia for this place. He'd buried a piece of himself here a long time ago, when he'd been just a boy. He'd never planned on coming back and unearthing it.

And yet, for all the pain he'd suffered here, Last Chance would always be home.


Despite her joke about being late to a funeral, Molly had no intention of being late for Ira Wolfe's wake. She had to hump to get Simon and his car delivered and then get home.

She raced through her shower, threw on a pair of slacks that weren't too wrinkled, and topped off her outfit with a gray cotton shell she'd knitted for herself using a seed stitch.

She headed into her mother's big country kitchen to collect the casserole Momma had made last night. Miz Charlotte wouldn't need too many casseroles, seeing as she probably had a housekeeper up in that big house of hers who would do her cooking and cleaning during this sad time. But still. Momma was of the opinion that when somebody died, it was a moral obligation to cook a casserole.

Molly didn't entirely share this view, mostly because she couldn't cook worth a durn.

She was just putting the mac and cheese into a grocery sack when her brother Allen sauntered into the kitchen wearing a pair of garnet and black plaid boxers and a University of South Carolina Athletic Department T-shirt. He looked like he had just rolled out of bed, even though it was four-thirty in the afternoon. He scratched his head, mussing the cowlick he'd had since he was two. "Have you seen my sunglasses?" he asked.

"Don't tell me you've already lost the Oakleys. You spent your entire paycheck on them."

"Don't be that way, Mol. I just misplaced them is all." Allen shuffled to the refrigerator, pulled out the milk carton, and took a couple of long, deep swallows that made his Adam's apple bounce.

"That is totally disgusting." Molly's voice assumed the big-sister tone that Allen had learned to ignore at a depressingly early age.

Allen wasn't very mature for twenty-three. His twin brother, Beau, on the other hand, had been born responsible. Beau had just completed his first year of law school, and he was working as an intern in the governor's office up in Columbia. Everyone reckoned that Beau had a bright future in politics.

Allen, not so much.

Allen rolled his gorgeous amber eyes and managed to look adorable even with a milk mustache. He'd always been adorable, which explained why he got away with so much.

He put the milk down on the counter and frowned. "Oh, uh, I forgot. Momma called around nine-thirty this morning with a message for you."

"Why would she do that? I had my cell phone."

"I have no idea. I was groggy, you know. It was a late night last night. Anyway, she told me to tell you that she loves you, and then she told me where I could find the message she left."

"Find the message? You mean she wrote me a note?"

"Yeah." Allen shuffled over to the little desk in the corner of the kitchen where Pat Canaday, Molly's mother, kept the household bills and her personal papers. He picked up an envelope and handed it to Molly.

Molly stared down at the white envelope bearing her name written in Momma's flowing script. This couldn't be good. The hair on the back of her neck and along her arms danced a little jig. Momma hadn't been very happy the last few months. She hadn't said much. She almost never talked about her feelings. But something was wrong. Momma had gone to town with her meditating. She'd even set up a meditation corner in the spare room.

Anyone who meditated that much must have a whole lot on her mind.

Molly's heart pounded as she tore open the envelope and read.

*Molly, darling,*

*I'm off to see the world. I would have liked to see it with your daddy, but he's gone fishing. Again. I'm not going to wait for another football season to come and go. Again. So I'm going by myself. You'll need to take care of the shop. I know you don't want to, but it will be good for you. Take care of your little brothers, too. Your daddy can obviously take care of himself.*

*Love,*
*Momma*

*P.S. You know I've been meditating about this situation. I've even tried praying about it, too. And at the moment it seems like leaving is the best thing. But just because I've failed to control my temper, doesn't mean you shouldn't keep trying to control yours. You should read my meditation book. And you can use my thinking corner if you like.*

*P. P. S. I left the book on the kitchen counter, along with my recipe box. You're going to have to learn how to cook.*

Molly blinked down at the stationery with rosebuds embellishing the edges and bottom of the page. She shifted her gaze to the kitchen counter. Sure enough, there was Momma's recipe box sitting right on top of a well-thumbed copy of *One Minute Meditations*.

"What's the note say?" Allen asked, as he pulled a jar of peanut butter from the pantry, opened it, and scooped some up with his finger.

She scowled at her brother. "Do you have any idea how gross you are?"

He shrugged like he didn't really care about her opinion. "What's it say?" he asked through the peanut butter in his mouth.

"It says she's ticked off with Coach, and she's gone to see the world."

"Momma's ticked off? Really? That's kind of interesting, isn't it?"

"I don't know, but I have a really bad feeling about this." She handed the note to her brother who proceeded to get peanut butter on it, which was more or less par for the course. Molly pulled out her cell and dialed her

mother's number. Momma's unmistakable ringtone—
Bert and Ernie singing "Rubber Ducky"—sounded from
her desk drawer. Molly opened the drawer and discovered
Momma's phone with a sticky note attached to it that said,
"You didn't think I was dumb enough to take my phone,
did you?"

Just then, the landline rang. Molly picked up the hand-
set from the old-fashioned phone bolted to the kitchen
wall. "Hey."

"Molly, is that you? It's Kenzie. I'm desperate for a
skein of carmine red alpaca, but there's a sign on the front
door of the yarn shop that says 'Closed Until Molly Real-
izes She's in Charge.' What in the world does that mean?"

Molly rested her head on the wall beside the phone
and squeezed her eyes shut. "It means my mother has run
away and expects me to fill her shoes and run the Knit &
Stitch." No doubt this was Momma's way of forcing her to
become a true southern lady—the kind who cooked casseroles, never lost her temper, and was always gracious
and polite. In short, the kind of woman who didn't have
a burning desire to fix cars or a five-year plan to open a
body shop.

"Oh, well, that's okay," Kenzie said. "You know more
about yarn than your mother does. Can you open the shop,
please? I'm desperate."

"Uh, no. Not right now. I've got to go to Ira Wolfe's
wake."

"Oh. Okay. But what about the Purly Girls meeting
tomorrow afternoon? You're going to open up for that,
right?"

Oh, brother. Molly was going to murder her mother the
next time she saw her. If there ever *was* a next time.

# CHAPTER 2

The funeral home's foyer was dark and smelled of lemon oil polish. Simon checked his baggage with the cloakroom attendant and made his way into a large room with big bay windows hung with heavy draperies. The drapes blocked all but a little crack of sunshine.

He checked his watch. After all his worry, he was half an hour early, and all alone with the guest of honor.

Daddy was stretched out in a bronze-colored coffin wearing his purple and yellow Davis High Football booster shirt. The coffin's lining was also in the school colors. Simon wondered how Mother felt about this. She had never been a big Rebels fan.

Simon stared down at the corpse, so peaceful in death. His father had been a handsome man, with piercing blue eyes and a strong chin. His eyes were closed now, and the dark hair that Simon remembered had gone to gray. Daddy's big hands were crossed on his chest, and he still wore his wedding ring.

What irony. Mother and Daddy's marriage had been

a disaster. The two of them could hardly speak without igniting an argument. And Simon had lived his life between their battle lines.

A familiar futility settled in his gut. It had taken years to learn how to recognize this feeling. And it sucked big time that he found himself unable to reason the pain away. He wanted to be numb. He wanted not to care. But instead, the wounds of his youth opened and bled.

He checked his watch again and paced the room to the window. He pulled away the drapes and stared out at a colorful garden filled with an abundance of flowers. If only he could escape to that bright place.

He wanted to get out of here. He needed to get back to his painting. The Harrison commission loomed over him like the sword of Damocles. He should never have let Gillian negotiate that deal, but he and Gillian had been in the appeasement phase of their relationship. He'd let her have a little bit of control, and then he'd realized that it was a mistake. Now Gillian was gone, and only the problematic commission remained.

"Oh my goodness, Simon, is that really you?"

He turned to discover a thin, sixty-something woman with carefully coiffed white hair and hazel eyes. She wore a simple black suit—the kind old ladies wear to funerals.

Who was this person?

"Don't you know me, honey? It's Aunt Millie."

He blinked a few times. She had changed. The last time he'd seen her, Aunt Millie had tipped the scales at 170 pounds, easy. But this woman couldn't have weighed more than a hundred pounds soaking wet.

He couldn't move, which was okay because Millie wasn't paralyzed. She hurried forward, threw her arms around him, and held on fiercely. He remembered then. Aunt Millie had always been a refuge.

"I'm so sorry about your daddy, son." She patted his back and then smiled through her unshed tears. "I'm so glad you're here. Your uncle Rob is bringing your mother up the back way. I know it will warm her heart to see you here."

Simon's insides went free falling. He hadn't seen his mother for eighteen years.

A moment later Mother entered the room, her hand wrapped around Uncle Rob's forearm as if she needed his support. Mother had not changed. She had celebrated her sixty-fifth birthday this year, but there wasn't a single gray hair on her head. In some cynical corner of his mind, Simon knew that Mother probably kept a weekly appointment at the local beauty shop, but that didn't matter. She was Mother. Still.

She turned her gaze on him, and it was like getting hit with a shotgun blast. All the unpleasant memories of living with Mother and Daddy tumbled through him. And yet he wanted to run to her and hug her. He had missed her, even if he couldn't stand being with her.

"Mother." He took a few steps toward her, but he didn't get close enough for an embrace.

Charlotte Wolfe took a step back, her big brown eyes growing wide and fearful. "Who are you?"

The words burned right through his middle.

"Now, Charlotte," Aunt Millie said in her most patient of voices. "It's your boy, Simon. Don't you remember him? He's come home to take care of you."

Simon opened his mouth to protest, but before he could utter a word, his mother shook her head. "No, he's not Simon. I would know my boy. Simon would never wear his hair long like that, or go around unshaven. Don't you try to fool me, Millie." Mother clutched Uncle Rob's arm and looked up at him with a wide stare. "Ira, you tell Millie she's wrong."

Uncle Rob, Mother's older brother, stared down at his sister with a look of pity. "Darlin', Ira's passed. Don't you remember? It happened on Saturday. He had a heart attack."

She blinked a few times, and her eyes seemed to brighten just a little. "Oh, yes, I remember." She turned to stare at the casket, her expression resolving itself into lines of grief. Uncle Rob escorted Mother to a seat on the opposite side of the room and hovered over her.

Aunt Millie sagged where she stood. She looked tired. "So now you know," she said. "Charlotte is having a very bad day today. I'm sure it's the shock of Ira's passing. There are some days when she's almost herself. Don't you worry, she'll remember you eventually. You haven't changed that much. You still look like the Polk side of the family."

"How long has she been like this?" His voice sounded like it came from a very great distance. Here he'd been thinking he could breeze in for the funeral and make a quick escape. Obviously, that wasn't going to happen. It was like the ground beneath him had turned to quicksand.

"Charlotte's been fading away for about five years. It's progressed pretty slowly. And your father took good care of her. So today is hard."

"Daddy took care of her?"

"Of course he did."

"But they could hardly stand one another."

"That's not true. Your folks had their share of fights, but they loved each other. Your daddy adored her. And he was so good for her. He was a bighearted man, Simon. And you broke his heart badly."

"They broke mine first." His voice was hard and tight.

Aunt Millie patted his back. "Son, I don't really know what happened between you and your folks. I never could really understand it. I know they had dreams for you that weren't what you wanted, but that wasn't a good reason for you to leave and never come home. And now I'm afraid it's time for you to pay the piper. Your mother needs to be cared for."

Of all the things waiting for him here in Last Chance, this was the most unexpected. He had thought he was coming to say good-bye to his father, and then he'd go back to his nice, orderly life in Paradise. The truth was beginning to sink in.

"I guess I'll have to take her back to California with me. I'll find a retirement home or something."

Millie stiffened. "You can't do that. You can't take her away from the home she loves. She's put her whole heart and soul into that garden of hers. And you can't take her away from her friends in the garden club and the Purly Girls."

"Purly Girls?"

"She's taken up knitting. The occupational therapist said it would be good for her because gardening is getting difficult. She needs to be watched when she's using her tools. Last month, she pulled up all her daffodils. She thought they were weeds. So we've been encouraging the knitting."

"She can knit in California. That's where I live. I realize she needs to be taken care of. But I'm not moving back to Last Chance, Aunt Millie. I'm just not."

"Listen to me. I love you, but if you take your mother to California and shove her into a nursing home, I will be so disappointed in you. I will not let you warehouse her."

"I didn't say I was going to shove her into a nursing home. I'll find a nice place for her with a mountain view."

"Simon"—Millie invested his name with a world of censure—"that would be exactly like warehousing her."

Millie was right, of course, and that thought wrapped itself around his neck and squeezed. Then Millie went on to tighten the noose.

"You know, son," she said, "you're going to have to stay for a little while anyway. There are legal issues. Eugene Hanks wants to talk with you about your father's will. And your uncle Ryan is very agitated about the financial situation at the dealership. You know his bank loaned your daddy a lot of money."

"What are you talking about?"

"Your daddy's business is practically bankrupt."

"How could a Ford dealership be failing in a place like Allenberg County?"

"The economic downturn hurt business, I guess. Your uncle Ryan has been talking about forcing the dealership into receivership. Of course, if you were willing to stay and help run the business, your uncle might change his mind. And it's important to save the dealership. There are about forty people who work there. It would be a disaster for this town if Wolfe Ford went out of business."

He looked at his watch again. He didn't know where else to look. Aunt Millie was crazy if she thought he was going to go into the business of selling cars. The bank would never go for it. Simon was an artist, not a car salesman. And he had a very big commission due in two months. He didn't have time for this.

He looked up toward the casket. His mother sat dry-eyed and hunched-shouldered by his father's corpse. Hell and damnation. How had it come to this?

He rudely turned away from Aunt Millie and went searching for the outside door—the one that led to the garden he'd seen through the windows. He sat down on a bench in the warm sunshine and watched a couple of goldfinches as they visited a bird feeder. They were the same color as the coreopsis that grew in clumps along the perennial border. He tried to clear his mind and focus on nothing at all.

But the coreopsis sent him back in time.

He remembered the day his mother had taught him the name of that flower. He'd been a little boy. He used to love spending time with Mother in the garden, getting dirty and learning the names of the flowers and the colors that went with them. All those different shadings of yellow, from buttercup to Carolina lupine. He'd learned them all at his mother's knee, along with an appreciation for how colors go together. He used that knowledge every day he painted.

And now the woman who had taught him this one, important thing didn't even recognize him.

Despite all his efforts to dam them up, a flood of tears deluged him.

Molly stood beside Ira's casket gazing down at his body. He looked pretty good for a dead man.

Ira Wolfe had been one of Davis High's biggest boosters. His contributions had refurbished the football field, paid for the new lighting system, and kept the team in uniforms. Which probably explained why the dealership was having some financial problems. Ira was generous to a fault.

Her vision smeared with unwanted tears. Who the heck was she crying for? Ira for being dead, Momma for being gone, or herself for having her life scrambled? Jeez louise, this was pitiful. She never cried. About anything. It was one of her life rules. No one would take a girl mechanic seriously if she cried. Ever.

"Thank you for coming." The voice was deep and accent-free. She turned. Well, hell. Simon Wolfe obviously didn't have any rules about crying. His eyes looked puffy and bloodshot.

And they widened in surprise. "It's you," he said. "I should have realized." His gaze traveled upward, taking in her hair, which she'd left down because she'd been too late to wrestle with it. She really needed to whack it off.

Simon's gaze dropped and lingered for more than a moment. Holy crap, he was ogling her boobs.

A totally unwanted body flush knocked her sideways. Whoa. What was that all about?

Guys in Last Chance never ogled her. She wasn't pretty or graceful or anything like that. So of course, guys talked cars and sports with her rather than looking or touching or making themselves nuisances. Over the years, she'd had a couple of friends with benefits. But they were just bed buddies. And besides, she wasn't interested in girl-boy entanglements. They were a big waste of time and always managed to get messy and emotional.

She needed to put distance between herself and this

guy who was old enough to be a member of the 1990 dream team. Which made him practically middle-aged.

"Uh, look," she said in a no-nonsense voice, "there's something I need to tell you. See, your daddy loaned me some space in his garage, where I've just started working on a full body restoration of a 1966 Shelby Mustang that I found in a barn up in Olar. I work there after hours, and I'm aiming to get the car finished by September for the Barrett-Jackson auction in Vegas. I'm hoping to hit pay dirt with this car so I can quit working for LeRoy and start a restoration business of my own. So, anyway, when you get around to taking a tour of the dealership, I just want you to understand that the Shelby belongs to me and my partner, Les Hayes, who's your daddy's chief mechanic. Don't be thinking that that car is one of your assets. Oh, and I have a set of keys to the building. So don't freak out if you see me there late at night, okay?"

The curls at the corner of Simon's mouth deepened into a semi-smile, which looked a bit incongruous given the state of his eyes. "I'm not planning to take a tour of the dealership," he said. "And I'm not all that interested in cars."

"Not even a Shelby Mustang?" Her incredulity showed in her voice.

"Not even a Shelby Mustang. My plan is to wrap up things here just as fast as I can and head back home. I think you should plan on the dealership being closed or sold."

"You're going to close the dealership?"

The muted conversations in the room halted, and a dozen heads turned in their direction. Oh, crap, she'd practically shouted the words, hadn't she?

"Uh, sorry," she said in a much smaller voice, even though she felt like screaming her outrage at the sudden reversals in her life. "But you can't let that happen."

"There's nothing I can do to prevent it."

"But I'll lose my garage space. Not to mention the fact that half of my friends own F-150s and go to Wolfe for their warranty service."

"What do you expect me to do, Molly? I'm an artist, not a car salesman or mechanic. I have no business running a car dealership."

Well, that was obvious. She just hadn't put all the puzzle pieces together until right this minute. Of course Ira's death was going to screw up everything.

"But what are you going to do with your momma?" She was grasping at straws now. This was the man who'd run away from home and never come back. Not once. Not even at Thanksgiving or Christmas.

"I don't know. But I do know I'm not staying, and I'm not going to take over Daddy's dealership. I'm not a car guy."

"Which makes you really odd for a man, you know that?"

Annoyance sparked in his dark eyes, and Molly immediately regretted the rancor in her words. Why couldn't she keep her mouth shut? Or learn how to deliver a put-down with a saccharine voice, like a southern belle. Unfortunately, she was missing the Scarlett O'Hara gene.

"I'm not the only odd one here," he said. "I'm willing to bet you don't know how to sew or knit or cook."

"Ha! I do so too know how to knit."

"Oh?" He frowned, his dark gaze cataloging her. "Don't tell me. You knitted that sweater, didn't you?"

"I did."

"It's very nice." He said this with another obvious glance at her boobs. Her internal thermostat went wacky again. Or maybe the funeral home's air-conditioning was on the fritz.

She was tempted to let him think she was some kind of super woman, capable of changing spark plugs and whipping up an apple pie all in a day's work. But actually, she didn't want to be a super woman. So why was she arguing with him?

She met Simon's gaze directly, squared her shoulders, and told the truth. "My mother owns the Knit & Stitch, the yarn shop in town. She taught me to knit when I was little, and I took to it. I blow at cooking and sewing, though, and I don't even care."

"Well, half odd is better than all the way odd," he said in a teasing tone.

Jeez louise! This conversation had taken a strange and uncomfortable turn. It was time to extricate herself. "Look, I'm sorry for your loss. I loved your daddy. He believed in me when no one else would, and he gave me a place to see if I could realize my dreams. I told him a million times that he needed to quit smoking those cigars, and..." Her voice wobbled the minute she thought about Ira standing in the middle of the showroom with an unlit cigar clenched in his teeth. She was never going to see him there again. He was never going to stop by and admire her body work. She was on her own now. And about to lose her garage space.

Her nose filled up with snot, and the urge to bawl became almost unbearable. She sniffled back her suddenly overflowing nasal passages. She was not going to cry. Not even for Ira Wolfe. He wouldn't want her to cry over him. Not in a million years.

Ira would just want her to finish that Shelby and get going building her business.

And wouldn't you know it, right then Ira's too-handsome and somewhat odd son reached into his pocket and pulled out a fine linen handkerchief. He held it out for her, his eyes filled with kindness and deep empathy. "You know, Molly, I could say the same thing about your father. He definitely believed in me when no one else did. I owe him a great deal."

She could refuse that hankie the way he'd refused to shake her hand earlier in the day. Or she could accept the handkerchief and his words as the peace offering they were intended to be.

She snatched the handkerchief and quickly blotted her eyes and blew her nose. She wanted to hand it back to him but realized that a snotty handkerchief was kind of gross. "Uh, I'll wash it and get it back to you," she said as she crammed the soggy cloth into the pocket of her slacks. "I guess I'll need to remember to bring tissues for the funeral tomorrow."

Simon glanced down at his father. "Me too."

# CHAPTER 3

A lonely fluorescent light illuminated a corner of the Wolfe Ford service center, lending the cavernous space an eerie quality. Molly hurried across the spotless gray floor, her sneakers squeaking with each step. She'd stopped at home on her way back from Ira's wake to change into her work clothes. She was brimming with news and gossip.

Les Hayes, Molly's best friend, was going to blow more than a gasket when he heard what she had to say. Heck, he was probably going to throw a piston, too.

She found him bent over the Shelby's engine compartment, which had been divested of the radiator, the battery, and all of the engine's hoses and belts. Tonight they were supposed to pull the block and the tranny. The plan from there was for Les to rebuild the engine while Molly started work on the body.

The car's seats and dashboard had already been pulled last week and sent to an auto upholsterer up in Columbia that Molly worked with.

"Hey, Molly," Les said without looking up from the engine compartment. "How was your day?"

"Probably the crappiest of my life."

Les looked up. Grease darkened his forehead and smudged one cheek, making his baby blues look bluer than ever. His curly brown hair puffed from around his Wolfe Ford hat. Momma always said that Les was a cool, tall drink of water. Yeah, branch water, maybe. He had an unpredictable temper.

Which made him a lot like Molly. They could fight like a couple of junkyard dogs sometimes over the right way to proceed on a restoration.

"What's wrong?" he asked.

"Well for starters, Momma ran away and left me in charge of the Knit & Stitch."

"Yeah, I heard about that. So now that you're *in charge*, are you going to reopen the store?" He said this with a wicked grin.

"Stop it. It's serious. I've got twenty messages from knitters in my voice mail. They aren't going to be happy when they find out I'm not going to reopen the shop."

"So don't fret about it."

"I'm not going to. Not about the yarn shop, anyway. We have much bigger problems. I just came from Ira's wake, and his son is planning to close the dealership."

"What?"

"That's what he told me. He's hot to get his daddy's estate in order, and then he's hightailing it back to Paradise."

"Paradise?"

"That's where he lives. It's in California."

Les laughed. His laugh was goofy and adorable and

kind of high-pitched and joyous. And seemed out of proportion to the crisis at hand. "Don't you laugh, Leslie Hayes. This is serious. What are we going to do if Wolfe Ford goes out of business?" She started pacing.

"Oh, I doubt it will go out of business. The family will probably sell it. There are a lot of Ford owners living around here who need warranty service. No one's going to leave those folks high and dry. So we can negotiate with the new owners, whoever they turn out to be."

She stopped pacing. "I wouldn't be so sure. You didn't talk to Simon Wolfe. He couldn't have cared less about the business. And he's not a car guy. He's always looking at his watch like he can't wait to leave. He could give a crap about the Ford owners in Allenberg County. I have a bad feeling about this. We're going to lose our garage space for the Shelby."

"Mol, you don't know that for sure, and you're just making yourself crazy worrying about something that hasn't happened yet."

"Maybe it hasn't happened, but we need to plan for it anyway. It's a shame we can't afford to buy the old Coca-Cola building yet."

Molly's long-range plan was to buy that abandoned building in Last Chance and turn it into a car-restoration business with a garage in the back where the old loading dock was and a showroom in the front. She had other dreams, too. Big ones. Like trying to interest Speed Channel in a show about a lady garage owner.

But first, she needed to restore the Shelby. Everything hung on that car. Finding it had been her stroke of good luck. The little old lady in Olar had no idea what was sitting in her barn. She'd wanted only four thousand dollars for the old car. Restored, the Shelby would probably sell for close to a quarter of a million.

"Maybe we can get a loan and use the car as collateral," Molly said. "I could talk to Dash Randall. He'd probably be willing to finance us. He loved what I did to his Eldorado and that old Ford truck of his."

"Jeez, Molly, you're getting way ahead of yourself." Les settled himself on a shop stool. "If we get a loan, that means we'll have to form a real, legal partnership. That costs money, too, and I don't want to go into debt. Besides, if the dealership closes, I lose my day job, which is another reason not to be thinking about borrowing money."

"Yeah, I thought of that. Maybe we could rent the Coca-Cola building instead of buying it outright."

"That still takes money. And we need tools and a lift."

"You've got tools in storage. Damn. I sure do wish your granddaddy hadn't sold his house and moved to Tallahassee. We could have used his old garage like we did for our first two cars."

"Yeah. Maybe old man Nelson has barn space we could borrow."

"I can't paint a car in a barn, you know that. It's too dirty. I'm gonna have to pay to have someone paint the car if I can't use the space here. I mean, even this space isn't as clean as I really need. I need a painting booth. But at least we can fake it here, and Ira has a killer air compressor."

"Well, I don't know." Les rubbed the furrows in his brow with his greasy hands. He did this when he was thinking, which is why his face was always dirty after a long day at work.

"I thought you were going to be furious. I know I am."

He shrugged. "There is nothing to be furious about. I'm sad about Ira. I'm worried about the people who work here. But venting anger on you or the car or the wall isn't going to change any of that. This is beyond my control. It's beyond yours, too."

"Well, I think it might be best if we didn't pull the tranny and engine tonight. It would be easier to move the car semi-intact."

"Okay. So you wanna go get a beer?"

The next morning, Molly dragged herself off to the Kountry Kitchen because there was no milk for her coffee or cereal. Obviously, Allen had consumed it all and hadn't given a single thought to replacing it—something that would never have happened if Momma had been home. Momma had a built-in radar that alerted her to milk shortages, pantry emergencies, and overflowing laundry baskets.

Molly had not inherited this knack for homemaking.

And she was exhausted. She and Les had sat up for hours, drinking beer while they tried to figure out what to do next.

"What can I get you besides coffee?" Ricki Wilson, the waitress, asked as she filled Molly's coffee mug.

"State-of-the-art garage space and someone to manage the Knit & Stitch," she muttered, then took a big slug of coffee. She could practically taste the caffeine.

Ricki put the coffee carafe on the counter. "How much does the job pay?"

Molly blinked up at the waitress. Her hair was platinum almost all the way down to her roots. She wore a standard pink uniform from right out of the 1950s. And boy, she sure did fill out that dress. "You mean you're interested in managing the Knit & Stitch?"

"If the pay is right."

"I can't afford to pay anyone, Ricki."

"Well then, your goose is cooked. Because, usually, people only work for a salary."

Molly thought about this for a moment. "I guess I could hire someone. But I have no clue how much I could afford. I mean, until yesterday afternoon, Momma had it covered."

"Yeah, I heard all about how your momma left town. At lunch yesterday, everyone was talking about that note your momma left on the front door of the shop."

Molly held out her cup, and Ricki refilled it. "If Momma leaving town and putting a snippy note on the door of the Knit & Stitch is the biggest news in town, that's just pitiful. There are much bigger problems. Simon Wolfe told me last night at his daddy's wake that the Ford dealership is going to be closed."

"No way." Ricki leaned in. This was obviously more important gossip.

"Yup, it's true. He's not even interested in selling it. He's just going to close its doors and whisk Miz Charlotte back to Paradise, California, where he lives." Molly's pulse started pounding in her forehead. She didn't even care whether this headache was caused by Simon Wolfe's insensitivity or last night's beers. She chose to blame Simon. He was at the root of her car trouble. "Do you think if I drink enough coffee this problem will disappear?" she asked Ricki.

"Which one? The yarn shop or the car dealership?"

"Both."

"Nope. But you could hire me to manage the yarn shop and that would solve that problem." Ricki's voice had dropped to a near whisper, and she glanced over her shoulder to make sure T-Bone Carter, her boss, didn't hear what she was saying. "I'd do anything to get a job that doesn't require me to be on my feet all day."

"Do you know anything about knitting?"

She shook her head. "No, but I could learn. I know all about cash registers and such. And I'm reliable."

Molly had to give her that. Ricki had been very reliable since she'd returned to Last Chance a couple of years ago. Before that, maybe not so much. Everyone in town knew how she'd broken Clay Rhodes's heart way back when and how she'd come back to town looking for a second chance that didn't happen.

"I don't know if I can afford you," Molly said. "If the dealership closes, I'm going to have a lot of expenses."

Ricki pulled a pen from her apron pocket and wrote something on her pad. She put the paper in front of Molly. "That's what T-Bone is paying me in base wages. And it's not even minimum wage. He's counting on me getting tips to make ends meet."

Molly looked at the number. It was shameful. Still, she had no idea if the yarn shop could support an employee. "Ricki, let me think about this, and I'll get back to you."

Molly finished her breakfast. She had a few minutes before she had to be at Ira's funeral at Christ Church. She wanted to take down the note on the Knit & Stitch's door and put one up that said "Closed for the Foreseeable Future."

And then, time permitting, she wanted to take another

look at the abandoned building on the opposite corner of Chancellor and Palmetto Avenue. It had once housed a Coca-Cola bottling business. Arlo Boyd, the main commercial leasing agent in town, had been trying to find a tenant for years. With no success. The "For Lease" sign in the big front windows had been there so long it was sun-faded.

Once, a long time ago, people could stand on the sidewalk and watch the bottling process through those big picture windows. Molly didn't remember that time, but she'd heard people talk about watching the glass bottles moving down the assembly line, filling up with soda, and being capped off, while a handful of people managed the process.

It wouldn't take much to turn the front portion of the building into a showroom for restored cars. And then people could once again stand on the sidewalk and peer in at something amazing.

Molly wanted that building. She had dreamed about it for so long that it almost felt as if it already belonged to her. Maybe Dash Randall, the not-so-silent partner in Angel Development, would give her a loan to make her dream come true.

But she couldn't go to Dash on her own. Les had to agree, since they jointly owned the Shelby. And right now, Les wasn't worried. He seemed to think everything would work itself out.

She left the Kountry Kitchen and headed up the sidewalk. But when she reached the Knit & Stitch, Kenzie Griffin was waiting at the front door with her eighteen-month-old baby on her hip.

"I'm not open," Molly said, her voice kind of snotty

and short-tempered, but that didn't deter Kenzie in the least.

"I've got to have another skein of alpaca," Kenzie said. "I've called every yarn store in a fifty-mile radius, and no one but you has what I need."

"But I'm not open."

"Molly, be reasonable. I'll just pop in and get the yarn and then I'll be gone."

"Yeah, and you'll tell your friends that I let you get the yarn, and then everyone will think the store is open. But it's not. Momma may have left me *in charge,* but she failed to think about the fact that I already have a full-time job at the Grease Pit."

"But you *have* to open the shop. The Purly Girls are coming this afternoon, and you've got knitting lessons scheduled for folks. People love this store. You can't close it down."

Guilt gnawed at her innards, even though, technically, Momma had closed the store, not Molly. But that stupid note had let everyone know it would be Molly's fault if the store didn't reopen.

And here she'd been all ticked off at Simon for closing the car dealership because his daddy was gone. But hadn't Momma put her in the same darn place? Even worse, Molly could practically hear Momma's voice whispering like Jiminy Cricket in her ear. Momma would tell her that she needed to be nice, and sweet, and reasonable. But at what cost? That was the question. Tension coiled up her backbone, and her already stiff shoulders tightened a little more.

"I can't be two places at one time. I'm only human." Her voice came out like a whine, and she regretted it. She didn't like whining. She liked being honest and direct.

"Oh, Molly, I'm sorry. Let me help you, okay?" Kenzie said.

"How?"

Kenzie's husband was an engineer who worked at de-Bracy Ltd. They rented a tiny house north of town, waiting for their new home to be built. She didn't have a garage or a lift.

"Let me mind the store today," Kenzie said. "Annie needs a set of DPNs, and Lola May needs some of that pink Baby Ull. She's frantic because it's for Jane's baby, and the child is due any minute. I can handle it. And Junior can nap in his stroller."

Kenzie was solving the wrong problem. But hey, if it got the knitters of Last Chance off Molly's back, that was one less thing to worry about.

"Okay. It's a deal. And the yarn you need is on the house, 'cause I don't think I can afford to pay you." Molly pressed the store's keys into Kenzie's hand. "Just take Momma's stupid note off the front door, please. And I'll see if I can get away from the Grease Pit a little early to help you with the Purly Girls meeting at four o'clock. It might be tough, though, since Bubba's going to be off all day. If I don't make it, you can drop off the keys at the Grease Pit after the meeting."

She turned and escaped down Palmetto Avenue like a coon with a dog on her tail. She didn't have much time before the funeral, and she needed to beat feet before any more knitters showed up and sidetracked her from her main purpose—finding alternative garage space for the Shelby before Simon closed down Wolfe Ford.

# CHAPTER 4

Daddy had lived for football, and the Davis High School Rebels, old and young, came out for his funeral in droves. There were at least half a dozen members of the 1990 championship team there, including Stone Rhodes, the quarterback, who was now the sheriff of Allenberg County. He came with his new wife, Lark Chaikin, a Pulitzer Prize–winning war photographer who had retired from the battlefield and was reinventing herself as a fine-arts landscape photographer. Her debut book, *Rural Scenes*, sat on Simon's coffee table back in Paradise. He had been thoroughly bewitched by her photos of the South Carolina swamps.

Stone wore his sheriff's uniform, but the other members of the team had donned their Davis High jerseys. In fact, the sanctuary was awash in purple and gold flowers.

It might have been a Rebels reunion except Coach was missing, still off fishing somewhere in the wilds beyond the reach of cell phones. Simon was disappointed. Coach had been the one who'd kept him together in high school, even though he had only been the kicker. There wasn't anything Simon wouldn't do for Coach. Even now, so many years later.

Coach's daughter was there, sitting in the back of the church, wearing the same outfit she'd worn yesterday and looking a little wrinkled but as pretty as ever.

She was grown up now, and he kept glancing over his shoulder to where she sat in the back pew. Each time, he caught her staring at him. He was so aware of her stare that the back of his neck started to burn, as if her laser-beam glare were searing its way through his spine.

She was angry. He didn't blame her. But there was nothing he could do about it.

After the service, the family hosted a buffet brunch at Mother's house, out in her garden, which had always been one of the prime spots on the annual garden tour. The garden looked a little neglected these days, but Simon may have been the only one to notice. Mother had been fastidious about two things in her life, her appearance and her garden. She still looked great, but maintaining the garden was now beyond her abilities.

Mother drifted through lunch in a fog. She hardly spoke, and she hadn't yet recognized Simon. Several times during this long, difficult day, she turned to Aunt Millie or Uncle Rob and asked why someone with such long hair was present in her garden.

In the face of this sad turn of affairs, Simon retreated into the shade of the oak trees at the back of the yard. He was hiding out, even though he knew he ought to be playing host. But that would require taking over from his uncle Ryan, who seemed to want to be in charge of everything.

Besides, it had been so long since he'd spent any time in Last Chance that he didn't recall names or faces. So it made sense to let Uncle Ryan manage things.

The day wore on. The crowd dwindled down to family. By two o'clock, the May heat had driven everyone inside.

They sat quietly, not really having much to say to one another. Cousin Charlene, a veterinarian, got called away on an emergency. Cousin Rachel, who was three months' pregnant and clearly exhausted, hovered over everyone trying to keep the family from going entirely silent.

And then Uncle Ryan dragged Simon off to Daddy's study for a man-to-man talk about "things." His uncle spent a good hour explaining why he had rounded up all of Daddy's creditors and was going to file in court to force Wolfe Ford into a receivership. He said it was because of the outstanding loans owed to the bank where Ryan was the manager.

"You have never shown any interest in this family or its business, Simon," he said in a censorious tone. "You're patently unqualified to run a car dealership. So it only makes sense for the bank to take it over and see what can be recouped from the mess your father made. Your daddy may have been loved by the football team, but he was a terrible businessman. I suspect, in this economy, it will make more sense to liquidate the business instead of searching for a buyer."

Ryan had always been just a little coldhearted. And clearly, he wasn't at all worried about Daddy's employees or customers. He only cared about the money. But then he came from the Polk side of the family. Simon distinctly remembered his grandfather, who had been a banker, too. Grandfather had been cool, aloof, and stern. And Grandfather had made money his god. Mother and her brothers had all been affected by having a father who was that way.

He escaped Uncle Ryan only to be cornered in the kitchen by Bubba, Rachel's husband, a mechanic at Bill's Grease Pit and clearly the other family black sheep. "You can't let Ryan bully you, Simon. You have to stand up to him. There are forty-some-odd people working at the dealership. They're going to lose their jobs. And it's worse than that. The folks who own Fords will have to drive a long, long way to get warranty work done on their vehicles. At the very least, you have to convince him to sell the business, not liquidate it."

This was the longest speech Bubba had made all afternoon. He was an interloper in the family, even if it was clear that Rachel adored him. It had probably taken a lot of courage for Bubba to corner Simon and speak his mind.

But what could Simon do? So he told Bubba the same thing he'd told Uncle Ryan. He was leaving just as soon as he could get things wrapped up. Daddy's will would have to go through an elaborate probate process.

And he'd have to plan for the expense of Mother's long-term care in California. That undoubtedly meant selling the house, which would break Mother's heart. But his choices were limited. And the house was Mother's main asset.

At about three o'clock, Mother roused herself from her stupor. She got up and went to her room, emerging fifteen minutes later wearing a bright flowered dress and carrying an equally bright tote bag.

"Well," she said to everyone. "I'm off to my meeting."

Aunt Millie got up. "Uh, honey, today might not be a good day to go."

Mother's eyes grew round. "Nonsense. We meet every Tuesday afternoon. It's my Christian duty to go. Besides, we're knitting poppies for the VFW to sell on Memorial Day, and this is our last meeting before the holiday."

She pulled away from Aunt Millie and headed toward the front door. She got there and stopped. Her shoulders sagged, and she looked like a puppy dog standing at the door waiting for a master who had been away too long. "I forgot. Ira won't be coming to pick me up, will he?" she said in a low voice. For all the emotion it packed, it remained steady.

Simon couldn't let her stand there by herself looking that way. He remembered earlier times—when he'd been five or six. He'd shared a special relationship with his mother, once. And in some deep way he understood her need to escape the people in this room with their various agendas. "It's all right," Simon found himself saying. "I'll take you to your meeting. It's at the Knit & Stitch, isn't it?"

Mother looked up at him. "Who are you?"

"I'm S—" He stopped. If he told her he was Simon, she'd get upset. She had been doing that all day. "I'm a friend of Millie's."

"That's right," Millie said. "He's come to help you out for a little while."

"Oh." She nodded. "How kind of you to take me."

At three-forty-five, Molly left Bill's Grease Pit and hightailed it up Palmetto Avenue to the Knit & Stitch. LeRoy, her boss, wasn't all that happy about it, seeing as she'd missed part of the morning because of Ira's funeral. But Kenzie had left her a frantic message on her voice mail. Molly needed to go.

The Purly Girls were, by and large, a bunch of very sweet ladies who were all gradually losing their minds. For some of the old gals, this trip to the yarn shop and Sundays at church were the only times they got out. Momma made a big production of Purly Girls meetings, serving sweet tea and cookies.

That was so not going to happen today.

She hit the shop's door at a dead run, hoping she could untangle whatever crisis Kenzie was having and still make it back to the Grease Pit. She wasn't dressed for the yarn shop. Although she had scrubbed her hands before leaving the pit.

She opened the door to hell.

"Oh my God, no, Junior!" was the first thing Molly heard as she entered the shop. And with good reason.

Eighteen-month-old Junior was running laps around the little table in the middle of the store where knitters came to sit and work on projects. Clutched in his fat little hand was the end of a skein of gray Himalayan yak, and the yarn was spooling out behind him as he ran around and around the table, effectively tying the chairs to it.

His mother, wearing an exhausted expression, chased after him while the little demon giggled and evaded her grasping hands. His usually calm mother let forth a string of profanity that was enough to turn Molly's ears blue.

And that's when she realized that someone, presumably Junior, had ripped the labels off the alpaca and merino skeins that were stored in the low shelves in the front of the store. The labels lay strewn across the carpet like autumn leaves.

And someone had mixed up all the colors.

She strode into the store and cut off the little bugger

as he began his fifth lap around the table and chairs. She extricated the yarn from his fat hands, picked him up by his armpits, and handed him back to his frazzled mother.

"Oh, God, Molly, I'm so sorry," Kenzie said. "Lola May came by to get her baby yarn, and while I was talking with her, well…" She surveyed the labels strewn across the carpet at the front of the store.

"And then Cathy called to find out if we still had a specific dye lot of the yarn she's using for Jane's baby blanket. And he got into the yak. Honestly, we were doing great until about half an hour ago, except for the juice incident."

"Juice incident?"

Kenzie's freckled face turn a shade of red that clashed with her carrot-colored hair. "He kind of spilled it."

"And…"

"He used a skein of cashmere to mop it up, but it turns out cashmere isn't all that absorbent, and uh…"

"Where did he spill the juice, Kenzie?"

"It ran from the counter into your Internet router. The router kind of sparked and then went dead. And then, of course, the credit card thingy stopped working. So when Lola May bought her Baby Ull, I couldn't run the credit card. But I did take her credit card number down. Maybe you can get your credit card thing fixed and run the charges tomorrow?"

Molly wondered if it was situations like this that had Momma spending all that time in her meditation corner. Because right at the moment, Molly was ready to strangle Kenzie and her adorable baby. She gave the demon child her evil eye. Which didn't help the situation because the kid started squirming and kicking and then howling.

And Kenzie, who apparently was not one of those firm

or demanding mothers, put the child down as she said, "I'll just get the scissors and free the chairs."

But Junior had other ideas. The kid took off at a dead run toward the front of the shop, clearly thinking of making an escape. He timed it perfectly—just as Simon Wolfe, wearing the same dark suit he'd worn at his father's funeral, opened the door for his mother.

The kid managed to evade Charlotte, but Simon was too quick for him. He caught Junior before he could take even one step out onto the sidewalk. And then, with a laugh, he held the demon child way up over his head. The kid squirmed and giggled. "You don't look like a Purly Girl to me," he said in that deep, accent-less voice. It was a weird kind of scene, because Simon didn't look like the kind of guy who had any experience with children. And yet he tucked that kid under his arm like a football, and the kid giggled as Simon followed Charlotte into the shop.

As always, Charlotte looked elegant and fashionable and above it all as she glided in like royalty. Molly couldn't miss the family resemblance between Simon and his mother. And yet Molly couldn't imagine Charlotte handling a demon toddler as effectively as Simon had. In fact, Molly couldn't imagine Charlotte having any kind of interaction with anyone younger than about twenty.

Charlotte stopped in her tracks and surveyed the litter on the carpet, the giggling infant, and the yak-tied table and chairs.

"What is going on here, Molly?" she asked. "Where in the world is Pat?"

"Good question. I'm hoping she sends postcards and lets us know."

Charlotte blinked but didn't respond. No doubt Molly's

snarky comment had confused her. But, lady that she was, Charlotte put on a good front and pretended she hadn't heard anything.

"Come on in, Charlotte. You're a little bit early," Molly said on a sigh, then turned just in time to see Kenzie frantically cutting through the strands of yak to liberate the table and chairs. Her bottom lip was quivering, and she looked like she was about to start bawling.

"It's okay, Kenzie," Molly said as she pulled out a chair for Charlotte. "Now, Miz Charlotte, you make yourself comfy. I'm afraid I don't have any cookies right at the moment, but maybe I can pop down to the doughnut shop and get some Bavarian creams for today's meeting. How's that sound?"

"I like Pat's cookies," Charlotte said with a sniff, then aimed her gaze at Molly's hands. "Molly Canaday, your fingernails are filthy. Go clean them at once." Charlotte shivered in revulsion.

Was it shame that made Molly curl her fingers into her palm? Was it shame that made her feel Simon's presence like a weight in the room, dragging her down? She had washed her hands. But of course, her nails were cut down to the quick, and there was always just a little bit of residual grease along her torn and ratty cuticles. Bottom line, Molly didn't care if her hands were dirty. But she resented Charlotte for pointing them out for everyone to see.

"To whom does this belong?" Simon asked, cutting through the alien emotion that was making Molly's face flame hot. She turned. He was standing there in all his sartorial splendor, bearing the demon under his arm. The boy hung limp and subdued.

"Oh, my God," Kenzie said. "I'm so, so sorry." She

rushed forward and took the toddler from the man. A suddenly tractable Junior settled in his mother's arms and put his little red head down on her shoulder. He aimed his angelic smile at Simon.

And the apostrophes at the corner of Simon's mouth curled up. Obviously, the guys had bonded.

"Are you Charlotte's son?" Kenzie asked.

"That man is not my son!" Charlotte said. "Millie hired him to do some odd jobs around the house."

And just as quickly, Simon's smile disappeared. He gave both Molly and Kenzie a little shrug that seemed filled with both resignation and something else—was it sadness? But he covered over the emotion almost as quickly as it flashed in his eyes.

"Do you want me to run down to the doughnut place for you?" he asked. He cast his gaze over the yarn labels and the tangled mass of yak in Kenzie's hands. "I could take the baby with me. What's his name?"

"We call him Junior," Kenzie supplied. The little demon seemed to know a friend when he saw one. He reached out for Simon. And the man took him in his arms again like he knew how to handle an eighteen-month-old.

"I'll take my time," Simon said, casting his gaze over the havoc that Junior had caused.

"Oh, that would be wonderful," Kenzie said.

"Wait," Molly said. "What are you doing here? No one expected—"

He gave Molly a direct and deeply unsettling stare. "Mother insisted on coming. I think she needed to escape from the family. And that's a feeling I understand pretty well."

"Oh. Well." The words dried up in her mouth. He

wasn't even trying to hide from his history, was he? She suddenly didn't know quite what to make of this man.

"It's okay, Molly. I'll go get the doughnuts."

And he turned on his heel, the baby riding his hip. He headed out the door and almost ran over Savannah White, who was dropping off her aunt Miriam Randall.

Simon put Junior down on his feet, and the two of them ambled up the street in the direction of the doughnut shop.

Savannah and Miz Miriam came into the yarn store.

"My goodness, Charlotte, was that Simon just now?" Miriam asked as she settled herself into one of the chairs.

"That man is not my son. Why is everyone saying that? I just told Molly, he's a handyman and chauffeur that Millie hired for me."

"Wow, Miz Charlotte," Kenzie said, "for a handyman he sure does dress nice. That suit he was wearing looks like Hugo Boss, or maybe Kenneth Cole. And he's like some kind of Pied Piper. I mean, Junior took one look at him and stopped misbehaving. How'd he do that?"

Savannah turned and gave Molly a funny look.

"What?" Molly asked. "Do I have grease on my face again?"

Savannah nodded. "Yeah, maybe just a little on your right cheek."

Molly wiped her cheek with her hand. "Guess I'll go wash my face. And my hands." And then after the meeting, she'd have to make a quick trip up to Orangeburg for a new router. Never mind the laundry, or the grocery shopping, or finding someone without a toddler to mind the Knit & Stitch. Or her job at the Pit. Or what she was going to do with the Shelby.

She headed toward the small storeroom at the back

of the shop, but before she could reach it, Kenzie said, "I promise. I'll pay for all of the crochet hooks."

Molly turned. "Crochet hooks?"

"Well, I put Junior in the storeroom for a minute when Annie Jasper came by for some superwash merino. I'm afraid he opened up a few packages of hooks. He was building a house with them, you know, sort of like Lincoln Logs?"

"Right." Molly nodded and headed into the storeroom. "A few packages" turned out to be more than a dozen, and the crochet hooks were scattered everywhere. She headed into the bathroom in the back and inspected herself in the mirror.

There wasn't a speck of grease on her face. So why had Savannah given her that goofy look? Why had she lied about the grease? Molly looked down at her hands. They were pretty clean, too.

She turned on the tap and started washing them again, cognizant that all of this was part of Momma's grand plan to turn her into some kind of girlie-girl who wanted to run a knitting shop instead of a body shop.

Junior was fearless and opinionated and not the least bit worried about being with a stranger.

Simon wondered if he'd ever been this fearless or this sure of himself. He could remember when he was four or five, walking to town with Mother. He'd been required to walk at a steady pace—not too fast, not too slow. He'd been required to hold Mother's hand at every intersection, even when he'd been eight or nine, as if Mother had tried to keep him a baby. She had never understood just how humiliating many of her rules were for an active boy.

But he'd never rebelled. For some reason, he'd never found the courage to break away until he was an adult.

Of course, he had managed to escape from time to time, especially in the summer, when Luke Raintree liberated him. And since Luke was the grandson of a former governor, Mother had allowed Simon to spend endless unsupervised hours out at the Jonquil House, the Raintree family's summer home on the Edisto River.

A happy sigh escaped his control as warm, sun-drenched memories tumbled through his mind. He hadn't thought about Luke in a long, long time. He'd suppressed a lot of those memories. Now he was stunned to discover that some of them weren't painful.

No doubt he was thinking about Luke because Junior had red hair and freckles. And Junior seemed to have the same *joie de vivre* that Luke had possessed in vast quantities. Luke was the kind of person that drew people to him. He was a natural-born leader.

Simon swung the toddler up onto his hip, just before the kid raced into traffic. "So, kiddo, are you going to be a leader one day?"

"No!" the toddler said emphatically and squirmed. "Down!"

"Not in the middle of the street." He pointed to the truck going by. "You'd get smashed flat."

"Mah fat," Junior parroted with an emphatic nod of his head. "No no." He waved his finger in the air and looked so adorable that Simon laughed.

"What an unexpected delight you are," Simon said to the kid. And he meant it. He had no desire to be a parent. God only knew what damage he might do to some unsuspecting child. He had no good parental role models. But there was something about the innocence of children that always cheered him up.

Just so long as he could hand the kids back to their parents when they soiled their diapers. He gave Junior a little sniff test. Thankfully, the kid passed.

They crossed the street so Simon could walk by the old Kismet movie theater. It was shrouded in scaffolding, while the sounds of drills and saws wafted out from the open doors. Simon remembered sitting up in the back row with Luke and Gabe Raintree watching horror movies and eating Dots. Simon hated the black ones, but Luke had loved them.

It made him happy to see The Kismet rising from the ashes. The last time Simon had come to Last Chance, the theater had been closed. It was like an omen to him then.

*And now?*

He was pondering that question when the past found him.

Zeph Gibbs came sauntering out of the movie theater wearing a pair of frayed overalls and looking a whole lot older than Simon remembered.

Simon stopped in his tracks, and Junior squirmed and said, "Down."

"Zeph?" Simon said.

The old black man turned. "Well, I declare." A big smile stole over his face. That smile hadn't changed one bit. "What in the world are you doing with Junior?"

The kid stopped squirming. Instead, Junior rested his head on Simon's shoulder and played coy. Then he got distracted by the handkerchief in the pocket of Simon's suit jacket.

"I'm taking him off his mother's hands for a while.

He trashed the Knit & Stitch, and the girls have a meeting going on over there. I've been sent out for doughnuts. Zeph, how are you doing?"

"Oh, I'm fine. Just the same as always. I heard about your daddy. I'm so sorry."

Simon looked up at The Kismet's marquee. "So you're working here. Doing carpentry?"

"I am."

"Do you go hunting much?"

"I do. And fishing. I built myself a little house out near the swamp. Near the governor's place."

Junior dropped Simon's handkerchief onto the sidewalk. "Uh-oh," the toddler said, looking down at the object like a redheaded angel.

Zeph picked up the handkerchief and handed it back to the baby.

"Do the Raintrees ever go out there anymore?" Simon asked.

Zeph shook his head and studied the concrete sidewalk. "No, sir, the old governor is long passed, and Gabe—well he's famous now. Lives in Charleston."

Simon should have known better than to ask. Of course the Raintrees hadn't come back. He'd even read one of Gabe's novels a few years ago. It was too dark and violent for Simon.

Suddenly all those happy memories turned gray. And the painful ones percolated to the top. He needed to get away from Zeph before they overwhelmed him. "Well, it's nice to see you again, but I've got to get going. I've been sent on an errand, and you know how Mother can be. I'll be here in Last Chance for a while settling Daddy's estate."

Zeph nodded but didn't look up. "It might be best if you didn't come out to the Jonquil House or anywhere out that way."

Simon understood. The memories had to be painful for Zeph, too. So he nodded and headed on down the sidewalk.

# CHAPTER 5

After the Purly Girls meeting, Molly fired up Momma's computer and took a look at the yarn shop's profit and loss statement.

Jeez Louise, Momma was doing much better with her business than she'd let anyone know. To hear Momma talk, the shop had been barely making a profit. But to Molly's astonishment, the Knit & Stitch had been bringing in modest yet steady income for a long time. Further investigation of the accounting software revealed that Pat Canaday had been socking away the profits and living entirely on Daddy's paycheck.

On Friday afternoon, just three days before she left, Momma had taken a huge chunk of cash out of her money market account. With that much money in her pocket, she wasn't coming back anytime soon.

This discovery left Molly reeling. Maybe Momma hadn't gone to see the world like she said. Maybe she'd taken all that cash and moved off to some other town and was planning to permanently set up shop there. Molly suddenly missed her momma something fierce. Surely Momma wasn't gone for good?

She wasn't going to cry over it. No, sir. The way Momma had slunk out of town had been hurtful and maybe just a little bit hypocritical. Momma talked a great line about being mindful and calm and collected, and all the while she was orchestrating her getaway. Well, running away didn't seem like a very good way to deal with problems. And Momma running away made Molly hopping mad. So mad that she actually thought about hauling out that dumb book Momma had left for her and trying one of those one-minute meditations.

But there was a silver lining in this disaster that Momma hadn't fully thought through. The shop was earning enough to support an employee. Of course, that would eat into any profits Molly would pocket, but if she could hire someone to manage the store, then whatever was left over could be plowed into the Shelby, or maybe used to rent the Coca-Cola building. Maybe things were looking up.

So Molly called Ricki Wilson, and the next morning at o-dark-thirty they met at the front door of the yarn shop. Molly had Ricki fill out all the necessary employment forms and then gave Ricki the one-hour training session on the point-of-sale equipment, which Molly had repaired last night.

Then she escaped, intent on getting a cup of coffee at the Kountry Kitchen—there still wasn't any milk in the refrigerator at home—before heading off to work.

As she left the store, her attention was drawn down the block, where Simon Wolfe was peering through the big picture windows of the Coca-Cola bottling plant while simultaneously talking on his cell phone. Molly immediately went on guard.

She didn't like anyone peering into those windows. That building was hers, and Simon needed to keep his distance.

He'd already upset things in this town, even if he *had* taken Junior off Kenzie's hands yesterday afternoon and come back with doughnuts and a completely tamed toddler.

Kenzie had been flabbergasted when Simon had taken a seat in the couch at the front of the store and quietly played with Junior for the better part of half an hour.

So he was the Pied Piper when it came to demon children; she still didn't trust him. He had no right to be investigating her building.

She needed to know what he was up to. So instead of heading toward the Kountry Kitchen, she strolled up the street toward the abandoned building. As she got closer, she could hear what he was saying into his cell phone.

"Well, it's got windows. They don't face north." He stopped talking and looked up at the sky. "They face east. I suppose it would do." He backed away from the windows and started pacing, listening to whoever was on the other end of the line.

This morning, he'd traded in his wool slacks for a pair of faded blue jeans and a white shirt with the sleeves rolled up to expose sinewy forearms with a road map of veins traveling across them. His Toms lace-ups were beginning to fray at the toe, but they gave him an air of shabby urban elegance that didn't belong anywhere in the vicinity of Last Chance.

He was still talking into his phone. "This building is probably the best I can do. And it's only short-term. But I have to get back to work, so I need you and the painting here ASAP."

Molly listened unabashedly as he discussed plans for the next several weeks with someone who was probably his assistant. It didn't take her long to realize that he was going to see if he could lease her building and turn it into some kind of studio.

What the heck? He had hundreds of square feet in his daddy's house, which was practically a mansion. Why did he need to rent commercial space? She needed to put a stop to this right away.

When he finally finished his call, she stepped right up to him, hands on her hips. "You can't lease this building. It belongs to me," she said bluntly.

Molly had no idea what a sardonic stare was, but she reckoned that the look she got from Simon probably qualified as one. Although she had to admit maybe his look was more surprised than anything else. After all, there was a big, if faded, "For Lease" sign in the building's window. She scrambled to explain. "I mean, it doesn't belong to me . . . yet. But it will. Soon. I'm going to put a car showroom and garage in there. So you can't have it."

He stood there with this hard-to-read expression in his eyes and those infernal curls at the corners of his mouth doing their thing. He said nothing, though. It was annoying how much Simon could say without opening his mouth.

"It's too big for a studio anyway." Molly forged onward, laying out all her arguments. "You don't belong here."

"You're right about that. But I'm here. For a while anyway—while Eugene Hanks wades through my father's affairs. And I need a place to paint."

"You could paint at home."

"No, I don't think so." He didn't elaborate, and Molly got the feeling that arguing about that would get her nowhere.

"Well, you can't paint here. It's mine." She turned on her heel and walked away, painfully aware that she had just sounded like some kind of pitiful little kid facing down one of the big boys on the playground. Only Simon hadn't behaved like a bully. A real bully would have mashed her flat or said something mean or ugly about her butt or her hair.

No, Simon didn't do any of those things. He'd just stood there looking at her from out of those big, brown eyes. Okay, so they didn't look sardonic; they looked kind of puppy-dog-ish. Which was annoying as hell because Molly had always wanted a puppy but Momma was allergic. And sad puppy eyes were like kryptonite to her. One look and she was rendered soft and pathetic and... girlie.

Damn.

Simon watched Molly as she headed back down the sidewalk, her dark curls lit up by the morning light, and her hips swaying in a pair of baggy pants. She had a long, confident stride, like a person who knew exactly where she was going in life.

He admired that.

She was a piece of work all right. She always had been. Even as a little girl in her overalls, standing with her daddy on the sidelines of every Rebels game.

He let go of a breath. It was all ancient history, better forgotten, like those summers with Luke Raintree. He'd spent years pushing those memories deep. No sense in dredging them up now. He was getting out of this place as soon as he could.

He turned and inspected the old building. The place was run-down, practically decrepit, and way too big for him. But it had the advantage of having large windows and being close to his parents' house, without actually being in it.

He couldn't paint at home. Mother would have a fit. His art had always been a bone of contention. Even more important, Mother didn't know who he was. She vacillated between treating him like a servant and a thief.

In a sad way, he *was* a thief. And Aunt Millie and Aunt Frances weren't above trying to guilt him about it, while Bubba thought he should just drop everything, go to war with Uncle Ryan, and assume management of the car dealership.

But none of those actions made any sense. He couldn't live permanently in this town. He was willing to stay in order to unsnarl his father's finances. He would try to convince Uncle Ryan to sell the dealership instead of liquidating it, but he wasn't becoming a car salesman. And of course, he'd have to see about selling Mother's house and making an informed decision about her future care.

That might take weeks or months.

But Simon didn't have weeks or months. He needed to focus on finishing the Harrison commission, which was due to be installed at the end of July in Harrison's new country estate in Sonoma.

He needed a sizable temporary studio to finish the painting. And he didn't have time to screw around. So Angel, his assistant, was going to bring the unfinished painting all the way across the country.

He looked down Palmetto Avenue. When he was a

teenager, he couldn't wait to get away from this place. The feeling hadn't changed.

He needed to get back to Paradise. But before that, he had a meeting with Eugene Hanks, and then he needed to visit Arlo Boyd at the real estate office and see if the owner of the building would rent it to him cheap.

Molly was in a terrible mood when she finally arrived at work. The parts had arrived for the piece-of-crap Hyundai, just as the rental car agency informed them that they would be sending a tow truck from Orangeburg. It appeared that Simon Wolfe didn't actually need a rental car anymore since he had his daddy's Taurus, not to mention all the vehicles on the lot at Wolfe Ford.

She turned her attention to Lessie Anderson's fifteen-year-old Chrysler, which needed a tune-up. Molly was hip-deep in motor oil when her cell phone rang. She ignored it.

It rang again.

And again.

She climbed out of the service pit, wiped her hands on a dirty rag, and fished the phone from her pocket. She didn't recognize the number. She was about to put the phone on silent when it rang again.

"Who the hell are you and why are you calling me?" she bellowed into the phone.

"Uh, it's me, Ricki. You said I should call?"

"Oh, um, I'm sorry. I didn't recognize the number."

"I'm not using the store's phone. There seems to be something wrong with it."

Great. One more thing on Molly's to-do list. "Besides the phone, what's the problem?"

"Where do I find merino, and what the heck is it?"

Oh, brother. "Merino is a kind of wool."

"Oh." There was a long pause on the other end of the line. "Yes, but all this yarn is made of wool, isn't it?"

Molly saw red. She opened her mouth to say something really snotty. But she stopped. Ricki wasn't actually the person she was angry with. Momma was the main villain. Ricki was just an innocent bystander.

She took a calming breath and decided to treat this as a teachable moment. "Ricki, yarn is made from all kinds of fibers, like cotton and silk and even bamboo."

"Really?"

Les Hayes came strolling into the garage. Les was supposed to be at work. What was he doing here? His big baby blues looked worried, even in the shade of his ball cap.

"Look, Ricki, I gotta go."

"Oh, well, Lola May called, and she's looking for dye lot 9824 of superwash merino."

"Uh, Ricki, how could Lola May call if the phone isn't working?"

Another long silence stretched out. "Well, uh, I kind of broke the phone. I mean I was trying to see if the yarn in the front was what she was looking for and the wire kind of came out from the phone."

"Great."

"No, it's kind of not great, because the phone keeps ringing and I can't answer it."

"Unplug it, Ricki." Molly no longer hid her exasperation. "I gotta go now." She put the cell on silent mode and turned toward Les. "What are you doing here?"

"We have a big problem."

Molly hoped he was talking about Momma leaving town and Ricki being clueless about yarn, because Molly didn't need any more problems. "What is it?"

"The bank closed the dealership. Everyone was sent home—without pay. They gave us directions to the unemployment office. I'm headed there after lunch."

Given the magnitude of his announcement, it was really rather remarkable that Les's voice was steady, and he didn't even sound panicky.

"Damn it! They didn't waste any time, did they? And we don't have anyplace to work on the Shelby. You got any ideas? When do we have to clear it out of there?"

"Uh, Molly, you don't understand. The Shelby is locked up with everything else on the premises. And even though we have a bill of sale for the car, apparently it doesn't matter. Ryan Polk was the one who made the announcement, and he told me that, as far as he was concerned, the Shelby is an asset of the dealership."

"Well, that's ridiculous." The pitch of her voice headed toward the upper registers. Her hands started to shake, and the tops of her ears started to burn. She was furious. How could Ryan Polk do such a thing? He knew darn well the Shelby didn't belong to Ira.

Greedy bastard.

"I tried to argue with Mr. Polk," Les said, "but he had a bunch of security goons with him, and they were armed. Everyone was forced to leave with about five minutes' notice. Molly, we aren't going to get the car back anytime soon, and we're going to have to fight the bank tooth and nail."

She pulled a rag out of her pocket and started wiping grease from her hands. "We'll just have to go talk to

Eugene Hanks. Or maybe we could take a contract out on Simon Wolfe."

"It's not Simon's fault," Bubba said, climbing out from under the Chevrolet he was working on.

"Of course it's Simon's fault."

Bubba shook his head. "No. It's not. Rachel's uncle is in some kind of big hurry, and Simon has no power to stop him. I mean, Simon's daddy owed Ryan's bank a lot of money. I don't think Simon set this in motion. I really don't."

"But he's in a hurry to leave town," Molly insisted.

"I know that. But it wouldn't matter if he were staying," Bubba said. "Ryan isn't going to let Simon lay his hands on the dealership. That's pretty clear. And I doubt Simon would be successful fighting over it in court since the business owes the bank all that money. The only good news is that the business is separate from Ira's personal finances. Simon is planning to stay because he was named executor of the will, which means he has control over what happens to the house. It's a good thing Aunt Charlotte's house is protected from the bank, otherwise I wouldn't put it past Ryan Polk to turn his own sister out. Course Simon is probably going to sell the house and move her off to California. So either way it sucks to be Aunt Charlotte."

"Simon probably wants to pocket the money from the sale," Molly said.

"Nah. Not Simon. I don't think money motivates him. I think he's just stuck here between his mother and his uncle. I kind of feel sorry for him. I'm telling you, some of my wife's kinfolk could be described as money-grubbers. It's not easy being related to those people, even by marriage. You should hear the conversations I sometimes have with my mother-in-law. Honestly, the Polks can be pretty narrow-minded when it comes to cash."

Les plopped down on a shop stool and changed the subject. "Bubba, you think LeRoy might hire me? I've got a lot of contacts with F-150 owners. There are going to be a lot of them looking for a reliable service center now that the dealership is closed."

"You should talk to him," Bubba said.

"Les, we need to make a plan for getting the Shelby back and finding a place where we can work on it. Why don't I take you to dinner tonight at the Pig Place? I mean, Momma's gone and—"

"Uh, well…" Les's face turned red.

"What?"

"I, uh, kind of have a date with Tammy Nelson."

"With Tammy? Of the horse teeth?"

He gave her the stink eye. "She does not have horse teeth. They are just really white."

"And big. Almost as big as her—"

"Don't say it, Molly." Les hopped off the stool. "I'm going to go talk to LeRoy. Is he in?"

"Yeah, but we need to—"

"Molly, take a big breath and calm down, will you? There isn't anything we can do about the Shelby right now. So there isn't any point in letting it make you angry. And I have a date with a pretty woman, which I'm not going to break. Maybe tomorrow we can talk to Eugene, but I don't have the money right now to hire a lawyer. Do you?"

"No, but we can't let Ryan Polk steal our car, can we?"

# CHAPTER 6

Molly hadn't planned to attend tonight's meeting of the Last Chance Book Club. She didn't have anything nice to say about their book selection this time. Besides, she had planned to work on the Shelby.

But the bank had screwed up that option. And when she got home from work, she found her lazy, no-account brother sleeping on the couch, dirty dishes in the sink, and laundry overflowing the hamper in the bathroom.

She probably should have gone grocery shopping or tackled the laundry, but that would have ticked her off worse than she already was. So she took a shower, made herself a grilled cheese sandwich with the last remaining piece of American cheese, and headed out for her meeting.

Thank goodness Savannah White was on refreshment detail this week. She arrived with the most amazingly delicious apple strudel.

Molly found herself standing around the refreshment table with several club members including Jenny Carpenter, Arlene Whitaker, and Rocky deBracy, the wife of the English baron whose textile machinery plant was single-handedly creating an economic renaissance in Last Chance.

"Honey," Rocky said to Savannah as more members of the club trickled through the library doors, "you have to enter this strudel in the pie contest at this year's Watermelon Festival."

Savannah gave Jenny a little smile, as if she knew that Jenny's string of pie-baking victories was about to come to an ignominious end. "Oh, I don't know," she said sweetly. "It's not my recipe. It's my granny's. And I think she already won a few blue ribbons at the festival."

Jenny maintained her composure. And why not? Jenny's pies were as amazing as Savannah's strudel. Molly was impressed by the baking prowess of both of them. When it was Molly's time to bring refreshments, she always stopped at the doughnut shop.

Jane Rhodes waddled in carrying her knitting bag and looking like an over-inflated hot-air balloon. "Hey, honey," Arlene said, draping an arm around her niece-by-marriage, "when are you going to have that baby?"

"I don't know. I'm already three days past my due date, and I'm tired of people looking at me slant-wise and asking me why I'm still here. Like I'm going to disappear once baby Faith is born." She ran her hand over her baby bump.

"So you've settled on a name?" Rocky asked. The baby in question was going to be Rocky's niece.

Jane nodded. "Yeah. But I'm starting to think that she's holding out until I finish this sweater." She reached into her bag and pulled out a pink baby sweater that was missing one arm. Jane had been working on this sweater for weeks and weeks.

She gave Molly a pleading look. "I'm desperate. How do I pick up the stitches around the armhole again? You walked me through it on the first arm, but then I forgot how to do it. And I was going to go ask your mother, but I saw the notice on the door. Where is your mom?"

"That's one of those unanswerable questions," Molly said. "Apparently she's gone to see the world. And she didn't think she needed to take Coach with her."

"Well, good for her," Arlene said. "Don't get me wrong, Moll. I love your daddy. He's a great football coach and all, but he's been ignoring your momma for some time."

Molly didn't respond to this. Because the more she thought about the situation, the more she realized there was blame on both sides. Coach had ignored Momma, but it wasn't right for Momma to take off without a word and leave everything on Molly's shoulders. She clamped her mouth shut and took Jane's knitting into her hands.

She immediately relaxed. What was it about knitting that always calmed her down? She felt the same way when she was working on a car. Whenever her hands got busy, her brain slowed down, and she could live in the moment.

She was deep into a knitting lesson when Nita Wills, the town librarian, called the group together. Hettie Marshall Ellis had arrived. Hettie was the CEO of Country Pride Chicken, the second largest employer in Allenberg County. She had also recently eloped with Reverend William Ellis, the pastor of Christ Episcopal.

No one in town, much less the book club, knew how to deal with this new reality. Hettie was often regarded as the Queen Bee of Last Chance, but that seemed like a very unlikely role for a minister's wife.

When everyone had settled down, Nita kicked off the book discussion. "I have a number of questions about our selection this time, but before I start, does anyone have a question of their own?"

"Yeah," Molly said, "why on earth did we pick this book?"

A titter of laughter met this comment, but Nita wasn't smiling. "I take it you didn't like the book."

"Nita, the book is over a thousand pages. I got to page two hundred and threw the paperback against the wall. Honestly, this was the most depressing thing I've read since *The Road*. Why do we read these books?"

"She's got a point," Arlene said. "I mean, I'm all for capitalism and freedom and all that, but honestly the author goes on and on about it. And she seems to think that anyone who gives to charity is either misguided or downright evil."

Lola May snorted. "Arlene, didn't you know that the best way to help poor folks is to let rich folks get richer?"

"Well, that is the morality that Ayn Rand espouses in this book," Nita said.

"Well, it ain't very moral," Lola May countered.

Cathy Niles let go of a long, mournful sigh. "Can we read something light and fun next time? I really liked it when we read *Pride and Prejudice*. I'd like to read a love story that doesn't involve the characters having long-winded conversations about original sin, morality, and free love. I don't know about y'all but I don't find any of that even remotely romantic."

"That's the point," Nita said. "We're reading to—"

"Nita, the book is just BS, and frankly someone should have edited it. It was boring," Savannah said.

Everyone looked in Savannah's direction. The use of even abbreviated profanity was frowned upon, especially with a minister's wife in attendance.

Savannah faced them all with cool aplomb. "I'm sorry, y'all, but the ideas in this book are just mean. For instance, if folks followed Ayn Rand's philosophy, The Kismet would have been torn down and replaced with a new, shiny, soulless multiplex. Instead, Dash helped Angel Development put money into the old theater, even though we all know it's probably never going to show a profit. But having a theater will build up our community. And that's important. Sometimes the community is just as important as the individual. And sometimes an individual needs help."

"Hear, hear," Molly said. "If it weren't for Ira Wolfe and his generosity, I wouldn't be anywhere near getting my own business off the ground. Of course, I can't say the same about his no-account son, or Ira's brother-in-law. Did y'all hear about how the bank closed the dealership?"

Everyone nodded except Savannah. She just stared at Molly, kind of the same way she'd stared yesterday at the Purly Girls meeting.

"Savannah, I know I don't have grease on my face this time. What is it?"

Savannah blinked. "Oh, nothing. I was just thinking." Savannah turned toward Nita. "We should stop reading dystopian fiction. It's depressing everyone, especially since things are improving here in Last Chance. I know we talked about reading *Hunger Games* next, but I really don't want to spend time with kids who are forced to kill each other for the amusement of the state."

"Me neither," said Cathy. "And you know what? It's kind of disturbing that every other book you pick up these days at the bookstore has a vampire or a werewolf or kids run amok. Doesn't anyone read the sweet books anymore? You know, like *Little Women*?"

"*Little Women*?" Hettie finally spoke. "My goodness, I haven't read that since I was twelve. I did love that book."

"I've never read it at all," Arlene said. "But I did see the movie. I loved Christian Bale, but I could never understand why Winona Ryder threw him over for Gabriel Byrne."

While Arlene was speaking, Savannah stared across the table at Molly. Her gaze was intensely probing. Just before Molly was about to check to see if she'd spilled cheese on her T-shirt, Savannah turned toward Nita. "You know, I think we should read *Little Women*."

"Could we talk about this book first, before we select the next one?" Nita said.

"No," Hettie said, looking around the table. "Is there anyone here who finished this book?"

Jenny Carpenter was the only one who raised her hand. But that hardly counted because Jenny had no life beyond teaching algebra at the high school. And, truth to tell, Jenny had been kind of depressed since Reverend Ellis had run off with Hettie. So of course she'd had time to read a book with a thousand pages.

Hettie stared at Nita. "I rest my case. Who wants to read something sweet like *Little Women* next time?"

All the hands went up. Of course, more than half the ladies of the book club were members of Christ Episcopal. So if their minister's wife, who also happened to be the second largest employer in town, suggested a book, it was a lead pipe cinch that everyone would agree to read it.

• • •

"Hold up a minute, Molly," Savannah called. Molly was heading toward her canary yellow Charger, parked in the lot behind the library.

She turned as Savannah hurried up to her. "What?"

"Uh…" Savannah stood there for a moment looking awkward.

"What the heck is it? Do I have BO or something?"

Savannah shook her head. "No, it's just that I have something I need to tell you."

"About what?"

Savannah danced from foot to foot and continued to look awkward. When she spoke, her words came out like a racing freight train. "It's a message from Aunt Miriam."

Wariness scrambled over Molly's backbone. "From Miriam?" she asked. Crap, she didn't need another surprise today.

Savannah's aunt was practically legendary. She was one part fortune-teller, one part busybody, and she'd made it her life's work to find soulmates for every blessed single person in Last Chance. She'd been implicated in several recent weddings. Miriam also had a hand in matching Savannah up with Dash Randall. Molly glanced at the big, fat diamond on Savannah's hand. The wedding of the decade was planned for the first week of June.

Molly wanted nothing to do with one of Miriam Randall's predictions. She didn't believe in that crap, which put her in the minority. If Miriam made a forecast, the church ladies of Last Chance—and that was a majority of the female population—would be working overtime to get her hitched up to someone.

Yuck.

"Don't look so astonished and petrified." Savannah was actually wringing her hands, which seemed like a bad omen.

"What is it? Are you about to tell me that I should be looking for a man just like my father? I'm not sure that's what I want. I mean, look at where it left Momma."

Savannah frowned. "Uh, well, I'm not sure. He might be like your father. I mean, well, most men like football, don't they?"

"Yeah, I guess. What exactly did Miriam tell you?"

"She told me you should be looking for someone who has known you for a long time. Since you were little."

The forecast was a little underwhelming. And also annoying.

"Great. So every past member of the Davis High School football team is a possible match."

"Uh, well..." Savannah's voice faded out.

"Or are you trying to tell me that I belong with Les? Because if that's what you're saying, you can just forget it. Les is my friend. We are not romantically involved. In fact, he's on a date right now with Tammy Nelson."

"Tammy? With the teeth and boobs?"

"Yeah. I'm thinking the boobs are the main attraction. Les is a pretty simple and straightforward kind of guy."

"Uh, well, I don't know," Savannah said in a rush, like she was suddenly trying to get away from Molly.

"Do me a favor. Tell your aunt not to repeat this crap, okay? I've already got problems out the wazoo. I do not need a bunch of busybodies trying to turn me into a bride. I am not bride material."

Ricki Wilson tapped her right heel forward and then her toe. She crossed her right foot behind her left and rocked to the Wild Horses' cover of "Boot Scootin' Boogie." As always, she danced right near the stage where she could keep an eye on Clay Rhodes, the fiddler in the band and the man she let get away.

The Wednesday crowd at Dot's Spot wasn't near as big as it would be on Friday, but it was big enough that she could dance without being alone. Which was completely ironic because she was as alone as a body could get.

She had lost Clay years ago when she'd decided to dump him in favor of the richer and older Randy Burrowes, the talent scout for the record label Clay had signed with back when he was eighteen.

Her decision had cost Clay a lot, because he'd walked away from that record deal. And she'd gone on to marry Randy.

She'd lived a pretty high life for a while. And then she reaped the seeds of destruction that she'd sown. Randy started cheating on her with a younger woman. And then the bottom fell out when she (and the law) discovered that Randy had embezzled a whole bunch of the record label's money.

She'd come crawling back to Last Chance, utterly broke and looking for a second chance with the only man who'd treated her with respect. But by then, Clay was in love with someone else.

Ricki knew it was stupid and ugly to hate Jane Rhodes, but she couldn't help herself. Jane was just so sweet. And Ricki was not that kind of woman. She never had been.

Well, at least she wasn't waiting on tables anymore. When she took that job at the Kountry Kitchen a couple of years ago, she thought it might be a nice place to meet men. Like that old Suzy Bogguss song about "Eat at Joe's." But it hadn't worked out.

Plenty of men ate at the Kitchen, but very few of them were unattached. And the best of the bachelors, like Bubba Lockheart, Stone Rhodes, and Dash Randall, had up and gotten the marriage bug. Sadly, none of them had chosen her.

She wasn't ever going to find Prince Charming at the Kountry Kitchen. She wasn't going to find him at the Knit & Stitch either, but at least working there would be easier on her bunions.

In fact, tonight she wasn't at all footsore, and that made line dancing so much more fun. Line dancing was just about the most fun a woman could have by her lonesome.

Just then, as if to point out the sorry state of Ricki's life, the Wild Horses changed tempo. Clay started singing a soft, sad ballad and playing a truly weepy violin.

Damn him.

All the line dancers headed for their tables. One or two couples stayed on the floor. She turned away and headed toward the bar, where the usual cast of characters were hanging out. She took the open seat next to Roy Burdett, who was telling a long and involved fishing story to Arlo Boyd. It was kind of amazing how Roy and Arlo could talk fishing twenty-four seven.

Dot put a glass of tonic and lime in front of Ricki and leaned in. "So, I heard T-Bone is in a snit because you left."

"I got a better offer."

"Yeah, honey, but what happens when Pat Canaday comes back?"

Ricki didn't want to think about that. "Who says she is coming back?"

Dot frowned. "Pat loves Coach."

"Well, if she loves him so much, why'd she walk out on him?"

Dot rolled her eyes toward Roy and Arlo. "Maybe because he took one too many fishing trips," she whispered.

"That's just dumb. If I had a husband, I wouldn't get mad at him for going fishing. A man needs his hobbies."

"I reckon," Dot said and moved down to refill a few drinks.

The band took a break, and Ricki was thinking about doing something heinous, like flirting with a married man, when Les Hayes came through the front door looking like the last pea at pea-time.

He stepped up to the bar right beside her and ordered a longneck Bud.

Les was nice looking when he cleaned himself up.

He was wearing a pair of new blue jeans and a striped golf shirt. His nails were cut down to the quick, and they looked remarkably clean for a man who worked on cars for a living.

Of course, Les was easily seven years too young for a woman Ricki's age, but a cat could always look at a king, as her momma used to say. And looking at Les was not a strain.

"Hey," she said. "How's it going?"

"Lousy."

"I'm sorry."

He gave her a long gaze. And damned if Ricki didn't feel like it was the first time Leslie Hayes had ever really seen her. A slow smile touched his lips. His mouth was just a tiny bit crooked. And he had a set of very sexy laugh lines.

Not to mention the sky blue eyes.

"Well, thanks, Ricki."

"What's wrong?"

"Ryan Polk and the First National Bank sent Wolfe Ford into receivership, which means me and thirty-nine other people just lost our jobs."

"Oh, I'm sorry."

"And then Tammy Nelson stood me up."

"Tammy Nelson? What were you doing with her? I thought you and Molly Canaday had a thing going."

He shrugged. The movement said more than his words. "Nope. No thing with Molly. And Tammy said she wanted a man with a steady job. She said she was getting too old to waste her time on an unemployed person." He tipped up his beer and demolished it in several long swallows.

"Tammy couldn't be more than twenty-eight," Ricki

said, staring down at her tonic water so that she wouldn't get mesmerized by the movement of his Adam's apple as he swigged his beer.

"Yeah, and that means her biological clock is ticking like a time bomb. Her parting shot was something about wanting to have babies with a man who could afford them."

"Oh, that's low."

He nodded. "It's okay. I wasn't all that interested in Tammy—at least not in having babies with her anyway."

"Yeah, I can imagine exactly what you were interested in."

This brought forth the smallest of chuckles from him. He had a funny, nerdy kind of laugh.

Molly needed to watch out if Les was paying attention to Tammy's bustline. Not that it was easy to ignore Tammy's bust when she poured her girls into tight sweaters. But still. Les and Molly belonged together. Everyone knew it.

The band returned from their break and struck up a soulful rendition of the "Tennessee Waltz."

"Dance with me," Les said.

Ricki's heart squeezed in her chest, and for the first time in eons, something inside her—something that had been frozen over for a long time—cracked. Emotions flowed. She wanted to dance with him. With all her heart. She found him attractive. But he was too young for her. And besides, she was working for Molly now. Leslie Hayes was off limits.

She already had a lot of misdeeds on her spiritual scorecard. And messing around with Les Hayes was going to set her karma back big time.

"Uh, no, thanks, Les. I gotta be running." She put a few dollars down on the bar for her drink and hopped down from the stool. "You take care, now, you hear," she said.

Then she turned and walked away from the first man who had asked her to dance in a good five years. It was one of the hardest things she'd ever done in her lonely, lonely life.

Zeph Gibbs stood in the shadow cast by the door frame of the old Coca-Cola building. He kept a vigil there, his gaze trained on Dot's Spot. The neon beer signs in the honky-tonk's small windows cast a glow over the sidewalk across the street. He cataloged the people going in and out.

Mostly regulars like Roy Burdett, but there were some surprises tonight, like Les Hayes. Les wasn't much of a drinker, but Zeph reckoned it was only natural for a man to want a couple of belts when he'd lost his job.

A shiver ran up Zeph's spine. The ghost, which had haunted him for years, was restless tonight. So was the dog—a tiny thing that looked like a cross between a Yorkie and a Maltese. The critter shouldn't have survived the swamp. But she had, probably because the ghost had found her first and scared off the predators.

Zeph had to wonder about the person who left a tiny dog like this out where she was prey for gators and snakes. No wonder the poor thing was shivering. She wasn't even full growed, and she already knew how brutal the world could be.

He stroked the pup and spoke nonsense to her for a long time. Eventually she relaxed and fell asleep.

But not the ghost. He never slept. And things had been worse the last few days, since Simon Wolfe's return. The ghost had become edgy and nervous. As if it expected something to happen now that Simon was back.

It wouldn't be good if the ghost decided to haunt Simon. And Zeph could certainly see why the ghost might want to do that. No, that needed to be avoided at all costs. It was Zeph's job to keep the ghost contained until Simon left town. And right now, that meant finding a home for this pup. The ghost always calmed down when one of its strays was taken care of. So Zeph had pushed things up a little bit. He'd made a snap decision.

Zeph stirred from the shadows, crossed the street, and headed into the alley between Dot's place and the dry cleaners. The alley opened into a parking lot. Across the way stood a small two-story house with an external fire stair leading to a second-floor apartment.

There was a small, weed-overgrown garden at the back with a couple of concrete planters that hadn't seen living plants in some time. Zeph pulled out the remnants of long-dead flowers, then laid down a couple of rags that he'd tucked into his shirt to keep them warm.

He placed the dog on the makeshift bed, then backed into the shadows at the corner of the building. He checked his watch. On Wednesdays and Fridays, Ricki left the bar at ten-thirty.

He didn't have to wait very long, and he wasn't surprised when the dog woke up right on cue. The ghost had something to do with that. The critters could see the ghost, even better than Zeph could.

Ricki came walking across the lot on those high-heeled boots she always wore to Dot's. Before she could put one foot on the stair leading to her apartment, the dog raised her head and gave a little halfhearted bark.

Ricki gasped in surprise and turned toward the planter. The dog barked again and started shivering.

And that was all it took for the bond to be forged.

Molly ducked out of work on Thursday morning around ten-thirty, just as soon as she'd finished rotating the tires on Clyde McKeller's Buick. She hurried up the street and into Arlo Boyd's real estate office.

She probably should have had an appointment, but these were desperate times. Adelle Clarke, his receptionist, looked up from her workstation computer as Molly came through the door.

"Hey," Molly said, "is Arlo available?"

"He's back in his office reading the paper and eating his midmorning doughnut. Thursdays are pretty slow. You can go on back."

Molly headed down a hallway, past a break room, and into Arlo's standard-issue real estate office. The room had a faux-wood desk, blue carpet, and a conference table where Arlo helped his clients make deals and offers. Arlo had once been a really big dude. Big enough to be a linebacker on the 1990 Rebels dream team. But that had been a long time ago. His love of doughnuts and cigarettes had caught up to him. He was balding and paunchy and red-faced, and he was headed for an early coronary just like Ira. She caught him finishing a big, juicy Bavarian cream doughnut.

"Hey, Arlo," Molly said. "I only have a minute. I've gotta get back to work. But I wanted to find out how much it would cost to lease the old Coca-Cola building."

Arlo used a paper towel to dab the Bavarian cream that

had leaked from the corner of his mouth. "Sweet Jesus, what is going on in this town? That building's been vacant for decades, and now, suddenly, in the space of three days, I've got two people wanting to lease it and a third who's about to make an offer to buy it."

"What? Someone is buying it? Who?"

"Well, the offer isn't all the way in yet. To be honest. And I'm not at liberty to disclose that. But it doesn't matter because the building is no longer available for lease. It's been leased for the next three months."

"Three months? You leased it for only three months?"

He speared the last few doughnut crumbs on his Styrofoam plate and conveyed them to his mouth with his finger. "Well," he said after savoring the last morsels with half-closed eyes, "the building's been vacant for a decade. I wasn't about to look a gift horse in the mouth. In fact, I would have taken the horse even if he'd been toothless and ready for the glue factory."

"But that building's mine."

"Uh, no, not really. The building belongs to the First Bank of South Carolina, and they've been trying to off-load it for years. And it would appear that there is a buyer for it. Although the buyer is a mite ticked off that it's been leased."

"Who did you lease it to?"

"Simon Wolfe."

"Dang!" She stomped her foot, turned around, paced three steps and then back. She wanted to put her fist through the wall. But that would probably hurt. A lot. "I'm gonna kill him."

"Uh, don't do that Molly. Stone would have to arrest you, and it would break Coach's heart."

"Ha. This is not funny."

"Well, honey, you just bide your time for a while and maybe someone else will kill him for you. For a dude who's been here for less than a week, he sure has managed to tick off a lot of people. You take my aunt Rose? She has a brand-new Ford Fusion, and she's going to have to drive eighty miles to get that car its warranty service. Sure is a sad time."

"Then why did you lease the building to him?"

"Easy. He's a teammate. And the way I remember it, we wouldn't have ever made it to the state championship without his foot. So I owed him one. And the building was empty, and he didn't even want me to do any cleaning or upgrading, which was kind of a godsend because the place is a mess. And also, the bank would have been furious with me if I hadn't."

Molly made an inarticulate sound that verged on a Rebel yell.

"Honey," Arlo said, "relax. Maybe I can find you something else. What are you looking for?"

"Garage space. Someplace to start a restoration business."

He snorted. "Well, you just wait and Wolfe Ford will eventually be available. After Ira's family strips it clean."

She glared at him.

"All right," he said with a professional grin. "I'll just do a little search for you and see what might be available. How's that?"

Molly let Arlo appease her. "All right."

"Good, I know where to find you. I'll give you a call tomorrow sometime, okay?"

"Okay."

She turned and trudged right out of the real estate office, across the street, and up into Eugene Hanks's law office. If she was going to spend the money to rent commercial space, she had better get her hands on the Shelby, and fast.

But when she found out that Eugene couldn't represent her, on account of the fact that he was already representing Simon Wolfe, she was, really and truly, ready to commit murder.

# CHAPTER
## 8

On Saturday, a week after his father's untimely death, Simon sat amid the flowers in his mother's perennial garden. He'd spent the last few days making himself useful by weeding the bed, edging the garden's border, and staking up foxgloves and delphiniums. This morning, he was hiding out with his sketch pad, doing studies of the flowers while Mother got ready for her garden club meeting.

The gardening aside, he felt like a prisoner in this house. Not only had Mother failed to recognize him, but, thanks to Aunt Millie, Mother was convinced he was the new combination handyman, caretaker, gardener, cook, butler, chauffeur, and footman.

He didn't mind taking care of his mother or her garden, but he hated every minute she treated him like an employee. His emotions were so deep and complicated he didn't even have words to express them. It was painful to realize that the scars of his childhood still festered.

He was itching to paint. But his painting equipment wouldn't be there for another couple of days. His assistant was on his way with the unfinished Harrison commission. At least he had a place to set things up. The old Coca-Cola bottling plant was way too big for him, but the lease had been cheap, and Arlo Boyd had allowed him to take a short-term deal on the place.

He added shading to his sketch and let the morning sunshine soak in. It was hot here, in a humid way that he'd forgotten. Northern California could get hot, too. But not the same way. This humidity wasn't comfortable, but it was bone-deep familiar.

His cell phone rang. He checked the ID—no one on his contact list, but the area code wasn't local.

Maybe this wasn't another nasty call from someone who owned a Ford and now had to travel eighty miles to get it serviced by a dealership. Molly Canaday had been right. There were hundreds of people with F-150 pickups who were ticked off about Wolfe Ford's closure. Unfortunately, they mostly blamed Simon, even though the real villain was his uncle Ryan. It didn't matter who was at fault; the town's animosity had been justifiably earned. And Simon felt it every time he ran down to the BI-LO for groceries.

He continued to stare at the caller ID for a moment, then decided to take the call. He wasn't a villain. The least he could do was listen to people vent. It wouldn't change a thing, but maybe folks would come to realize that he wasn't afraid of hearing what they had to say.

He pressed the talk button. "This is Simon Wolfe." He braced himself for another round of verbal abuse.

Instead a low and slightly husky female voice said, "Hello, Simon. You and I met at your father's funeral."

"Who is this?"

"It's Lark Chaikin, Stone Rhodes's wife."

He closed his sketch pad. "Oh, hello. I'm a fan of yours."

Silence for a beat. "A fan? Really?" There was a definite northern edge to Lark's accent.

"Yeah, I have a copy of *Rural Scenes*. I love your images of the swamps. I recognized some of the local scenes the moment I picked it up at the bookstore."

"I guess that means you spent a lot of time in the swamps."

He chuckled, thinking about Luke and Gabe Raintree. "Yeah, I did. So, what can I do for you?"

"Well, I heard from Arlo that you leased the old Coca-Cola building."

He had forgotten how fast news travels in Last Chance.

"Only short-term. I need a place to paint while I settle Daddy's estate."

There was another slight hesitation before Lark spoke again. "Look, Simon, I'm calling because I've had my eye on that building as studio space for a while now. I was thinking it could be transformed into a number of studios."

"Are there that many artists in Allenberg County?"

"Well, no," she said, "but there's you and me, and I looked you up. You're up and coming, as they like to say."

He focused his gaze on the tall, showy spikes of foxglove. "Uh, my press clippings exaggerate. I can assure you that, while I'm not starving, I'm also not Thomas Kinkaid."

"But I spoke with Rory Harrison, and he says you're brilliant. And if Rory Harrison likes your work, then you are probably more than merely up and coming."

Wow, she was well connected. "Okay, I'll bite. Why exactly did you call?"

"It's complicated. I'm part of a group of investors interested in renovating the downtown district. And we've had several conversations about the Coca-Cola building. It's turn-of-the-twentieth-century commercial architecture and ought to be registered as a historic site. And abandoned, like it is, it's a terrible eyesore. So I thought we might use it to create an artists' colony."

"An artists' colony in Last Chance? Are you nuts?"

She laughed. "Well, probably. But there's precedent. Up in the Washington, DC, area, where I lived for a while, there was an old factory that the city of Alexandria renovated into studio space for working artists and artisans. I'm thinking our Coca-Cola building would be perfect for the same thing, on a smaller scale. Having a place where people can buy art and crafts on a year-round basis could be wonderful for the town's economy."

"Uh, well, that's a fabulous idea for an urban area like DC, but I don't know about Allenberg County. And besides, I'm not staying. I'm just leasing the place for a short time."

"Oh."

"I have a life in California."

"Oh. Well. I just thought with your mother and all..."

"I'm sorry."

There was a long silence on the other end of the phone before Lark spoke again. "You know, I don't give up so easily. I'd like to have lunch with you. If not to talk about this project, then to just connect with an up-and-coming artist. At the Red Hot Pig Place? This noontime?"

His mother came through the French doors at the rear

of the house. She was all dressed up for her garden club meeting, and she gave him a wave through the windows. "Uh, lunch is out. Mother's garden club meeting only lasts until eleven-thirty or so. But I could meet for a quick cup of coffee at the Kountry Kitchen if you could be there in half an hour."

"That's perfect."

It was past nine o'clock when Molly finally dragged herself out of bed. Even sleeping in, she'd only managed about five hours of shut-eye last night. She'd stumbled home at four in the morning after spending hours at the Grease Pit making up time. She'd been pretty disorganized the last couple of days what with attending funerals, putting out fires at the Knit & Stitch, and looking for a lawyer who could help her get her car back. Thank God it was Saturday—her day off.

She opened her dresser drawer and was greeted with a vast emptiness.

Crap. She was out of clean underwear. And, not surprisingly, her laundry basket was overflowing. Not to mention that dirty clothes littered her bedroom floor.

She stared at her unwashed laundry for a long moment. Momma always took care of the laundry. Just like she took care of the grocery shopping. Who the hell was supposed to do that stuff now?

She knew the answer. It sure wasn't going to be Allen, and Beau was off working in Columbia.

She hoisted the laundry basket up and headed to the small laundry room right off the kitchen. She didn't get very far.

The living room was a disaster area. Empty beer bottles and cans were strewn across every horizontal surface.

Pizza boxes littered the floor. Someone had been sick in Momma's schefflera. And the entire room reeked of beer and vomit.

Worse than that, some guy Molly didn't recognize was sprawled on the couch wearing nothing but his plaid boxer shorts. He was snoring with his mouth wide open.

Molly had missed all this destruction when she'd come home in the wee hours. She'd come in the side door and never switched on the light. Which was probably a good thing, because she needed her sleep. Thank God, Allen's no-account, redneck friends hadn't decided to use her room for something nasty.

Or maybe they had, and she didn't even know it.

Disgust and the overpowering odor of vomit made her gag. She was on the verge of rushing to the bathroom for a moment. She concentrated on breathing through her mouth and hollered. "Allen!" The guy on the couch didn't even budge. She let her voice move up the range from holler to yell. "Allen, you get your ass out here this minute."

Nothing but silence.

She dropped the laundry basket and headed toward the bedroom hallway. Allen's door was locked. She banged on it.

She heard a distinctly female voice say, "Allen, honey, wake up."

"Is he alive?" Molly yelled through the door.

"Uh, yeah," the voice said. "But he's kind of passed out."

"Oh, good," Molly muttered. "That means I can kill him when he wakes up." She turned away from the door, picked up her laundry, and headed toward the laundry room.

Where she discovered destruction that only a group of drunken fools could unleash. The room reeked of beer. There were empty bottles and cans everywhere. But that was nothing compared with what those boys had done to Momma's state-of-the-art, front-loading LG washing machine—the one Coach had given Momma for their anniversary a month ago. The one that had disappointed Momma because she had expected two tickets to someplace exotic.

The sleek, stainless-steel machine had been disconnected from the water and pulled out from the wall. It looked as if someone had taken a baseball bat to it. The control panel had popped off and hung upside down by a few wires. The stainless veneer on the washer's top had come off and lay bent on the laundry room floor. The door had been taken off its hinges and leaned against the far wall.

Molly peered into the machine's basket.

Someone had thrown a sizable rock into it. No doubt the a-holes had turned the machine on with it tumbling inside.

She stood there not really knowing what to think or feel. She was so surprised and angry that she went numb, except for the little hole in the middle of her forehead where it felt like someone was jackhammering. Of course the boys had been drunk. And all of Allen's friends were rednecks. They got into trouble on a regular basis.

But Momma's washing machine? Really?

She coldly headed toward the front closet where she found Allen's old aluminum baseball bat. She walked down the hall and vented all of her emotions on Allen's doorknob.

Eventually the lock gave way. She stalked into the room, which smelled like old socks and sweaty sex. Her brother was just waking up. He squinted up at her.

"Hey, Molly, wazzup?"

"You murdered Momma's washing machine." She lifted her bat. The naked girl with red and purple hair, smudged eyeliner, and press-on purple fangs gave a little squeak and then slid from the bed onto the floor. She had some kind of weird tattoo all down her back that was not terribly attractive. She started gathering up random pieces of black leather clothing.

"Uh..." Allen winced. "You're not going to actually use that bat, are you?"

Molly stood there trembling, her whole body on fire. What the hell was she going to tell Coach when he got back from his fishing trip? What the hell was she going to tell Momma?

Then it occurred to her that Momma might not be all that heartbroken to see the washer in little bits and pieces. And then she thought about how maybe Allen was just as upset about Momma being gone as she was. And maybe in some drunken rage, he'd taken all that anger out on the damn washing machine. Maybe Momma should have left him a book on meditation, too.

And then it occurred to her that no amount of meditation could make this situation any better. Besides, who had time for it? Especially since she now had a boatload of laundry and no washing machine.

She threw the bat at the wall. It hit the only window in Allen's room and shattered it. Allen's bed buddy squealed and headed for the hills.

"Hey, what did you do that for?"

"Because otherwise I might have broken your head. And that wouldn't have made me feel any better. Did it make you feel better to destroy Momma's washer?"

She didn't wait to hear her brother's explanations. She simply turned on her heel and left Allen's bedroom just in time to see the girl head into the bathroom and slam the door.

She shouldn't have broken Allen's door. She shouldn't have thrown the bat. She'd only contributed to the destruction that Allen had unleashed.

Molly went into her room and slammed the door behind her. She was not going to cry. Crying was for sissies. She was going to get herself dressed, without clean underwear, and she was going to go to the Wash-O-Rama next to the Knit & Stitch. She would dump the dirty clothes into the washer and then she'd go sit down quietly in the store and knit for an hour.

She picked up the book Momma had left her. Maybe she would actually try to read *One Minute Meditations*.

And maybe then she would stop feeling so angry.

Thirty minutes later, Molly found herself lugging laundry—both hers and Allen's—from her Charger into the Last Chance Wash-O-Rama. She started dumping clothes into washers and then realized that she didn't have any change for the machines.

She stood there gazing down at the five full machines, feeling angry and discouraged. She was so exhausted her head felt kind of spacey and her back hurt and her legs felt like lead.

She needed coffee. Bad.

She turned on her heel, leaving her clothes where they

were, and headed toward the Kountry Kitchen, a few doors down the block.

It being Saturday morning, the place was busy. But today, T-Bone Carter, the proprietor and main short-order cook, appeared to be having his own very bad day. Floretta Kemp, his new waitress, looked harried, and orders were piling up in the pass-through between the kitchen and the dining room. Meanwhile Flo seemed utterly confused as to which order belonged to which customer.

Molly felt a twinge of guilt. She'd unleashed this chaos on T-Bone by hiring Ricki. Of course, Momma was responsible for this. It was a classic case of unintended consequences.

She stood just inside the door for a moment, watching the flustered waitress move from table to table. The usual Saturday crowd was there with one exception. Lark Chaikin and Simon Wolfe were sitting together in one of the front booths sipping coffee and looking surprisingly chummy for a couple of people who were total strangers.

She wanted to march up to Simon and give him a little piece of her mind. But that wouldn't help her calm down, would it? And making a big spectacle of herself here in the Kitchen wouldn't get her Shelby back either.

She headed toward the counter, where there were seats available. But she didn't get very far before Lark called her by name.

"Molly," she said, "I just found out you were thinking about buying the Coca-Cola building. I wish I had known that."

It was a real good thing that Molly didn't have Coach's shotgun at that moment, because she probably would have aimed it at Simon Wolfe and pulled the trigger. It was bad enough that Momma had deserted her, and Allen had destroyed the washing machine, but Simon was the personification of every other bad thing that had recently happened in her life. He hadn't done a thing to stop the bank from taking over Wolfe Ford, and now he was sitting there telling Lark Chaikin all about her own plans for the Coca-Cola building. Such as they were.

Damn him.

A true southern lady would smile at a moment like this and say something sweet and benign and completely bitchy. But Molly wasn't good at that. She was good at telling the truth. "Well, it looks like I'm out of luck," she said, "because Simon has leased the place, and even after his lease is up, Arlo told me that someone else has already made an offer to buy the place."

She couldn't help herself. She gave Simon the stink eye and turned away from them. She found a seat. She had to wait five minutes before Flo came over to take her order, and then another ten minutes before the coffee finally arrived.

In the meantime, she had nothing better to do than to eavesdrop on the conversation going on in the booth behind her.

And that's when she discovered that it was Lark Chaikin who was planning to buy the building so she could create some kind of froufrou artists' colony. Great, just what Last Chance needed—a bunch of hippies getting subsidies so they could live their bohemian lifestyles, make cheesy art, and sell it to tourists.

Last Chance was getting more citified every day of the week. And Molly wasn't all that happy about it.

But she couldn't stop it. Lark was on the Angel Development board of directors. And she was related to Tulane Rhodes, the NASCAR driver whose wife, Sarah, was the mover and shaker behind the efforts to rebuild Palmetto Avenue's business district. Lark had the inside track. And Simon Wolfe was exactly like one of those citified artist types that Lark wanted to attract.

Molly was sunk. Officially. She didn't have the Shelby. Her best friend had lost his job. Her mother had flown the coop. Arlo was having a hard time finding acceptable garage space anywhere in Allenberg County. Her lawyer of choice had been hired by the enemy. And she didn't even have any clean clothes.

Life could not get much worse.

Except that it did, the moment Ricki Wilson opened the door and cried, "Someone, come quick, Jane's having her baby at the Knit & Stitch."

Molly turned in time to see Ricki, wearing a short skirt in a leopard print, a really tight tank top, and a pair of high-heeled boots that had probably stayed in the back of her closet when she'd been a waitress. She was dancing from one high heel to another, and she was hyperventilating.

And so was the tiny, shivering dog in her arms.

"Oh God, Molly, you have to come. She's screaming in pain."

"Did you call nine-one-one, or Doc Cooper?"

Ricki just stood there dancing from foot to foot with a deer-in-the-headlights kind of expression.

"Jeez Louise. Ricki, go run down to the hardware store and tell Clay."

Ricki crumbled. "I can't do that," she sobbed. Her yappy little dog started to bark in addition to shivering.

"I'll do it," Lark said, standing up and racing to the door.

Molly was not happy with Lark Chaikin, but she *was* Clay's sister-in-law and had a reputation for being cool under fire.

Molly jumped up and headed out the door. She got five steps down the sidewalk before she realized Simon was following her.

"Are you some kind of ambulance chaser or something? I don't think Jane needs some strange man with her right at this moment."

He didn't give her the benefit of a reply as they raced down the sidewalk to the Knit & Stitch. Molly pushed through the door and found Jane on the floor making funny, squeaky noises and breathing hard. The carpet underneath her was wet. Thank God it wasn't bloody because Molly, as tough as she was, didn't think she could deal with blood right at the moment, even if she hadn't had her breakfast yet. She sure wasn't ready to witness childbirth either. In fact, the whole childbirth thing gave her a serious case of the willies.

Before Molly could do or say anything, Simon was down on his knees beside Jane talking to her in a low, quiet, calm voice. He held her hand and touched her baby bump like he knew what he was doing.

Who the hell *was* this guy?

Jane's body arched in a contraction. Simon lifted up her maternity dress and in one swift move had her panties off.

Clay, Jane's husband, came rushing into the store and got down on his knees beside his wife. She was crying. She seemed to be really, really worried about something bad happening to the baby. But Clay was steady, like he always was.

And Simon...well, Simon had taken charge like he knew exactly what he was doing. He kept telling Jane to breathe, but Jane was too busy freaking out.

Molly backed away. This was beyond her. She reached for her cell phone, just as she heard the siren of an emergency vehicle. She put her cell phone back in her pocket and looked through the front windows where Ricky and her dog (since when did Ricki have a dog?) were pacing back and forth like they were the expectant father, except that Ricki was crying and her mascara was running down her cheeks. Clay's baby being born right there in front of her was obviously causing Ricki a whole lot of psychic pain and heartache.

"I need a blanket or something," Simon said, pulling Molly's attention back to the issue at hand.

Molly grabbed the bright pink display blanket that Momma had knitted using Baby Ull yarn from Denmark. It was a sissy, lacy, girlie thing. Perfect for little Faith, who was about to make her debut.

She handed it to Simon and allowed herself to look at what was really happening. There was blood on the carpet now, and Jane wasn't breathing hard. She was red-faced and pushing. And the top of the baby's head was clearly visible.

Things happened incredibly fast after that. The baby started crying, hard and loud and kind of angry, before she was all the way born. Simon steadied the little one with his long-fingered hands as Jane gave one final push. The baby slid out, and Simon tipped the wet and slippery newborn over onto Jane's tummy and covered it with the blanket. The baby was crying like it was the end of the world.

Clay was crying, too, but in an entirely alpha-man kind of way.

"He's going to be fine. He's big and pink and loud," Simon said.

A moment later the afterbirth slipped out, making a big mess on Molly's carpet. Simon let the blood drain out of the umbilical cord and then used a piece of superwash merino to tie it.

Jane raised her head. She had stopped freaking out. But she didn't exactly look all that Madonna-like. "What do you mean, 'he'?" she said, frowning.

Simon blinked. "It's a boy. Were you expecting something else?"

Clay stopped crying. "It's a boy?" He lifted the sissy pink blanket and checked. "Uh, how in the Sam Hill did the ultrasound technician miss *that*?"

"It's a boy?" Jane asked.

"It's a boy," Clay responded.

"Oh, my God, Clay, we painted the nursery pink."

# CHAPTER 9

Simon stood at the small sink in the back room of the Knit & Stitch, washing his hands. He was surrounded by plastic bags stuffed with yarn. The place practically smelled like lanolin.

"So are you gonna tell me where you learned how to do that?" Molly stood in the doorway to the stockroom, her arms folded across her chest, obscuring the message on her T-shirt. She looked like she'd just rolled out of bed.

Her hair was all tumbled and curly and vaguely uncombed. She had pulled it through the back of her ball cap, but that hardly kept it under control. Her T-shirt was slightly wrinkled, and her oversized sweatpants bagged around her hips and ankles.

She looked like a candidate for that reality makeover show Gillian used to watch all the time. Even so, there was something incredibly feminine about her. She looked utterly fetching standing there studying him with eyes that reminded him of the paint pigment called "ancient earth," light brown with just a touch of tarnished copper green.

His fingers itched to touch her hair. He wanted to take her out into the sunlight and study its color. It was quite dark, but strands of burgundy and claret ran through it. She would be magnificent naked, her pale skin almost translucent except for a dusting of pale freckles.

"You going to answer my question or stand there looking shell-shocked? Because I'll tell you something, I am definitely shell-shocked. Childbirth gives me the heebie-jeebies. So I'm kind of blown away that you just walked right in and took charge. Where did you learn to do what you just did?"

"From Coach."

Molly rolled her eyes like a teenager. It underscored the vast difference in their ages.

"What is it about ex-Rebels?" she asked. "You all worship at Coach's knee. And I know he's a take-charge kind of guy, but the thing is, Coach doesn't know crap about delivering babies."

"Oh, that." He looked away. He didn't like talking about this. It was like excavating ancient pieces of himself long buried.

"Yeah, that," Molly said. "Where'd you learn to do that?"

"I studied medicine in college. For almost six years."

"You're a doctor? I thought you were—"

"I'm not a doctor," he interrupted. "I never finished my internship or residency. And that's all there is to discuss."

"But—"

He held up his still-damp hand. "Molly, I didn't do anything. When a baby has decided it's time to be born, sometimes all you have to do is play catch."

She chuckled. "Now you're sounding like Coach. He'd

probably say you need a wide receiver with a good pair of hands."

She glanced at his hands, and he had the sudden desire to hide them behind his back. Instead, he tore off a length of paper towel and dried them. "Yeah, well, as you may recall, I was not a wide receiver," he said, dropping the damp towel into the trash can.

He checked his watch. Great. He was running late. Mother wouldn't forgive him for being late. She had always told him that punctuality is the politeness of kings. He hadn't really understood what she meant as a boy, but as a man, he'd learned. It was incredibly rude to waste other people's time.

"I gotta go. I left Mother at Lillian Bray's for the garden club meeting. But I need to pick her up before she starts to worry."

He headed toward the front of the shop with Molly trailing after him. He got within three feet of the front door and realized he was in trouble. A surprisingly large group of females had gathered in the front of the shop. Their numbers were so large that they had spilled out onto the sidewalk. The minute he made his appearance, they started clapping.

Earlier this morning, he'd felt like a pariah in this town, blamed for things that he hadn't done. Now they were applauding him for doing absolutely nothing but catching a baby. Jane had done the work this morning.

His face heated as he edged his way toward the door, checking his watch again. But he needn't have bothered because the door swung open with a little jingle, and Mother came into the shop arm-in-arm with an ancient, white-haired lady wearing rhinestone-studded eyeglasses.

The old lady had been at Tuesday's Purly Girls meeting but he didn't remember her name.

Mother stared at him, blinking, as if she were trying to place him in time and space. The old woman with her gave him a sober look out of a pair of sharp brown eyes.

"Simon," the old woman said, "looks like you didn't throw all that medical training out entirely."

"Do I know you?" he asked.

She flashed her dentures. "I'm Miriam Randall. You remember me, don't you?"

He said nothing as the memories clicked. He remembered. Miriam Randall had been the eccentric and colorful chairwoman of the Christ Church Ladies' Auxiliary. Which made the tableau in front of him all the more surprising, because Mother tended to look down on eccentric and colorful people. He was pretty sure there had been a time when Mother would have died before being seen arm-in-arm with Miriam Randall.

The little old lady reached out and grabbed one of his hands. Her palm was dry and slightly cool. Her hands were badly flexed with the telltale swellings common to rheumatoid arthritis, but her grip was strong and her eyes were darkly bright.

"Son, I'm mighty glad you've come back home. And it's just a wonderful thing that you've arrived right on time."

"Well, I didn't do much. I—"

"Oh, I'm not talking about Jane's baby, although I suppose it was handy that you were on the scene. Oh no, I'm talking about everything else."

Mother cocked her head. "Simon?" she said in a quavery voice.

"Yes, Mother, it's me." Something eased in his chest, but not all the way. Mother stood there looking uncertain and confused.

"You know," Miz Miriam said, "you might take down your defenses, son."

"What?"

The old woman leaned in, and Simon felt an uncanny tremor move through him. Like when kids sit in a darkened room conjuring ghosts from out of their imaginations. He went cold for a moment.

"Sometimes," Miriam said, "it's not the things we've done that lead to regrets. It's usually all the stuff we didn't do."

Her words cut a swath through him, triggering memories he had locked behind a steel door. He glanced away, right into Molly Canaday's greeny-brown eyes. She was angry at him, he knew, but in spite of that, he found kindness there. He'd always found kindness in Molly's eyes. Even when she'd been a little girl.

Miriam turned toward Mother. "You should be proud of your boy, Charlotte. He delivered a baby right here at the Knit & Stitch not twenty minutes ago."

"Simon?" Mother, who never showed much emotion, had tears in her eyes. Simon didn't know what to make of that. His own insides were threatening to unravel.

Mother took a couple of steps forward and ran her hands over his shoulders. It wasn't a real hug. Mother didn't do that sort of thing, not even in private. But she got close enough for him to inhale the scent of the floral soap she'd always used. It was some interesting blend of lavender and herbs, and it triggered even more memories.

But like everything in Last Chance, time had moved

on. She wasn't really the Mother he remembered. That Mother would never cry in public. This Mother was like some facsimile of the real one. Or maybe just a memory-induced artifact of the past.

She backed away from him, her eyes suddenly alive and bright. "I'm so glad you're home. Maybe you could talk to Doc Cooper and get a job at the clinic."

He said nothing. Mother may have recognized him, but she was still living in that past he'd escaped a long time ago.

"Now, don't you fret, Charlotte. I'm sure Simon will figure it out. It's all about timing, you know."

"What's about timing, Miriam?" asked one of the other ladies, whose name Simon didn't know.

"Well, love for starters. And marriage, too. In fact, you could say life is a matter of timing."

All the ladies turned their attention toward Miriam, and that's when Simon remembered that Miriam Randall had a reputation as a matchmaker. Oh, boy, he needed to get out of this shop and fast. The estrogen level was so high it was practically toxic.

"Uh, ladies," he said in a big, announcement-type voice, "if you don't mind, Mother and I have an appointment that—"

"I don't remember an appointment," Mother said. She turned toward Miriam. "Do you have some advice for Simon?"

"I do," Miriam said, turning her bright eyes on him. "You know son, hindsight isn't always twenty-twenty. Sometimes what you think you know can box you in. So even though something seems improbable, that doesn't mean you shouldn't take a risk. Like I said, sometimes it's not the things we do, but the things we choose not to do that make all the difference."

Another tremor rushed through him. The old woman had just laid him bare in a couple of sentences. He needed to escape. Now.

But Mother had other ideas when he tried to steer her toward the door. She took a step and then looked back at Miriam. "I don't understand what you're saying," she said. "What kind of wife should Simon be looking for?"

"The one who can change his mind," the old woman said.

The women in the room started talking, but Simon breathed a huge sigh of relief. There wasn't a woman alive who could change his mind about marriage.

Hours passed before Molly could extricate herself from the Knit & Stitch. Word of Jane's delivery spread like wildfire, probably because Ruby Rhodes, the proprietor of the beauty parlor, was the new baby's granny, and the Cut 'n Curl was the hub of all real news in town.

And then there was the surprise of the baby's sex.

The child was not supposed to be a boy. And his arrival precipitated a run on the yarn store, not merely to see the freshly shampooed carpet where the blessed event had transpired, but mainly to buy blue yarn.

The knitters of Last Chance were in a complete dither. Pretty soon a dozen of them had congregated. They sat around the table or relaxed on the battered couch in the front of the store while they cast on projects from booties to blankets. Of course, Ricki was not that much help, except for ringing up sales and keeping Muffin, her yappy and clearly psychotic dog, from treating the skeins of cashmere as chew toys.

With all that knitting going on, of course Ricki wanted to learn, and it was in Molly's best interests to teach her. Before she knew it, Molly was ensconced at the work-table, giving knitting lessons and answering questions about the morning's events.

"Is he really as handsome as everyone says?" Kenzie asked.

"Who? Simon or the baby?" Molly said, feeling trapped. This is precisely what Momma wanted for her. And it was like the gods and Simon Wolfe had conspired to put Molly in her place. Although it was true that they were ringing up a lot of sales that afternoon. Heck, she was going to have to reorder more baby blue Ull superwash.

"Did you hear what Miriam Randall had to say?" Lola May asked.

"Uh, well, sort of. I mean she kind of dissed him for staying away so long, which he so deserves."

"How can you say that? He saved Jane's life and the baby's, too," Cathy Niles said.

"He didn't save her life. He just caught the baby. Although he did that with a lot of competence and calm. Babies scare the willies out of me, but apparently they don't bother Simon." Molly leaned toward Ricki and pointed at her knitting. "Honey, you should be purling that row."

"Well, I don't want to know about his competence," Cathy said. "I want to know what kind of woman he's supposed to be looking for."

"The woman who can change his mind," Molly said.

"Huh?" All the women around the table looked up from their work.

"That's what Miriam said. It's not really much to go on. If you ask me, Miriam's losing it."

"What makes you say that?" Cathy asked. "Her forecast for Simon is probably true. He's got to be pushing forty pretty hard, and he's never been married. So either he's gay or he's just never met the woman who could change his mind." Cathy had such a sweet faith in romance. It was sort of pitiful, really.

"Well, that's my point," Molly countered. "Miriam's forecast is so vague it could be anyone. It's hardly even advice."

"You don't know. It might have some deep inner meaning to Simon."

"Right. Well, if Miriam isn't losing it, then why did she send Savannah to deliver her forecast to me, instead of delivering it herself?" These words popped out of Molly's mouth before her brain caught up with them.

But Molly realized her mistake a nanosecond later. All the knitting needles and crochet hooks stopped, and every single customer looked up at her.

"Miriam gave *you* matchmaking advice?" Cathy said.

"Well yeah, but it came from Savannah who said she was delivering a message from Miriam, but since when does Miriam use Savannah as a messenger?"

"What did she say?" asked Lola May.

The avid look on the faces around the table made it clear that Molly wasn't ever going to keep this a secret. Half these women were members of the Christ Church congregation, and the other half were members of the garden club. If she didn't tell them what Savannah said, they would ask Savannah directly, and the truth would be told.

She sighed. "All right, she told me I was destined to marry someone I'd known all my life."

Laughter exploded around the table. "Well," Cathy

said after catching her breath, "that's not exactly a very startling marital fortune, is it? I mean, everyone knows you and Les are going to get married one of these days. We're just waiting for Les to get around to making *you* change *your* mind."

Molly stood up. "Ladies, I hate to disappoint you, but I am not going to marry Leslie Hayes. But I *am* going to go next door and see about doing my laundry."

Molly escaped the Knit & Stitch with the laughter of her mother's best customers still ringing in her ears. Well, they could laugh all they wanted, but Molly was not marrying Les. In fact, she wasn't marrying anyone if she had her way. She was too busy trying to build a business to be sidetracked by romance.

Besides, she was a dunce at romance. Sex was okay, but romance was kind of icky.

She strolled into the Wash-O-Rama and started looking for the laundry she'd abandoned this morning. She eventually found it in three of those rolly metal baskets supplied by the Laundromat. It was her lucky day. She'd busted a window with a baseball bat, witnessed a birth, and no one had stolen her abandoned dirty clothes.

She rolled the laundry over to a bank of washing machines and started to fill them.

"You aren't going to wash the jeans with the whites, are you? If you do, that handkerchief I loaned you will end up blue and that would be embarrassing for you."

She looked up from the hankie she was holding to find its owner standing a few feet inside the Wash-O-Rama. He had changed clothes, no doubt because of the blood from this morning's events. But the jeans still fit perfectly and the sleeves of the blue oxford cloth shirt were turned up over his muscular forearms.

"Are you about to give me a lesson in laundry?"

The apostrophes at the corner of his mouth curled. And that was so annoying because she wanted to punch him in his handsome face, except that he had a winning smile, had tamed a toddler, and had delivered Jane's baby. So he clearly wasn't evil.

"Do you need a lesson in laundry?" he asked.

She looked away. Why was he here? "Don't you have someplace to be, like forcing people from their jobs or something?"

Her barb hit the mark. She knew because he compressed his lips as if he were holding in some wicked comeback. For an instant, she wished he would just say whatever nasty thing he'd trapped in his mouth. But he didn't.

He paused and drew in a breath. And for an instant, it seemed as if he was actually capable of achieving all that transcendence crap Momma was always talking about, right after she'd finished meditating. It was a pretty neat trick. Molly sincerely wished she could figure out a way to keep her cool like that.

When he spoke again, there was no emotion in his voice. "My uncle Ryan closed the dealership. Not me. There was nothing I could do to stop it." She wondered what emotions, besides being ticked off, he was trying to control.

He strolled into the Wash-O-Rama and began removing her clothes from the washing machines.

"What are you doing?"

"I'm ensuring that you don't turn this underwear blue."

He held up a pair of her lacy bikini underpants. They looked very tiny in his big hands.

Uh-oh, no one was supposed to know about that underwear. "Those aren't mine," she said quickly. She could have sworn someone had just taken a blowtorch to her face.

He twirled the panties around one of his long, elegant fingers. "Excuse me but aren't you the only girl living at your house these days?"

"They belong to Allen's skanky girlfriend." It was the best lie she could think of on short notice.

He studied the panties. "They're La Perla. Not exactly the kind skanky women buy. And not the kind of panties you should wash in the same load as blue jeans."

"Okay, so his girlfriend isn't a skank. And I'm sort of amazed you even know they're La Perla."

His lips quirked just a little as he picked up another pair of panties. These were a really pale shade of pink. "These belong to the skank, too?"

She nodded. And if she'd been made out of wood, her nose would have gotten a few inches longer. He put the panties in a pile in one of the baskets. "You don't machine-wash stuff like that unless your washer has a delicate cycle. You might let your brother know that for future reference."

He continued pulling out clothes and sorting them by colors, dropping each new pair of panties and her bras into a pile by itself.

"What are you doing here?" she asked, after about a minute of this odd humiliation.

He looked up. "Settling my father's estate."

"No, I mean here, at the Wash-O-Rama?"

"I came to collect my laundry."

"So your mother doesn't have a laundry in that mansion of hers?"

"The dryer is busted. Apparently it's been broken for some time. Daddy was using a clothesline. I guess he didn't want to be seen in a Laundromat."

"And in contrast, you seem well acquainted with them. Do you always sort other people's clothes?"

"I'm sorting your clothes because I need to apologize to you."

Whoa. Hang on. That was a surprise. "Uh, yeah, you do need to apologize for a bunch of things. But which things were you thinking about?"

He continued to sort her laundry as he spoke. "I rented the building you wanted. And I'm sorry your boyfriend lost his job."

"Les is not my boyfriend. He's my partner."

Simon nodded. "Sorry. I just got the impression from everyone that—"

"Les is not my boyfriend."

"Okay. I stand corrected. And like I said, I'm sorry I leased the building you wanted, but it's only short-term."

"Whatever," she said.

All she could think about was how her life had become one great big mess. It was like Simon arrived in town and her luck went south. It might have been cathartic to unload on him, but it would have solved nothing. Instead, she tried to be mindful, the way Momma was always talking about. She hadn't actually read *One Minute Meditations*, but trying to be aware of her feelings gave her just a little bit of control over them.

"You have change for the machines?" he asked.

She dug in the pocket of her sweatpants and hauled out a mess of quarters she'd gotten from Flo at the Kountry Kitchen, after the excitement this morning. He took them from her hand, his fingers brushing over her palm for an instant. The touch was brief but it kind of lingered on her skin. And for some inexplicable reason, she curled her fingers up in a fist in order to capture and hold the sensation.

Why did this man unsettle her so deeply?

She folded her arms across her chest and leaned her hip on one of the empty washers. The silence became awkward as he methodically started each of the machines. The quiet room suddenly roared with the sound of rushing water.

"So I heard you're thinking about selling your momma's house."

"She can't live on her own." There was a sadness in his words that Molly hadn't been expecting. A little bit of her anger evaporated. His life had taken a big left turn last week, too. He'd lost his father, and it wasn't Simon's fault that Ira was dead. Ira had done that to himself, by smoking too much and not getting enough exercise.

She needed to remember that kindness was the opposite of anger. And she'd been battling her anger for years. So maybe instead of standing there stewing about it and trying to meditate on it, she could just do what Momma was always telling her to do.

Just be nice.

"If you're looking for help with your momma," she said, "there's the senior center in Allenberg. You should talk to Shevon Darnell. She's the one who organizes the Purly Girls meetings every week. Your daddy used to bring Charlotte to the meetings by car, but most of the girls come on the senior center bus."

He looked up at her then, his deep brown eyes going liquid. Vulnerability flickered across his face and vanished almost immediately. And then he turned his back on her and headed down the row of dryers, towing a rolling basket behind him. She watched him for a long time as he took his clothes out of the dryer and carefully folded each item.

She wanted to dislike him. She wanted to be angry at him. But the picture folks were painting of him—as some kind of callous, insensitive idiot—was wrong. She'd watched him play with Junior. She'd seen the way he'd been with Jane. She'd heard his heartfelt apology. Maybe Bubba had been right about him. He wasn't like Ryan Polk, even if he had that unmistakable Polk family look about him.

And she had to admit that watching him fold laundry was turning her on. Probably because she was so laundry-challenged. That had to be it. Didn't it?

She didn't wait around to explore those hot tingly feelings for more than a moment. Instead, she escaped the Wash-O-Rama and returned to the Knit & Stitch, where she allowed herself to be sidetracked into teaching Ricki how to make increases and decreases.

When she finally returned to the Laundromat a couple of hours later, she found her laundry neatly folded in her laundry baskets.

With all her lacy, unwashed panties piled on the top.

# CHAPTER 10

It was almost seven o'clock by the time Molly finally got home from the Knit & Stitch, the Wash-O-Rama, and the grocery store. She was exhausted, both physically and mentally.

She hauled her groceries up the front walk and braced herself as she opened the door, expecting to find the living room in the same disastrous state as when she left.

The scent of Febreze almost knocked her over. Someone had cleaned, dusted, vacuumed, and scrubbed the place. She hurried into the kitchen, laden with grocery bags, only to discover that it also sparkled as if Momma were still living at home. Not to mention that the carcass of the washing machine had been removed from the adjoining laundry room.

That's where she found Les, wearing battered jeans, a flannel shirt with the sleeves cut off, and an old, sweat-stained Atlanta Falcons hat. Les was in the last stages of hooking up a new washing machine. Of course, it wasn't exactly new off the showroom floor, like the front-loader Allen had destroyed last night. It was obviously secondhand.

She peered at the knobs. Oh joy, it had a delicate cycle. She wouldn't have to go commando tomorrow.

And then her joy faded. Because if she had a washing machine at home, she couldn't justify hauling her laundry to the Wash-O-Rama where she could accidentally-on-purpose run into Simon and maybe get him to sort her darks from her lights.

While she watched.

She shook that image out of her head and focused on Les. "What are you doing here?"

"Allen called this morning."

"And you came over and cleaned up his mess?"

Les finished hooking up the water and then shoved the washer into its space by the wall. "I had nothing better to do."

"Did he help?"

"Some."

"Les, you're amazing. You're sweet. I can't believe you did all this. But you should have let Allen clean up the mess he made. You're not doing him any favors, you know. Where is he now?"

"I have no clue. About noon, he got a call, and he told me it was an emergency. He took off on his motorcycle."

"Typical. I bet he left right before you were about to clean the barf out of the schefflera."

Les shook his head. "No. As a matter of fact, I made him and his friends clean up all the vomit."

"Good for you, but I bet you did most of the work. You'll need to tell me how much I owe you for the washer and—"

"It's okay. Allen took care of that."

"He did? Really?"

Les nodded.

"So you don't know where he is?"

Les shook his head. "Nope. I reckon he's over at Kacey's place."

"Kacey?"

"Kacey Travers, she lives in Allenberg. She's a grocery checker at the BI-LO. She's pretty new in town. I think she was married to someone who left her high and dry right in the middle of Allenberg without a dime to her name. I think Allen's been helping her out."

"Right. And sleeping with her on the side. She looks a little skanky to me. Who dyes their hair red and purple?"

"Don't be ugly, Mol. She's an okay girl, just kind of young and down on her luck."

Molly held her tongue. Les was kind to a fault. And she loved him for it.

"I heard you had a busy day," he said, changing the subject. "I stopped by Lovett's Hardware, and Arlene Whitaker told me all about Jane."

"Yeah, talk about having a mess to clean up. You know childbirth is not a very pretty thing to watch."

"No?" He was smiling now.

"No. It's terrifying. And Jane was freaking out, and... well... can we talk about something else?"

"You hungry? I got a pizza in the oven." Les headed into the kitchen and started pulling out glasses and silverware like he actually lived here. He slipped on an oven mitt and pulled the pizza out.

It was another domestic moment in which Molly found herself the observer. What was it about the guys in her life? They didn't seem domestically challenged, whereas she was a total bust when it came to cooking and cleaning and laundry-doing. She caught herself. Simon wasn't actually in her life, was he? He'd only done her laundry.

And seen her underpants.

Humiliation exploded in her middle like a Molotov cocktail, burning her face and neck and all the way down her back. Those panties were a secret.

Except, of course, Momma had seen her underpants plenty, because Momma did the laundry around here. Molly had never thought about that. Maybe Momma had misunderstood about those panties, and the matching bras. Maybe Momma thought her lacy underwear was a sign that Molly wanted to be more girlie.

Which of course she didn't. She just liked nice underpants.

Les had a bottle of wine and a candle to go with the pizza. Holy God, this was shaping up into something terrifying.

"Les, what on earth are you doing?"

"Sit down, Molly. I want to talk to you."

"Uh, I'm not sure I want to sit down." But she sat in one of the kitchen chairs, and he sat facing her.

"Arlene told me something else when I ran up to the hardware store for a new doorknob."

Oh boy, she knew what was coming. "Uh, Les, honey, I know Arlene probably told you about what Savannah said to me the other night at the book club. But honestly, you can't put any store in that nonsense about Miriam Randall. I mean, of course she's going to tell me to go look for someone I've known my whole life. I mean, I live here in Last Chance. So it stands to reason that, if I ever get married, it's probably going to be to someone I've known my whole life. But whoever it is—if I get married—I'm going to love him with all my heart."

He blinked, and Molly realized that she'd once again failed to cushion her words. Why couldn't she be good at sweet-talking? Heck, every southern female seemed to be born knowing how to soften the worst of blows. Except her.

Les's bright blue eyes held steady and true. Which was unusual for him. Usually when she unloaded on him, he unloaded on her, and then the two of them were in an argument.

But instead of unloading, Les gave her a moony look and said, "I love you, Molly. I've loved you for years and years, and I reckon it's time to say it out loud. And before you point out that I'm unemployed, you should just know that I've got some real prospects. You know, irons in the fire and all that. So, anyway, when Arlene told me what Miriam said, well, I just knew the time had come."

Oh, crap.

It took a moment for Molly to get her act together. Les's words had more than merely stunned her. They'd rocked her world. And not in a good way. It was like she'd just been shaken by an earthquake registering eight-point-oh on the Richter scale.

"Les, honey, you're a great guy. Really. I mean, you're way too good for me. Just look at what you did today. That was thoughtful. And I'm grateful. Sort of like that day Foster Boyd spit in my face…" Damn, she was babbling. She closed her eyes and tried to concentrate. It was really hard.

She finally opened her eyes and gave him the most earnest stare she could muster. "I just don't love you. I mean, I love you like a brother, not a husband."

He reached out and covered her hand with his. "Don't be stupid, Mol. We're perfect together. We're friends. How many couples start out that way?"

She looked down at his broad workman's hands and couldn't help but compare them with Simon's. They both had very talented hands. Good-looking hands. But their hands were as different as night and day. It was wrong to be thinking about Simon right now. Or maybe the fact that she was thinking about Simon was the root of the problem. Because she found Simon attractive and sexy. And Les, not so much.

"Uh, Les, you make a good point about us being friends. And I'd like to keep it that way."

He let go of her hand and placed both of his on the table in front of him, palms down. He said nothing, but Molly could read his growing annoyance even though he was trying to hide it.

She hated hurting him. He was her best buddy. "I'm really, really, really sorry. Please don't be disappointed. It's sort of like that old George Strait song, you know? 'You Can't Make a Heart Love Somebody.'"

"Is there someone else?" he asked.

"Les. Come on. You know the answer to that without asking. In fact, if you thought about it, instead of getting all caught up in Miriam Randall's mischief, you'd realize I'm the kind of woman who isn't ever going to fall in love and get married. It's not for me. I'd be a crappy wife all the way around. You'd be unhappy with me. Heck, any man would be unhappy with me. I'm not an easy person to love."

"That's not true, Molly."

"Of course it's true. I'm blunt, and I'm never ever going to be sweet. And I'm not comfortable around kids. I don't think I'd be a very good mother. And we argue all the time. In fact, we're arguing right now."

"That may be, but one day you are going to fall in love."

"No, Les, I'm pretty sure that's not ever going to happen."

"You're wrong, Mol. If Miriam tells you that there's a soulmate waiting for you, you will find him. It will happen. I only wish you'd open your eyes and see that I'm the guy. Because, honey, you're the only one I want."

"Les, please. Cut the drama. You don't want me. A few nights ago, you were all over going out with Tammy Nelson. Be sensible."

"I don't want to be sensible. I want you to see it my way. Marry me, Molly."

"No, Les. And one day, when you look back on this, you'll thank me for saying no. You will, I promise."

He stood up, knocking over a wineglass. It shattered on the sparkling floor. "I don't think so, Mol."

"Trust me, you'll get over this. You'll find some great woman who really appreciates you. Someone who's girlier than me. Someone with a sweet temper who can bake and stuff. Someone who wants to get married, unlike me."

"You know, Mol, one day some guy is going to walk into your life and sweep you off your feet. And then you're going to feel like you can't live without him. I hope he tells you no, because then you'll know exactly how I feel right this minute."

The Purly Girls had knitted a grand total of 103 poppies, all out of inexpensive crimson Red Heart yarn. And today, on the Sunday before Memorial Day, a few of the girls had gathered in the fellowship hall at Christ Church to sell some of the poppies on behalf of the American Legion. Similar sales were occurring this morning in every church in the county. Later this afternoon, a brigade of vets would be putting American flags on soldiers' graves in every cemetery. There were four large cemeteries in Allenberg County, and at least a dozen small graveyards, some containing soldiers from as far back as the Revolution.

Molly had gotten roped into organizing the sale and the flag distribution at Christ Church. This was something Momma did every year, and with Momma gone, naturally Molly was nominated. It wasn't as if anyone asked either. They just assumed.

Of course, with the Shelby still locked up, she had the time. And staying busy would keep her away from Les, who attended church with the Baptists. After he'd left last night, Molly had rattled around the house like a loose marble in a cigar box. She'd finally settled down with some knitting and watched TV for a while. But her heart was sore.

Not broken, just bruised. She didn't want Les to be mad at her. But she sure as hell wasn't going to marry him just because Miriam had some idiotic forecast for her.

She pushed thoughts of Les to the back of her mind and focused on the task at hand. Molly stood behind a card table where a couple of Purly Girls had showcased their poppy pins. Some of the poppies were a little misshapen, but the congregation didn't seem to mind. Charlotte Wolfe and Luanne Howe were handling the sales, which had been pretty brisk. Charlotte was managing to make change without any problems. But Luanne, who was eighty years young, seemed to think she was at the kissing booth at the Watermelon Festival. She had already laid big ones on Reverend Ellis, Hugh deBracy, and Dash Randall.

At least Luanne still had sense enough to know a handsome man when she saw one.

At the moment, Luanne was making eyes at Simon Wolfe, who had come to church this morning dressed in a dark gray suit that looked like it had been hand-tailored for him. His tie was silk, his shirt starched, and his shoes shined. He sure didn't look like a starving artist.

He sauntered over to the table. "Oh, hello," Charlotte said, smiling up at him. "I don't know you, do I? Are you one of the new people who works for the textile mill?"

Molly's heart tumbled when she saw the hurt in Simon's eyes. Jeez, he was always kind of self-contained, but if you looked really hard at his eyes, they gave him away every time. Now that she'd seen him in action taming toddlers and delivering babies, not to mention sorting laundry, he really didn't seem to fit the mold of a hardass who would walk away from his family and never look back. Or the kind of man who would callously shut a business and throw people out of work.

Luanne stood up. "Hey, honey, I'm going to enjoy kissing you. Kisses are only five dollars."

"Luanne, I wish you would stop saying that. We aren't selling kisses now. We're selling poppies, and they are only three dollars." Charlotte gave Luanne the evil eye.

It bounced right off Luanne, who leaned across the table and puckered up.

Simon put a five-dollar bill on the table. "Ms. Howe,

you make my heart sing," he said. Then he stepped around the table, took Luanne into his arms and dipped her, like some Hollywood swain. He laid a pretty tame kiss on the old lady's lips then put her back on her feet and steadied her.

Luanne opened her eyes and smiled up at him, revealing a mouth shy of a few teeth. "Oh my, who are you?"

"A friend of Millie Polk's," he said, the corners of his mouth displaying those sexy, adorable apostrophes that made Molly's RPMs head into the red zone. But she wasn't about to admit that to anyone. Simon wasn't her type. For one thing, he was a snazzy dresser and she wasn't. Who wanted to be with a guy who was always checking himself out in a mirror?

Not that she'd seen Simon do that, but really, turned out like that, he probably was hopelessly vain.

"Oh, I remember you," Charlotte said. "You're the hired help. You have no business kissing Luanne." She picked up his money and handed it back to him. "We don't do business with your type."

Oh, boy, Charlotte's ugly side had just come out. "Now, Miz Charlotte," Molly said, "we're going to take his money because we're selling poppies for the VFW. You remember that, don't you? And it's not your place to decide who Luanne kisses."

Charlotte's frown deepened. She handed the five-dollar bill to Molly. "All right. For the VFW." Then she turned toward Simon. "You're fired, young man. You tell Millie I want someone else to take care of things. I don't need a man in my house who goes around assaulting older women."

Simon's smile faded. "All right, I'll tell her," he said in

a calm voice. Then he turned and walked away without even picking up a poppy or his change.

Half an hour later, Molly found Simon sitting on the bench by the big magnolia that screened the graveyard from the church parking lot. He was contemplating the red earth over his father's newly made grave.

"I'm sorry about the ugly things your mother said to you," Molly said as she sat down beside him. She had a box filled with small U.S. flags. Her helpers were scheduled to arrive in about twenty minutes.

Glorious May sunshine had sent the temperature up into the eighties. Distributing flags would be hot work, so Molly had changed out of her dress slacks and into a pair of comfy combat shorts and a Willie Nelson Farm Aid T-shirt.

Simon was still wearing a suit, and he hadn't even taken off his jacket.

She handed him a knitted poppy and two dollar bills. "You forgot your poppy and your change."

He studied the knitted flower. "Why do people wear poppies on Memorial Day, anyway?"

"It comes from that poem. You know, about World War One—*In Flanders fields the poppies blow. Between the crosses, row on row*...I had to memorize that poem in ninth grade, I think. Momma always organizes a poppy knit-along every year. I inherited it this year, since she ran away from home."

"Keep the change." He pinned his poppy to his lapel. "Your mother ran away?"

She put the two dollars in the envelope destined for the VFW. "Yeah. She took off a few days ago. And it's mostly Coach's fault."

"Coach, really? That surprises me. I always thought he was a stand-up guy. But I guess that's marriage for you."

"Have you ever been married?" She had been dying to ask that question, because Simon had to be almost forty years old.

He snorted a laugh. "No. And I never intend to be. You'd have to be certifiable to get married."

"And yet most people do."

"And half of them go on to get divorces, and God alone knows how many others are miserable." He gave her a long look. "But I suppose a person of your age is probably out there looking for Mr. Right?"

She shook her head. "Actually not. I'm much more interested in starting my own business. But that's going to be hard to do if I'm permanently saddled with the Knit & Stitch. Honestly, Momma has seriously screwed up my life."

"Well, that's hardly surprising. Parents are notorious for screwing up their children's lives."

"Did your parents screw up your life? They seemed like pretty good people. I adored your father. And he adored your mother," Molly replied.

"You're kidding, right? My parents were miserable. Living with them was like living through World War Three. I probably deserve medals for the crap I went through."

"Really? That surprises me. Ira was devoted to your mom."

"Yeah, well, he used to argue with her all the time when I was a kid. And I was always in the middle of those arguments, somehow."

"Is that why you left home?"

He stared silently at his father's grave, and then he changed the subject back to poppies. "You know, I haven't worn a poppy on Memorial Day since I left Last Chance. It's not a big thing where I live now. I'd forgotten all about it."

Darn it, he wasn't going to answer her question, was he? Her curiosity would go unsatisfied. She masked her disappointment by making small talk. "A lot of city people have forgotten the true meaning of Memorial Day," she said.

"I'm not a city person. Paradise is a small town about the same size as Last Chance. But they don't knit poppies for Memorial Day there."

"Well, I reckon we hang on to our traditions harder than they do."

"Not every tradition is a good one."

They lapsed into silence. And she was just itching to turn the conversation back to his parents and their marriage. Because Simon's perception of Ira and Charlotte was different from everyone else's. If ever there was a man devoted to his wife, it was Ira Wolfe. When Charlotte started losing her mind, Ira had stepped up and cared for her in ways that would warm anyone's heart. And Charlotte adored her husband. It was kind of cute the way her eyes would light up every time Ira came through the Knit & Stitch's door to pick her up. That man spun her world. And Ira seemed to be the only one who could soften some of Charlotte's snootiness.

Just then the quiet of the late-spring day was shattered by the strains of "Livin' la Vida Loca" supported by a bass so deep it rattled the church's stained-glass windows. The sound swelled as a red Jeep Wrangler, trailing a U-Haul, pulled into the church parking lot. The driver killed the engine and turned off the radio. The day was returned to the birds and their much quieter music.

"Finally," Simon said as he got to his feet. He headed toward the break in the hedge that led to the parking lot.

Molly stood up to get a better view. She knew most every car in Allenberg County, and no one drove a red Jeep Wrangler. The women of Allenberg were smart enough to want a car with a better suspension, and the men knew a sissy car when they saw one.

Her gaydar started pinging even before the driver stepped from the Jeep. But once she got a good look at him, it went right off the scales. The fabric of his white guinea-tee stretched over a sculpted chest and exposed a pair of biceps that could only be achieved by hours in the gym. His dark hair looked perfectly tousled from his drive with the top down. His skinny jeans had neatly frayed slashes across the knees and backside. And jeez, he had one tight-looking behind.

In short, he was so pretty he might as well be a girl. But when he walked up to Simon and gave him a hearty slap on the back, everything kind of slowed down. No way. Simon was *gay*?

Boy, her gaydar must be slipping. She had never once considered the possibility that Simon was gay. But it looked like she had missed something important.

Maybe Simon wasn't some idiot who left home and broke his parents' hearts. Maybe it was the other way around. She doubted very much that either Ira or Charlotte would have been pleased to discover that their darling son was a homosexual.

# CHAPTER
## 11

Molly spent Memorial Day in bed. She almost never did anything like this, but there was no point in getting up. She didn't want to run into Les at the Memorial Day parade, she couldn't do any work on the Shelby, and she was not about to open up the yarn store the way Momma did every year, hosting a little sidewalk sit-and-stitch while the parade passed them by.

She turned off her phone because the knitters of Last Chance were upset that she'd blown off this tradition. She didn't want to explain to anyone that this was Momma's tradition. Not hers.

So she stayed in bed and consumed an entire package of Oreo cookies while reading *Little Women*.

Molly's frame of mind suited the book. Jo March, the book's heroine, valiantly battles for her independence through the first half of the book. And from Molly's viewpoint, the novel would have been perfect if the author had just stopped right there.

But no, Louisa May Alcott had to write part 2, which

chronicles Jo's slow, inevitable slide into marriage and domesticity. Cathy Niles probably loved this ending, although, knowing Cathy, she would probably be unhappy that Jo tells the young and passionate Laurie to take a hike and then turns around and marries the stodgy old Professor Bhaer. As far as Molly was concerned, Jo was an idiot to get married at all. And to give up her dreams of writing for a living so she could have babies was a big disappointment. No way that would happen in the twenty-first century.

Molly was just turning over the last few pages when Coach came stomping through the back door. "Hey, darlin', I'm home," he shouted.

Obviously Coach hadn't noticed that Momma's Ford Fusion was not in the garage. He shouted again, and Molly lay there in bed wondering if she could hide in the closet and pretend she wasn't home. She didn't want to be the one to tell him that Momma had gone AWOL.

But who else would do it? Allen? Not likely. Her younger brother hadn't been home for a couple of days. She'd called his cell phone, and he'd curtly told her that he'd moved in with Kacey.

Molly brushed the cookie crumbs from her T-shirt. There was no point in putting off the inevitable.

She headed into the kitchen, where she found Coach staring at the replacement washing machine.

"Where's the new washing machine?"

"It broke," she said vaguely. She'd given the whole washing machine incident a lot of thought over the last couple of days. She understood why Allen had destroyed the washer. He'd been angry. And while his behavior had been immature, she wasn't about to tattle on him. Siblings stuck together when it came to stuff like this.

"How could it break? It was only a few months old."

She shrugged like a guilty teenager. "It did."

Coach put his gigantic hands on his hips. He was a big man who had once played football for Georgia Tech. He stood a good six foot five, wore a size thirteen shoe, and had not let his belly go to fat. His real name was Fredrick, but he'd been called Red from the time he'd been a toddler on account of his flaming red hair, which was fading to ginger these days. He'd broken his nose at least five times playing one sport or another, and now it meandered down his freckled face and gave him a truly intimidating demeanor.

Especially when he glowered, which he was doing right now.

"Where's your mother at?" he asked.

Molly swallowed. "Uh, well, um, see…Daddy, she's gone."

He blinked, probably because Molly almost never called him Daddy unless she was trying to weasel her way out of a misdeed. Only in this case, she was trying to weasel her way out of Momma's misdeed, which was really screwed up.

"What have you done?"

"I haven't done anything. Momma's gone to see the world."

"What?"

Molly turned and padded across the kitchen in her hand-knit slipper socks. She found Momma's peanut-butter-smeared note and handed it to Coach.

She watched the red flush run up his cheeks as he read it. His hands were shaking by the time he finished.

He looked down at her out of a pair of bright blue eyes.

"This is all your fault," he said. "She left so that you would quit all this nonsense about starting a car-restoration business and start helping her with the store."

Coach's words poked at the unhealed wound that had been there since Molly was five. And for once, Molly wasn't going to let him get away with it, even if what he said was sort of true. Momma's note had made it clear that she was unhappy with Coach, too.

"No, Coach, this is not just about me," she said. "Momma's been saving up money for a world cruise for a long time. Anyone who was paying the slightest bit of attention to her would know that she really wanted to go see Europe. Hell, she thought you were going to give her a cruise or something for your anniversary this year. But instead you gave her a washer and a dryer so she could more efficiently wash your dirty underwear. And then you disappeared for two weeks with your fishing buddies like you do every year.

"And, by the way, while you were out with your bass-hole buddies, Ira Wolfe died, and no one could even reach you. You missed the funeral."

"Ira's dead?"

"Yeah. He is. And the dealership is closed, and Momma is gone. You know, Coach, you can be a real idiot sometimes. And I resent the fact that your idiocy means I have to turn myself into Momma for you and Allen and everyone else in town."

She turned and headed back to her room, the tears she'd been fighting all day suddenly filling her eyes. The last damn thing she wanted Coach to see was her having a big, fat, girlie crying jag.

So she slammed and locked the door and had a good cry anyway.

• • •

Molly's life completely unraveled on Tuesday morning when she showed up for work at Bill's Grease Pit only to find Les there, wearing work overalls and a guilty look on his face.

Before she could even say good morning, LeRoy called her back into his office. He didn't mince words. "Molly, I know you're a good mechanic, but since your momma left town, you've been less than attentive to your job. Last week was an unmitigated disaster."

"C'mon LeRoy, that's not fair. I was here on Friday until four in the morning, and—"

He held up his hand. "Look, Molly, the last week has been hell. Ricki's been calling you every five minutes. You're constantly running up the street to unsnarl some yarn tangle, and the only reason you had to put in the overtime was because you were hardly here during working hours."

Molly didn't say anything. What could she say?

"Look," LeRoy continued, "I'm sorry, but I've got a chance of a lifetime to pick up some Ford customers who have never done business with me."

"So that's why Les is here."

"Yes. He's got a file with the names of Wolfe Ford customers in it. Those folks are angry about the dealership closing. Les has been working on those people's cars and trucks for years. They trust him. Do you have any idea how many people own Ford trucks in this county?"

"So you hired him."

"I did."

"He's good at what he does," she admitted.

"I know. But the thing is, I can't afford to have him and you here at the same time."

"Why not? We argue a lot, but then—"

"Molly, it's not because you argue. Les is worth more money than you are, and if I pay him what he was getting over at the dealership, I just can't afford you. And besides, there are folks around here who don't want you to touch their cars. They don't trust you. And I'm always having to argue with them about your qualifications. With Les, I don't have that problem, plus he brings in customers I couldn't get otherwise. And besides, it's not like you don't have something else you could do, now that your Momma's gone. Honestly, T-Bone Carter and his customers would be thrilled if you took over your momma's shop and sent Ricki back to the Kountry Kitchen. In fact, there's a whole mess of people who would be overjoyed."

Molly seethed. Her face burned, and her heart raced, and she wanted nothing more than to sock LeRoy right in the face. In fact, her fists balled up so tight that her short fingernails almost dug holes in her palms.

But socking LeRoy was out. Not only was he bigger than her, she couldn't afford to burn any more bridges.

She forced herself to stop feeling and to start thinking. This was the sort of thing Momma was always telling her to do. It's what she meant about being mindful.

So Molly tried to bring logic into play. She tried to think things through for once. Thinking calmed her, just a little bit.

LeRoy was only being a sensible businessman. Les had a better reputation as a mechanic than Molly did. And truth to tell, Les was a better engine man than Molly would ever be. Molly's gift was with body work. That's why they were such a good team when it came to restoring old cars. Their strengths fit together. Until Miriam Randall had messed up everything with her marital advice.

So she couldn't even argue the point, because LeRoy knew the truth as well as she did. "Yeah," she said in a surprisingly calm tone of voice, "everyone in town will be overjoyed...except me and Ricki."

"C'mon, Molly, don't be that way. It's just business."

She turned on her heel and stalked into the garage, wondering if Ira Wolfe would have ever conducted his business this way. The answer was a resounding no, but then Ira's business had ended up in receivership.

She found Les in the pit doing an oil change on Thelma Hanks's SUV. "Did you know you had stolen my job when you came over on Saturday and installed that new washer and asked me to marry you?"

"C'mon, Mol, don't take it that way. You've got an alternative job, and I don't. I needed this job more than you did."

Her anger spiked again. "I asked you a question, Les. Did you know you'd stolen my job when you asked me to be your wife?"

"Yeah." At least he had the dignity to sound a tiny bit contrite. Like maybe the idiot understood how badly he might have hurt her.

The calm feeling she'd almost managed to find disappeared. "So when, exactly, were you going to tell me about that?"

His face got red. At least he felt some shame. "Look, Molly, you're the one who encouraged me to talk to LeRoy."

She had. She knew it. "Yes, but I had no idea it would

cost me my job. And besides, you weren't honest with me on Saturday night."

"Unlike you. You were brutally honest."

"Why are you being such an a-hole?" she asked.

His blue eyes stilled, and he gave her an earnest stare. "I know you think I'm to blame for this. Or at least that I'm being a jerk. But the thing is, Molly, if I didn't do something to wake you up, how on earth was anything ever going to change? I know you don't believe it. But I love you."

"Wake me up?" God, he was sounding like the stupid note Momma had left on the front door of the Knit & Stitch.

"Molly, listen," he said in a voice that was obviously struggling for calm, "this is going to work out. Just you wait and see."

"How? By me giving in and marrying you like Jo March married Professor Bhaer?"

"Huh?"

"Never mind. I'm not ever going to marry anyone. And whatever kindness I was feeling toward you is now utterly gone. You stole my job. And Simon Wolfe stole my building. And his greedy uncle stole my car. What the hell did I ever do to deserve this?" She screamed the last bit and then turned and headed up Palmetto Avenue toward the yarn store. She was out of control.

She desperately needed to knit something. Maybe if she started knitting she could regain her composure.

She looked up from the pavement just in time to see Simon's pretty boyfriend maneuvering a dolly with a big wooden crate on it. He was moving the crate into the Coca-Cola building.

Her building.

Crap. Double Crap.

The only thing left to her was the damn Knit & Stitch. Only now she had to fire Ricki. Because if Molly was out of a job, then she'd have to rely on the yarn shop income to get by.

It just wasn't fair.

It felt a whole lot like that time right after the twins were born. She'd been five years old, the apple of Coach's eye. He took her to every football game, even the away games. She had labored under the mistaken notion that she was actually an essential part of the team.

And then her brothers were born.

And it was over. Coach wasn't all that interested in her anymore. And to make up for it, Momma had stepped in with her knitting needles and her embroidery and her sewing machine. Molly would never forget the day when the twins were about four months old, and she came home after a weekend at Granny's to find her bedroom transformed. It looked like someone had vomited Pepto-Bismol on the walls.

She might have forgiven Momma for doing that to her. But it was Coach who had painted the room. With that room, Coach had made his position clear: Molly was supposed to become Daddy's little girl instead of a stand-in for the son he wanted. But she had shown him, all right. She'd gone right on being herself. She had decided to do the things she liked. And that included watching sports, and working on cars, and knitting. Everyone thought it was crazy for a tomboy like her to love knitting, but Molly didn't see how one thing excluded the other.

She unlocked the door to the shop and went inside.

The lanolin-rich aroma of the wool comforted her. She actually loved being here at the shop. But she didn't want to manage it or make it her whole life. That was what Momma never could understand.

It was early still—an hour before opening. She headed through the shop's dim interior to the cubby behind the counter where she'd stashed one of her many knitting projects. This one was a raglan-sleeved baby sweater she'd started on Saturday, when Jane's baby had turned out to be a boy instead of a girl.

She settled herself into the couch at the front of the store and started knitting, her needles clicking in the early-morning quiet. The repetitive motion soothed her. And she almost achieved that state of mindfulness that Momma was always talking about.

She didn't know how much time had passed when someone knocked at the shop's front door. She checked her watch. It was nine-forty, just twenty minutes until opening. Ricki was nowhere to be found, which was almost a blessing in disguise. Molly was dreading the moment she was going to have to let Ricki go. She hoped LeRoy was right, and Ricki could get her old job back.

She hopped up from the couch and peered through the front window. Simon's boyfriend was at the door. There was no way he wanted to buy yarn, was there?

She opened the door and looked into his perfect face. He had dark, almost blue-black hair that fell, just-so, over his forehead. His cheeks were like blades, his mouth as puffy as a porn star's, his nose narrow at the bridge and manly at the tip. No wonder Simon was hot for him. He was movie-star handsome.

"The shop doesn't open until ten," she said. She knew

it was bitchy, but for some reason she wanted to lash out at him, even though he was merely an innocent bystander in the train wreck that had become her life.

He gave her a wink. A wink! Wow. "Do you carry Jamieson's Spindrift?" he asked in a voice that had just a little Latin lilt to it. "Please say that you do. I ran out of one of the colors for a sweater I am knitting. And I have been driving across the country and didn't have time to find a good-quality yarn shop."

He winked at people, and he was a knitter. Double wow.

"Uh, yeah, we carry a limited supply of Jamieson's wool." She opened the door. "What color are you looking for?"

"Just one moment. I will go get my bag. I don't know the color exactly, but maybe we can match it." He jogged up the street and returned a moment later carrying a magnificent brown leather satchel that may have actually been made by Coach. He dropped the bag on the table in the center of the store and pulled out a spectacular intarsia crew-necked sweater in a very large size. It was knitted in the round and only lacked an inch or so of cuff on one sleeve to be finished.

"Wow. That's amazing. You knitted that?"

"Well, I have been knitting since I was very little. My aunt taught me, and now she says I am a yarn whisperer."

Molly stared at him. "That's what people say about me."

"Then you know how it is." He pointed to the unfinished cuff. "I do not remember what color I need for this."

"Let me get a couple of skeins and see if we can match." She headed off to the specialty yarn area. Jamieson's yarns had a zillion colors. She picked up several skeins of various shades of gray and brought them back to the counter.

"Well, let's see, it looks like slate to me."

"Ah, yes, that matches. Thank God."

"You're in luck. We don't carry all of Jamieson's colors."

"You have saved my life. Rodrigo's birthday is next week, and he is already unhappy that I am not going to be home for it."

"Rodrigo?"

"He is my boyfriend. Let me introduce myself. I am Angel Menendez. I work for Simon Wolfe."

"So your boyfriend is *Rodrigo*?" she found herself asking. She left off the rest of the question.

"I guess you do not have many gay men who have come out here in South Carolina."

"Uh, no, but I'm okay with it."

"And you are the pretty girl who works at the yarn shop?" It was his way of asking for her name.

"Oh, I'm sorry. I'm Molly Canaday, and I don't work here. My momma owns the place but she's out of town. I work at the . . . Crap." Pain knifed through her.

"You work where?"

She let go of a gigantic breath, and her shoulders sagged. "I guess I do work here since this morning, when I lost my job at the Grease Pit."

His eyebrow cocked. "Oh, I am so sorry. The Grease Pit? What kind of place is that?"

"The auto repair place down the street."

He grinned, showing off a set of straight, pearly white teeth that could not be entirely natural. "So, you are a mechanic and a yarn whisperer?"

"Yeah, well, right now I'm here selling yarn."

"And that is not so bad, is it?"

Molly headed toward the cash register. "So you only need one skein?" she asked, changing the subject.

He nodded, then dug his wallet out of his back pocket. He continued to examine the shop while she rang up the sale. "I am so happy there is a real yarn store here. I did not think there would be one. I'm very fussy about my yarns."

"Who isn't," she said. He was completely sweet and engaging. And his boyfriend wasn't Simon, but some big dude named Rodrigo. For some reason, that knowledge gave her a lift in what was otherwise starting out as a terrible day.

"So you brought Simon's things, then?" She found herself asking, hoping to lure Angel into a little bit of harmless gossip.

"I did. It took more than a week to drive across the country. I ran out of yarn in Kansas City and could not find a shop that carried Jamieson's anywhere."

"So you're staying for a while?"

"Until Simon has taken care of his father's affairs. Actually, I think getting away from California will be good for him. He is basically on the rebound, and I think his current painting is not his best work. Maybe a couple of months."

"On the rebound? Really?"

Angel leaned in closer and dropped his voice, as if he were imparting the choicest morsels of gossip, which was precisely what Molly had hoped for. "His girlfriend, Gillian, dumped him about a month ago. He says he is not heartbroken, but he lies. He also thinks he can fool me into believing that he is perfectly fine. But he is not. He wears all of his emotions right there for anyone to see if you look carefully. And the painting does not go well."

"His girlfriend dumped him?" Why was her heart suddenly pinging around her chest?

Angel laughed. "You thought he was gay, didn't you? Everyone thinks that, and I can see why. The man is so particular about his clothes. He drives me crazy. He is almost as fussy and demanding as Rodrigo." Angel picked up the calendar flyer that listed all of the shop's special events, classes, and meetings. "Ah, the Purly Girls. I think Mrs. Wolfe is a member."

"She is. The old ladies come from the senior center on Tuesdays. We'll be having a meeting this afternoon."

"I hope it is not limited to old ladies."

"You want to join the Purly Girls?"

"I love charity knitting." He grinned. "And Simon wants me to accompany his mother."

She handed him his purchase. "Well, I guess I'll see you this afternoon. We're starting prayer blankets now that we've finished our Memorial Day poppies."

"I will see you then. Thank you very much for opening the store early for me."

He turned to go.

"Wait, are you staying at Charlotte's house?" she asked.

"Oh, no. Simon says Mrs. Wolfe is kind of scared about strangers. For now, I have a room at the Peach Blossom Motor Court." He made a face.

"Oh, my God, you slept there last night?"

"And the night before that."

"I can't believe Simon told you to get a room there.

The place is roach-infested. You should be staying with him in his mother's gigantic house."

He gave an exaggerated shrug. "Well, that is not possible. And there is no other place in town to stay."

"Wait, I have an idea."

She pulled out her cell phone and speed-dialed a number. "Hello, Ruby, is the apartment above the Cut 'n Curl available?"

The studio space was much larger than Simon needed and much dirtier than he expected. He and Angel lost a whole morning running up to Lovett's hardware for mops and detergent and window squeegees. By lunchtime, they had the front windows cleaned, the concrete floors mopped, and the bathroom bearable.

Even so, it was a relief to be here doing something productive instead of puttering around the house, waiting for Daddy's will to be probated and getting the house ready to put on the market, while simultaneously keeping an eye on Mother, who usually didn't have a clue who he was.

Today was the first day she would be spending at the senior day care facility in Allenberg. Since it was Tuesday, he'd pick her up later this evening at the Knit & Stitch, after the Purly Girls meeting, which is where he wanted Angel to befriend her.

He was counting on Angel to be her combination chauffeur, nursemaid, and knitting buddy, while Simon concentrated on getting the Harrison commission finished and dealing with the business of winding up his father's affairs. It was a truly lucky thing that his assistant was gifted with a set of knitting needles.

Angel would be fine with that. Simon had never met a person who made friends quicker than Angel Menendez. In fact, it had taken him almost no time at all to score an apartment above the Cut 'n Curl, where Simon was sure he'd fit right in.

Simon was just putting up his big easel when Lark Chaikin came strolling through the door. She was accompanied by a little girl of eight or nine with a bright blond ponytail, wearing pink shorts and a One Direction T-shirt.

"So," Lark said, taking in the space, "I see you've dusted a bit. Haley and I were in town, and we thought we'd come over and see how you're settling in."

Lark made it sound very neighborly, but he was certain she was here to talk him into something he didn't want to do. And besides, he didn't want or need distractions right now.

"I'm fine," he said without elaboration.

"And so, apparently, is your assistant. He's made quite an impression on my mother-in-law."

He frowned trying to figure out who Lark's mother-in-law was. It had been a long time since he'd lived here. The relationships among people were still a little vague.

"Ruby Rhodes," Lark supplied in answer to his unasked question. "The owner of the Cut 'n Curl? Stone's mother?"

"Ah." He nodded and finished tightening the last screw on the easel.

The little girl had wandered over to the wood crate

holding the Harrison canvas. "What's in there?" she asked, turning to give Simon an adorable, wide-eyed look out of a pair of dark brown eyes.

And, once again, the past came out of nowhere and hit him upside the head. The girl had to be Sharon McKee Rhodes's daughter. She looked just like her late mother.

"Your mother was Sharon McKee," he said. It wasn't a question. Funny how he still remembered Sharon. She'd been pretty and blond and always on Stone's arm, when she wasn't organizing something. The whole graduating class of 1990 had been utterly blown away when Stone had run off with Sharon the year she was the Watermelon Festival queen.

"She's in Heaven," Haley said.

"I heard about that. My daddy's in Heaven, too," he said.

"And I heard about that, too. I'm really, really sorry. But I'm sure he's happy in Heaven." She turned and looked at the crate. "What's in there?"

"A painting."

"Really? It's big."

The canvas was five feet by seven feet—intended to hang above the massive fireplace in Rory Harrison's new Northern California retreat.

"Can I see it?" the kid asked.

"It's not finished."

"Are you painting it?"

"Yes, I'm painting it." He checked his watch, then realized that it was a rude thing to do. Gillian had scolded him on any number of occasions for that little nervous tic. He really didn't want to be rude to Sharon and Stone's daughter. She was a cute little thing.

"I can see you're busy," Lark said. "We didn't mean to keep you from your work. We just came to see how you were doing and to welcome you to Palmetto Avenue. You're likely to get hit up by the merchants' association."

"I'm not a merchant."

Lark turned her back and cast her gaze over the space. "But you could be." She turned her attention to the little girl. "C'mon Haley, it's lunchtime. Let's go get that milk shake you wanted."

She reached out her hand, and Haley skipped across the floor and took it. Lark draped her arm across the little girl's shoulder. There was something about the way Lark embraced the child. It made his insides go liquid. Lark had come to this child late in her life, and the girl clearly adored her. What was this longing inside of him? It wasn't for the past. Not at all. But somehow Last Chance and all these connections had unlocked it.

And suddenly he wanted this moment to last just a little longer, before he had to face the painting that was giving him such trouble.

"Wait," he said.

They both turned.

He squatted down, the better to be on Haley's level and spoke directly to the little girl. "If you like, you can help me take the painting out of its shipping crate."

"Really?" The little girl's face lit up, and that made Simon feel ever so much better about himself.

"Sure."

He stood and picked up the crowbar sitting beside the crate. He loosened a couple of nails and popped off the end piece.

He let Haley help him slide the canvas out on its edge.

Lark stepped forward, took a corner, and helped him carry it to the large easel.

Once it had been secured, all three of them stood back and regarded the work-in-progress. "Wow, very south-western," Lark said. Simon read the disappointment in her voice. He wanted to reiterate that it wasn't finished. But she already knew that.

Haley stared at it for a long time. "It looks kind of like where Wile E. Coyote lives."

The child had hit the nail right on the head. No matter how many times Simon tried to re-create the Painted Desert, it always ended up looking like a cartoon backdrop.

"I guess," he muttered. "It's a painting of the desert."

"Why are you painting deserts?" Haley asked.

"Because Mr. Harrison wants a painting of a desert."

"Mr. Harrison?"

"He's the man who is going to buy the painting when it's finished."

"Oh." Haley paused and continued to study the paint-ing. "Mr. Harrison must have a mighty big house for a picture that humongous."

"He does."

"Well, if I ever get a big house, I'm going to buy pic-tures of other things. You know, like birds in the swamp. Sorta like Lark's pictures. Did you know her pictures are so good they made a whole book of them? I reckon selling a book of pictures is better than selling just one big one." There was no mistaking Haley's pride in her stepmother. And Simon had to agree. Lark's book, *Rural Scenes*, was a masterwork of photography. In his opinion, some of her work rivaled that of Ansel Adams.

He looked over at Lark. She didn't seem at all

embarrassed about what Haley had just said. Judging by the spark of amusement in her dark eyes, Lark knew the Harrison commission was god-awful. "Don't let Haley fool you," she said. "She is way more perceptive than you might expect."

Lark turned and took Haley by the hand. "C'mon, sweetie, let's leave Mr. Wolfe to his work."

The two of them left him to stand there contemplating the disaster that was the biggest commission of his life.

Angel found him there ten minutes later. "You know, boss, standing there looking at it will not make it any better." Angel handed him a can of soda and a sandwich wrapped in waxed paper.

"What's this?" Simon asked, holding up the sandwich.

"Ham and American cheese with no mustard, only mayo, and no lettuce but only tomatoes. By the way, your hometown is quite a lively place."

"Lively? You're kidding, right? They roll up the sidewalks at night."

"That may be, but during the daytime there is much excitement. There was a catfight at the café between a woman named Flo and another one named Ricki. I am not absolutely sure, but I think Ricki had been working at the café until she got a job at the yarn shop. But then her job at the yarn shop disappeared because Molly, the very nice proprietor, lost her job at the garage and had to fire Ricki from the shop. So Ricki wanted her old job back, and the owner of the café was happy to give it back to her, but the new waitress, Flo, was making it hard for him to do that."

Angel unwrapped his sandwich and took a bite.

"Molly lost her job at the Grease Pit?"

"You know Molly?" Angel spoke with a partially

full mouth. For a gay guy, he really needed better table manners.

"Yes," Simon answered. "Molly is Coach's daughter."

Angel frowned. "Ah, the famous football coach. The man you admire so much. Football is very big in this town."

"Yes. But she lost her job?"

"That I heard straight from her mouth when I stopped by the yarn shop this morning. I also heard from your aunt Millie, who I ran into at the Cut 'n Curl when I was moving my things in, that your uncle Ryan is trying to steal a car that belongs to Molly and her boyfriend, Les, who used to work for your father."

"Les isn't Molly's boyfriend."

"No? Everyone says he is."

"She told me he's not."

Angel studied him for a very long, pregnant moment during which Simon knew that his assistant was adding things up and coming to conclusions that might be embarrassing. Angel had a knack for reading his most intimate feelings that was often quite useful and sometimes downright annoying.

Angel swallowed another bite of his sandwich. "Well, according to the ladies at the Cut 'n Curl, Molly is as good as engaged to this man. But maybe they don't know the whole story, because Les is the one who took Molly's job at the Grease Pit. So perhaps this love affair between Molly and Les has hit a bump in the road."

Simon studied his assistant. "How do you do this?"

"What?"

"Walk into a place, a party, a gathering, and learn everything there is to know in the space of an hour?"

"I spent more than an hour this morning talking to people. I mean you sent me to Lovett's Hardware five times. And Ruby's son knows everything that goes on here. By the way, he is very grateful to you for delivering his baby. He told me that, if it weren't for the fact that the baby has been named after his late uncle Pete, they might have given him the middle name Simon. But Peter Simon sounded too biblical. Ruby plans to invite you and Molly to dinner. I gather the both of you delivered this baby. She is very cute, the owner of the yarn shop."

Simon's head was spinning, but he should have known that Angel would fit right in with the notorious gossipers of Last Chance.

"Molly doesn't own the shop," he said, forcing his correction into Angel's stream of information.

"Oh, yes, I forgot. She is just filling in for her mother. But according to Dash Randall, who I met at the hardware store, Molly has great skill in restoring classic cars. Have you seen his Eldorado?"

"No, I haven't."

"Well, it is magnificent." Angel paused for breath and then continued. "And, as I said before, your aunt Millie says that your uncle Ryan has taken possession of a car that Molly was in the process of restoring. And Millie's friend Thelma told me that Molly wanted to hire her husband, Eugene, who is your lawyer, but she could not because Eugene is already working for you. So Molly has many problems, it would seem."

"Wait a second, are you talking about the Shelby?"

"What is a Shelby?"

Simon rolled his eyes. "A very valuable automobile. My father gave Molly space at the dealership to restore this car. She made a point of telling me about it on the day of my father's wake. She wanted to make sure I didn't get any ideas about trying to take it from her, just because it was there at the dealership."

"Well, apparently your uncle Ryan is trying to take it away. I heard that this car might be worth one hundred thousand dollars. Is this true?"

"It may be worth more than that."

"Wow. No wonder your uncle wants the car."

"Well, it's not his to take." Simon turned away and looked out at the traffic passing on Palmetto Avenue as he tried to tighten his internal tourniquet. No matter how hard he tried to hold it back, anger bled through him.

Angel continued on. "Everyone in town thinks that he can take the car. Everyone is talking about it. They are also saying that you rented this space even though Molly wanted it."

"Whose side are you on?" Simon asked, his voice small and cramped.

"I am not on any side. I am just reporting what I hear. This is a very interesting town, Simon."

"Well, don't believe everything. There's a gossip on every street corner." He threw his half-eaten sandwich into the trash bin. He had suddenly lost his appetite. "You stay here. I've got something I need to do." He headed toward the door.

"Simon, the only thing you need to do is finish the painting."

"Not before I have a chat with Uncle Ryan about a car."

For a small-town banker, Uncle Ryan sure did have one heck of a fancy office, complete with cherry paneling and a desk as big as an aircraft carrier. Simon took a seat in the burgundy leather chair in front of the massive and surprisingly uncluttered desk. He felt diminished, as if the desk had been put up on a platform and the legs of the chairs shortened just a bit.

"So you're finally showing some interest in your father's affairs. It's about damn time." Ryan steepled his fingers and leaned back in his swivel chair. He looked satisfied, as if he thought he'd won a round in a game of high-stakes poker.

Simon drew in a deep breath and let it out slowly, forcing his emotions to still. In the walk from the Coca-Cola building, he'd let his anger overwhelm him. Now he needed to gain some control.

For all his efforts to stay calm, Simon still wanted to rage at the man. He didn't quite understand why the whole Shelby situation had angered him so deeply. But it had.

"I came here to tell you to give Molly Canaday her car."

"Why should I do that? She owes the dealership rent on the space she was using."

"You know good and well that Daddy wasn't charging her rent for that space."

"Well, speaking as his banker, he should have been."

"You can't change the rules on Molly like that. It's not fair, and it's not legal. She didn't sign a lease or anything. You don't have a leg to stand on. And you're just using your position and your wealth to bully her. It's not right."

"Possession is nine-tenths of the law. If she wants the Shelby back, let her get a lawyer and fight for it."

"She can't afford a lawyer."

Ryan shrugged. "Well, that's her tough luck, because I believe I already have a buyer for the Shelby, and you'll be pleased with the amount. Even unrestored and in pieces, the buyer is willing to pay a hundred grand for it. That will clear a lot of your father's debt."

"That's bull. You can't sell it without a title, and the title isn't in the dealership's name. Ryan, don't be a jerk. Give her back the car."

Ryan leaned forward. "Why do you care?"

"Because it was my father's business, and Daddy was trying to help Molly. He wouldn't be happy with this situation. Who are you to come in and make her life miserable?"

"I'm your daddy's banker."

This back-and-forth made Simon antsy and uncomfortable. He wasn't going to win this argument. Shooting verbal missiles at Ryan and ducking when he fired back would never solve Molly's problem. He'd learned a long time ago that arguments settled nothing. It was a man's actions that made the difference. So he stood up and stalked to the door.

But he couldn't resist one last barb. He was so furious that the words escaped him even though he knew they would do him no earthly good. "You're an asshole, you know that, Uncle Ryan? You've always been an asshole."

Ryan stood up and looked down his long, frugal nose. "And you are a no-account loser. Sort of like your daddy was. It's a damn shame my sister married your father. He was beneath her. And like him, you'll never amount to anything. You're almost forty and look at you—you dress like a queer, you've got hair like a hippie, and you're just scraping by. It was no loss when you left this town, and no one will care when you leave it again."

Simon stood there staring at his uncle. This was

nothing less than what Mother had said on the night Simon had told his parents that he was giving up medicine in order to pursue his dream of becoming an artist. And Daddy, who used to argue with Mother from sunup to sundown, had stood there and let her say it. The last thing Daddy wanted was a son who wanted to paint for a living.

So there wasn't much new in Ryan's cruel words. And still, after all these years, Simon wished he could spring across the room and pop his uncle right in that long nose of his. But letting anger escalate to violence had horrible consequences, and it wouldn't get Molly her car. The braver man walks away. The wiser man finds an alternative.

"Give the car back to Molly," Simon said, forcing his voice to go low and almost soft.

"When hell freezes over."

Ricki hugged Muffin to her chest and walked down the sidewalk, trying as hard as she could to keep her head high and the tears from her eyes.

Deep within the rational folds of her mind, she knew that T-Bone couldn't take her back as a waitress because then Floretta would be out of a job. And besides, Ricki didn't really want that waitress job anymore. She was tired of being on her feet all day, and when she worked at the Knit & Stitch, she could have Muffin with her.

And that was important. Because even in the space of a few days, Muffin had become her best friend. She had fallen in love with that poor, pitiful dog. They were kind of alike. Someone had gotten tired of Muffin, just like Randy had gotten tired of her.

They had both been thrown away by someone they loved.

But she needed a job, even if it meant leaving Muffin at home. She couldn't pay the rent on the apartment she leased from Dot Cox without a job. And owning a dog required additional expenses. She'd already had Charlene Polk give Muffin a complete checkup and all her shots and a bunch of lab work. Her free dog had cost her a hundred dollars that she'd put on her nearly maxed-out credit card.

She stalked into the garage area of Bill's Grease Pit, where Bubba Lockheart was bent over the open hood of a car. "Where the hell is he, Bubba? I'm gonna kill him."

"Who?" Bubba asked.

"Who do you think? I'm looking for Les."

Bubba's eyes widened as he took in her leopard-print Michael Kors knockoff dress, her little red strappy shoes, and Muffin's matching leopard dog collar.

"What do you want Les for?" Bubba asked.

"It's none of your business," she replied.

"Hey, Ricki." The voice came from under the car in the adjacent service bay. She bent over and found Les, looking all greasy and masculine, peering at her from the service pit from whence Bill's place got its name.

"I need to talk to you," she said.

He dropped the tool he was holding and headed up the ladder at the end of the pit. A moment later he appeared around the end of the car, using a rag to wipe off his hands.

"What's the problem?" he asked, cocking his head a little and giving her the same once-over inspection she'd just gotten from Bubba. His gaze unleashed a torrent of lust that was just wrong.

Leslie Hayes was a boy. And besides, he was Molly's boy.

She stroked Muffin's head and tried to calm herself and the dog. The dog was shivering real bad now. Muffin only did that when she was scared. And she only got scared when Ricki lost her cool. Like the other day when Jane went into labor.

She pulled her mind back to the issue at hand. And steeled her body against its suddenly raging hormones. She was too old to have hormones. She needed to get a grip.

"How could you take Molly's job?" she asked.

"Because I needed a job. I mean, I didn't know LeRoy was going to fire Molly when I took the job. But hell, Ricki, I need the work."

"So do I, and now that Molly has lost her job, she has no choice but to work at the yarn shop. Which means she can't afford to keep me on."

"Oh. Well, that's okay. T-Bone will take you back."

"No, he won't."

"What?"

"If he took me back, then Flo would lose her job. He's not going to take me back. And besides, I don't want to go back. And Molly doesn't want to work at the Knit & Stitch."

"Oh. Well, I don't want to be unemployed."

"Leslie, you're an idiot. Don't you know that Molly loves you? How could you do this to her?"

"No, Ricki, she doesn't love me. She's made that abundantly clear."

"Well, of course she has. You just took her job. That's not a very good way to say I love you. I want my job at the Knit & Stitch back."

"But you weren't very good at your job at the yarn store. I mean, I heard that Molly was always running up there to get things untangled."

She stood there holding a dog who was one second away from totally freaking out. She felt useless as she stared down Leslie Hayes, who had only pointed out the obvious: Ricki wasn't good at anything. Once, when she was young, she'd been good at being pretty. But that didn't cut it anymore. And more than anything, Ricki wanted to feel competent.

"I'm learning to knit, same as I learned how to wait tables. I'm not stupid." Her words were like a declaration or something.

Les's face turned kind of red underneath all that grease. "I didn't mean it that way."

"I liked my job." Her lips started to quiver. Tears filled her eyes, and these were genuine tears, not the kind of tears she'd once used to keep Randy in line. "And Molly never once told me she was unhappy with me. Not once. She was teaching me." The tears rolled down her face.

"Uh, Ricki, don't cry, honey. Maybe I could talk to Molly." Les checked his watch. "It's almost quitting time. Maybe we could go up to the Knit & Stitch and talk to her right now. Okay?"

"Now?"

"Sure. I'll just go wash up a little, and we'll see if we can get Molly to take you back."

His smile made everything seem like it was going to be okay. "All right," she said through a sniffle. She reached into her purse, pulled out a tissue, and blew her nose. Her mascara must be a complete mess. "I'm sorry."

"It's okay, honey. Let's see what we can do."

Molly sat at the little table in the Knit & Stitch, the Purly Girls surrounding her. They were all busy knitting away at prayer blankets in various shades of Red Heart basic acrylic yarn. A box of red velvet cupcakes sat in the middle of the table. Angel had brought them along with a note from Simon to his mother, who'd come today on the senior center's bus. Molly thought Simon was sweet to remember that the girls liked to have refreshments when they came to knit. Angel said Simon himself had bought the cupcakes at the bakery in Allenberg this morning when he'd dropped his mother off at the senior center.

Molly was finding it difficult to stay angry with Simon. He was so thoughtful. And his assistant was a good teacher and extremely patient. So all in all, this week's meeting was coming off without a hitch, in stark contrast to last week's complete disaster.

"I think Russell is having an affair," Luanne Howe said in a quavery voice. She was knitting her blanket in the variegated colorway called Favorite Jeans.

"Really?" Mary Latimer responded. Mary might be almost eighty-five but she still had a surprisingly girlish voice. She leaned forward, never missing a stitch, ready to get the juicy gossip. "What tipped you off? Did you find someone else's underwear in his car or something? You know that happened to Grace Watkins. That man of hers was fooling around something terrible."

"No," Luanne replied, "it's nothing like that. It's just that he's been ignoring me." She turned to Miriam Randall, who wasn't knitting because her hands were badly afflicted with arthritis. "Do you think I should hire a private investigator?" Luanne asked.

"I don't know. That can get expensive," Miriam said. Thank goodness she didn't remind Luanne that her husband of forty years, who had been the morning voice of WLST, the local radio station, had died last spring. All the members of the Purly Girls were widows. It was kind of sad, really. And Luanne missed Russell something fierce. This idea of him cheating on her wasn't anything new.

Miriam picked at her red velvet cupcake. The old lady had been off her feed recently. Miriam had lost her husband just a few months ago, too.

Mary Latimer leaned toward Luanne. "Well, I say you should definitely hire a private eye. You don't want to end up like Grace."

"How did Grace end up?" Angel asked.

Mary blinked a few moments. "I don't remember."

"Oh, for heaven's sake, she ended up divorced. But she got her revenge. She got the house and the car and the dog," Charlotte said. "And then she went off and got a boob job."

"You think I need a boob job?" Luanne asked.

"Hush up. Your boobs are just fine," Mary said. "If Russell doesn't know a good pair of boobs, he's blind."

"Well," Luanne said, "he's been having some trouble with his eyesight, you know."

"Well, he doesn't have to look at them. I mean, it's all about—"

The front door opened, thankfully cutting short Mary's discussion of breast enhancement in the older generation. The girls stopped talking as Les and Ricki strode into the store. Les looked out of his element standing amid the shelves of yarn, wearing his greasy coveralls. And Ricki looked like a slightly trashy fashion plate who, judging by her messy mascara, was about to come apart at the seams. Her dog looked exactly like that, too.

"Hey," Molly said getting up from the table. She braced herself for what was surely going to be an unpleasant conversation.

"You have to take Ricki back," Les said.

"I don't have to do anything."

"But if you don't, she's going to be unemployed."

Molly was about to point out that technically she, herself, was unemployed. Then Ricki said "please" in a whiny voice. And her little dog started whining, too.

"We all thought T-Bone would take her back, but he won't," Les said.

"We all who, Les?"

Her best friend hung his head. And it was kind of impossible to be all that angry at him. He thought he and LeRoy had it all worked out. Typical.

What the heck was Molly supposed to do now? Momma would be so calm in a situation like this. But all Molly wanted to do right now was scream.

Angel came to her rescue. "Um," he said rising from his seat at the table, where he'd been finishing up his gorgeous sweater, "I don't mean to interrupt this discussion, but what Ricki just said is not exactly true."

He came to stand beside Molly and continued, "I think T-Bone would take Ricki back, but Ricki wants to bring Muffin to work with her." He smiled at the dog.

And damned if the dog didn't stop shivering and smile back.

And then she defected. She launched herself out of Ricki's grasp and right at Angel. Good thing he had skills as a dogcatcher.

The pooch immediately settled into his arms, while the man began to croon baby talk to her. It was a clear case of love at first sight.

"That's my dog." Ricki's voice sounded brittle.

"I know. But you can't take her to work at the Kountry

Kitchen. It would be a health code violation," Angel said in what Cesar Millan, the Dog Whisperer, would probably call a calm, assertive voice.

Les turned toward Ricki. "You said T-Bone didn't want you back."

"Well, not on the terms I wanted. I can't leave Muffin alone." She gave the dog a desperate look. "She chews things when I'm not looking. She destroyed my only pair of Fendis. But without her, I…" Ricki almost choked. It was clear that despite the dog's misbehavior, Ricki loved Muffin.

"Well," Les said, completely missing the emotionally charged moment, "you're not really unemployed then. You can confine her in your apartment's kitchen until she's housebroken, and you can walk her on your breaks or something."

"But she'll be lonely." There was such aching sadness in Ricki's voice.

"Oh, that is no problem. I have a perfect solution," Angel said.

"You do?" Les, Ricki, and Molly practically spoke in unison. Meanwhile, the Purly Girls were knitting like a bunch of Madame Defarges at a public execution.

"Of course," Angel said. "I will babysit Muffin."

Ricki's gaze bounced from Angel to Muffin and back again. She burst into tears. And before anyone could say another word, she ran right out of the yarn shop. Molly was impressed by how fast Ricki could move on those spike heels.

But that wasn't nearly as impressive as the way Les took off after her.

"And so it begins," Miriam said.

"What begins?" Angel asked, turning toward Miriam.

Miriam gave him a long, assessing look from behind her rhinestone-studded trifocals. "Your love affair with Muffin," she said.

Luanne giggled like a schoolgirl, but Angel seemed not at all perturbed as he stroked the head of the little, useless dog. "I have wanted a dog for a long time. Alas, Rodrigo is not a dog person."

Miriam regarded him soberly. "And that should tell you something right there, young man."

Whatever comeback Angel was about to give Miriam was cut short by Simon's arrival. He burst through the door, making the little bell jangle like an alarm. His brow was folded into a scowl, his dark eyes looked bright and angry, and his jaw had a hard-as-steel look to it.

"Molly," he said, "I need you."

Miriam giggled at this sudden display of alpha-male behavior.

"For what?" Molly asked.

He glanced at his mother and then back. "I need you to come with me right this minute." He turned toward Angel. "Take care of Mother."

And with that he locked his long, masculine fingers around Molly's arm and started to pull her toward the door.

"Stop that man," Charlotte said, standing up. "He's a molester and a thief." She shook her finger at Simon, and for a fleeting instant Molly saw the hurt in Simon's eyes.

"Mrs. Wolfe, it's okay," Angel said, stepping between mother and son. "It's just a fight between Molly and her boyfriend."

Miriam giggled again, and Molly tried to pull away.

But Simon put the kibosh on all her attempts at escape. He had some really powerful hands.

"Molly," Charlotte cried, "don't go with that man. He's no good for you. You can see that, can't you? I mean, look at all that hair. Your father would never approve of a man with hair that long."

Which, actually was sort of true. Even so, Molly was tempted to tell Charlotte to put a sock in it for what she'd just said. Since when did she require Coach's approval—for anything? And then she realized she didn't need Coach's approval because Simon wasn't her boyfriend. Which was a good thing, wasn't it?

"Don't be difficult," Simon whispered. "I'll tell you what's going on when we get outside. There are too many gossips in this room." He cast his gaze toward Angel and then back to Molly.

"I'll be back in time for tonight's knitting class," she said to the Purly Girls, who looked as if they hadn't seen this much excitement in years.

"I wouldn't count on it," Miriam said.

# CHAPTER 13

Simon didn't want to drag Molly to the sidewalk. He didn't want to argue with her either. His argument with Uncle Ryan was already one argument too many. But when people started behaving like idiots, sometimes a man just had to act. Otherwise the anger could eat right through him, like acid.

"Stop being difficult," he said. "I'm here to help you."

He loosened his grip on her arm, and she pulled away. His hand felt empty the moment she escaped.

She whirled on him. "I don't like being manhandled."

"Sorry. But what we're about to do requires stealth."

"You call manhandling me out of my shop stealthy?"

"No. But explaining why I need you out here would have been stupid. The biggest gossips in Last Chance are in your shop right at this moment. I didn't want to discuss my plans in front of them. We're about to commit grand theft. Sort of."

"What?"

He turned and headed down the sidewalk toward Bill's Grease Pit. "Do you want your Shelby back or not?"

"Are we going to break into Wolfe Ford?" Her voice carried, and half a dozen pedestrians on Palmetto Avenue turned to stare.

"Keep your voice down," Simon whispered. "And don't act suspicious."

"Right. But what exactly are you talking about?"

"My uncle Ryan is an a-hole. That's what I'm talking about."

"Well, I'm glad you and I agree on something," Molly said.

"Why didn't you tell me Uncle Ryan was trying to steal your car?"

"I told you days ago that the car didn't belong to the dealership."

"I know. But you didn't say one word to me about how Ryan had locked it up and was insisting that it belonged to the dealership in payment of rent due. That's just ridiculous. I talked to Les and Bubba, and they both confirmed that Daddy wasn't interested in charging you rent for that garage space."

"Oh, is that the excuse Ryan used for hanging on to the car? He stonewalled me when I spoke to him about it. He pretended my bill of sale wasn't good and that I would need to go get a lawyer."

"You should have told me."

"I didn't think you would give a darn, to be honest. I thought you were just in a big, hot hurry to get back to Paradise."

He stopped and looked down at her. Her eyes were as amazing as her hair. Their color was so unique and changeable. He wanted to get lost in that look she was giving him. And suddenly all the rage disappeared, replaced by the simple need to make things right for her. "I'm sorry. Sometimes I can be very aloof. It's just my way of staying out of arguments."

"But you're getting into the middle of this one?"

He nodded. "Yes. I am. We're going to get your car, right now. I don't like bullies."

"But—"

"Hush, we can't talk here."


Molly struggled to keep up with Simon as he strode down Palmetto Avenue toward Bill's Grease Pit, where Bubba Lockheart was waiting in the parking lot, leaning up against the flatbed truck, idly tossing and catching the keys.

"Hey, Molly, I'm real sorry about what LeRoy did. That was low, in my opinion, even if Les is a great mechanic."

"It's okay," she muttered.

"Well, no, it's not, which is why I told Simon that I'd be happy to help you liberate the Shelby. Anything for Coach's daughter, right, Simon?"

"Absolutely." Simon gave Molly an I'm-up-to-no-good, devilish kind of smile that didn't show any teeth. This time it made her feel light-headed, but maybe it was just the excitement of finally doing something about the car situation.

Or maybe it was the fact that Simon was drop-dead gorgeous. And his take-charge attitude was sexy. Especially since he'd dressed for a car heist in skinny black jeans, a black T-shirt, and a pair of boots that had been polished to within an inch of their lives.

He looked bad. All he needed to complete the outfit would have been one of those Celtic-motif tats around his upper arm. Sadly, he appeared to be tattoo-free.

"Hey guys," Bubba said, "I have a question. The dealership is all locked up. How are we going to get in? I'm not down with breaking windows or anything like that."

Simon reached into his jeans pocket and pulled out a shiny brass key. "We'll use this. It's way more civilized than breaking and entering."

"You have a key?"

"I reckon I do."

"How did you get that?" she asked.

"I told my uncle's secretary, Miz Linnette, that Mother and I were heartbroken about not having Daddy's football memorabilia—you know all those team photos he'd hung all over the dealership. Not to mention the game ball from the 1990 championship season. Miz Linnette may work for my uncle, but I reckon she's just about the biggest Rebels booster there is, now that Daddy's passed. I promised her the autographed team photo."

Bubba snorted a laugh, and Molly found herself taking another look at Simon Wolfe. Maybe he hadn't lost his southern accent or attitude. He'd just used the word "reckon" twice in a row.

When he talked like that, it was deeply seductive. But she ought to resist. She was still Coach's daughter and could get in a lot of hot water with her daddy for stealing things. Even if the stuff she was stealing was her own property.

"You know, maybe we should rethink," she said. "I really want that car back, but we're going to get into trouble. I mean, when the car turns up missing, everyone is going to know it was me who stole it back. And I'll bet Miz Linnette hasn't given a key to anyone else. So they're going to know that Simon helped. And since the Shelby is in bits and pieces, naturally they'll assume that Bubba or Les helped with the truck. And I don't even want to think about the crap I'm going to get from my daddy for doing something like this."

"I don't care what people think, not even Coach," Simon said with cool resolve. "I'm not going to let my uncle steal your car, Molly, and we have to do it this way because he told me this afternoon that he's got a buyer for it."

"But he can't sell it. He doesn't have—"

"He can sell it, and he will. He'll find some dirty, underhanded way of doing it, and he'll pocket the money. And it will be a done deal while you're still interviewing lawyers. So it's now or never. He can't accuse you of stealing your own car. And I have permission to be in the dealership. It belonged to my daddy. So what if I let you in to get your belongings, too. What can he do to you?"

"Plenty. He's got the money to hire lots of lawyers."

"And you have a bill of sale and a title."

"Coach is not going to be happy about this, and—"

"Why not?" Bubba asked. "Simon's got a point. I mean, it's not stealing if you're just taking back what's yours to begin with. The only thief in this scenario is Ryan Polk."

"But we still have a problem," Molly said. "Once we take the car from the dealership where the heck are we going to stash it?"

"We're going to stash the car at the Coca-Cola building," Simon said.

"But you've rented it already."

"That place is cavernous," he replied. "You can have the area right by the loading dock. It's perfect garage space. And I'll take the front room with the windows."

"Oh, my God. Thank you, thank you, thank you," Molly threw her arms around Simon's neck and gave him a big hug and a kiss.

But something went seriously haywire with that kiss the moment her lips touched the stubble on his cheek. She got stuck there and made the double mistake of breathing in. Bad move. His scent was intoxicating.

And then he put his arms around her waist and held her there for just the smallest fraction of a moment. A moment that expanded in time so it was long enough for Molly to feel the pressure of his thighs. Long enough for her to taste his cheek with the tip of her tongue. Long enough for her hormones to pitch a full-out, no-holds-barred female tizzy.

Time started flowing again, and she pulled away. But her face felt like it had been blowtorched.

Ricki ran from the Knit & Stitch without any real conscious thought of where she was going. She just needed to run—to get away from Muffin's defection and the sorry state of her life. She'd thought things were looking up for her, and then, *wham*, here she was dogless, and jobless, and all in the space of a few hours.

It would have been much better if she'd been wearing a pair of running shoes, or even the Skechers she used to wear at the Kountry Kitchen, because the heel of one of her little red shoes got caught in a sidewalk crevice. Her ankle turned, and her leg collapsed, and down she went, right onto her leopard-clad butt.

She must have cried out in pain or something, although really it was mostly her butt that hurt. Anyway, the next minute, Les Hayes was there being all big and manly and surprisingly tender. He took charge, and that was nice. He wouldn't let her get up.

"You could have really broken or torn something. I'm taking you to see Doc Cooper."

"I'm okay, really."

But Les was exactly the kind of tenderhearted, take-charge guy she had a weakness for. So when he hoisted her from the sidewalk and started walking toward the clinic, she let him. It took him almost ten minutes to walk there, and he didn't falter once. "You must work out," Ricki said as he carried her through the doors.

"A little." A blush ran up his cheeks. She inhaled him. He was one part gasoline and two parts de-greaser, with a hint of good clean soap. He didn't smell like Randy, that was for sure, but boy, there was something about him that ran circles around her ex.

Probably the fact that he was twenty-five years younger. That cooled her jets a little bit.

A moment later Les deposited her on one of the examining room beds. Annie Jasper, the nurse, bustled in, and Ricki gave her all the details of her fall. Les hovered beside the bed.

"Did you try to put weight on it?" Annie asked.

"No."

"No?"

Ricki glanced at Les. "Uh, well, Les picked me up and carried me here."

Annie turned around and gave Les one of those measured looks. "Really?"

"Yes, ma'am," Les said, and his face got pink again.

"Does it hurt to move it?"

"Not really. Not anymore, I mean."

"Right." Annie gave Ricki one of her stern looks. "Why don't you hop down from there, gently, and see if you can walk it off."

"Okay."

She slid from the bed and gave the ankle a little test. Of course it didn't hurt. But with Annie Jasper staring at her, she suddenly felt like the biggest jerk in the universe, not to mention one of those cougars who prey on younger men. "It seems to be okay."

"Annie, you need to check her over top to bottom. She took a bad tumble. I saw it happen," Les said.

Bless his heart, Les cared.

Annie glared at her, and Ricki had no problem interpreting that look. The whole town would be saying very mean things about her tomorrow morning. About how she was making a play for Molly Canaday's man. And with Ricki losing her job, people would put two and two together and come up with the wrong answer.

God, could her life have gotten more complicated in the space of twenty-four hours? She forced one of her waitress smiles to her face. "I guess I'm okay, Les. Thank you for being so chivalrous. But I think I can make it home now."

"I'll walk with you." This was not a request, and it really worried Ricki when Annie Jasper rolled her eyes.

But there wasn't any way she was going to get rid of Leslie Hayes. Under other circumstances—like in a big city where nobody knew anybody's business—Ricki might have let herself enjoy the sudden attention of a very handsome man. But this was Last Chance, where everybody passed judgment on everybody's business, so there would be no enjoyment of this moment.

"Thanks, Annie," she said and headed toward the door. Les trailed after her.

She had taken a few steps down the sidewalk in the direction of her apartment when her cell phone rang. She pulled it out of her purse and checked the number. It was Molly.

Damn, was she already checking up on Les? She gave him a glance where he strolled beside her, looking kind of grim. "It's Molly," she said, then she pressed the talk button.

"Hey, Molly." She tried to keep her voice as neutral as possible. She was starting to think it had been a very bad idea to make such a scene during the Purly Girls meeting.

"Honey, I'm sorry about your job. Really and truly. I don't know if I can afford to hire you back, but right now I need you."

"You need me?"

"Yes, I do. I have an errand I have to do, and I left Angel in charge of the shop. He may be able to knit like nobody's business but I don't really know him, you know what I mean?"

"Uh-huh."

"So I'm hiring you back. I need you to go keep an eye on things and help Angel. And I need you to stay open for the gals who come in this evening for knitting lessons."

"But, Mol, I don't know how to teach anyone to knit."

"It's all right. Just get Angel to do it."

"Okay."

"You're the best, Ricki. And I promise I'll find some way to get your job at the Kountry Kitchen back for you. Don't you worry, now, you hear?"

Ricki refrained from telling Molly that she didn't want

to go back to waitressing. She liked knitting a whole lot better. But beggars couldn't be choosers, and Ricki had been a beggar for a long time.

She turned toward Les. "I gotta go back to the store. Molly's rehired me just for tonight."

"Oh. Uh, well, that's great." They had reached the parking lot at Bill's Grease Pit, where Les's truck was parked. "I guess I gotta go then."

She stood there awkwardly. "I'm sorry I yelled at you."

"It's okay. I probably deserved it. I'm glad your ankle is okay."

"About that, I—"

He held up his hands. "I still think Annie Jasper should have called for an X-ray or something. My heart stood still when I saw you topple over."

"It did?"

He nodded, and his cheeks got just a little red again. Man, he was cute when he blushed like that.

"Well, thank you for carrying me. That's the nicest thing anyone has done for me in ages and ages. Maybe ever."

He smiled. And when his mouth quirked up like that, it stole Ricki's breath.

"Maybe I'll see you sometime down at Dot's Spot."

"Maybe you will."

# CHAPTER
## 14

Simon liked order in his life. He kept his drawers and his closet and his work organized. Every day, when he stepped into his studio, he knew where all his tools were, and he knew which part of a painting he was going to attack. He knew what he wanted to accomplish. He set goals for himself. He worked hard. And he always got up early in the morning.

It was barely dawn on Thursday morning when he opened the Coca-Cola building, made himself a strong cup of coffee in the old coffeemaker he'd borrowed from his mother, and regarded the Harrison commission.

All his focus and all his organizational skill could not save him from this disaster. The colors were wrong, the heart of the painting was missing, and he felt no deep, burning desire to finish it. He was lost and had no notion of how to get back on track.

He stood there a long time, paralyzed by his indecision, until someone started banging on the front door. It was surprising that anyone was awake at six in the morning. But this was Last Chance, where farmers got up early and listened to the agricultural talk show on WLST.

Simon was pretty sure a farmer would have better things to do at six in the morning than bang on his studio door. Unless, of course, the farmer was ticked off about having to go eighty miles to get warranty service on his truck.

Simon was also pretty sure Uncle Ryan wasn't out there disturbing the early-morning peace. Ryan kept banker's hours.

By the violence of the pounding, his morning visitor was in a most unfriendly mood. So Simon ignored this interruption of his working day.

The banging stopped, thank goodness, only to be replaced by a rather urgent tapping on the front window. "Simon, open the damn door," his visitor shouted in a slightly husky voice.

A jolt of recognition marched through Simon. He would know that voice anywhere. He looked up. Coach Canaday stood on the sidewalk glowering at him through the big picture windows.

Coach had gotten older and a little grayer, but his face, with its wandering nose, looked the same. His eyes were still piercing, and he still commanded immediate respect just by standing there.

Coach was an early riser, too. Simon had learned the value of getting up at the crack of dawn from the man himself.

He hurried to the door and let Coach in. He expected a slap on the back, or a handshake, or at least a "Hey, how've you been?" But he got none of that.

Instead, Coach stalked into the middle of his makeshift

studio, glanced at the disaster on the easel, and then turned toward Simon with a scowl.

Simon remembered that look. Coach could be a hard man at times. But he was always fair. Coach praised more often than he scolded, which was why his players loved him. But Heaven help the player who got on his wrong side.

"I have a bone to pick with you, boy," Coach said.

"Sir?" It was funny how Simon immediately dropped back into old ways in the face of Coach's disapproval.

"Don't you act like you don't know what I'm talking about."

Simon didn't have a clue, so he said nothing. Silence was always a good policy when Coach was on the warpath. Ducking worked, too, because Coach was known to throw things when he got mad.

"I'm talking about my daughter."

"Oh." Of course he was. Molly had even warned Simon that this was coming. How could he have forgotten?

"Don't you 'oh' me. You know darn well I have a policy that no player of mine messes with my daughter."

"Sir, I don't remember that policy. As I recall, Molly was about four when I was a member of the team. She was our good-luck charm. I used to rub her head before every kick."

"Exactly my point." The look on Coach's face could only be described as "furious father."

"She's not four now, sir. She's a grown-up. And I'm not *messing* with her."

"No?"

"No, *sir.*"

"Then why is it all over town that you got her involved

in some kind of fight with Ryan Polk? She doesn't need that kind of trouble."

"Sir, my uncle stole her car. I only helped her get it back."

"You know, it might have been better if you hadn't."

"But—"

"Look here, there are things going on that you don't have any idea about. My wife walked out on me because of that car. And now I've got my daughter's name being run down by the town's biggest banker. And to make matters worse, she's here camping out with you." Coach pointed a finger at Simon's chest.

Simon held his temper. "She's not camping out with me. She's working on her car whenever things at the Knit & Stitch give her time. And it's only temporary. I'm leaving just as soon as my daddy's will is probated and I can put Mother's house on the market."

"Son, maybe you don't get it. My daughter has been talking about you nonstop for two days. She's pretty naive. And a guy like you, who is still a bachelor at forty, is either not playing for the boys' team or you're hard on women. Either way, I don't want you messing with her head. And that doesn't even count the fact that you're thirteen years older than she is. Back off! She belongs to Les Hayes. At least Les is her age, and from what I hear Miriam Randall has predicted that Molly and Les belong together. You're messing things up around here for her, and I won't have it."

Well, this was disconcerting news. Not the part about Molly and Les, but the part about how Molly had been talking about him. Because Simon had been *thinking* about Molly. More or less nonstop. In particular, he'd been thinking about the way she'd felt in his arms for that one brief moment when she'd kissed him on Tuesday. That had not been a thank-you kiss. It had not been a kiss between old friends. Simon's lips may not have been involved in that kiss, but that kiss had been sexy as hell.

And kind of scary. Because Coach was right. Simon was too old for her. He knew this without being told. And the last thing he wanted was for Molly to get a crush on him. Because he didn't think he could resist. And he sure as hell didn't want to hurt Coach's daughter.

He forced a smile to his lips. "I understand, sir. And I promise that I'll discourage her attentions. But I don't think it's possible to discourage her about the Shelby. And I think if you talked to Molly, you'd discover that she thinks she belongs to her own self, not Les or you or me or anyone else. All she wants is to restore that car, sell it, and start a business. In that way, she's a whole lot like your wife. And I screwed up her plans by leasing this place, and my uncle tried to steal her dream. So it was the least I could do to help her get her dream back and give her a little space where she could work on her car. I guess in that way, I'm a little like my daddy."

This was not the right thing to say to Coach. "You were a huge disappointment to your father. You have no right to even claim kinship to Ira in my book. You walked out on him. Same as my wife has walked out on her family. So don't you go comparing these things, you hear?"

"Yes, sir." What else could he say? He'd burned his bridges eighteen years ago. And he knew, good and well, that he'd disappointed his parents. But his parents' dream for him was not his own. Any more than Coach's dreams for his daughter bore any resemblance to what Molly wanted for herself.

---

And this, pure and simple, was the most important reason that Simon never, ever wanted to be anyone's parent.

"You keep your hands off my daughter, you hear?" This time Coach pushed his index finger into Simon's chest like he was arguing with a referee.

"I promise. I will."

Simon's life settled into a certain equilibrium in the week after his confrontation with Coach. He ignored Molly to the best of his ability. He tried to concentrate on the Harrison commission, and he waged a silent war on Uncle Ryan, using some basic but stealthy tactics in the form of the master gossip Angel Menendez.

It only took Angel four days before every single soul in Allenberg County knew that Ryan Polk, the receiver for Wolfe Ford, was more interested in liquidating the business than finding a suitable buyer.

It was almost funny to see Last Chance's own version of the Occupy movement set up camp outside Ryan's office at the bank. Of course, Occupy Last Chance had a large number of middle-aged church ladies in its ranks who had probably voted steady Republican in the last five elections. But they had one thing in common—they all owned Fords.

The public demonstrations did the trick. The dealership's creditors put pressure on Ryan to quit trying to liquidate and start trying to find a buyer. And bless Stone Rhodes for being completely unwilling to arrest anyone for the removal of the Shelby from the Wolfe Ford premises—especially when Molly produced a bill of sale and a South Carolina title.

Not everything was rosy in Simon's life, though.

Mother continued to think he was some kind of thief or murderer. The probate courts moved like molasses in January. And the vast majority of citizens were convinced that Angel was his lover—no doubt a rumor spread by Coach. A rumor Simon made no attempt to dispel. It was hard to prove a negative. And besides, maybe if Molly thought he was gay, she might keep her distance.

So Simon spent his days staring at the monstrosity on his easel, trying, vainly, to find the enthusiasm to finish it. Which might have come more easily if he didn't have to contend with the noise coming from the back of the Coca-Cola building, where Molly—wearing safety goggles, her hair in complete disarray, her body hidden in oversized jeans—was having the time of her life taking apart an automobile. Just knowing she was there was a huge distraction. He kept peeking in when she was welding or sanding or doing other amazing things.

Today he was trying not to peek. Today he was sitting on the stool in his studio, flipping through photographs on his iPad trying to find some inspiration.

He'd been with Gillian when he took these photos of the Painted Desert, the Grand Canyon, and the Petrified Forest. Gillian hovered at the edges of each photo like a ghost.

He resented her. Gillian had negotiated the deal with Harrison. Simon should never have allowed her to take the lead. Harrison had dictated elements of the painting he wanted, and Gillian had agreed to all of them without even consulting Simon. And when Simon had learned the details, he'd been upset. But he'd sucked it up and signed the deal anyway. Because, as Gillian pointed out, Harrison had put a lot of money on the table.

Why had he agreed to do this painting? Money had never motivated him before.

Short answer: to make Gillian happy. And he had, for some strange reason he couldn't quite understand, wanted to please her at that particular moment in his life.

But she'd read his actions all wrong. Three weeks later, on the grand tour of the Grand Canyon, she'd laid down her ultimatum. She wanted a wedding ring. She wanted kids. But Simon had been honest from the start. No marriage. No kids. Ever.

The final argument had been practically historic in its dimensions. But Gillian had finally believed him. And the next day, she and her ticking biological clock left him to deal with Rory Harrison all by his lonesome.

"So, are you ever gonna actually work on that? Or do you get your kicks standing there giving it the evil eye?" Molly strolled into his space sipping on a Diet Dr Pepper, her face just a little dirty, her clothes a little dusty, and her amazing hair tempting as always. He both loved and hated these moments when she wandered into his studio. He had promised Coach that he would discourage her friendship, but damn it, he enjoyed spending stolen moments with her.

"I was not giving it the evil eye," he said.

"Yes, you were. So are those photographs of the ex-girlfriend? By the look on your face she must have done you wrong." She strolled over to peek at his iPad. He powered it off before she could see the image of Gillian, smiling into the camera with the Painted Desert behind her. Like every woman he'd ever known, Molly knew darn well he was heterosexual. So the whole hiding-behind-Angel thing wasn't working.

At all.

He glowered up at Molly.

She responded by grinning. He almost fell off the stool. Molly's smile was like a weapon.

He held her gaze, forcing her into an impromptu staring contest which he ultimately won when she turned away, strolling over to his stereo. She unplugged his iPod and began searching through his music.

"Don't you have anything a little livelier than Bach?" she asked.

"No." Being blunt with Molly was a tactic he was employing to absolutely no effect.

Molly returned his iPod to the speaker dock, where she flipped through his playlists. A moment later the soft baritone of David Wilcox singing "Rusty Old American Dream" filled the room.

She laughed. "It's a song about a car that needs to be restored," she said.

"Yes. It's also a song about growing older." He refrained from pointing out that Wilcox's music could never be taken quite literally. There was a haunting metaphor in every song. And right now Simon was like that rusty car, and Molly was like the young man who wanted to bring it back to life. And he kind of wanted that to happen, only it couldn't. It would be so unfair to Molly.

She studied him with her head cocked, as if she were thinking deeply. He had trouble not looking at those tarnished-copper eyes. "Simon, you need some fresh air."

"I do not." He stared at his painting. It made his stomach churn. Damn, he'd run out of Rolaids. He'd been popping a lot of them lately. "I need to make an end of this..." Words failed him.

"It's crap. You know it. I know it. Angel knows it. Heck, anyone walking by and glancing in your windows knows it."

"Thanks for the vote of confidence."

"You know, the painting would probably be ten times better if you didn't try to paint the woman out of the scene."

He tried to pretend he didn't understand her meaning. "What are you talking about?"

She gave him a squinty-eyed look that was utterly adorable. "Your attempts to hide the photographs you're working from have failed. So is that woman the one who dumped you?"

"Dumped me? Who told you—"

"Angel. He says you're heartbroken. Are you?"

Oh, great, his assistant had blown his cover. No wonder Molly wasn't buying the whole gay thing. "No, I'm not heartbroken."

"No?"

"No. And I wasn't dumped. I walked out on her."

"Ah. And why was that?"

"None of your business." He put his iPad down with more force than was necessary. He turned and gave her his own rendition of a squinty-eyed look. "Don't you have something to do?"

She took a swig of her soda. "Yeah, but I'm feeling antsy today." She nodded toward the windows. "It's a beautiful June day out there. Angel and Ricki have the Knit & Stitch running like a well-oiled machine. And I don't have LeRoy breathing down my neck. So I was thinking of knocking off early."

"Well then, don't let me stop you."

"You don't want to knock off early? Heck, you started at the crack of dawn. It's amazing how much time you waste in here, Simon. Really. And all work and no play makes Jack a dull boy. So come on, live a little. Let's play hooky."

"No."

She glanced at the painting. "Really? I would think you'd want to escape from that monstrosity."

"Everyone's a critic," he muttered. "And I don't have time to play hooky." He said this forcefully, even though deep down he wanted to escape from the Harrison commission.

Which was probably why Molly refused to give up. She had this uncanny ability to read his mind or something. Instead of leaving, she threw her Dr Pepper can in his wastebasket and then picked up his most recent sketchbook. She flipped a few pages, while the tiniest of enigmatic smiles played around her mouth. God, she was beautiful.

And young. "Do you rifle through my things when I'm not around?"

She shrugged but didn't look up from the sketches. "Not often. You're usually around. But a girl's gotta satisfy her curiosity one way or another, doesn't she?"

Something stirred in his belly. He was insanely flattered that Molly was curious about him, even though he knew it was madness to feel any curiosity about her. He said nothing in response to her obvious bait.

"So," she said, "I'm trying to figure out why every sketch in this book—even the ones dated before you got here—appear to be scenes from down on the river. And yet the big official painting looks like something you'd find at a roadside art stand somewhere in Arizona."

The critique stung. Especially because it was true.

"Good question," he said.

"Right. So, see, I've got a couple of fishing poles in the back of my car and a cage full of crickets. I think you need to go down to the river and do some fishing. It's guaranteed to clear your mind."

Or overwhelm him with sad memories. Those memories had been trying to claw their way into the sunshine for some time—ever since he'd picked up Lark's coffee table book.

"I've never been overly fond of fishing," he said. "To be honest, all I ever manage to catch is mosquito bites."

She laughed. "Okay, you bring your sketch pad, and I'll bring the fishing poles and bug spray. It's June, the days are long, and the fishing is good in the afternoon. Then afterward we can stop off at the Red Hot Pig Place for dinner. I'll buy you a beer."

It sounded like a wonderful way to end his day. "I can't, Molly. I have to pick up Mother after her meeting."

"Not to worry. Angel has everything taken care of. Your momma's in expert hands. In fact, I'm letting him and Ricki handle the Purly Girls all on their own this afternoon."

He knew when he was being railroaded. "You and Angel have consulted on this, haven't you?"

"Sorta. We're both of the opinion that you should burn this canvas and start again with something like this." She looked down at the sketch pad.

He hesitated, caught between his promise to Coach and the knowledge that he probably needed to go down to the river and wash away the bad memories. Maybe that was the only way to make peace with the past. And of

course, it would give him time with Molly. Innocent time.
She'd be fishing. He would sketch. They would hardly
talk. Nothing else would happen. Nothing else *could*
happen.

"So," Molly said in her siren voice, "are you game?"

The setting sun gave definition to the river's current.
It gleamed on the surface eddies like flickering sprites.
It edged the Spanish moss cloaking the cypresses. And
glowed like a halo on Molly's dark mane of unruly hair.

She looked like the essence of summertime, standing
on the public pier, barefoot with a fishing rod in her slen-
der hands.

Simon's heart pounded as he captured the moment
with his pencils. His hands, his eyes, his insides suddenly
remembered how it felt to have passion for his work. It
had been so long. It felt as if this place of haunting and
mysterious beauty had been waiting for him. That surprised him.

He had expected the place to depress him. To remind
him of things he wanted to forget. And it did, in some
ways, but like everything here in Last Chance, his memories were like artifacts, overlaid with something else. The
place wasn't exactly the same as when he'd last stood here.

He drank in the scene with all his senses. Not just
the light, but the babbling of the river and the buzzing of
the dragonflies; the soft swish of Molly's reel as she cast
and the little click as she reeled in; the warm, humid wind
that kissed his face; the scent of copper on the air.

"So," Molly said into the long silence, "you've been
working like a fiend."

"And you haven't caught anything."

"Doesn't matter." She leaned her fishing rod against a tree and strolled back to the little clearing along the river-bank where they'd set up a couple of lawn chairs.

She collapsed into one. "Oooph, it's hot in the sun." She opened a small cooler and pulled out a Dr Pepper. "You want one?"

He shook his head.

She peeked at his sketch. "Oh, my God. Please tell me my butt is not that big."

It amused him to think that Molly, who seemed not to care at all about how she dressed, was still woman enough to worry about the size of her butt. "It's not big. It's perfect." His heart stalled the moment the words left his mouth.

"Perfect? Get real. I swear, Simon, if you paint a pic-ture of me from the rear I will never forgive you."

"I'm sure it's just your baggy pants," he muttered, put-ting his pencils away.

"You think my pants are baggy?"

He ground his teeth together, his mood suddenly sink-ing. There was no way to make her happy. He'd watched his father have the same ridiculous conversations with Mother. And over the years, he'd had his own impossi-ble conversations with the women in his life. They never liked the way he told the truth.

He turned the conversation. "I'm getting hungry. You said something about the Pig Place and a beer?" He had become a master at the pivot.

"You're changing the subject, aren't you?"

"Yup," he said, as he started putting his sketchbook and pencils into his field backpack.

"Okay, you're right. My pants are kind of baggy,"

she said in a little voice. "But that makes them really comfortable."

"It's okay, Molly. I didn't mean to—"

"But in any case, I don't want anyone recording me or my butt for posterity, or posterior as the case might be. It kind of creeps me out."

Her shoulders slumped, and she gave him a woeful look that he might have mistaken for a female pout. But on Molly, that sad-adorable look touched something deep inside him. "Why does it creep you out?"

"Because I'm not pretty. I don't have a great body. And I'm not particularly photogenic. Or in this case, sketch-o-genic. The idea of people looking at some image of me and making fun is just creepy."

This admission stunned him. "But you're beautiful. One day I'd love to paint you without—" He stopped speaking. This was the kind of talk Coach would frown upon. He'd been thinking with his heart again.

She gave him her squinty-eyed look. "You'd like to paint me without...what?" She stared at him for a long moment as the truth settled in. "Without my clothes? Oh, my God. You want to paint me naked?" She got up and stalked away toward her fishing gear. She was visibly upset.

And he wasn't exactly sure what to do about it. If he told her he was only joking, it would underscore her own self-doubts. If he told her the truth, he'd be breaking his word to Coach. But someone needed to tell Molly that she was stunning.

So he prayed that Coach would forgive him for telling Molly the God's honest truth. "You'd be lovely. Backside and all," he said.

"Did you paint that other chick, Jill or whatever her name is?"

Her question zinged through him. "No. I never wanted to paint her."

"So that's the reason you painted her out of the photograph?"

"Molly, we're not talking about Gillian right now."

"Why not? You keep looking at her photo. You say you're not heartbroken but you really are, aren't you?"

"Christ," he swore. "Will you please stop it? I'm not heartbroken. I'm trying to recapture the spark of something I felt the day I took that photo."

"Something you felt for her?"

"I don't know..." He hesitated for a moment. "No, not for Gillian. It's something else entirely. When you stand on the rim of the Grand Canyon, something moves inside you. Like awe. Like lightning. I took dozens and dozens of photos that day. I look at them now to try to capture that feeling I had. If I can find that feeling, I'm sure I can finish the Harrison commission. *But* I can't find it in the photos. It's disappeared. And that has me running scared. I've been worried that I might never find that spark again. The thing is, though, I felt that spark right here. Just now."

"You're teasing me, and that isn't nice. Let's go get a beer and pretend we never had this conversation."

No, he wasn't going to do that. Molly needed to know the truth, no matter what limits her daddy had set.

"I'm not going to pretend anything," he said. "I stopped pretending eighteen years ago, when I told my parents that I didn't want to be a doctor. I say what I mean, and I mean what I say. So if I tell you that I think you're beautiful, I'm not teasing you or handing you some line.

I'm telling you the truth as I see it. And that spark I felt, just now, happened as I watched you fishing. So it's about you as much as it's about this place."

She kept right on packing her things. His words bounced off that armor she'd pulled around herself. He knew that armor well. He had his own shell.

But damn it, he wanted to crack her open. He wanted to see what was really inside. And she needed to respect the fact that he was telling her the truth. He didn't give one damn what Coach might say about it.

And then it hit him—one of those deep memories he'd been reluctant to face—he and Luke Raintree shucking their clothes and diving into the Edisto River. They were thirteen, maybe. And it was before Luke had lost his life. Before Simon had donned his armor.

He could almost feel Luke's ghost behind him, reminding him of how easy it had once been as a boy to just be himself. How happy he'd once been in this place, before life had taken its toll. Before he'd learned to hide himself from the hurt.

Maybe there was a lesson here for Molly. Maybe if he forced her out of that defensive shell she'd built around herself, she'd learn that she was beautiful, and utterly unique.

He started unbuttoning his shirt, and by the time Molly turned, he'd almost divested himself of his jeans. The look on her face was priceless. For a moment, she must have thought he was some old pervert. But he didn't let her startled expression stop him.

"Last one in the river is a rotten egg," he shouted as he finally lost his boxers. And then he took a flying leap into the freezing-cold water of the Edisto River.

• • •

Jeez Louise! Simon was an amazingly good-looking man with his clothes on. Without them, he was…Well, she didn't have any words, because all the words left her mind as she watched him jump into the water.

He wasn't built like a muscle-bound linebacker. Oh, no, he had a body like a kicker, with broad shoulders, a flat belly, and strong legs. The years had been kind to him. Or maybe he worked out on a regular basis.

She'd been skinny dipping a time or two. She knew how this worked. Only a wus would stand up here fully clothed. But she didn't want to bare it all in front of Simon. For some reason, allowing him to see her naked was scary as hell.

He surfaced and shook his head to clear his eyes of water. He grinned up at her as he treaded water. His teeth were beautifully white, sort of like the wolf at the little piggie's front door.

"Are you scared?" he asked.

Damn him. He was really perceptive for a guy. "Taking off your clothes was completely unfair."

"Was it? I was mighty hot. And the water is cold."

"Mighty? Man, you're getting your southern back, aren't you?"

"My southern?"

"Yeah. And I hate to tell you but it's attractive on you."

"Really?" He laughed. It was the first time she'd ever heard him laugh. He started swimming upstream. He was a strong swimmer. He made excellent progress against the current.

She stood there envying him. Guys never had any problems dropping their drawers. Her brothers were completely shameless in that department.

"Hey," she yelled.

He stopped swimming and let the current carry him back to the pier where she was standing. "What?"

"I need to make something clear, okay?" she said.

"Okay."

"I don't do relationships."

"Oh. Well, neither do I."

"What about Gillian?"

"Molly, I don't want to talk about Gillian."

"But I do."

"All right, Gillian was a big mistake. She broke the rules."

Molly didn't know whether she liked this response. She tended to hate rules on general principle. Especially the rules that said a woman's place was in a yarn shop and not a garage. "What rules? And who made them?" she asked.

"My rules."

"Oh. And what are your rules?"

"I don't do relationships, commitment, marriage, children. Gillian knew that going in. And then she changed her mind. I didn't."

"Oh." Molly found Simon's attitude and honesty remarkably refreshing. "I think I like your rules."

"You do? That would make you the first female I ever met who had that reaction. But it's neither here nor there, because I'm way too old for you. You do know that, don't you?"

She thought about that for a while. "No, I don't know that. I think you're hung up on age. What difference does it make? Especially if you don't do long-term relationships."

His reaction was priceless. She had definitely scored a point with that one. Although she wasn't sure she wanted to score any points on him. This wasn't a football game. In truth, she was hopelessly attracted to him, which was why she hadn't yet shucked her clothes.

He recovered his cool and gave her another one of those sexy smiles. "So are you going to get naked or stand there on the sidelines afraid to jump in? The only issue at hand is skinny-dipping. Not Gillian or my age. And also I really want to see what kind of underwear you have on. I have a theory that you're wearing La Perla."

Heat crawled up Molly's face. She was so busted. She might as well confess. "Okay. The underwear was mine. Why are we doing this exactly?"

"Because you wanted to play hooky. And, I'm sorry, whenever I came down here as a boy it usually ended up with everyone losing their clothes and jumping in."

"So you're just trying to get me naked."

"You're giving this entirely too much thought. You're a chicken. It's clear."

Oh, boy, that was a dare, pure and simple.

"You're scared to bare it all, aren't you?" he asked, punctuating the point.

She shook her head. "It's just complicated."

"How?"

"I'm Coach's daughter."

"Ah. Yes you are. So I'm going to have to be very careful with you. I admire your father. But I still want to see you naked." His words were seductive. Most guys just ran for the hills the minute Coach's name came up.

"Honestly," she said, "he has a rule that I'm not allowed to date any football players. I hesitate to think what Coach might do if he found out I got naked with one, even if it was just to go skinny-dipping."

He snorted another laugh. "And do you always do what Coach tells you to do?"

"Are you nuts? You *have* seen him when he's angry. Have you ever defied him? Ever?"

He gave her the strangest look. "Yes, I have. And there's something else I remember about your father. He always used to say that the best way to live your life was to dive right into it without fear."

Damn. Simon had it all figured out, didn't he? And that line about diving in just happened to be something that Momma said all the time. Coach had merely borrowed it. Momma had certainly lived by that credo. She'd gotten tired of waiting on Coach, and she'd just gone off and dived in and left everyone else on the shore.

Well, if Momma could do it, then Molly could do it, too. Because, right now, Simon Wolfe looked like an adventure worth having. She'd be a fool to stand here like a 'fraidy cat.

So she pulled off her T-shirt. Simon's dark eyes seemed to light up the moment he caught sight of her lacy La Perla bra. "Nice," he said drawing out the syllable until it sounded like the hiss of a snake.

Her nipples tightened. "If you tell anyone about my underwear, I swear I'll murder you."

"Your secret is safe with me."

She undid her pants. This time he didn't say a word. But there was a hungry look in his eyes that made her skin go warm.

He watched her strip in silence—a silence that got deeper and tenser with each item of clothing she lost. A silence that was so wide and so deep and so hot that Molly thought she might just combust before she got all the way naked.

Thank God the Edisto River was freezing cold.

Molly broke the surface, her curls slicked back, making the angles of her face sharper. The brown river water turned her eye color to raw umber, and drops clung to her eyelashes. Her skin was like alabaster, with a dusting of delicious freckles across her nose and shoulders. Simon wanted to swim over there and kiss her.

But he couldn't do that. Skinny-dipping was as far as this was going. So he kept his distance, treading water just enough to keep himself stationary against the pull of the current.

"Oh, my God, you didn't tell me the water was freezing," she said with a big eye roll. She was so young.

His cheeks hurt from the big smile on his face. "You're a local girl. You know how cold the Edisto is."

"Yeah, I guess. But it's been a while since I went swimming in it."

"Me too."

They bobbed there, each of them fighting the current.

"Too bad we're not swimming at the country club. We could drift down to the float," he said.

"So did you ever make out with anyone on the float?" she asked.

"Naked?"

She giggled. Her lips were turning blue. The water was really cold. "It would be hard to swim naked at the country club, especially in the light of day."

"I kissed Annie Roberts when we were both fourteen

and wearing bathing suits at the time," he said. "It was during the Watermelon Festival. She didn't like my braces. And besides, even then she was more interested in Nick Clausen."

"She's Annie Jasper now. And Nick died."

"I heard about Nick." A little fissure opened in his heart. As much as he tried to square this place with where he'd grown up, the images didn't fit or overlap.

He pushed those thoughts away. "And you? Did you make out on the float?"

She shook her head and then dived under the water. She surfaced a few yards upstream and started swimming. He followed her. They swam for a few minutes, until Simon's muscles started to burn.

"So what now?" she asked as she let the current pull her back down toward the public pier.

"Now we go put on our clothes and get some dinner at the Pig Place." As much as he wanted to suggest something else, he still planned to keep his promise to her father. He was glad he'd gotten her to drop her defenses, get naked, and go swimming. But he had no intention of "messing" with her as Coach had so inelegantly put it.

"You get out first," she said.

He chuckled. "No, I don't think so."

She turned and splashed water in his face.

He retaliated.

The splash fight soon escalated into a full-out dunking war in which he discovered that Molly was one part mermaid. She eluded him, swimming upstream, mostly submerged, her long hair trailing out behind her as she swam. She was sneaky and fast and could stay under for a remarkably long time.

But he had more stamina than she did. And fighting the current required lots of that. He caught her at last, but the moment his fingers encircled her arm, his desire to dunk her evaporated, replaced by a yearning that was almost adolescent in its intensity.

She stopped fighting him and snaked her hands around his neck. The slide of her skin warmed him. Her lips were cold, her mouth was hot. And even in the freezing water, desire pumped through him the minute he got his first taste of Molly Canaday. She kissed him back with complete abandon, as if the Edisto had washed away the mask she wore most of the time, as it surely had washed away the promise he'd made to her father.

Heaven only knew how far he might have gone if Zeph Gibbs hadn't rescued him from his own stupidity.

Zeph stood on the beaten earth by the public boat launch watching the young'uns in the water. Painful memories whirled and tumbled through him. He wanted to hide deep in the woods where the ghost couldn't find him and punish him for remembering.

The ghost was edgy, and now Zeph knew why. The ghost was jealous of the living. And he would be particularly jealous of Simon. Simon could still go swimming. Simon got to kiss a girl.

"Is that you, Simon?" Zeph called. He knew it was Simon out there with Coach's daughter. He knew he shouldn't be here invading their privacy.

But he had to stop what was happening, before the ghost did something bad. The ghost had learned how to haunt real good in the last few years, like a poltergeist from right out of one of those books Gabe Raintree wrote. And Zeph sure didn't want that ghost to get a notion to haunt Simon. That boy had been through enough. He didn't need the ghost making things even harder.

The young'uns broke apart. The ghost settled some.

"Zeph?" Simon's voice.

"It's me. It's your old Zeph. I hate to interrupt but can I have a word with you?"

Simon said something to the girl and took a couple of strong strokes toward the shore. He emerged, the water streaming down his sides. He was all growed up now. Not even really a young'un anymore. Which made Zeph feel ancient.

Simon reached for his jeans and tugged them up. They didn't slide so good over his wet skin, and he had to hop on one foot and then the other. The memories assailed Zeph.

Simon finally took a few steps forward. "What is it?" he asked.

Zeph looked toward the girl who was still treading water. "You and me should walk a little ways, so Coach's daughter can get her clothes on."

Simon looked toward the water and gave a little shout. "I need to talk with Zeph, Molly. I'll be right back."

Coach's daughter didn't say nothing back. Zeph and Simon took a little stroll down the path. The ghost was still agitated. "Uh, Simon, I know it's none of my business, but do you know what you're doing?"

Simon snorted a laugh. "No, not exactly."

"I figured. Well, take it from me, you don't want to be messing with Coach's daughter. That's just dumb. You're too old for her. And I hear you're just staying for a little while, and that girl has Last Chance stamped all over her, if you know what I mean."

"I guess I do," Simon said, and Zeph believed him. There was a yearning in his voice for things he could never have. Zeph knew about that feeling. He knew it very well.

"You need to take that girl home."

"I guess." Simon let go of a long breath. "I forgot how beautiful it was out here."

Zeph didn't like hearing that. He didn't want Simon out here. It would upset the ghost. But if he told Simon the truth, they'd call him crazy. And then some do-gooder would try to get him locked up in some VA hospital.

So he had to lie.

"This place isn't like it was when you were a boy," Zeph finally said. "The Jonquil House is falling down; people don't come here that often. And there are snakes in the river. You want to be careful."

"I'm not afraid of snakes. As I recall, Gabe was the one who was afraid of snakes."

"That's right. But a man is just plumb stupid not to be afraid of some things, Simon. So I'd suggest that you keep your distance from that girl. And you keep your distance from this place. You hear me?"

A frown folded down across Simon's brow. "You told me that before. What's wrong?"

"Not a thing. Just you and the girl shouldn't ought to be skinny-dipping like that in broad daylight. It's just not right, and it's not safe, and I doubt her daddy would be happy about it."

Simon's shoulders stiffened. "All right. I'll keep that in mind." He turned and walked away.

And that almost broke Zeph's heart in two. But at least the ghost was satisfied.

Molly's hair dripped down the back of her neck, soaking her T-shirt. Without a towel, any hope of staying dry was impossible. She probably should have thought about this before shucking her clothes.

As it was, she was trying to figure out her tumbling emotions right at the moment. If Zeph hadn't shown up, Simon's incredible kiss would have probably led her right to the Peach Blossom Motor Court or someplace equally skanky. That might have been fun. But of course, it would have gotten her into hot water with her father.

She was lacing up her sneakers when Simon returned.

Her heart thumped in her chest, and little explosions of heat blazed through her to see him walking on bare feet with his chest exposed. His long, elegant toes matched his beautiful hands. But his naked chest—well, there were no words that were up to the task of describing it, or the way just looking at him made her feel all hollow and melty inside.

She wished he hadn't put on his pants.

"So," Simon said, his voice low and gruff. He drew the one-syllable word out. It might have been a sigh, or a question, or a punctuation point. It was hard to tell.

He stood on the other side of the clearing by their lawn chairs. She wanted him to come closer and kiss her again, but the moment had come and gone. She felt oddly bashful, even though she was completely covered up now.

She shouldn't mess with him. The logistics were bound to get very complicated. She was living at home now. When she'd been in college, sleeping with guys had been pretty easy to manage. But carrying on with someone you weren't ever going to go steady with, much less marry, was difficult in Last Chance.

Besides, she was Coach's daughter. And he had rules. They were stupid rules, but he took them seriously, and besides, he was pretty depressed right at the moment. He'd been sitting at home with the television on, not moving and not speaking to anyone. Momma's leaving had hit him pretty hard.

It was a shame. Because Simon had a killer body, and he seemed to be laboring under the illusion that she was attractive. It was a deadly combination.

"We better go," she said.

"I guess going to the Pig Place is out, huh?"

She pulled her hair to one side and tried to wring a little more water out of it. "Maybe not such a good idea. I'm all wet, and we'd have a hard time explaining that. I swear, one of these days I'm going to whack all this hair off. It's just a nuisance."

"Don't." It was a fierce whisper, if ever she heard one.

"It's okay. I'm always threatening to cut my hair, and I never have the courage to go through with it. I'm not sure why." She picked up her tackle box and gear while he put on his shirt and folded the chairs.

It was late in the day, but not quite dusk. Simon looked like a veritable god moving around in that golden afternoon light. Molly decided that she could spend the rest of her days watching Simon move. He was still an athlete.

They headed down the narrow path that led to the parking area at the end of Bluff Road. "So," she said, just to make conversation in the silence that had sprung up, "are you and Zeph special friends or something?"

"We were, I guess, back when I was a boy and Luke Raintree was still alive."

She looked over her shoulder. "You knew Luke?"

"I was there the day he died."

"Oh, my God." She stopped and turned. "When I was

in high school, we used to come down here sometimes and hang out at the Jonquil House. It's all abandoned now and really creepy at night. Perfect for scaring the bejesus out of little kids. Everyone used to say that Luke Raintree haunted the place."

Something flickered in Simon's brown eyes and then disappeared behind his perfect, mild-mannered mask. He started walking again, but his whole body seemed to have gone stiff. Boy, she must have hit a nerve. Not to mention the fact that it was weird to be with someone who had actually known Luke Raintree. He'd died a long time ago.

She followed after him. "Uh, I'm sorry, I guess. You knew him well?"

"Luke Raintree was my best friend until the day his brother shot him dead."

Simon found it a little strange to be sitting in the passenger's seat. But Molly clearly loved driving her vintage Charger, and there was something about the way she casually held the steering wheel with one hand. It was sexy as hell.

Which was a thought he needed to ice right now.

They said almost nothing as she drove him back to his mother's house in town. Just before he got out of the car, he turned toward her and said, "I didn't mean for that kiss to happen. You know it would be crazy, and probably dangerous, for the two of us to go down that road, don't you?"

"Dangerous?"

"Yeah. I have no desire to get on Coach's bad side."

"What does Coach have to do with it?"

"He came by to see me the other day, specifically to

tell me to stay clear of you. He thinks you've got a crush on me."

There was still enough light for him to see the blush that rose to her cheeks. "That's silly," she said emphatically.

"Look, kiddo, you don't want to have a crush on me. I'm hard on women. And I'm too old for you. And besides, I'd rather be your friend."

She looked up. Something strange burned in those changeable eyes of hers. "That's good. Friends are good."

"So we understand each other?"

"Absolutely." She looked away, and Simon had the terrible feeling that she was going to leave this encounter thinking she was unattractive or undesirable.

But he'd given Coach his word. And when Coach and Zeph were in agreement, the moral path was clear. "I'll see you tomorrow," he said and got out of the car.

He didn't turn to look over his shoulder as she peeled out of the driveway with a little bit of wheel spin and flying gravel. Molly had a temper, and he'd just ignited it.

Thank God Zeph had come along when he had. It wouldn't be the first time Zeph had saved him.

It was just a shame that Zeph hadn't been there to save Luke.

And that errant thought stopped him in his tracks. He stood there on the porch steps like a man who'd been struck by lightning. Memories he'd pushed under for so long suddenly swirled up, like mud from the river bottom.

There had been another day, when he was thirteen, when Zeph had pulled him out of the abyss and sent him home. Simon had stood right here on the porch steps, his world shattered, his heart breaking. He'd needed someone that day.

And there wasn't anyone who cared.

The sounds of his mother and father arguing reached him even through the front door. He'd stood there, tears running down his face, knowing that nothing good ever came from an argument. He'd bypassed the door and hid out in the shed, crying his eyes out until there wasn't anything left to cry.

By nightfall, all of Last Chance had heard the news that Governor Raintree's grandson had been tragically killed in a hunting accident. But by then, the hot argument between Simon's parents had run its course. And his parents had entered the chill phase. Each of them had gone off to their individual places upstairs. They'd put on their separate television sets, at the highest volume possible, so they didn't have to hear each other moving around. They had staked out their territories. And the war was on.

Mother and Daddy's really big fights—the ones that had turned into pitched battles—may have started as screaming matches but they always ended in silence, punctuated every once in a while with hurtful verbal darts.

The day Luke died, they'd been screaming. The day Luke was buried, they weren't speaking. And both of them were so focused on their battle that neither of them had the time or inclination to think about Simon or the pain he felt.

The heavy sigh caught him almost unawares, along with the telltale tension in his neck and shoulders. The memories of that horrible day seemed to haunt this place. Had haunted it for years. He hated coming in the front door.

This time, the house was quiet. Daddy's Taurus was in the driveway so he knew Mother had gotten back from her meeting. As usual, Angel had everything under control. Simon entered the big, formal foyer. It was dark in here, but a light gleamed from the kitchen. And the sound of laughter was coming from that general direction.

Simon stood riveted to the wide, butternut plank flooring for the longest of moments, listening to his mother laughing. Out loud. With abandon.

He had to investigate. Mother had never been a big fan of people who laughed out loud, not even in private. Mother always kept her emotions under wrap.

The kitchen in the house bore little resemblance to the one Simon remembered. Mother had spared no expense redoing it. The place gleamed with stainless-steel appliances, granite countertops, slate flooring, and white farmhouse cabinets. Arlo Boyd had practically salivated over the kitchen. He'd said it made up for the pitiful laundry room, with its ancient washer and broken dryer. He said the house would bring good money when Simon was finally allowed to list the place for sale.

Right now, Mother was sitting on a stool at the center island. She was sipping what appeared to be a strawberry milk shake through a straw. And in between sips, she was giggling—giggling!—at Angel, who was juggling three bananas.

Simon had seen Angel's juggling prowess before. It was impressive. His assistant had a dream of running away one day and joining Cirque du Soleil. Angel said the circus costumes were to die for.

Mother startled the minute Simon walked into the room. Angel stopped juggling.

"You're early," Angel said.

"Who are you?" Mother said.

And something snapped. "Mother, you know good and well who I am. It's Simon, your son. Angel, here, is my assistant."

"You are not my son."

"I most certainly am. I'm sorry you don't remember me. Probably because you never had much time for me after I reached the age of eight or so, unless it was to tell me what was expected of me. And when I failed to do the expected, you simply forgot I existed." The last words came out hoarse and angry.

He took a giant breath, turned, and walked out of the kitchen. The moment had come and gone. And he'd been the one to destroy it. This is what came from getting angry. But who the hell was he angry with? Mother? Luke? Coach?

Or was it only himself?

Molly slipped into the side door, intent on reaching her bedroom before running into Coach. Because if she ran into him she might just give him a piece of her mind. He seemed to think she was still a little girl or something. What gave him the right to warn Simon off? If she wanted to have a fling with a handsome, older, experienced man, it was her own damn business, not Coach's.

Of course, she'd be an idiot to have a fling with Simon, but lust was pretty toxic to brain cells. And there wasn't any doubt that she had developed a first-class case of lust. And that meant it couldn't possibly be anything so childish as a crush. Like that time in high school when she'd become infatuated with her English teacher.

Crushes were not usually mutual. But Simon had enjoyed that kiss as much as she had. Not to mention the way he'd sweet-talked her out of her panties.

And that just wasn't fair—not if he had already been warned off by Coach. Heck, he was the one who started it by getting naked. Where did he think it would go?

Damn. It was really a toss-up as to whom she was most annoyed with. Either way she just needed some alone time in her bedroom. Maybe she could sit quietly, like the book said, and empty her mind, while simultaneously achieving a transcendent moment of mindfulness. Or maybe she could find something unbreakable to throw.

Her plans unraveled the moment she walked through the door. Coach was sitting at the kitchen table all alone. The kitchen was semi-dark, illuminated only by the small utility light above the stove. He had a shot glass in front of him, and he was drinking from a bottle of Woodford Reserve bourbon.

Molly's anger-filled balloon deflated.

Coach drank an occasional beer or glass of wine, but Molly had never seen her father with a shot glass in his hand. This was shaping up like something from out of one of those sad country songs, about cheating women and drinking men.

This was not supposed to be happening in her family. Her parents loved one another. They were good, church-going people. And Coach was a role model for just about every male in Allenberg County, even Simon who had just delivered a sermon to her on the wages of sinning with an older man. Coach preached personal responsibility and abstinence. And his players toed that line, to a man.

He turned and looked up at her. His eyes were puffy

and bloodshot, like maybe he'd been crying, which was a really disturbing turn of events.

"Why's your hair wet?" he asked.

Well, of course he noticed. Coach might be buzzed or drunk, but Molly's wet hair was waist length and had pretty much soaked her T-shirt.

"I went swimming," she said, while simultaneously trying to decide just how honest she wanted to be. She had a bone to pick with him. But picking it while he was consuming bourbon was maybe not a smart idea. Not that Coach was likely to become violent or anything. It was just that he seemed so lost without Momma.

"Who were you swimming with?" he asked. Coach was a mind reader. Everyone said so.

She decided not to lie. Lying would just make a bad situation that much worse. So she stared him right in his bloodshot baby blues and said, "I was swimming off the public pier with Simon Wolfe."

He looked up. "You went swimming with that old queer?"

Rage tickled her backbone, and she could practically feel it snap upright. Any sympathy she'd been feeling for him evaporated. "Coach, you should know better than to use a word like that. It's demeaning. Don't they teach you sensitivity or something down at the high school? And besides, Simon is not gay."

"Ha! Shows how much you know. You're infatuated with a queer, who isn't really interested in you. You're making a big mistake. Les is the guy for you."

Well, this was a fine kettle of stinky fish, wasn't it? It was irritating as hell that everyone thought Simon and Angel were together. Not that Molly had any problems with guys being with guys. But Simon was clearly not gay. And more important, Coach was acting like a bigoted idiot and a bully.

"Daddy, just use the word 'gay' or 'homosexual,' okay?"

"Okay, why the hell were you swimming with a homosexual?"

"Because he dared me to take my clothes off." She put her fists on her hips. If Coach wanted to have this fight, well then, bring it on.

"He what?" Coach looked up from his bourbon.

"We went skinny-dipping in the river. And Simon is not gay. And I resent the fact that you warned him off. If you really thought he was gay, why'd you do that?"

"Did you and he . . ."

"That is none of your business."

He hit the table with the flat of his hand. "It damn well is my business if you're living in this town and in my house. I'm not going to have a daughter of mine sleeping around or getting naked in public. Especially if she's doing it with someone who is old enough to be her father."

"Simon isn't old." The words escaped Molly's mouth before she really thought about them. But once said, their truth was self-evident. She didn't think about Simon's age. She'd completely forgotten about it. He was a guy she wanted to get to know better. He was interesting, but more important, he was kind. She'd seen that innate kindness in everything he did, from playing with Junior Griffin, to remembering sweets for the Purly Girls, to folding her laundry, to helping her liberate the Shelby.

He'd gone out of his way to make her feel powerfully feminine today. And the feeling was exciting and intoxicating. She didn't see him as an old man, even if he was thirteen years older. Even if he was more than forty and she was twenty-eight.

"I should tan your hide, girl, for behaving like that. And I sure as hell need to have a man-to-man with Simon."

Like Coach had ever spanked her in his life. She wasn't really worried. But she knew for certain that Coach was going to give Simon a piece of his mind. And Simon, being an ex-Rebel and all, would listen to him. Rebels, ex- or otherwise, always listened to Coach. Honestly, being Coach's daughter was murder on her social life.

Molly folded her arms across her chest. She was tired of this crap. And besides, Coach was the one sitting there getting drunk. All she'd done was go skinny-dipping and kiss a guy in the middle of the freezing Edisto River. It wasn't like she'd gone off to the Peach Blossom Motor Court with Simon, as much as she might have liked to. Nothing had happened today. And Simon had made it clear that nothing was ever going to happen. So it was done, over, finished. And Coach was going to get his way. Again.

And she'd go along with the rules because she was a good girl and always had been.

And then it occurred to her that she wasn't the only person who had misbehaved in this room.

"Daddy," she said, knowing that calling him that would get his attention, "why are you sitting here in the dark drinking liquor?"

Muscles bunched along his jaw but he said nothing. Coach was not going to give her any kind of explanation. She might as well give up.

"Have you had dinner?" she asked, taking pity on him.

"No." There was a peeved note in his denial. Molly refused to feel guilty. But she decided to show him mercy.

"I'll see what we have in the fridge." She turned away from him and hit the lights. Coach flinched in the sudden brightness.

"So, how did the second day of football camp go?" she asked as she opened the fridge. The cupboard was kind of bare. But there was a carton of eggs. Molly had very few skills in the kitchen, but she could scramble eggs.

"I stayed home today. Dash Randall covered for me," Coach said.

She turned, egg carton in hand. "You missed football camp?"

"I wasn't feeling too good. I had a headache."

"Daddy, did you drink last night, too?" Molly had been very late getting home. She'd been putting in some serious hours on the Shelby to make up for lost time.

Coach made no reply to her question.

"You *did* get drunk last night, didn't you?"

Coach looked up at her with bleary eyes and echoed Molly's own words of a few moments before. "It's none of your damn business."

She put the eggs down on the counter with a little more force than was entirely necessary.

"Yes, it is my business." She put her fists on her hips.

"How you figure that?"

She was momentarily stumped by this question. Because, really, if Daddy and Momma wanted to ruin their lives, it was their business. Just like it was her business if she snuck off to the Peach Blossom Motor Court with Simon for an afternoon of sin.

She and Momma and Daddy were all fully grown adults.

But it was still her business if Coach went on a bender. Because she loved Coach. And Momma, too. Even when they misbehaved.

"It's my business because we're family," she said at last.

"Some family," Coach muttered. He snatched the glass off the table and downed a big swallow of bourbon.

She held her tongue and concentrated on scrambling up some eggs and cheese for the two of them. She snagged a Dr Pepper from the refrigerator and joined Coach at the kitchen table. "Here, you need to eat something."

He looked down at her offering, which was admittedly a little browner than it should have been. He gave an indifferent sniff.

She dived into her own eggs. They tasted okay, even if they didn't look all that appealing.

"Why don't you know how to cook?" he asked. His words were just a little slurred.

"I'm not interested in cooking."

"But why?"

"I don't know. I'm just not interested."

"You should be interested."

"Well, I'm not."

"You know this whole thing is your fault."

Molly continued to chew her rubbery eggs. For once, she decided not to rise to his bait or mouth off. She was going to be as calm and rational as she could be. She was going to be mindful of what came out of her mouth.

She looked up from her food. Coach was staring down at his bourbon. "You know, Daddy, you're kind of right.

Momma wants me to be different. She wants me to learn how to cook and to help her mind the store. And I guess I've let her down in that respect. But it isn't all my fault that she's gone. Her note made it clear that she was tired of waiting on you, too. She wanted to go on a vacation with you, but you went fishing."

"I've been a good and true husband to her. I love her. How could she walk out?"

"Do you love her, or do you just like clean laundry?"

"What's that supposed to mean?"

"You gave her a washer and dryer on your wedding anniversary. That's not a very romantic gift, you know?"

"But—"

She held up her hand. "Daddy, listen to me. Since she's been gone I've come to realize just how much Momma does around the house. She washes the clothes, gets food on the table, and she's also the sole proprietor of a successful business. She's an amazing woman. And none of us really appreciates her." Molly let go of a big breath. "So if she took off to tour the world or whatever, it's because none of us gave her a reason to stay."

Her father pinched the space between his eyes and took a deep breath through his nose. And then he burst into sobs. And for the first time in her life, Molly comforted Coach instead of the other way around.

# CHAPTER
## 16

It was Tuesday evening. The Purly Girls had come and gone, and Ricki was feeling happier than she had in a long, long time. Molly had trusted her enough to let her handle the meeting alone.

Almost. Angel had been there to help the girls with the actual knitting part of the meeting. But Ricki had been in charge otherwise and that made her feel a million times better about herself. Being a clerk at the Knit & Stitch was way better than waiting on tables. And there were fringe benefits—she was learning how to knit. And it was fun.

She tidied the shop then snapped a lead onto Muffin's collar, locked up, and headed for her apartment behind Dot's Spot.

She wasn't prepared when Muffin suddenly crouched down and started growling and shivering simultaneously. Ricki looked up, and there was Les Hayes strolling down the sidewalk on the other side of Palmetto Avenue. Muffin was watching him like he was the devil incarnate.

Ricki watched him like he was a really handsome, unattached, sexy-as-sin male human being.

She and her dog were clearly not on the same page about Leslie Hayes.

She scooped the dog up into her arms, gave a quick look both ways down Palmetto, and jaywalked.

"Hey, Les, wait up."

The big man turned, hesitated, and then gave her a mouthwatering smile. By the sudden spark in his baby blues, he was happy to see her. "Oh, hey, Ricki. I see that Molly's taken you back full-time. I'm glad about that."

"Yeah, I guess she decided to work on the Shelby while she has the space at the Coca-Cola building."

"I'm glad you didn't end up unemployed. I was only jobless for a couple of days, and it really sucked."

Muffin yipped and then growled. Les gazed down at the dog. "She's kind of high-strung, isn't she? I had a dog once. His name was Rex. But he was a big ol' coon dog. He didn't shiver like that."

"You know, it's strange. She's usually so sweet."

"Not around me, she isn't."

Ricki thought about that for a moment. Les was right. Muffin was always growling at Les. It was like a sign. A very bad sign. "Maybe you remind her of whoever it was that abandoned her."

"She was abandoned?"

"Yeah, I found her sleeping in the planter by my apartment. Who would throw away such a sweet dog?"

Les shrugged. "So, uh, are you headed for Dot's?"

Ricki hadn't actually been headed that way. The Wild Horses usually didn't play at The Spot on Tuesdays, and she only went down there when they played. It was really sad the way she still carried a torch for Clay. She needed to get over that. He was married and had a baby now.

"Is that where you're going?" she asked.

He nodded. "I kind of don't know what to do with myself since Molly and I had our falling-out. Why don't you come with me? I could buy you a beer."

"How about a glass of wine?"

"Whatever you like."

She ought to keep her distance. Les belonged to Molly. And besides, Muffin didn't like him for some reason.

But Ricki liked him a lot. A whole lot, in fact.

"Okay. I just have to take Muffin home," she said. A little wave of guilt passed through her. Muffin would be lonely. And Muffin seemed to think that Les was someone Ricki should stay away from.

But guys as handsome as Les didn't ask her out for a beer every day of the week. In fact, it had been years since anyone, handsome or otherwise, had actually offered to buy her a drink.

And she was getting too old to turn down offers like that.

Jane brought baby Peter to the book club meeting on Wednesday, and he immediately stole the show. For once, Molly wasn't bombarded with knitting questions during the refreshment phase of the meeting, which featured a couple of Jenny Carpenter's pies this week. Instead, the book club members passed the baby around like frat boys passing a bottle. And really the women got just as happy as frat boys.

The baby had some kind of magic impact on all of them. They made cooing sounds. They smiled and giggled.

And it all made Molly incredibly nervous.

That baby was tiny. And she was sure someone was going to drop him on his head or something. She wanted them to put him down in a safe place.

And then Cathy, who was the designated holder of the moment, turned to Molly and said, "Here, you take him. You practically delivered him."

"Uh, well…" Words failed her. She wanted to point out that she'd watched while Simon had taken charge and that watching Simon deliver the baby had been sort of life-changing. At least her feelings about Simon had altered in that moment. Her feelings about babies, not so much.

But she didn't say any of this because, the next thing she knew, Cathy was putting the baby in her arms.

The moment that soft, warm weight hit her, something kind of hitched inside of her. It was scary as hell, but kind of wonderful, too. Even so, she stood there superglued to the linoleum tile, afraid to move. Peter looked up at her, slightly cross-eyed, and the corners of his little, toothless mouth curled up.

"Look, he's smiling," Cathy said.

"It's just gas, for goodness' sake," Lola May said.

Jane peered down at the child. "He *is* smiling," she affirmed. "He likes you, Molly."

Molly wanted to admit that she kind of liked the baby, but she had an image to maintain.

And then Pete stretched his little baby body, gave a sigh, closed his eyes, and went blissfully to sleep.

"Wow, Molly, you might be a baby whisperer in addition to having skills with yarn," Jane said. "I've never seen him just lay back and go to sleep like that. He's kind of a wakeful little critter."

Molly wanted to smile, but she was still sort of afraid to move.

"Do you mind holding him for a while?" Jane asked. "I mean the meeting is about to start, and if I take him back, he'll wake up."

"I'm a firm believer in letting sleeping babies lie," Nita said. "So why don't we get started, since little Pete is being such an angel for Molly?"

Molly carefully took a seat and adjusted the baby's weight. It was kind of hard to focus on Nita with the child in her arms. She just wanted to look down at his sleeping face. He was a most miraculous baby. Probably because he was the only baby Molly had ever held in her life.

Nita kicked things off. "I thought I'd get tonight's meeting started by asking y'all how you felt at the end of *Little Women* when Jo sets aside her literary career to marry Professor Bhaer and help her husband run a school?"

"If you want the truth," Cathy said, "I think she was an idiot to turn up her nose at Laurie. Why would any woman in her right mind do that?"

"Do you think she would have maintained her literary career if she married Laurie?" Savannah asked.

"I don't know, and I don't care," Cathy said. "I just felt let down at the end when she marries that big, German oaf. She could have had everything, including a rich husband."

"Who she didn't love," Hettie said. "I think the worst thing in the world is to be married to someone you don't love. I really admired Jo for telling Laurie no. That took real courage for a woman in the eighteen hundreds. And I applaud Jo's parents for not forcing her into a marriage with Laurie. Many parents would have, you know, given how rich he was."

This speech from Hettie Marshall Ellis made everyone a little uncomfortable because Hettie's first husband had been a rich man her parents had picked out for her.

"That's true," Rocky said. "But would you have given up being the CEO of Country Pride Chicken in order to marry Bill?"

"He didn't ask me to."

"But what if he had?" Rocky persisted.

Hettie clasped her hands in front of her. "If the only way to have Bill was to give up the chicken plant, I think I would have done it. But that's beside the point. A man who truly loves would never ask that."

"Ha!" said Lola May. "Maybe not your Bill, but I gotta tell you, all three of my exes were resentful of my work outside the home. They weren't resentful of the money I made, but they thought I should work and cook and clean for them. Which is why they are all exes, and I'm never going to get married again."

"I think you just made my point, Lola May," Hettie said in a soft, lady-like voice.

Lola May sniffed.

"You've been mighty quiet," Nita said, turning her sharp brown eyes on Molly. "I would have expected you to have something to say about this book. In particular."

Molly had been paying more attention to Pete than the conversation, so she was caught a little off guard. Still, *Little Women* was the kind of book that kind of stuck in your head. The last few days her mind kept turning back to it.

Molly envied the love portrayed among the March

sisters. She had always secretly wanted sisters. Maybe if she'd had a girlie sister like Amy or Meg, she could have been more like Jo. And no one would have expected so much of her.

"Well," she finally said, "I sure don't blame Jo for telling Laurie to take a hike."

This elicited a number of chuckles around the room.

"What's so funny?" she asked.

"Oh, nothing," said Rocky. "It's just that everyone's been wondering whether you were influenced by the book when you turned down Les's proposal."

Molly gazed from face to face. Her so-called friends were all smirking, except for Savannah, who seemed very serious right at the moment. "No, I wasn't influenced by the book. I read the book *after* Les proposed."

"He's very disappointed," Cathy said.

Molly turned her gaze on Savannah. "I don't want to lay blame, but this is partially your fault. If your aunt hadn't meddled and told everyone I was going to marry someone I'd known forever, Les wouldn't have gotten the wild hair up his butt to actually propose. Honestly, his proposal came from way out of left field."

"Really?" Jenny asked, while Savannah didn't look surprised at all.

"Really. I haven't even kissed Les. And believe me, the idea of kissing him is mildly repulsive. So I don't know what he was smoking when he sprang his whole marriage thing on me. And now he's all ticked off because I won't marry him. And he's been a total jerk about the Shelby. He won't help me with the engine. To be honest, he owes me a lot. I mean, he took my job at Bill's. If you must know, I'm deeply disappointed in Les. He's been sort of mean to me the last few weeks." In marked contrast with Simon, who had been nothing but kind.

"Now, Mol, don't get down on men. They have their good points, too," Jane said, smiling down at little Pete, who was still sleeping away in Molly's arms.

"I have nothing against men. Hanging with the guys and watching football is great. I enjoy the company of guys. But not when they start acting like little girls whose feelings have been hurt. Honestly, Les is behaving like a total drama queen.

"And as for the protagonist in this book, I thought Jo was at her best when she vowed never to marry at all. The story would have been perfect if Jo stayed a spinster— maybe running the school on her own, without a man. But I guess that would probably have gotten the book banned in the eighteen hundreds."

"Don't you want to get married?" Jenny asked.

Molly hung on to little Pete and held her ground. "No. I'm completely happy on my own. I love my independence. Why should I give that up for a man?"

The women around the table gave her a bunch of pitying looks, even Lola May who was constantly swearing off men and then falling in love again.

Savannah broke the silence. "Molly, honey, you don't *need* a man, any more than Jo March did. But there will come a day when a man is going to knock you on your butt, just like Professor Bhaer knocked Jo for a loop. And you'll care about him. And when you fall, you'll fall hard, because that's the way you are. You'll live and die for this love, Molly. You might even be willing to give up your Shelby for him."

"You know, Les told me the same thing. But he was wrong and you're wrong. That's not ever gonna happen."

Especially with her father running around town telling any guy who might be even remotely sexy to keep his distance.

"I'm sorry, hon, but I'm afraid that it is." Savannah gave her a big smile. And for just one instant, Molly could see the resemblance between Savannah and her great-aunt Miriam Randall.

Molly stuck around after the book club meeting, enduring way too much teasing from her friends about the things Savannah had said. But she needed to talk to Nita about something. She'd been stewing about what had happened yesterday down at the river, and while Coach was partly to blame, it wasn't all Coach's fault.

Something had changed in Simon the minute Zeph Gibbs interrupted them. It might be as simple as Simon coming to his senses, or it could be something way more complicated. Simon had been kind of broody afterward. And what he'd told her on the walk back to the car had kind of taken root in Molly's head.

And of course, she was fascinated by Simon Wolfe. She wanted to know everything about him. And since he wasn't willing to talk about himself, she had to go snooping. Which, of course, lent credence to what her father had told Simon. She did have a crush on him. A big, sexy, grown-up girl crush.

"Are you waiting on me?" Nita finally asked as the two of them tidied up the refreshment table.

"Uh, yeah, I have a question."

"About the book?"

"No. About something totally off topic. You and Zeph Gibbs went to Dubois High School together, didn't you?"

Nita's face lit up with surprise. "We did. I've known Zeph since we were both little children. You have a question about him?"

"Yeah. He worked for the Raintrees, didn't he?"

"He did. He was the caretaker at the Jonquil House. He was also a hunting and fishing guide when the governor brought his political friends down every year to shoot quail. He wasn't so strange then. Why do you ask?"

"I was down at the public boat ramp yesterday with Simon Wolfe. I was fishing. He was sketching." She left out the skinny-dipping part. "Anyway Zeph came around, and he and Simon took a walk and talked for a little bit. And afterward, well…"

"Ah." Nita's eyebrows rose. "I forgot."

"What?" Molly felt like a bloodhound on the trail of something really important.

"Simon and Luke Raintree were great friends. Not that Luke lived here all the time. But Governor Raintree was always bringing his grandsons with him on his hunting trips, and the boys spent most of the summer here. Simon and Luke were the same age. There was a whole mess of white boys that age, including Stone Rhodes, who hung out together." She chuckled. "A lot of those boys went on to become members of the 1990 championship team."

"But about Zeph? Did he—"

"I know what folks say about Zeph. How he came back from Vietnam all messed up, and I reckon some of that is true. He might have been a doctor or a lawyer if he'd had the money to go to college and get out of the draft. But he had to go, and he went. And it changed him. Made him more solitary, I guess. But he used to come to church regularly. He was still a part of the community. But after Luke died, well..."

"Was he there when the accident happened?"

Nita sank down into one of the chairs. "I believe he was."

"But yesterday, Simon told me he saw Luke's brother shoot him. I never heard any such thing before."

"Mercy. I never heard any such thing either. I heard that the brothers were hunting with Zeph and one of the guns went off by accident. I never heard anything about Simon being there. Are you sure you have it right?"

"Simon told me himself. And the way he said it, he made it sound like Luke's brother was at fault. Almost as if he were suggesting that Luke's brother did it on purpose."

"You know, Luke's little brother is a very famous man now."

"He is?"

"Gabriel Raintree."

"Oh, my God. The writer? The dean of horror?"

"Yes, ma'am. And he wouldn't have been any more than ten years old when the accident happened. Gabe may have been holding the gun that killed Luke, but I don't think Gabe killed his brother on purpose. It was just a terrible, terrible accident. And as I recall, the governor put the blame square on Zeph for letting it happen."

Molly stood outside the Cut 'n Curl early Saturday morning, hoping that no one would see her as she snuck inside. Of course, it was completely stupid to sneak into the Cut 'n Curl. After all, everyone would know when she showed up at Dash and Savannah's wedding later this afternoon.

With short hair.

But still. Molly could count on the fingers of one hand the number of times she had actually set foot in the Cut 'n Curl. For just about all of her life, she'd been happy to wear her mop of curly hair in a ponytail, or braids, or pigtails, or pulled through the back of a baseball hat.

But after the swimming fiasco, she had finally come to the conclusion that waist-length hair was just a royal pain in the neck. Quite literally.

And since Savannah and Dash were getting married today, it seemed like a good time to have her hair whacked off. She didn't actually want to think too deeply about this plan, because somewhere, lurking deep inside, was this notion that she might be able to turn a certain male head, if only she would do something about her appearance.

But the minute she set foot inside the Cut 'n Curl she realized the foolishness of this notion. She shouldn't have to change herself to turn heads, should she?

And besides, the Cut 'n Curl was like alien territory. The place was wallpapered, painted, and upholstered in various shades of pink, Molly's least favorite color ever since Momma and Coach had forced her to live in a pink room. The place smelled sweet, too. Like the cosmetic counter at Belks. She stood just inside the door, her hands jammed into the comfy, deep pockets of her Dockers.

She wanted to run.

And would have, too, if Ruby Rhodes hadn't turned, taken one look at her face, and smiled. "Well, hey, stranger," she said. And then she left her station, where she was doing unspeakable things to Hettie Ellis's hair that involved a substance that looked like mud.

Ruby walked right up to Molly with a serious look

in her green eyes. "Honey, you don't have to be scared. We're going to pamper you today." She turned over her shoulder. "Aren't we, girls?"

The girls turned out to be Hettie, Jane Rhodes, Miriam Randall, and the bride, Savannah, whose hair was covered in tinfoil or something very much like it. Jane was bent over Savannah's hands, giving her a manicure. Little Peter snoozed contentedly in one of those baby car seats with the handle. He was wearing a pink onesie. Everyone, except Peter, looked up and nodded, like they had rehearsed.

Molly's heart started thumping, and her hands kind of went cold and then clammy. She tried to turn away and make an escape. But Ruby's arm was stronger than it looked.

"You're not running, honey. We've all had a conversation about this, and we've decided that it's time for an intervention," Ruby said.

"What?" Molly's voice cracked.

"A beauty intervention," Hettie said.

"Uh, I think what Hettie really meant to say was that we are going to enhance your natural beauty," Ruby said as she firmly, but gently, directed Molly to the seat beside Hettie's.

"Enhance? Uh, Ruby, I just want a haircut. I absolutely refuse to have mud put on my hair."

"A haircut?" All the girls said this word in unison, and then little Peter woke up and started to fuss.

"Sit," Ruby directed. "You are not cutting your hair. My goodness, Molly, your hair is your crowning beauty. And we are going to put mud in it. In fact, I plan to use quite a bit of henna on you."

"Henna?" Molly had no idea what henna was.

"It really is mud," Savannah said with humor in her voice. "But you won't believe what it's going to do to your hair. And I have a feeling once Ruby is done with you, you are not going to escape anyone's notice."

Before Molly could say another word, the front door opened, and Rocky strolled in carrying a garment bag. "Oh goody," Lady Woolham said, "she actually came."

"What the heck is going on here?" Molly said. She might have stood up, but Ruby had a firm hand on her shoulder.

"When Savannah found out that you made an appointment for this morning, she asked us if we would all come together to make you look beautiful. So sit yourself down. We are not letting you escape."

Molly stared at Savannah. She looked like she was channeling a young Phyllis Diller with her hair all gooped and foiled up. It was almost horrifying when Savannah grinned. "Honey, I don't want you to come to my wedding wearing khakis."

"Or ugly shoes," said Rocky.

"Or your hair in a big messy bun on the top of your head," said Ruby.

"Or your nails all torn and tattered," said Miriam.

"Or your face without any makeup," said Hettie.

"Or your eyebrows all bushy like that," said Jane. Jane actually shuddered.

"But I don't want to be made over," Molly said in a small voice.

"Of course you do," Ruby said. "And besides, it's on the house, on account of the fact that you were so cool under fire when Jane went into labor."

"But I—"

"And I know I made a mess of your yarn store so this is my way of paying you back," Jane said. And Jane was so utterly sweet it was kind of hard to argue with her.

"And besides," Savannah said, "you are always helping the knitters of Last Chance whenever they have a problem. This is our way of saying thank you."

"But—"

"No buts, honey," Ruby said. "Your daddy is really down in the dumps because of what your momma did. And I know it would do him good to see you all primped and polished and wearing a pretty dress."

"A dress?" Molly's heart really started to hammer in her chest.

"Yes, ma'am," Rocky said. And with that, she unzipped the garment bag to reveal a berry blue dress that looked like it was made of silk. "This is Rachel Lockheart's dress. I figure you and she are about the same size. She can't wear it, of course, now that her baby bump is starting to show. I've got accessories out in the car."

"Accessories?" Molly squeaked.

"Oh yes, honey, I've got some bracelets and a necklace and some earrings. You are going to knock Les right on his fanny."

"But I don't want to knock Les anywhere."

"Probably a good idea," Miriam said.

Suddenly all the girls in the shop turned to stare at Miriam.

"What?" Ruby said, looking over her shoulder at the old woman, who was wearing a pair of pink jeans, a purple paisley-print blouse, and red Keds slip-ons.

Miriam gazed up at Molly, her deep brown eyes

gleaming behind her trifocals. "Honey, one day, pretty soon, I've got a feeling that you'll get tired of your independence. It's a fine thing to be independent. But it can get mighty lonely sometimes."

"Really Miz Miriam, I'm fine with being independent. I like it."

"I know. But I think you might find something a whole lot sweeter, if you quit hiding your light under a bushel basket."

"What?"

"Honey, you're like a chestnut burr, all prickly on the outside, but sweet on the inside. You need to let folks see that side of you."

"Why? So some guy can move in and insist that I do his laundry for him? No thanks, Miz Miriam."

"Marriage is a lot more than that," Savannah said.

Molly decided to zip her lip. It was Savannah's wedding day, and it would be kind of ugly and inappropriate to express her views on the topic of marriage. And really, she couldn't refuse this offer so earnestly made by her friends. They meant well. They truly did. Just like Momma and Coach had meant well when they painted her room that time.

So she settled into the chair and endured it as Jane and Ruby and Rocky tried to transform her into a more beautiful rendition of herself.

Ruby refused to whack off her hair and instead smeared it with real, actual mud, which had the effect of bringing out the red highlights. They trimmed off her split ends, and then curled her hair, and put it up in a completely ridiculous do. They polished her nails, then applied makeup and blusher to her face. Finally, they dressed her in the purple-blue dress with a plunging neck-line that was practically indecent. The borrowed silver necklace, earrings, and bracelets made her look like a decorated Christmas tree.

The blue pumps with modest heels were the last indignity Molly had to suffer. Hettie said they made her ankles look slim and sexy. As far as Molly was concerned, they were torture devices.

The girls spent almost as much time on Molly as they did on Savannah, and boy howdy, did they work on the bride. When it was all over, Ruby surveyed the both of them.

"You'll do," she said with a satisfied grin.

At which point Miriam patted Molly on the shoulder, leaned in, and whispered. "Honey, the one you're looking for is going to be a little late for the party. You may have to wait on him for a while. But don't you fret, he'll get there eventually."

# CHAPTER
17

Dash Randall had really tricked out his stables for a big party, but the bathrooms were just a little primitive in Ricki's estimation. There was only one small one near the stable's office, and the line for it was pretty durn long.

If she hadn't been squeamish about using a porta-potty she wouldn't have had to wait. But porta-potties didn't come with mirrors. And really, for a big wedding where everyone in town had been invited, you'd think Dash and Savannah would have rented out the VFW hall over in Allenberg or something, instead of holding it up here like a summer barbecue.

She danced on her high heels as the line inched forward, cursing herself for the Diet Coke she'd drunk right before the wedding ceremony. She should have used the ladies' room at the church. What had she been thinking?

She finally got her chance to use the bathroom. Then she checked her mascara in the teeny, tiny mirror above the sink. She was a mess.

She pulled a tissue out of her purse and blotted. Why did

she even bother to put on mascara? She always cried at weddings. And the way Dash had looked at Savannah, as if she hung the moon, well it just made Ricki tear up something awful. She didn't ever recall Randy looking at her that way.

On that sour note, she fixed her face as good as she could manage then she headed over the patchy grass by the corral to the big green and white circus tent that had been set up for the wedding reception. Thankfully there was a dance floor, so her high heels weren't constantly sinking into the ground.

She found her table, only to discover Les Hayes standing there. He wore a nice gray go-to-meeting suit with a white shirt and a red silk tie. He'd obviously visited Danny Madison's barbershop. He looked positively corporate with his curls all shorn that way.

Her insides went all jittery. She hadn't said a single word to Les since the night he'd bought her a glass of wine at Dot's Spot. And she still didn't really know how to act or what to say around him.

At least he hadn't seen her yet. He was concentrating on something, or someone, across the dance floor. Ricki followed the direction of his gaze.

Damn.

"Is that Molly?" she asked. "Or has Coach gone and gotten himself a sweet young thing?"

"It's Molly," Les said in a voice that sounded a little peeved or something.

"She looks beautiful, doesn't she? I don't think I've ever seen her in a skirt before. And Coach looks like he's having a great time escorting her."

"She looks like she's dressed up for Halloween," Les said.

"Now, that's just ugly. And it's not true."

"I don't much care for girls who get all dressed up in lace and bows." He turned his baby blues on her, and she had this horrible sinking feeling in the pit of her stomach because her dress was made of vintage lace in a dusty rose color. It was one of the few dresses she hadn't put on consignment after Randy had dumped her. She'd bought it from her favorite Nashville specialty shop. It was one of a kind, and she'd spent an obscene amount of money on it—more than she made in two weeks working at the Knit & Stitch.

Les must have realized what he'd just said because his face got red. He really did blush a lot, didn't he? It was kind of cute.

"Uh, Ricki, I didn't mean that…" He ran out of gas, just as the Wild Horses started playing the "Tennessee Waltz."

And then he interrupted himself. "Ricki, would you dance with me?"

She was not going to turn Les down a second time, even if he didn't like girls in lacy dresses. But then at her age, Ricki was hardly a girl.

"I declare, is that you, Molly?" Lillian Bray, the chairwoman of the Ladies' Auxiliary, asked as Molly and Coach reached the reception tent. "I hardly know you, honey. Bless your heart, don't you look just like a girl?"

"You can say that again," Coach said with a big grin on his face. He'd been grinning like that from the moment Molly came home from the beauty shop. She was glad she'd made Coach happy. He'd been so sad recently. But it was a shame she had to dress up like someone else to do it.

Why did people have to be this way? It was almost as if they thought she had become a better person, just because she was wearing a dress. But she didn't feel like a better person. She felt like her same old self, only less comfortable. The dress was short and made her feel exposed. She kept tugging down at the hem and up at the V in the neckline. She also lived in constant fear that the clip-on earrings would come flying off. They looked valuable, and she didn't want to lose them. She kept checking them, even though they hurt her earlobes and were hard to ignore. But most of all, she was waiting for the moment when she could take off her pumps and go barefoot.

Molly scanned the gathering crowd. Les stood across the dance floor, staring at her with an odd, unreadable expression on his face. He didn't look like he approved of her new look. And the idea that Les might disapprove of her getting dressed up made her feel even worse. He turned his gaze away from her and toward Ricki Wilson, who looked entirely comfortable in a girlie-girl dress. Then Les did the most amazing thing—he took Ricki's hand and hauled her onto the dance floor.

What was up with *that*? When did Les ever learn how to waltz?

She tore her gaze away and followed Coach toward the table that had been assigned to him and Momma. Molly had been separately invited to the wedding and seated at a different table, but she'd promised Coach that she would stand in for Momma today. No doubt that's why Coach abandoned her to talk football with Dale Pontius almost as soon as they started across the dance floor. Molly could certainly hold her own in any given discussion of football, but the men obviously didn't want her company. No doubt that's because she was wearing a dress and standing in for Momma.

Coach had been abandoning Momma at events like this for years. Molly always thought Momma allowed it because she had no interest in talking football or fishing. But maybe that wasn't true.

And then Molly wondered why the heck Coach had even wanted her to stand in for Momma, if he was going to abandon her so quickly.

Without her so-called escort or her best friend, Molly took to the edge of the dance floor and watched the dancers. The band had picked up the tempo, and it sure looked like Ricki was teaching Les the steps to some stupid line dance.

Crap.

She missed Les. Usually she and Les hung out at dances like this. They would stand at the edges like companionable wallflowers and make fun of the dancers. Which was sort of mean, but it sure was fun.

How could Les be out there dancing? It just wasn't part of his usual MO.

*Enough.* She wandered over to the bar, where she got herself a glass of wine, and then she simply went with the flow. She was standing in for Momma so she joined a group of knitters and talked about the differences between cashmere and possum yarn. The conversation was definitely good for business. She'd probably sold some possum. But she couldn't shake the feeling that she was morphing into her mother, and while she loved Momma, she didn't want to become her.

Molly was feeling pretty low by the time the bride and groom arrived and the party really got started. She took her place in line for a plate of barbecue and headed back to her assigned table, where she found Coach already chowing down as if he hadn't had a decent meal in days.

Which was probably true, but she refused to feel guilty about it. Stone Rhodes and Lark Chaikin had been assigned to their table as well, which made perfect sense since Stone had been the famous quarterback of the 1990 championship team. Arlo Boyd and his wife, Janice, were at the table, too, since Arlo had been one of the linebackers. There were two empty seats.

Maybe the rest of the evening would be okay. Sitting with a bunch of former Rebels would be fun. These guys could talk Gamecock football until the wee hours of the morning. But right now, Stone and Daddy were too busy eating to talk—not that Sheriff Rhodes was much of a talker at any time. Arlo, on the other hand, was leaning in Lark's direction and the two of them were having a detailed conversation about the restoration of downtown Last Chance, and Lark's plans for the Coca-Cola building.

That's when Molly learned that Lark had, indeed, purchased the building. And boy she sure had a bunch of plans that she intended to put into action just as soon as Simon's lease was up at the end of August. So Molly was going to have to get her butt in gear and finish the Shelby restoration fast. Otherwise she'd be on the prowl for garage space. Again.

Her mood took another nosedive. Molly yanked the earrings off her ears and put them in her borrowed purse. The blood returned to her earlobes, making them feel hot, itchy, and abused.

If she'd been Momma, she would have engaged Janice in some inane conversation involving recipes. But Molly wasn't Momma, and she had no earthly idea how to start a conversation with Janice.

Instead she followed Coach and Sheriff Rhodes and focused on the barbecue, which was terrific since it came from the Red Hot Pig Place. But on her first bite, she managed to spill some sauce on her dress.

She quickly stuck her napkin in her water glass and started to blot it with cold water.

"Oh, dear," Janice said, "that's gonna stain."

Molly gritted her teeth. Janice was an ex-Carolina-cheerleader. And while Molly hated stereotypes, Janice kind of fit the cheerleader mold. She was perky and sweet and always dressed well. She and Arlo had several kids, and Janice was probably a complete expert on laundry and stain assessment in addition to being the chairwoman of the elementary school PTA.

Molly kept blotting and looking down. If she looked up, she was going to combust and say something nasty to Janice, who wasn't guilty of anything except being all the things Molly wasn't. And Molly didn't even know why that bugged her. She needed to get out of there and compose herself. She was just slipping her feet back into her uncomfortable shoes when warm breath feathered over her cheek and a deep voice said into her ear, "Who *are* you?"

The anger fled, replaced with far more combustible feelings. She looked up from the spot on her dress.

Simon wore a light gray suit, a striped shirt, and a red tie. As always, he was dressed to impress. Molly envied and admired him for looking so comfortable. The apostrophes at the corners of his mouth appeared, and his dark eyes sparked with something deep and hot and wicked.

She'd seen that look in his eyes the afternoon they'd gone skinny-dipping. And she'd seen that look evaporate, too. She hadn't seen him since that day. He worked in the early hours of the morning, and she worked in the afternoons. Whether they had been avoiding each other by chance or design was hard to say. He'd rejected her that day, and yet she could see desire in his eyes.

He put a plate of barbecue at the empty place beside her, and then Coach went and ruined everything.

"Simon," he said with that daddy-on-a-warpath look in his eye, "you and I need to talk, and I kind of resent the fact that you've been avoiding my phone calls these last few days."

"I'm sorry. I've been busy getting Mother's house ready to sell. I'm happy to have that talk, but maybe not here." Simon met Coach's stare. The contest waged for a full fifteen seconds before Coach actually looked away.

Wow! That had never happened before.

Simon took his seat and started eating.

"How's your mother doing?" Stone asked. And Molly wanted to give the sheriff a hug for choosing that moment to speak. Otherwise there would have been a really awkward silence.

"She's doing as well as can be expected. I'm late to the party because I tried to get her to come with me. But she refused. She doesn't know me or trust me much. She was sure I wanted to kidnap her and do terrible things to her."

Stone's eyes darkened. "I'm so sorry." No one else said a word, and suddenly the much-dreaded awkward silence was upon them again. But Stone, who was no great conversationalist, heroically launched himself into the fray again. "I want to thank you for what you did for my nephew," he said.

"It wasn't anything. Jane did all the work. How's the baby doing?"

"He's great," Molly said, glad to have something positive to say in the difficult situation. "He's cute as a button. I got to hold him at the book club meeting last week, and he was at the beauty parlor today. Honestly, Stone, he's the most perfect baby ever. And he even looks good in pink."

Lark laughed. "Poor Jane. Everyone gave her sissy clothes at her baby shower, and she's such a frugal soul she's gone right ahead and used some of them."

"Not when Clay's looking," Stone said, with just the smallest crack of a smile at the corner of his mouth. He turned toward Simon. "I'm still impressed by how you handled that situation. I only had to deliver one baby in my life, and believe me, I don't ever want to do that again."

"Who's looking after Charlotte?" Lark asked.

"She's in good hands," Simon said. "She's taken a shine to my assistant, Angel Menendez—you may have met him; he's Ruby's tenant. He does errands for me, and he's been helping Ricki at the Knit & Stitch."

Coach decided to join the conversation, and not in a good way either. "Oh, everyone knows about your assistant, Simon. I gather he fits right in with the gals at the beauty shop and the Knit & Stitch."

Stone's effort at small talk was undone. Everyone turned back toward their meals, and the conversation faltered. Embarrassment flared through Molly. When had Coach become so intolerant? Had he always been this way? Had she just missed it? Or was he just coming completely undone without Momma to keep him on track?

She wanted to come to Angel's defense, but picking a fight with Coach in public would be stupid, no matter how shameful his words. So she clamped her mouth shut, bowed her head, and continued to worry the spot on Rachel's dress.

Just then, the Wild Horses struck up the song "Can I Have This Dance?" with its sappy lyrics about happily ever after and lifetime commitment. Clay Rhodes announced over the intro that this was Dash and Savannah's song—the first one they'd ever danced to, last spring at the Easter street dance. He called the bride and groom onto the dance floor for their first dance as husband and wife.

"I declare," Janice Boyd said, "it's so romantic. And aren't they perfect together? Just like Miriam Randall predicted." She dabbed her napkin to the corner of her eye.

Molly rolled her eyes in Simon's direction. He wasn't smiling as he watched the bride and groom take a turn around the dance floor. Between verses, Clay called all the other waltzers up. Of course, Lord and Lady Woolham took to the floor. His Lordship had gone to cotillion classes and was always ready to show off his stuff. He and Rocky were kind of cute together.

But then Les and Ricki came out, too, leaving Molly utterly confused.

Simon stood up and turned toward Molly. "Come dance with me."

Coach's disapproval ran right up her back, and she worried that her daddy might jump up and physically get between her and Simon. She hated being right in the middle. "You don't want to dance with me, Simon."

"Molly, I sincerely *would* like to dance with you."

She'd have hell to pay at home if she danced with Simon. And really, what was the point?

But then Janice put her foot in it. "Oh, go on, Molly. You're all dressed up like Cinderella at the ball. You might as well dance with someone who looks like Prince Charming, even if he is playing for the other team."

Coach made a noise that was halfway between a grumble and a cough. His position was clear—he didn't want any daughter of his dancing with anyone playing for the other team, or anyone playing for his team either. In fact, Coach would be happy if Molly would just lock herself up in a tower somewhere so no one would ever mess with her again.

So really, Molly had to dance with Simon. It was a matter of pride. For both of them.

She stood up and put her hand in his. His palm was warm and dry and sexy as hell. Her own hands were rough and callused. She was aware of this fact only because Jane had clucked over them the whole time she was working on Molly's manicure.

"I sure hope I don't trip over these shoes," she said as they stood on the floor facing each other. He was clearly waiting to catch the beat of the dance.

"Trust me, you'll be fine," said Simon, looking down at the blue satin shoes she'd borrowed from Rachel. He evidently approved of them. Or maybe he was admiring her thin ankles.

He took her in his arms, and in an instant away they went, not very gracefully because Molly had no idea how to waltz or even let Simon lead. But even if she stumbled and almost turned her ankle, she discovered that dancing with Simon was fun. Way more fun than standing on the sidelines with Les making rude remarks about people.

"Molly, you are so beautiful this evening that I'm almost afraid to speak with you."

"Ha, you're only afraid because you know darn well Coach is over there watching us like a hawk and disapproving of every minute."

"No. I'm not afraid of your father. But I swear, Molly, if you dressed like that on a regular basis, you'd be turning heads from one end of Palmetto Avenue to the other."

She looked up and met his dark eyes. "Don't tease me, please. I went to the Cut 'n Curl this morning to get my hair done, and Ruby, Jane, and Rocky Rhodes dressed me up. I think it was for their enjoyment, but I know I don't look like me in this dress. By the way, it's your cousin Rachel's dress, and I think I ruined it."

"I'm sure you look better in it than Rachel ever did."

"Ha ha. Very funny. Your cousin is gorgeous, and I'm not. I'm odd and strange. And I'm not falling for your line again, mister. So quit. If you want to know, I feel kind of like a dressed-up Barbie or something. Not that I ever played with Barbies, but obviously Ruby, Rocky, and Jane did. I don't even know how I got myself into this situation. I just wanted Ruby to cut my hair is all."

"Remind me to thank Ruby." He glanced up at her hair. "You haven't really done anything more than pile it on your head, have you?"

"I didn't do anything, except let Ruby mess around with it."

"Would you let me mess with it?" he murmured.

Oh, Heaven help her. He was seductive and irresistible. And a tease. He needed to stop with the lines. She knew good and well he wasn't going to cross Coach. No one in this town ever crossed Coach.

Except maybe Momma.

"No, you can't mess with my hair," she said as emphatically as she could. "You remember, don't you? Coach told you not to mess with me. So there will be no messing with anything. Especially since he's back there at the table glaring at you like you're evil incarnate. And the last thing I want to do is mar Dash and Savannah's big day with some kind of lowbrow argument. Coach is going through a really hard time right now."

Simon nodded soberly. "I hate arguments, too."

The waltz finished, and Molly expected Simon to escort her back to the table. But the band segued into a rousing rendition of "Save a Horse (Ride a Cowboy)," and Simon snagged her hand and kept her out there on the dance floor. "There is nothing wrong with dancing at a wedding," he said, his dark eyes intent.

He wanted to live dangerously. Molly wanted the same thing. So she got in line and followed Ricki, who seemed to know the steps to every line dance in all of creation. Before long, Molly had jettisoned her uncomfortable shoes and forgotten all about Coach and his sour mood. A mob of dancers took to the floor, and she started having a really great time.

She danced half a dozen line dances until she was out of breath. She escaped the dance floor with Simon and got herself a longneck Bud to cool off.

That's where Coach found her. He didn't look pleased. But it was what he deserved. After all, he had abandoned her before she had abandoned him. And besides, he'd abandoned Momma plenty over the years. So Molly was just evening the score.

"You'll have a headache in the morning," her father

said, scowling at the beer in her hand as if he had any moral leg to stand on, given his two-day bender earlier in the week. "You know your mother disapproves of that."

"Coach," she said in a surprisingly calm voice, "Momma is not here. And I'm thirsty." She raised the beer in a toast. "And it's a special occasion. One beer is not going to put me on my butt, especially with all the dancing I've been doing."

He glared, but not at her. The look he gave Simon was practically lethal. He turned back. "It's getting late. We need to go," he said in a business-like tone.

"It's not even dark yet. It couldn't be much past eight o'clock," Molly said. "I'm not ready to go."

"Yeah, well, we've got church in the morning."

"Everyone here has church in the morning."

"Well, we're going to be the ones who show up without hangovers." Coach put his big hands on his hips.

Damn it all to hell and back. Why did he have to be standing there like some kind of anti-godmother, forcing her from the ball *before* midnight? So he didn't approve of the older, wiser Prince Charming she'd been dancing with. Since when did he have veto power over anything she did or thought or felt?

Short answer: Since always.

Molly suddenly resented the hell out of it.

But she couldn't fight it. If she didn't go along with Coach, he might go home and drink himself silly. Or he might take it in his mind to shove Simon into the wedding cake, which would be a freaking disaster.

She had to go. She really didn't have a choice.

But just as she was about to give up the field, Simon

changed everything. In a calm and civil voice he said, "Don't worry, Coach, I'll look after her."

The two men squared off for a solid half minute of staring each other down. Simon wasn't nearly as large as Coach, but boy he sure had a penetrating stare when he put his mind to it.

Finally Coach pointed a finger at his chest. "I'm not happy about this. And I swear, Simon, if you don't get her home by midnight, there will be hell to pay."

He looked at Molly. "Don't do anything stupid." And with that, Molly's father turned on his heel and stalked away.

Simon didn't remember Coach as being so hard. He remembered him as being a positive force. But something had changed. Whether it was in himself or Coach, Simon couldn't say. But sadness welled up inside him as he watched his old mentor cross the ballroom in an uneven gait. Coach had had a few, hadn't he?

It didn't seem in character, somehow. Coach wanted to protect Molly. Simon understood that. But the guy was obviously not listening to his daughter. He got the feeling Coach wasn't very supportive of Molly's career path. And Simon knew exactly how that felt.

Simon gulped down his beer and pulled Molly back onto the dance floor. He knew a moment of complete joy when the pins holding up her hair began to fall out.

They danced for a long time, and when the last light of day began to fade, he took her by the hand and tugged her away from the tent. She came willingly, a fresh beer in her hand and no shoes on her feet. They strolled up a rolling hill behind the main stable far away from the party, which was beginning to wind down a little.

The cake had been cut. The bouquet had been tossed. The bride and groom had been sent off in a shower of rice. The old folks had gone home, but the Wild Horses kept right on playing music, and the young folks kept right on dancing. They would dance until the bar shut down, and knowing Dash, that wouldn't be for some time yet.

But it was quiet here a little ways away from the tent. And they had a great view of a red sunset sky.

"Red sky at night, sailor's delight," she said, taking a sip of her beer. "Want some?" She offered it to him.

He accepted the bottle and took a sip, letting the yeasty tang fill his mouth. It was cool, and he was thirsty. "I should have gotten one for myself."

"There's more where that came from."

"I'm sorry about the way your father acted before. I get the feeling he's not one hundred percent behind what you want to do with the Shelby. I find that kind of interesting, seeing as you two used to be inseparable."

She let go of a long, sad sigh. "That was before the twins were born. Back when you were a Rebel, I was a boy, and Coach was happy with me."

He chuckled. "You were a boy? You want to explain that?"

"I was allowed to do all kinds of boy stuff. I could climb trees, go fishing, and ride my bike on a hot day without a shirt on."

"I'd like to see you do that now."

She rolled her beautiful eyes in his direction. The purple sky made them look almost huckleberry blue. It was so amazing the way her eyes changed color all the time.

"Why is it that when I'm alone with you for five minutes the conversation always ends up being about one or the other of us getting naked?" She snagged her beer back and took a long swig.

"Don't get huffy with me. You were explaining about how you were once a boy."

"Yeah, I was. I mean I didn't know there was any difference between boys and girls. And then my brothers came along. And my innocence was lost."

"Your innocence?"

"Yeah. I realized they had something different than I had. And then Daddy got the wild notion to paint my room pink and buy me a bunch of Barbies. And suddenly, I wasn't allowed to run around without my shirt."

"I'm sorry."

She sighed. "I guess I made him semi-happy today. I got all dressed up for him. But this isn't me." She gestured to the dress.

"Sure it is. You're you, Molly. In all your glorious contradictions. And regardless of what you happen to be wearing...Or not."

"Contradictions?"

"You're a walking contradiction. A woman who can restore a car and knit a sweater, too. All that makes you unique and wonderful."

He took her hand in his. "You know, when I was a little boy, I used to work in the garden with my mother. I learned all the names of the flowers, and we used to talk about colors. And no one thought there was anything wrong with me enjoying the garden. And then I turned eight. And suddenly Mother didn't want me in the garden. And Daddy wanted me to play sports and be tough."

He gave her a mournful kind of smile. "I'm not complaining. I liked sports. I loved to swim out in the river with Luke. I liked playing soccer. Of course, my father never regarded soccer as a real American sport. I guess I gained back a little respect when I was recruited for the varsity football team. But I wasn't much of a football player. At least I wasn't the kind of player my father wanted me to be."

"You're kidding, right? Simon, you're the one who won the championship with that field goal. You were the hero of the game."

"No, Stone was the hero. He masterminded that final drive in the closing minutes. I just kicked the ball."

"But still, you probably hold all the Rebel records for field goals and PATs in a single season. You never missed. Ever. And we won games because you were always so steady."

"How can you remember this? You were like four."

"I don't really remember. But I've been a Rebels fan all my life. I know what's in the record books. And if you look up placekicker, you find your name after every record. Without you, that team would never have gone all the way."

He laughed, suddenly embarrassed. She certainly remembered things differently than he did. All he remembered was the anxiety every time he walked onto the field to do his job. He knew damn well that any miss would be remarked upon at home, and he was terrified of being tackled by some of the bruisers on special teams. It wasn't that he doubted his ability, he just didn't enjoy American football. Soccer was fun. But no one cared about soccer.

The only thing that held him together week by week was his faith in Coach and Coach's faith in him. He loved Red Canaday. That man had given him more confidence than any other teacher. And of course there had been Molly, Coach's daughter—and his good-luck charm.

"I rubbed your head for luck before every kick. And you would look up at me with those incredible big eyes of yours, and I knew I had to succeed because I couldn't imagine disappointing you."

He reached out to touch her hair. It was halfway piled up on top of her head, and his hand connected with the last remaining hairpins. He couldn't help himself. He started taking them out. One by one, unwinding the thick curly tresses. His heart started pounding. What was it about Molly's hair that turned him on? "Your hair was short then, and curly," he said.

He had to take a deep breath. Touching her hair was extremely arousing. And by this time, he'd divested it of all the pins. He ran his fingers through it, reveling in the texture. She shook her head to loosen it. It fell down, past her shoulders, like a glossy dark veil.

It was sexy as hell.

In the distance, Clay Rhodes was playing a sweet, mournful fiddle tune. The band was down to playing ballads for the remaining couples who wanted to slow dance.

He pulled her against his chest, tucking her head under his chin. She snaked her arms around his neck. They danced, out where no one could see them. The night grew dark, and the crickets harmonized to the distant fiddle.

When the song drew to a close, she looked up at him, moonlight in her eyes. He should stay away from her. Coach had warned him off. And even if Coach was less than what Simon remembered, he was still Coach. And this was still Coach's daughter. And he'd given Coach his word.

He should back away. He should take her home.

But he didn't. He couldn't help himself. He let the southern moonlight and Clay's fiddle carry him away.

And then he kissed her, and when his lips touched hers, he lost control.

# CHAPTER
## 18

Molly closed her eyes and drank in the sensations. Simon's mouth was warm and inviting. His hair flowed through her hands like silk as she pulled him closer, deepening his initial kiss.

Hunger of a kind she'd never known seized her. She wanted to eat him up, devour his sweet lips, taste the warm skin on his throat and his cheeks and his ears. She wanted to get closer.

His shirt and tie and jacket were in the way. And so was her dress, even though there wasn't all that much of it. She remembered the way his body had felt under her hands for those few moments in the river.

But it had been freezing cold then. And it wasn't now. The night had turned humid and balmy, as only an early-June night could. The moon was shining high above the Carolina pines. It was perfect in every way. Molly just needed to get Simon to spread his jacket on the sword grass at their feet so they could lie down.

She was about to make that suggestion when the Wild

Horses struck up "The Watermelon Crawl." The music boomed up in their direction, reminding her that they were hardly alone or in a private place.

He drew back slightly. "You want to dance?"

He was going to get noble again, wasn't he? He had told Coach that she'd be home by midnight, and it sure looked like he was going to make good on that promise.

She couldn't let that happen. For one thing, she was weary of having to follow Coach's orders all the time. And for another, Simon looked like a great adventure worth having.

He was experienced and older. He could probably teach her things. She just needed to jump in and take control. She needed to take a leap of faith or something.

So she smiled up at him, trying to channel a true, southern *femme fatale*. "Are you talking about vertical dancing or the horizontal kind?" She let her voice go low and husky.

This earned her a sultry grin. "Either is fine with me."

Was he giving up that easily? She pressed the point. "You ever seen the insides of the Peach Blossom Motor Court?"

He sobered. "I'm not going to have sex with you at the Peach Blossom. You can put that right out of your mind."

Damn. That was a definite misstep. Of course he wasn't about to take Coach's daughter to the Peach Blossom. "Is that a no to the sex or no to the motel?" What was she going to do if he told her he was putting the kibosh on getting naked?

He chuckled. "Uh, well, I don't have any objections to getting horizontal." With that, he swooped in and kissed her again. This kiss was in a whole different league than the one he'd just given her. He moved in like a marauder invading her mouth with the heat and energy of his tongue. She stopped worrying about the idea that he wasn't interested in sex.

She brought her hands up to the back of his head and pressed him into the kiss, hungry for the rasp of his stubble against her skin, yearning for something deeper, harder, and more intense. She arched back and gave him access to her throat, and he took advantage.

He traced her jaw, the pad of his thumb sending heat and shivers through her. Her knees almost buckled as he ran his fingers across her throat and then followed them with a string of searing kisses that made her feel feverish and alive.

His mouth trailed down to the hollow of her neck and then he bit her again, kind of hard and just wickedly good enough to make her buck against him, like something wild and untamed. That love bite awakened the tides inside her, and she ached for him down deep in her core.

He seemed to understand this because he pushed himself against her, bringing his hand down to the flare of her hip. A deep and inarticulate sound bubbled out of him as he pulled her closer and rocked his hips against her.

And that's when she knew Simon had lost his self-control. A little, wild part of her thrilled at the knowledge that he was capable of losing control in such an obvious and incredible way. He ground his hips against her, and all she could think in her inflamed brain was that he was magnificent when he let himself go like this.

"Molly, I really do want to get horizontal," he whispered in her ear.

"Me too. Where? Not here. There are too many people."

"Mother's house."

She pulled back a bit. "Your momma is at home. We can't—"

"My mother is not in her right mind. She won't know. We can sneak in like a couple of teenagers." He gave her a soft kiss on the nose. "Which is kind of exciting. It's been a really long time since I was a teenager, and I never had the gumption to sneak a girl into my room when I was younger."

"Gumption? Jeez, Simon, you're sounding more southern every day. C'mon, let's go." She snagged his hand and started pulling him in the direction of the parking lot and driveway. He pulled her up sharp.

"Before we do this, I need to say something."

"Please don't. I know Coach disapproves of you and me. But he's totally confused. He can't decide if you're too gay or too old for me. And he's wrong on both counts. Besides, I'm a big girl. I know you're not a forever kind of guy. So let's just have a little fun, okay?"

Holding Molly's hand was a carnal experience. The brush of her fingertips against his flesh ignited a conflagration inside Simon that toasted his brain and blew conscious thought to smithereens.

He held his breath and set a steady pace down the hill toward the parking lot. Daddy's Taurus was parked way down the driveway because he'd been late to the party. A tense silence had come up between them, which allowed Simon to actually hear the roar of his own blood in his ears. He was drunk on lust.

It had been so long since any woman had made him feel this way. He almost wished she would babble or do what other women did at slightly awkward moments like this. But Molly wasn't like that. She was direct. When he opened the car door for her and their gazes met, there wasn't the least bit of uncertainty in her eyes. Instead, she laid another scorching kiss on him before she slid into the front seat.

And even though Molly was completely incapable of flirting, she still managed to flash her legs at him. She had some really nice-looking legs. It was kind of a pity she hid them all the time.

She looked up at him. "Simon, for God's sake, shut the door and let's get out of here."

She was apparently in a hurry. He needed to slow her down. Because he figured this might be the only time they got to experience each other, and he'd be damned if he was going to rush through it.

He shut the door and slid into the driver's seat. Ten long minutes later, he pulled the Taurus into the garage that Mother and Daddy had added on to the turn-of-the-century Victorian that had been their home for decades.

He turned toward her. "You need to take off your shoes and be really quiet."

"I already lost my shoes somewhere at the party. They hurt like a son of a gun."

He wanted to laugh. She was so natural and fresh and real. "C'mon, follow me."

He opened the side door that led into the dark kitchen. The television was on in the den. Its blue light flickered in the hallway. Simon gave Molly a sign to stay where she was, and he continued down the hall to investigate.

Angel was sprawled on the couch snoring while some HBO slasher movie played. Simon made a snap decision to leave sleeping assistants where they lay.

He turned and motioned Molly forward while simultaneously giving her the universal sign for quiet.

She looked amazing in the flickering light, with a devilish smile on her face. He took her by the hand and pulled her the rest of the way down the hall to the stairs. Up they went in the near darkness. All was quiet in the direction of Mother's room. He turned in the opposite direction and pulled her into his own bedroom.

Moonlight, filtered through the magnolia tree in the backyard garden, gave the room a soft glow. The dappled light glimmered in Molly's hair. He turned toward her, curled his fingers around the back of her skull, and pulled her hard against his body. He kissed her then—not a romantic kiss at all, but a base statement of his needs and wants.

This was what she wanted. So she met his tongue with her own, simultaneously invading his mouth and inviting him in. Soon he had her backed up against the door, and the roar of blood rushing through his ears told him there would be no turning back.

And yet he needed to slow down and control himself. Down deep he wanted so much more than a quick coupling against a door frame. He wanted to pleasure her. He wanted to give her what she wanted, and he knew, even as she bucked against him and gave all the signals of a woman in the throes of some kind of frenzy, that it would be a mistake to confuse Molly with a really experienced woman. She might be liberated, but she wasn't experienced.

He braced his hands on either side of her head. "We need to slow down," he said in a husky voice.

She looked up at him out of eyes that glinted in the moonlight. "Why?"

He felt the corner of his mouth tip up. She looked like a fantasy come true. "Because we do."

She brought her fingers up to play across his chest, and he felt the burn down to his toes. She loosened his tie and pulled it through his collar. She tossed it aside. Then she started on the buttons of his shirt. "I don't want to slow down," she said.

He played with her hair, twirling it around his finger. "But I do."

She slipped another button through its hole. "You want to seduce me."

"Yeah."

She slipped another button loose, and her tongue peeked from the corner of her mouth. She did that sometimes when she was concentrating.

"Well," she said, "it won't be hard to seduce me because I surrender."

He combed his fingers through her hair, drinking in the herbal scent of her shampoo and the musky smell of woman. It felt like someone had put a band around his chest and was pulling it hard. He could hardly breathe.

She pulled the tail of his shirt from his pants and unbuttoned all the rest of the buttons.

"I don't think you're all that easy," he said.

She inched her chin up, and something flared deep in her gaze. "So I'm a challenge, then?"

"Yeah, Molly. You're a challenge."

He stroked her hair, and she lowered her gaze to his naked chest. He saw admiration in her stare, and it knocked him for a loop. That look made him feel all hot and bothered and ready for action.

She pushed the edges of his shirt over his shoulders, and

he shucked out of it, giving her full rein to touch him. She ran her fingers over his pecs and circled his nipples and stroked his abs, making his breath hitch in his throat. He had never been so turned on by a woman's touch, especially considering that she hadn't actually hit any seriously erogenous zones.

It became more than he could bear. "There's something not quite fair about this situation," he said as her fingers dipped down below the waistline of his pants.

She looked up at him as she started to undo his belt. "And whose fault is that? You've been so busy going slow that I'm leaving you in the dust."

"Guess I'll have to catch up."

"Last one naked is a rotten egg," she said. It was the same thing Luke always said when he was making a dare. And for just an instant, he lost his concentration.

"What is it?" she whispered.

"Nothing." He leaned in and kissed her again. His mind fogged nicely.

"No, it's something." She pushed him gently back.

He let go of a breath. "It's what you just said. Luke used to say that all the time. Last one in the river is a rotten egg. Last one up the tree. Last one down to dinner. Everything was a race to him."

"I talked to Nita Wills. She's an old friend of Zeph's. She didn't know you were there when the accident happened."

He rested his forehead against hers. "No one knows I was there when Luke died, okay? Except Zeph and Gabe, I guess." He whispered the words.

"You never told anyone?"

"No. And I'd really like to talk about something else, like maybe your underwear. Are you wearing La Perla?"

"Right. Sorry. It was just that look on your face a moment ago."

"Well, I'll just wipe that look off my face, okay?"

She stood up on tiptoes and started kissing his neck. "Does this help?" she whispered against his skin.

"Uh, yeah. That helps a lot."

He reached around her, the movement bringing their thighs into contact just as she succeeded in getting his belt undone. He drew in a sharp breath as mindless lust washed over him again. With trembling fingers, he found the zipper of her dress and drew it down.

He peeled the fabric away from her shoulders and midriff. The garment slid to the floor and pooled around her feet like a dark shadow. She stood there wearing the daintiest pair of silk panties and a matching lace bra.

He groaned aloud. "Oh, my God, that underwear is amazing. You look like heaven. Please tell me they're pink."

"Yeah, they are."

"You wear pink on the inside?"

She shrugged. "The pink ones were on sale."

He cupped her breast, feeling its weight, flicking his thumb over her nipple through the lacy cup. It pebbled under his ministrations, and she moaned.

He didn't think it was possible but his groin got tighter. He was almost in pain now, trying to keep up this snail's pace.

He kissed down the column of her throat. "You are so hot," he murmured against her neck, savoring her taste, fighting the urge to bite and suck and eat her up.

He pushed her harder against the wall, caught up in the glide of her skin against his. He felt the blood beat at his temples as she started working on the button and zipper of his pants.

She finally finished and started tugging on his trousers. They caught briefly on his hips and then fell to his ankles. He shucked off his loafers just as she touched him.

He lost it. He pushed her against the door suddenly wondering why he wanted to go slow with her. And oh, thank the Lord, she took care of his underwear. And he took care of her panties. Finally they were naked as a couple of jays and caught up in the rhythm of the moment.

"C'mon," he said after a few minutes of this. He pulled her across the room and up into the four-poster bed that Mother had put in his room once he'd left home. The bed was an antique, with a real canopy. It was kind of a sissy bed, but this wasn't his bedroom anymore. It was the room reserved for guests.

"Wow, snazzy bed, Simon. It's really kind of turning me on. Much better than the Peach Blossom."

He pulled back the goose down comforter and scattered the pillows, then pulled her down into the softness of the mattress so that she landed on top of him. She tried to roll off, and he wouldn't let her budge. He held her there, chest-to-breast, laid out thigh-to-thigh, sex-to-sex, forcing himself to go slow.

"You get to be on top," he whispered, looking up into her darkened eyes as he cupped her butt cheeks.

She gave him an impish smile. "Okay. I can definitely handle that."

And in the next few minutes, Molly Canaday proved that she could.

# CHAPTER 19

Molly nestled her head tight against Simon's chest and listened to his heartbeat. She felt safe, and content, and satisfied.

Dawn light edged the draperies. The soft illumination ate away at the shadows and revealed the room's floral wallpaper, the antique furniture, the Williamsburg print on the bed's canopy. She might have been sleeping at a very nice bed-and-breakfast, not someone's home.

Daybreak exposed the truth. This wasn't Simon's bedroom. It was the guest room where he was only a temporary resident.

Simon slept on, unaware of her thoughts, his hair spread out on the pillow, his chin sporting that oh-so-sexy shadow of stubble. He had just the slightest smile on his face, and there were threads of silver in his hair. It was funny, but she didn't think they made him look old. They were kind of a turn-on.

The two of them had behaved like a couple of crazy teenagers last night. And Molly would do it again in a

New York minute. She would have made the night last forever if she could have.

But time moves forward. She'd had her fun, and it was time to leave. She was still a little intoxicated—a little high on Simon, but highs like this don't last forever.

She crawled from the bed and collected her clothes, slipped into the adjacent bathroom, and put herself back together.

Sort of. She had managed to lose her shoes and purse. Near as she could remember, she'd left them at her table at the reception. What an idiot. She was going to have to talk to Savannah or someone to see if she could get them back. Otherwise Rachel Lockheart was going to be furious with her.

Simon was snoring in the most adorable way when she left the room and headed down the hallway. It had taken a lot for her to go. She had stood by the bed watching him sleep while the sky got brighter and brighter. But it was going to be bad at home. Coach might even be waiting for her with his shotgun. So she needed to get going.

By the time she made it to the main staircase, the sun was well up and streaming through the front windows. Boy, she was going to have a lot of explaining to do when she got home. But she'd have time to work on her story, because she was going to have to walk home. And even though her parents' house wasn't all that far away, walking on bare feet would add a new element to the traditional walk of shame.

She made it to the first landing on the stairs without being discovered. Then her luck, which had been pretty crappy lately, turned all the way bad. Angel was standing in the foyer watching her descend with an interesting and unreadable expression on his face.

Adolescent guilt and embarrassment seized her. She started trying to think of something stellar, or funny, or even remotely coherent, to say.

All she could come up with as she came down the last few steps was, "What?"

He continued to study her. "You have lost your shoes, Cinderella."

"I left them at the reception."

"Of course you did. And you look as if you need a ride home."

"Oh, Angel, that would be so helpful."

Five minutes later, Molly found herself riding shotgun in Angel's flame red Jeep as he drove right through the middle of town.

With the top down.

Flo and T-Bone, who were just opening up the Kountry Kitchen, saw her. She knew this because T-Bone waved. So did Kenzie Griffin, who was dashing into the doughnut shop. And Molly was dead certain that Lillian Bray kept surveillance cameras trained on the stretch of Palmetto Avenue running by her house.

Yup, Molly was definitely going to be dodging embarrassing questions this morning at church. Well, at least one good thing might come of this. People would quit thinking that Simon and Angel were lovers.

She turned toward Angel. "You aren't going to gossip about this, are you?" She knew damn well he was going to gossip. Angel might be a gay Latino from California, but he'd been adopted by every last member of the Last Chance old hens' network.

"Of course not," he said.

"Why do I not believe you?"

He shrugged and looked handsome in a chiseled sort of way.

Angel slowed the car as he turned onto the side street where Molly had grown up. "Chica, you *do* know that Simon is not a good one for falling in love with?"

"Ha! I'm not falling in love with him. Last night I was carried away by lust."

"Which is how you lost your shoes?"

"They weren't my shoes. They belong to Rachel Lockheart. I also lost Rachel's purse, with Lady Woolham's earrings and my driver's license in it. Which tells you just how badly intoxicated I was." She paused for a moment, collecting her thoughts, because she was not drunk last night, at least not on beer or wine. "You know, Angel, getting dressed up and going to a ball is a really dangerous thing for a girl like me. I'm just not cut out for stuff like that."

"Well, it's only dangerous if you mistake Simon for Prince Charming."

"Yeah, well, I didn't mistake him for a prince. And he didn't mistake me for a girlie-girl. So we're good. We had fun. But now it's over." Which was very sad.

"That's a good way to look at it, Molly. I've seen too many women break themselves on Simon's heart."

"But you said Gillian had broken his heart."

His shoulders lifted just a little bit. "Did I say that?"

"You did."

"Well, Gillian got farther than most women get. And I think Simon was just a little upset when she finally gave up on him. But his heart is very hard."

"You think?" Molly didn't think Simon's heart was hard, or cold, or anything like that. He was kind. He was generous. And he was an extremely considerate lover. Her insides started to melt just thinking about the stuff they'd done last night.

"Chica, don't let yourself fall. He is all of those things you are thinking about, but he is not a marrying kind of man."

Of course he wasn't. He'd been clear about that. And it was totally okay. "That's fine," she said out loud. "I don't want to get married. I was merely looking for some fun. And he provided it. But the thing is, here in Last Chance, people aren't supposed to just get together and have fun. If they get caught doing something like that, everyone starts planning their wedding for them. So it's really important that you don't say anything."

"*En boca cerrada no entran moscas.*"

"And what does that mean?"

He grinned. "Roughly translated, it means that my mouth is so tight not even a mosquito will pass."

"Good, keep it that way."

He slowed the Jeep and pulled to the curb beside her parents' house. "Nice Harley," he commented, as he inspected the bike in the driveway. The hog was parked right beside a silver Mazda 3 hatchback.

"Thank God. Allen is alive. I was starting to wonder."

"Allen is your brother?"

"He's been MIA for the last week or so. The Mazda belongs to Beau, Allen's twin, who didn't tell anyone he was coming." She leaned her head back on the leather seat, suddenly exhausted. She hadn't gotten enough (any) sleep last night. The only good thing about this scenario was that Coach wasn't sitting in the driveway with a shotgun.

"Would you rather I take you to breakfast? You and me being seen at the Kitchen would definitely throw some people off the scent."

She snorted a laugh. "Angel, honey, no one in this town is going to believe that you and I spent the night together."

Muffin growled the moment Les came wandering into Ricki's small kitchen. The dog kind of crouched down, shivering. And then she launched herself at his ankles, which thankfully were covered by a pair of dress boots.

Ricki was mortified by the dog's behavior. "Muffin, sit!" she commanded. But the dog paid her no mind.

The situation could have gotten out of hand. But Les didn't do anything to Muffin. He just stood there letting her growl and bark at him. Not that Muffin was all that frightening, given her tiny size. But if Les had wanted to, he could have just stomped on her.

"I think you need to pick her up or something," Les said.

Ricki wasn't sure she wanted to get anywhere close. Muffin had tiny, sharp teeth. Where was Cesar Millan when you needed him, anyway? "You know, I've never seen her behave this way with anyone but you. She really doesn't like you."

"I kinda got that idea last night when we had to lock her in the closet. It was hard to concentrate with all that whining." His face got red.

"It's okay, Les. You were fine. I had a lot of fun. And I'd really like to do it again."

Les's expression brightened. "You do?"

Ricki knew it was crazy to encourage him. After all, he was younger than she was, and her dog didn't like him one bit. But Les was sweet, and even though he was inexperienced, he had turned out to be a considerate and impressive lover.

A thought that brought heat to her face. She still couldn't believe they had ended up here, together, with the dog in the closet and the two of them naked.

"I better go," he said, eyeing the dog and backing away toward the apartment's door. Muffin followed him, her eyes all squinched up and her entire body radiating doggy annoyance. "She obviously hates me. It's probably a sign."

He reached the door and had it open before Ricki could respond. Damn it. She had wanted him to stay and have breakfast. It had been a long, long time since she'd had a Sunday morning free, and spending it getting to know Les a little better would have been all right with her.

But Muffin had ruined everything.

"I'll see you," he said as he bolted through the door, making a quick escape down the fire stairs.

Muffin stopped barking, turned, and trotted back to where Ricki was standing in the kitchen. The dog sat down and looked up at Ricki expecting adoration. Clearly Muffin was proud of herself for having run off the big, bad, sexy man.

Simon startled awake and knew three things immediately. Molly was gone. Coach was going to be furious with him. And he was going to be late for church.

He inhaled. Molly's scent assailed him. She clung to him, even in her absence, and a yearning came over him, adolescent and exquisitely sweet.

One night with her was not going to be enough.

And yet her absence underscored the point that one

night was probably all he would ever get. And then it occurred to him that it was really strange to be on the receiving end of a one-nighter.

Simon was a master at those. But he had rules about them. He never brought a lady home. He always left before dawn. He never left a note.

He had certainly broken all his rules last night, not to mention his word. He'd even known he was breaking the rules, and that made the encounter that much more fun. That much more dangerous.

He wanted that woman. It was an urgent, almost desperate, crazy kind of feeling. He'd never wanted a woman that much. He'd never enjoyed a woman that much.

Damn.

He got up, threw on a robe, and checked in on Mother, who for all her dementia was already dressed and waiting for him to take her to church. When she saw him in his robe, she gave him what for, accusing him of being shiftless, lazy, and a pervert.

Then she fired him—again.

Satisfied that she was all right, and that Molly and Angel were gone—which probably meant that Angel had driven Molly home—he headed off to shower and shave.

They made it to Christ Church just after the processional. Mother was not happy at being seated in the back. And Simon was disappointed to discover that Molly wasn't there at all.

Molly prepared herself for World War III as she let herself in the garage door, which was rarely locked. But Coach wasn't waiting for her in the kitchen, as she expected.

Hope blossomed inside her. Maybe she could pull off this whole teenager-sneaking-around thing without being discovered. She tiptoed through the kitchen and out into the living room.

Busted.

Coach was there. But so were her brothers. And the moment she set foot in that room, she knew that no one was worried about where she'd been last night.

Beau was sleeping on the couch. Only this was not her real brother; this was some caricature of him. He looked pale and gaunt, his cheekbones almost painfully jutting from his face. And his hair looked all patchy and mangy, like he was losing it.

Coach and Allen sat in the adjacent wing chairs, both of them looking like they'd pulled all-nighters.

Coach turned his gaze on Molly. She braced herself for the inevitable interrogation, but instead of asking her where she'd been all night, he simply said, "Beau has cancer."

"What?" A toxic mixture of adrenaline and guilt and God knew what else spilled through her. It poisoned the high she was riding, and she crashed to earth in truly painful fashion.

"It's non-Hodgkin's lymphoma," Allen supplied in a gruff-sounding voice. He looked up at her with such pain in his eyes. His face was identical to his twin's, or at least it had been. "The idiot thought he'd keep it to himself," Allen said. "He went into the hospital about a week ago for his first chemo treatment. But it knocked him out. Apparently he's been losing weight for weeks."

"Why didn't he say anything?"

"Because Beau never wants to be a burden. Because

I'm a fuckup. Because you're always busy with your cars and stuff. And Daddy's busy with football. And Momma..." Allen couldn't say another word. He just got up, stalked down the hallway, and slammed the door to his room.

Beau stirred and looked up at her. "Hey, Mol," he said, taking in her slightly rumpled appearance. "Nice dress, kiddo."

Molly sat down on the sturdy coffee table and took his hand. "You idiot. You should have told us. If you had, maybe Momma—" She bit off the rest of her words as reality came down on her. In Momma's absence, she was going to have to take charge. "So are you still trying to work?"

He shook his head. "I withdrew from the internship. And I don't know if I'll be well enough for classes in the fall. The docs told me the chemo would make me weak and sick to my stomach, but I didn't realize how weak and sick. I called Allen when I knew I couldn't do this on my own."

"You shouldn't have felt like you needed to do it on your own."

"I'm sorry, Molly," he said, giving her hand a squeeze. "I know I'm screwing up your life right now."

"Forget it, Beau. I'm here for you. I only wish Momma was here, too."

Beau closed his eyes and seemed to drift off. Molly looked up at her father and realized that she was still in a big mess of trouble.

"Now is not the time," he said quietly, "but imagine how Beau and Allen felt when they showed up here last night and you were out partying."

Molly read the front of the postcard. It said "Greetings from San Sebastian" and showed a gigantic, white sand beach with a crescent of blue-green ocean. On the back, in Momma's curly script, was a one-sentence message: "The Canary Islands rock, having a great time."

Molly stared down at the writing. Usually if Momma sent letters they closed with X's and O's, or at least a "Love, Momma." She'd done nothing like that. And even though there was only a tiny space for writing on the back of the card, she still could have squeezed in a couple of X's.

But the postcard hadn't been addressed to Molly, or Coach, or the twins. It was addressed to the Purly Girls in care of the Knit & Stitch. Ricki had picked it up at the post office and brought it right up the street to Molly at the Coca-Cola building.

"Do you have any idea where the Canary Islands are?" Ricki asked.

"They're off the coast of Spain. Momma used to talk

about going there all the time. I think it's the place where Columbus started his trip across the Atlantic in 1492."

Molly swallowed back the knot that was forming in her throat. She didn't know if that constriction was because she missed Momma or if she was incredibly ticked off at her.

Momma should be home right now. She should have at least left a forwarding address. Beau needed her.

Not that Molly wasn't willing to take care of Beau. That wasn't the case at all. In fact, Molly was so determined to take care of her younger brother that she'd used Momma's recipe cards to plan a week's worth of meals. She'd taken off her party clothes and gone grocery shopping and then made a meat loaf that was edible, even if Beau had only picked at the food. After dinner, Molly had sat down in the living room and read *One Minute Meditations.* And this morning, before she came to work, she'd spent fifteen minutes in the meditation corner in the spare bedroom where she worked doubly hard trying to get Simon out of her brain.

Even so, a few things were much clearer now that she'd thought things through in a purposeful way.

Molly handed the postcard back to Ricki and told her to post it on the corkboard behind the cash counter at the Knit & Stitch. "We'll show it to the girls when they come tomorrow." It was amazing how calm she felt—how resigned she'd become to Momma's defection.

Ricki went back to the shop, and Molly went back to welding some new sheet metal to a section of the Shelby's front quarter panel that had been eaten away by rust.

She didn't hear Simon when he came into her cavernous work space. She didn't need to hear him. The moment he arrived the atmosphere became charged, and gooseflesh prickled her arms and shoulders. She shut down the welder, removed her welding mask, and looked over her shoulder.

Simon stood by the door that led to his studio looking sexy and debonair in his paint-smeared 49ers shirt. In his hands, he carried a pair of blue shoes and a matching clutch purse. "I thought you might want these back," he said, lifting the items so she could see them.

He gave her the most perfect smile, like he might be channeling some storybook swain. "Actually, Angel got them back for you. He said you were worried about them. Then he made a completely gratuitous remark about Cinderella and suggested that I come in here and demand that you try them on, just to be sure they belong to the woman I danced with on Saturday."

Molly didn't know whether to laugh or cry. This was the last thing she'd expected him to say. She'd kind of hoped he'd treat her like the one-night stand she'd been. That would have made everything so much easier.

"They don't belong to me," she replied. "They belong to your cousin Rachel. I'll just take my driver's license and Lady Woolham's jewelry out of the purse, and you can return the shoes directly to her yourself."

Something dimmed in those big brown eyes of his. "All right." He paused a moment, managing for the first time to look slightly awkward. "Uh, I didn't see you at church on Sunday."

"I didn't go." She resisted the urge to ask him if the entire town was gossiping about them. If they were, she'd hear about it soon enough, and that would be a big problem given the current situation at home. Maybe she should have thought about all that on Saturday night. But of course, she hadn't known Beau was sick on Saturday night. It was darn annoying that half her family had been keeping secrets.

"Is something wrong?" Simon deposited the shoes and purse on the board she'd put up between two sawhorses. It wasn't the best shop bench in the world, but it was the best she could improvise on a temporary basis.

Damn. Her whole life felt temporary. She wondered if Beau felt the same way, and her heart turned over in her chest.

Simon took several steps toward her. "Something *is* wrong, isn't it? You regret what happened on Saturday."

"No, I'm fine, and I have no regrets, but obviously it can't happen again. My brother is really sick. I found out Sunday morning when I got home."

"Oh?"

She nodded, her whole jaw tight. "He's got non-Hodgkin's lymphoma. He's lost twenty-five pounds, and his hair is coming out, and…" Her voice got thin and reedy, and she couldn't pull enough air into her chest. She wanted to put the welding visor back over her eyes and get back to work. There was something kind of comforting about removing the layers of the car's surface until the rust was exposed. If only she could do that with her own self, and her own family.

"What can I do to help?" he asked.

"Not a thing." Her voice held steady, despite her raging emotions. Maybe those fifteen minutes she'd spent in Momma's meditation corner had done some good after all. "Unless you can find Momma and bring her home. But that's not going to happen. I see that now."

Simon sat down on the shop stool and opened his

arms. "Come over here." He was offering his wide, manly shoulder. She could find comfort there if she wanted to. It was a tempting offer. But she had to refuse it.

"No, Simon, I can't."

He cocked his head. "You can't or you won't?"

"It's the same thing. Look, Saturday night was fun. But that's all it was. We both know that, so let's not kid ourselves, okay? People in Last Chance do not have affairs. And you and I are not going to have one either. You were clear the other day down at the river, and I'm good with your rules. And besides, Coach thinks you're too old for me, and he has his own set of rules. Coach and I have been known to argue about stuff like this, but now is not a good time. Not with Momma gone and Beau so sick."

"I understand," he said, but for a second Molly had the feeling that she might have hurt his feelings or disappointed him or something.

"So we're good?" she asked.

He nodded. "We're good. I understand. You're right, Beau needs you all pulling in the same direction right now."

Simon stood and retrieved the purse and shoes. He opened the evening bag and found Molly's driver's license, which he put on the makeshift table. "I'll have Angel take all of these things back for you. It's the least I can do. I'm so sorry about Beau." And with that he turned his back on her and left her alone.

It had only been a few days since Dash and Savannah's wedding, but Ricki was starting to wonder if Les was destined to be a one-night stand.

She probably ought to put him in that category. Not

that she'd actually ever had a one-night stand before in her entire life. She'd been with Clay Rhodes, and then she'd dumped him for Randy, which in retrospect had been a real stupid move on her part.

Randy had not deserved her.

So, all in all, one-night stands were not something she was all that experienced in. And now that a few days had passed, and Les hadn't called, she was starting to worry. Should she call him? What would he say if she called? Would he tell her she was too old? Would he tell her that he was carrying a torch for Molly?

He probably *was* carrying a torch for Molly, but then Molly appeared to be carrying a torch for *Angel*, which was really sad because Angel was gay. And besides, everyone knew that Miriam had predicted that Molly belonged to someone local. So it couldn't be Angel.

Although it could be Angel's boss. Molly had danced a few dances with Simon Wolfe, but the idea of Molly and Simon together was almost as absurd as Molly and Angel. Simon was way too old for her. And besides, how could a guy who dressed like Simon end up with a woman like Molly? No way.

She gave Muffin a little pat on the head. The dog was sitting at attention by the Knit & Stitch's front door as if she knew Angel would be there soon. It was Tuesday afternoon, almost time for the Purly Girls to show up. So naturally Muffin was standing by the door, waiting. Muffin had a hopeless doggy crush on Angel. If anyone in town was carrying a torch for that guy, it wasn't Molly, it was Muffin.

Which was annoying as hell because the dog hated Les. Muffin was getting in the way of Ricki's love life, which was sort of amazing because, until recently, she'd been both dogless and love-life-less. And now she couldn't imagine being without either.

The bell above the door tinkled, and Muffin gave a little bark, but she was sadly disappointed. Because it wasn't Angel who came through the door.

It was Molly. Sort of.

"Oh, my God, what have you done to yourself?" Ricki said. "Please don't tell me Ruby did that to your hair."

Molly stood on the threshold, her hair cut off in a kind of spiky do around her head. She looked like a mangy dog. "Ruby had nothing to do with it. I took my sewing scissors to it."

"But why?"

"Because I was tired of dealing with it. And I figured if Beau was losing his in patches, then I could cut mine in solidarity. I've been wanting to get rid of my hair for ages and ages. I kept putting it off for some reason. But this morning I meditated about it and decided cutting it was a way of simplifying my life. Short hair is light and cool, and I like it," she said, although the expression on her face said otherwise. "It took no time to get it dry this morning. I'm thinking the boys have all the fun, Ricki. We need to remember that."

"But your hair, Molly, it was your best feature. And if you wanted to cut it, you should have gone to Ruby instead of going at it with your scissors."

She snorted a laugh. "Yeah, well, Ruby refused to cut my hair once so I had to take matters into my own hands. And if I'd walked into the barbershop, the tongues in this town would have been wagging faster than Muffin's backside." She gave the dog a pat on the head. Muffin ate up the attention like the little tramp she was.

Ricki made no further comment about Molly's hair, but she knew someone was going to have to make an intervention and get that girl down to the Cut 'n Curl to fix the damage. Without her beautiful curly hair, she looked kind of like a skinny little boy.

Maybe Angel was bi and he liked his female lovers looking that way?

Ricki pushed that thought way back in her head. No way.

"And I've got another idea," Molly said. "The hospital in Columbia where Beau had his treatment is looking for knitted hats for chemo patients. I'm thinking we should get the Purly Girls working on hats. And we can get the ladies of the book club who knit to work on some hats, too. In fact, a hat is the perfect project for you, now that you've got the basic stitches down."

Great. She was turning into a lonely old spinster with a gender-confused boss and a dog with a crush on a gay man. And now she was taking up knitting.

This was not what Ricki had been hoping for when she'd given up her job at the Kountry Kitchen.

Molly and Angel helped the Purly Girls cast on the knitting worsted they were using for their first set of Chemo Caps. Everyone was knitting a simple ribbed cap so it was easy to keep the girls on track while they reminisced about people they knew who had died of cancer.

The talk was disturbing as hell, and Molly felt on the verge of tears the entire time until Miriam Randall, bless her heart, changed the subject.

She turned her dark gaze on Angel, who had stopped knitting and was busy cuddling Muffin. "Who is Rodrigo?" Miriam asked.

He continued to stroke the dog's head. "Pardon me, ladies, I do not mean to shock anyone, but Rodrigo is my boyfriend."

"Ah," Miriam nodded. "And, based on what you've said before, he's not a veterinarian, or a dog trainer, or something like that, is he?"

Angel gave Miriam the oddest look. "Sadly, no. I think I told you that Rodrigo is not a dog lover. And not a cat lover either. He is basically not a pet person. Not even goldfish." He pulled Muffin closer to his chest and gave the dog a little kiss on her head.

Muffin lapped up the attention.

"That's a shame," Ricki snarked. It was pretty clear that Ricki was jealous of Angel's relationship with Muffin. And Molly thought *she* had a complicated life.

"It is." He held the little dog up so he could look her in the eye and speak more baby talk to her. "It's a very big shame, isn't it my little angel?"

"Ha!" Miriam said. "Angel's angel. That's amusing. But it's not at all amusing that your Rodrigo doesn't like dogs. It's not amusing at all."

Luanne Howe piped up. "Miriam, are you saying that Angel needs to get rid of his current boyfriend?"

"Oh, no, I couldn't do that," Angel said.

Miriam leaned forward and caught Angel by the upper arm. "Son, you listen to me. God did not put you on this earth to spend your life with someone like this Rodrigo."

"You do not even know him."

"Of course I don't know him. But that's not important. If he doesn't love dogs, then he is not for you."

"Is that a forecast?" Ricki asked. There was such a yearning in Ricki's voice. It was sort of pitiful.

"A forecast?" Angel looked at the ladies around the table. All of them, even the senile ones, were leaning in. When Miriam started talking about relationships, everyone listened.

"I have heard about this knack of yours," Angel said. "But I am happy with my boyfriend."

"Angel, you know that isn't true," Miriam responded. "You need to get a dog and lose Rodrigo. And I promise you that everything will turn out right."

"A dog? Really? What kind?"

"I don't know. Maybe one like Muffin."

He lifted up the pooch and spoke to her in a singsong voice. "You hear that, my little prima donna? I need to find a dog like you. But Miz Miriam does not realize that you are one of a kind."

The dog barked. She obviously loved being adored.

Molly refrained from making any comment about this turn of events. Thank goodness Miriam's matchmaking advice had distracted everyone. Otherwise she'd be hearing a lot of crap about her hair. And she didn't want to hear any crap about it because, now that she'd whacked it off, she was having some major misgivings. It was lighter and cooler and all that, but it was hard to hide behind short hair. And until that hair was gone, she hadn't realized how much hiding she'd been doing.

She employed one of the techniques in *One Minute Meditations* and tried to clear her mind of everything but the knitting. And to her astonishment, the technique worked, and she felt kind of centered. Which was a good thing, because otherwise she might be obsessing about Beau, or Momma, or her hair, or that moment when Simon was going to walk in the door to pick up his mother. She didn't want to see Simon. Telling him no yesterday had been one of the hardest things she'd ever done. But it had been necessary.

And now she wanted him to go back to California as quickly as possible. Because she was weak and God only knew how long her willpower could hold out in the face of such overwhelming temptation.

The bell above the door jingled, and Molly almost jumped out of her skin. Time had moved on without her. She'd been so centered on the knitting. She looked up, bracing herself for another encounter with Simon.

But it was Les. And he looked at her with this strange expression on his face. "Whoa, Mol, you look like you tangled with a buzz saw."

"Thanks," she said.

"Don't mention it. You look kinda cute, actually."

Ricki gave Les a look that was one part *I'm so glad to see you* and another part *Go away and leave before you hurt me more than you already have*. Molly, Angel, and Miz Miriam recognized this look and glanced at one another.

"Why are you here?" Ricki asked. She sounded truly ticked off. And so did her little dog. Muffin, who had been happily lapping up Angel's attention, suddenly turned into Cujo on a miniature scale. She crouched down on Angel's lap and growled at Les.

This only lasted for a couple of moments before Angel went into Cesar Millan mode. "Muffin," he said in a calm, assertive voice. And that's all it took. It was either the tone or the Spanish accent, but the dog turned her back on Les, looked up at Angel with adoration in her brown doggy eyes, and sat down on his lap.

"How did you do that?" Ricki asked.

Angel shrugged. "I do not know. She and I are sympatico."

Ricki turned back to Les, who was standing there looking more and more awkward by the minute. "Why are you here?" she repeated.

"Uh, um…" He gave Molly a desperate look and then turned back toward Ricki. "Uh, can I talk to you a minute?"

Ricki's face turned the color of the red knitting worsted she was using. "Les, I'm working and…"

"It's okay. You can talk to him if you like," Molly said.

"I'll watch Muffin," Angel added unnecessarily.

And that's when Miriam leaned toward Ricki and said, "Honey, it's now or never. You do realize that?"

Damned if a big smile didn't flower on Ricki's face. Not to mention that Les suddenly looked like a cat who'd just eaten the best goldfish in the tank. Ricki left her knitting on the table and followed Les out the door.

"Well, I don't reckon we're going to see them again this evening," Miriam said.

Luanne turned toward Miriam. "I'm confused. I thought Molly and Les were supposed to be the ones getting married."

"I never said that," Miriam replied. "You must be getting senile."

"Oh? But I could have sworn I heard it somewhere."

"Just because you heard it somewhere doesn't mean I said it," Miriam said as she gave Molly a knowing glance. It was like the old lady had a pretty good idea what she and Simon had been doing on Saturday night. And it occurred to Molly that Simon actually fit the forecast. He was a guy who had known her a long time ago. So long ago that Molly hardly remembered it.

But so what? There were so many reasons why she and Simon needed to back away from things. Miriam could prognosticate away, if she wanted to. But Molly was smart enough to know that her great love—the guy who was going to change her mind about kids and marriage—was not Simon Wolfe. In fact, given his relationship rules, it was a laughable idea.

She glanced at the clock. It was getting late.

Shevon Darnell entered the shop a few minutes later. "Hey y'all, it's time to go," she said in her big, booming, always cheerful voice.

The Purly Girls started getting their things together. All of them except Charlotte, who glanced at the clock behind the checkout with a worried look on her face. "Ira's late," she said. "I don't want to ride the bus like some old lady."

This earned her a couple of dirty looks from the other Purly Girls.

"Do not worry, Miss Charlotte," Angel said. "I am taking you home tonight."

"Where's Ira?"

"He has a meeting with Ryan," Angel said, not missing a beat. This must mean that Simon was with Ryan tonight. So Molly was safe. Why the heck did she feel so disappointed?

The Girls got on the bus. Rocky deBracy came by to pick up Miriam seeing as Dash and Savannah were off honeymooning. Then Angel bundled Charlotte and Muffin out the door.

Molly was left all alone in the Knit & Stitch, staring

at the damn postcard Momma had sent from the Canary Islands. A boatload of lonely tears filled up her eyes.

Ricki's internal alarm clock was still locked in at four-thirty, even though she no longer had to make it to the morning shift at the Kountry Kitchen. So consciousness arrived before sunup.

She awoke warm, inside the curl of Les's body. She opened her eyes to the alarm clock and the still-dark patch of sky at her bedroom window. The view between the curtains was narrow and familiar, and yet inside her heart there was something different, something new, something big.

She snuggled deeper into Les's chest, skin-to-skin. "Hmmm, that feels nice, baby," he said as he touched her breast.

Her body responded with a spiral of heat. But it was so much more than that. Her heart was pounding. She felt so alive. As if she'd been reborn last night.

As if God had finally handed her a second chance. Or maybe it was a last chance.

But she had to make the leap. She had to commit. She had to push her doubts about everything aside. She had to open her arms and accept it and not run. It had happened too fast. But if she didn't trust it, she might lose it again and never have another chance.

She had to be fearless this time.

"I love you," she whispered.

And he kissed her on her ear. "I love you back."

She rolled over slowly, meeting him face-to-face in the darkness. His eyes shone even in the shadow light. He was so handsome.

She kissed his chin, stroked his hair. "I mean it, Les. I want you in every way. And I don't want to sneak around. I love you, and I just want to be with you every minute."

"Yeah, me too. I can't stop thinking about you. And I'm still amazed that a woman as beautiful as you would be interested in me."

"I'm not that beautiful. I'm too old for you, but I'm not going to think about that."

"I like experienced women. And you are beautiful. In fact, you're so beautiful you're out of my league, but, honey, I'll do whatever it takes to make you happy."

She laughed. "You've already made me happy tonight several times. But over the long run, you'll have to make friends with my dog."

"Oh." His voice sounded flat.

"Oh?" Her voice sounded wary.

"Uh, honey, I was kind of thinking that maybe you could give Muffin to Angel. I mean she loves him, and she most definitely doesn't love me. I don't know why. I never got that kind of reaction from a dog before. I had a golden retriever named Rex for years and years. And we were great friends. We went hunting together and everything. But Muffin doesn't like me. She's scared of me or something. Maybe I'm too big for her."

"I'm not giving Muffin away. I love her."

"Uh, yeah, but—"

"I'm not giving her away." Randy had treated her like a dog that no one wanted anymore. She wasn't going to treat Muffin that way. Never. Ever.

# CHAPTER
## 21

Allen woke Molly in the middle of the night with a firm rap on her bedroom door.

"Molly, I need your help."

She came out of sleep all at once and quickly slipped from the bed. She opened the door.

"What's wrong?"

"Beau's got a fever. A bad one. We need to get him to the hospital right away. And Daddy's useless. He's been drinking."

Oh crap. Molly had read everything she could find about caring for someone going through chemotherapy. A fever like this could be life-threatening, given what the drugs and the disease were doing to Beau's immune system.

"Wrap him up in Momma's living room throw. I'll be dressed in a minute." She threw on her clothes. By then, Allen had contacted Doc Cooper on his cell. Based on his advice, they piled into Molly's Charger, and she drove them all the way to Columbia in record time.

The next few hours were horrible. Beau was isolated while they pumped him full of antibiotics and took images of his chest and lungs. He was having trouble breathing, and the doctors were pretty sure he had pneumonia. They were already talking about a possible bone marrow transplant, if he came through this crisis.

Molly didn't like the "if" in that sentence. Of course Beau would come through. And he had a perfect bone marrow donor in his twin. God could not be so uncaring as to let Beau die at the age of twenty-three.

She bypassed meditation and went right to prayer. But God seemed so far away. As if He didn't want to hear her prayers. As if He wanted to take back her brother, who was brilliant and sweet and kind. It wasn't fair. God should take her instead.

Molly refused to leave Beau's bedside while the fever raged. He was completely out of it, and every time he asked for Momma, Molly's heart cracked until it felt like a damaged egg inside her chest.

She had no idea how much time had passed when someone touched her too-short hair. Hair that, if the mirror was any judge, was standing on its end and making her look like someone who'd seen a ghost. The touch was incredibly gentle and warm. She dropped her knitting needles to her lap and looked up.

Simon stood just behind the uncomfortable hospital chair with a grave expression in his eyes. He must know the situation was dire.

Her throat closed, and her eyes teared up. She stood up and reached for him like someone groping in the dark. He wrapped his arms around her and just held her tight. "I'm here," he said.

And she hung on. She didn't really cry. But just being pressed up against his chest, just feeling his hand caressing her shorn head, was enough to give her strength. As if, somehow, the God she'd had trouble finding in her prayers had suddenly handed her this helping hand.

She had no idea how long she stood sheltered in his arms. Eventually it occurred to her that hugging on Simon in public was probably a bad idea. So she disengaged and looked up at him. "I'm better now. Thanks."

He nodded but didn't say anything. She turned away and picked up her knitting from where it had fallen on the floor.

"Momma?" Beau stirred in the bed, but he wasn't fully conscious.

Molly took his hot hand in hers. "I'm here," she said, repeating the words Simon had just spoken. She was stronger now. She could do this. She could be Momma's stand-in. She could hold the family together.

"I hate it when he calls out for Momma that way," she said.

"Your mother is on her way."

"What?" She turned to look over her shoulder.

Simon's dark eyes were filled with kindness. "Yesterday, based on that postcard she sent, I took a wild guess and started contacting Mediterranean cruise operators who call at the Canary Islands. I finally found her and got a message to her. She'll be landing in Atlanta at ten-thirty tonight."

"You did this yesterday? But I—"

"Your mother would have been very unhappy if no one had tried to get in touch with her. I know that she abandoned you. But I also understand why someone might need to run away and not leave a forwarding address. Then yesterday morning, I woke up and I couldn't stop thinking about the things Miriam Randall told me the day Peter was born. She said that sometimes it's the things we don't do that we regret most of all.

"I know you're curious about what happened the day Luke Raintree died. And the simple truth is that Luke was arguing with his brother, Gabe, over who got to use the new rifle. They argued all day. And I had any number of opportunities to get between them. But I didn't. Because when my parents argued and I tried to get between them, all that anger got aimed at me, and it hurt. So I didn't try to stop them. And they ended up playing tug-of-war with a loaded rifle."

"Oh, Simon. That wasn't your fault."

"I know. But I carried the guilt for a long time. I'm still carrying it. And that's why I had to do something about your momma. With Beau so sick, I knew your mother would regret not being here. And you and Allen and Coach would all regret not looking for her."

Another little wave of guilt slapped Molly. "Shoot. You're right."

"Don't feel bad, Molly. You're the one who's been trying to hold things together. Everyone can see it. And I, for one, admire you for it."

Simon held a piece of paper with Pat Canaday's name on it. He stood just outside the security gate, near the baggage return at Hartsfield Airport, trying to figure out how he'd gotten so deeply involved in this family drama.

Something had come over him the day before yesterday. He'd awakened in that preposterous canopy bed, breakfasted with his mother, who treated him like a stranger, and missed Molly like she was the sunshine.

He'd missed her when he'd opened his eyes. He'd missed her at the breakfast table. He'd missed her while he tried to fix the Harrison commission.

And all that time, all he could think about was the pain that Molly and her family were going through because her mother had run away. Those thoughts shamed and depressed him. He hadn't said good-bye to his father before he died. And as for mother, her words that night he'd walked away had turned prophetic. He truly *was* dead to her.

There had to be a way to make some kind of amends for what he'd done all those years ago by walking out. So he'd forgotten about the Harrison commission—again—and he'd worked the phones until he found Patricia Canaday and had a short phone conversation with her on a ship-to-shore connection.

He didn't think he would recognize Pat, but he was wrong. Molly was quite a bit like her mother.

Pat stopped in front of him. "You know, I don't even recognize you. Simon?"

"It's me."

"Well, look at you and me together. A couple of sad prodigals." She looked as if she'd been crying. Her eyeliner had smeared under her eyes, and her nose looked raw.

"Well, if you recall, the prodigal was welcomed back with love," he said. Although his family hadn't done any such thing. But Simon had every reason to believe that Pat's family would.

"Thank you for reminding me of that," she said, giving him a brief but motherly hug. "I can't believe what a fool

I've been, and I will be forever grateful to you for calling me on it."

Half an hour later, her bags tucked into the Taurus's gigantic trunk, Simon pulled onto the interstate heading toward South Carolina. He was hoping Pat would sleep, but she was too antsy to close her eyes.

"So, you came home for your daddy's funeral?"

"I did."

"And you stayed?"

He filled her in on the latest news from Last Chance, including the closure of Wolfe Ford, Molly's travails with the Shelby and the Knit & Stitch, and his plans to leave town just as soon as he could wrap up the major details of his father's estate.

"And when's that going to be?" she asked.

"Soon. The house is ready to put on the market, and Arlo said he had a 'major nibble' already from someone who wants to turn it into a bed-and-breakfast. I've also made arrangements for my mother at an assisted living place near where I live. California social services is already working on the paperwork. Uncle Ryan is in control of the business side of things. At least he's changed his mind about liquidating the dealership. I heard yesterday that he's in negotiations with Dash Randall and the only thing holding them up is that Dash is off in the Caribbean somewhere on his honeymoon."

"Does Molly know all this?"

He tightened his hands on the wheel. He hadn't expected Pat to jump right to that conclusion, but then what other conclusion would she jump to? He supposed he could tell her he was doing it for Coach's sake. But he had a feeling Molly's mother could see right through him.

"She knows my plans," he said. "And she can use the Coca-Cola building for the Shelby until the end of August. I rented the place for three months, but I'm not going to need it for that long. Hopefully, by then Dash will own the dealership, and he'll give her some space for her business."

"And did you stipulate that as part of the sale?"

Heat crawled up his face. "Well, I'm not in control of the sale. My uncle is. But I might have mentioned it to Dash before he took off on his honeymoon."

"Uh-huh. Yes, I can see things very clearly." Pat didn't sound so friendly all of a sudden. In a minute, she was going to give him the same speech Coach had delivered a few weeks ago. That speech about how he should back off and not mess with Molly. About how he was too old for her. About how he was too jaded for her. About how he was the kind of guy who walked away from commitments.

Yeah, he was that guy. And Molly knew it. And she'd already ended it. And he was going to live with her decision, because it was the right one. He had no business messing with Molly. She deserved someone younger and better than him.

"Look, Mrs. Canaday, I—"

"Call me Pat."

"Okay, Pat. Hurting Molly is the last thing I want to do. She's become a friend."

"A good friend?"

"A friend." He tried to invest this word with deeper meaning. He was not about to have a detailed conversation about what happened last Saturday night, or this Monday morning. Although he knew that Pat would figure it out eventually.

Pat said nothing in response to this. She merely turned her gaze toward the flashing white lines on the highway.

Despite Simon's good news, the day wore on, hour by hour, with little improvement in Beau's condition. Simon left at six to make the drive up to Atlanta—a good four hours.

Molly and Allen continued to keep vigil. Around midnight, while Allen was dozing in a chair, Beau let go of a long, rattling sigh.

And were it not for the monitors showing the steady rhythm of his heart, she might have thought that exhalation was a death rattle. His cheeks had gone deathly pale. But his respiration seemed easier. She leaned forward and touched his forehead. His brow was much cooler than it had been.

The fever was down, but she'd already been warned by the doctors that someone with a compromised immune system like Beau's might not be able to muster a fever in the face of an infection. She didn't awaken him. He needed his rest, and she chose to be optimistic. But she kept her eye trained on the clock.

If Momma's plane touched down at ten-thirty, then the earliest she could be here was three in the morning.

Time crawled. The monitors beeped. Allen snored. And she knitted, even though she could hardly keep her eyes open. She wasn't even sure what she was making anymore. It had started out as a sweater for someone approximately Simon's size. But now it was taking on afghan proportions.

Around two, Coach finally arrived, grim and sober. He didn't say a thing. He merely took Allen's place, while her brother went off in search of some coffee.

An hour and a half later, Momma came sweeping into the room.

There was a brief and somewhat awkward family reunion. And then Momma and Coach took their places at Beau's side.

Since the hospital only allowed two visitors at a time, Molly retired to the family waiting room. She was too tired to drive back to Last Chance and too emotionally unsteady to accept Simon's offer to drive her home.

Besides, if she did that, she'd be without a car, and she hated that feeling. In the end, Simon drove Allen home to get some rest, and Molly sat in the family waiting room, knitting until she fell asleep.

Coach roused her in the morning with the news that the doctors believed Beau was out of immediate danger. Then she and her parents had breakfast together in the hospital cafeteria. Whatever Momma and Coach had said to one another over Beau's prostrate form would remain a secret between them. They seemed like their usual, normal selves again.

But maybe their usual, normal selves hid something rotten. Molly couldn't get past the fact that both of them had let her down. She would have called them on it, except now was not the time.

For once, Molly held her tongue. There was no point in creating a big argument by expressing her disappointment in a public place. She screwed on her best face and best behavior. For Beau's sake.

And when Beau finally opened his eyes later that morning, it was to see both his mother and his father at his bedside.

Molly visited shortly thereafter to pat his hand and

give him the first Chemo Cap that she'd knitted for him. He asked to rub her short hair for luck, the way the members of the 1990 dream team had done.

She left him then. She planned to go home for some sleep and a shower and return for the evening watch.

She made it halfway down the hall toward the elevator before Momma caught up with her.

"There are a couple of things I need to say to you," Momma said as she pulled Molly into a big motherly hug that Molly deeply wanted to return. But she stood there, frozen and still angry. Momma seemed to realize this.

"First of all, I want to apologize for running out on y'all. I realize now how hurtful that was. And to be honest, I didn't really enjoy seeing all those sights all by my lonesome. And I will regret what I did for a long time. I just got so angry and, well, we've talked before about how destructive anger can be if you give it full rein. Which is what I did."

Molly said nothing. She was dead tired, and this was a terrible time for Momma to be making her grand confession. But she listened, even if she found it hard to look her mother in the eye.

"I should have told your father what I wanted. I should have made him understand. And when I decided there was no point in waiting for him, I should have told everyone I was going to follow my dream regardless. And I should have left a way for you to contact me."

"Yeah, you should have."

"And I shouldn't have put that note on the door of the yarn shop. I guess I was just feeling so disappointed in my family. It wasn't right to try to turn you into my clone."

Molly finally looked up. "Momma, my dream of starting a car-restoration business is not some kind of failing. It's not a problem. It's what I want. I wish you'd understand that."

"Honey, it's only that I sometimes think you sell yourself short. And I just thought that if I could force you into a different way of thinking, then maybe…" Her voice failed her.

"Maybe what?"

"I wanted you to understand that you can still be the master of your fate, even if it doesn't involve doing a man's job."

"But who says working on cars is a man's job?"

Momma rolled her eyes. "Okay. I was wrong. And I'm sorry."

"Good. I'll accept your apology."

Molly turned on her heel, still feeling a little angry, but her forgiveness was genuine.

"Darlin', there's one other thing."

"What?" Molly turned around.

"You and Simon Wolfe."

Crap. Momma would come home and immediately start prodding around the most sensitive issues. "What about us?"

"He's in love with you."

Those words zinged right into her middle like some kind of poisoned dart or something. She started feeling short of breath almost instantly. "He is *not* in love with me."

"All right, then he's infatuated with you. The way older men sometimes fall for younger women."

"Don't you think I *know* that? I'm not a fool."

"I'm glad to hear that. Your daddy says he thinks you

have a crush on him. He says Simon has been taking advantage of you. He says you and Les have had a falling-out and he's pretty sure it's because of Simon. I'm really unhappy to hear this."

"Momma, there is nothing going on between Simon and me. And before you meddle in my life any more than you already have, maybe you and Coach should concentrate on working out your own problems. And by the way, there are a lot of good reasons why Les and I have had a falling-out, starting with the fact that he stole my job."

She turned, took a couple of steps, and stopped. "Oh, there's something else," she said, looking over her shoulder.

"I'm afraid to ask," Momma said looking almost contrite.

"There have been some changes at the Knit & Stitch."

"Changes?"

"Yeah, I hired Ricki Wilson. And even after LeRoy fired me, I decided to keep her on. I figured I was getting free rent for the Shelby and free rent with you and Coach. So it was the right thing to do. She's turned out to be a great employee. If you sweep back into town and let her go, I will be so disappointed in you."

On Tuesday afternoon, six days after her return, Momma
stood in the Knit & Stitch cutting slices from the big sheet
cake she'd baked with the words "Bon Voyage Charlotte"
scrawled across the top in blue icing.

She handed a slice of cake to Jane Rhodes, who was
one of several Knit & Stitch customers who'd shown up
for this week's Purly Girl meeting, even though they
weren't officially members of the knitting club.

Everyone was dying to get the straight skinny on the
state of Momma's marriage. Not to mention the fact that
the knitters of Last Chance had all volunteered to knit
Chemo Caps. And everyone wanted to say good-bye to
Miz Charlotte.

Molly was really glad Jane had come. She'd brought
little Pete with her, and the baby was getting fat and adorable. He wasn't nearly so wobbly as he'd been the first
time Molly held him. And this time, instead of immediately going to sleep, he'd given her a couple of big smiles.
His eyes were changing color from dark blue to brown.

And he was starting to look a lot like Jane. Molly had given up her knitting to hold him. And Jane didn't seem to mind one bit.

"I have never been to California," Momma said as she sliced another piece of cake. "I hear it's very scenic, especially the northern part."

Charlotte didn't look up at Momma. She was completely focused on her knitting. "I don't want to visit California," she said. "I want to stay home."

"You do?" Momma said. "But there's a whole world out there just waiting for you. You'll see new things. I always wanted to get me one of those Airstream trailers and drive across the country and see the sights."

"I don't want to see any sights." Charlotte dropped her knitting and folded her arms across her chest. She looked more than sad; she looked a little scared.

"That Simon should be shot," Lola May whispered in Molly's ear. "The poor thing is being torn away from everything she knows and loves."

Molly wanted to come to Simon's defense, but it would have done nothing to help Simon's reputation. Everyone, except maybe Momma and Coach, was angry at him for taking Charlotte away from her friends and family. Momma and Coach were both kind of happy that he was leaving. Which was a depressing thought.

How could they both dislike him so much when he'd been the one to help bring her family back together? It made no sense.

Molly was solidly with the camp who thought he should stay. But that was a childish wish. Simon had been utterly honest with everyone. Even her. He had never intended to stay.

"Miriam, I have a question," Ricki said into the sudden lull in the conversation.

Miriam looked up from the knitting magazine she was perusing. Her big black eyes twinkled behind her upturned glasses. "Sure, honey, what is it?"

"Do you think dogs can match people up the way you do?"

"Well, sugar, I never thought about it, to tell you the truth. I mean when God has a plan, it usually works out in the end. And I figure dogs are close to God."

The look on Ricki's face was heartbreaking. "Oh."

"Honey," Miriam continued in a soothing tone, "the thing is, people are the ones who mess up when it comes to the Lord's plan. Not usually dogs."

The look on Ricki's face grew positively grim, and she gave Molly a little worried glance.

"Ricki," Molly said. "Don't look at me like that. I'm not interested in Les. I've told you this a dozen times."

Ricki's eyes grew round. "But everyone is saying that Miz Miriam—"

"You have to stop listening to everyone. You have to decide for yourself."

"But Muffin . . ."

"Ricki, get a grip," Miriam said. "I didn't ever say anything about Molly and Les. I've been quite plain about that to everyone. But do people listen? No, they don't. They get a notion in their heads and they run off like silly chickens."

"You didn't?" Molly was surprised. "But I was told you thought I was going to marry someone I've known forever."

"I never said any such thing. Savannah may have said

it. And I know it's confusing, but that's mostly Savannah's fault. I reckon she's kind of new at the whole match-finding thing."

"Wait, wait," Momma said. "Savannah is doing match-making now?"

"Well," Miriam sniffed, "she's got the sight, you know. And I'm teaching her. But the whole thing with Molly and Les was her doing."

"Thank you Miz Miriam," Molly said with a grin. She turned to Ricki. "See, there is no prior claim on Les. You can have him. And as for me, well, I. Am. Not. Getting. Married."

"Oh but you will…eventually. You may have to wait awhile," Miriam said with a smile. "And you're going to make a terrific mother."

Simon and Angel had packed up the canvases and stowed them in a U-Haul. They'd filled dozens of boxes. They'd taken a ton of crap to the Salvation Army. Everything was ready for their departure early tomorrow morning.

It was time to tell Molly good-bye.

Simon had been ruminating about this moment for several days. A part of him wanted to skulk out of town, like he'd done all those years ago. He'd been wounded then. And he still carried those scars. But they didn't hurt so much anymore.

And Miriam Randall was right. The biggest regrets in his life were the things he had chosen not to do or say, because he was scared to do them or say them. He would never regret the courage he'd found to give up med school and choose the life of his dreams. If he'd been afraid of speaking his mind, he would have ended up living his life half asleep. He'd made a choice. It had cost him dearly. But he would do it again.

And right now he wanted to see Molly one last time. He knew it would hurt. And he wasn't all that brave. But he also knew that if he didn't say good-bye he would regret it for years. They had been lovers for a single night, but before that they had been friends. She had unlocked something inside of him. And he was a better man for it.

So he strolled into the Knit & Stitch, ostensibly to collect his mother and Angel, but he'd come for one last glimpse of the little girl who'd given him the perfect season.

She was sitting on the couch at the front of the store, holding Jane Rhodes's baby in her arms. The child was fast asleep, and Molly looked so natural holding him. He knew down deep that Molly should have children of her own. She'd be a wonderful mother. She'd raise them to be courageous. She'd let them find their own way.

Molly looked up at him, and her mouth opened a little bit, and her cheeks pinked up. She looked down almost immediately in a vain attempt to hide the blush. It was hard to do, now that her hair was so short.

Was she embarrassed or attracted?

He didn't know.

It didn't matter.

Seeing her there with that baby in her arms reminded him of what he needed to do. It reminded him of the things that were not for him and never would be. He had avoided commitments like that for forty years. He would be an idiot to go longing after them now. He had no earthly idea if he could ever be a husband or a father. It was best not to even try. And certainly not to try with such a young person as Molly Canaday.

And besides, if he got down on his knee and spoke the things that had captured his heart these last few days, he'd only come between her and her parents and her brothers. He wasn't going to do that.

Coach didn't want him around. And who could blame the man. Molly deserved someone better and younger. Someone who wasn't so scared of that soft look in her eyes as she gazed down at that child.

"Simon," Miriam Randall said. "So, you're off to the West, then?"

"Tomorrow morning. I thought I'd stop by, collect Charlotte and Angel, and say good-bye to everyone. We'll be leaving early." He addressed this to the Purly Girls and the other women who had obviously come to give his mother a proper Last Chance send-off, complete with sheet cake and sweet iced tea.

Jane Rhodes hopped up from her place at the table. "I haven't really had a chance to thank you for what you did for me and Pete." She came at him, and before he knew it, he was getting a big, old southern hug.

"I didn't do anything. You did all the work." He gave her a little pat on the back.

"You need to give the baby a hug before you go," she said. And the next thing he knew Jane had taken her son from Molly's arms and was putting the baby right into his.

Pete was a lot heavier than the day he'd been born, and he seemed a great deal sturdier. It was incredible how quickly children grew.

The child gazed up at him. Innocent and new.

"Well I declare," Miriam said, "look at Simon smiling.

Charlotte, he's a good-looking man when he smiles like that."

Mother said nothing, of course. And a little part of Simon's heart broke.

"It's a shame you're leaving," Jane said. "Clay and I were thinking that you would make the perfect godfather for Pete. But we want someone who lives close by."

"Probably a wise choice," he said as he handed the baby back to his mother.

Jane turned toward Molly, who was looking down at her hands. "But, Molly, we did decide that we wanted you to be Pete's godmother."

Molly looked up with a combination of surprise and astonishment on her face.

"Good choice, Jane," Simon said, amused by Molly's discomfort.

"Uh, really? Me?" Molly said.

"Yes, you. Pete has really taken a shine to you. Every time I put him in your arms he relaxes and goes right to sleep. I think you may have some talents you don't even know about."

That was Jane Rhodes, the perpetual optimist. Except for that one moment when she had been in labor—when he'd seen the fear in her eyes. He was glad, suddenly, that he'd been there that day to catch the baby when he arrived. That he'd been able to reassure her that Pete was going to be okay.

"I see babysitting in your future, Molly," one of the Purly Girls said. "That should make you happy, Pat."

Pat grinned and nodded. "It does. It's about time Molly took an interest in babies."

Suddenly the estrogen level was more than Simon

could manage. Plus the shop was crowded and the things he wanted to say to Molly couldn't be said here.

But he sure as hell couldn't ask her out onto the sidewalk. They had only shared a fling. A one-nighter. A little fun between the sheets. He needed to wrap his head and his heart around that fact and move on.

So he turned his back on Molly and spoke to Angel. "We need to get going."

Angel let go of a long, dramatic sigh. "Ladies, I am sorry but the time has come for leaving. I just wanted to let you know how much I enjoyed being a member of the Purly Girls for the last few weeks. I will send postcards back from our drive across the country. And I will keep in touch on Ravelry.com." Angel gathered up his knitting and proceeded to hand out kisses and hugs with an abandon that Simon envied.

Simon turned back toward Molly, who was still sitting on the couch looking down at her hands.

"Good-bye, Molly," he said quietly.

She looked up, managing a smile that reminded him of the little girl she once had been. "Good-bye, Simon. Good luck with the Harrison commission."

He nodded. "Good luck with the Shelby."

And then it was time to go.

"Where's Muffin?" Ricki asked, her heart suddenly twisting in her chest.

"Well, shoot, I don't know," Pat said as she continued wrapping up the leftover cake. "I haven't seen her in a little bit."

It was almost six o'clock, and Shevon had picked up the Purly Girls shortly after Simon had come to collect

Charlotte and Angel. Molly had left to do some work on the Shelby. Now only Ricki, Miriam, and Pat remained at the Knit & Stitch.

Ricki searched the shop from front to back, the panic setting in. "What am I going to do? She's gone." She reached for her cell phone. "Maybe I should call Chief Easley and put in a missing persons report."

She started to dial, but Miriam stood up and plucked the phone from her hands. "No need for that."

"But—"

"Darlin', you need to sit down."

"Don't you care about Muffin?"

"She's fine. She escaped in Angel's knitting bag while Angel was giving out farewell kisses. Honestly, I hope that alpaca he bought for his cross-country knitting project isn't another sweater for that Rodrigo character. I think he'd be much better making Muffin a sweater."

"What?" Pat and Ricki said in unison.

"You heard what I said." Miriam managed one of her beatific smiles.

"That no-good, dog-stealing—"

"Now, Ricki, do not say something that you will ultimately regret. Muffin belongs with Angel. If he were staying a little longer, I might have been able to finesse this, but with him leaving so suddenly, I had to take matters into my own hands. I'm afraid I encouraged the dog to take a nap in that big, beautiful bag of his."

"What are you talking about?" Pat said.

"Sit, both of you. And quit looking at me like I'm one of the senile Purly Girls. I know exactly what I'm doing."

Pat and Ricki sat down. "I'm sure Angel is going to

discover Muffin soon and bring her back. And when he does, Ricki, you're going to give Muffin away."

"But I can't do that." Her voice sounded shrill even to her own ears.

"Of course you can."

"I'm not throwing her away. She's already been thrown away once. Do you have any idea how heartbreaking it is to be thrown away? How worthless it makes you feel? How lonely it is?" Her voice fractured along with her composure. She could no longer control her lower lip or her breathing. No matter how hard she swallowed, the big knot in her throat was growing bigger by the minute.

"Oh, honey," Pat said as she pulled her chair closer and gave Ricki a hug. Pat's hug was maternal. And warm. And safe. In the last couple of days, Ricki had come to realize that Pat was not going to fire her or let her go. It looked like Ricki had a permanent job at the Knit & Stitch.

Miriam moved her chair to Ricki's other side and took one of her hands. "Sugar, this is an intervention."

"An intervention?" She sniffled back her tears. She was not going to bawl like a baby.

"Yes, it is. And I'm telling you right now that giving Muffin to Angel is not the same as throwing her away. It's really more like Muffin is dumping you for someone else."

"What? But I've been—"

"I know you have. You took her to the vet, and you gave her a home, and you treated her well, but she fell for Angel. Almost the first time she ever saw him."

"But she's a dog, not a person."

"I know. But see, he needs her."

"He does?"

"Yes, ma'am. He needs her because, when he gets back to California, Muffin is going to make him brave enough to dump Rodrigo."

"She is?"

"Yes, ma'am. And he needs to dump Rodrigo so he can find his soulmate. And I'm pretty sure the Lord is going to send him a vet."

"Really?"

"I think so. So you see, letting Muffin go isn't like throwing her away."

"And besides," Pat said, "if you let her go with Angel, she'll get to ride in his Jeep all the way across the country. Can you think of a better adventure for a little dog?"

Ricki had to admit it sounded kind of fun.

"And here's the best part," Miriam said, leaning in. "You get to stay here and marry Les Hayes."

"Les?"

"That's right. I think the two of you are perfect together."

"But he was mean to Muffin. And he's too young for me. I mean, Randy dumped me for someone really young and—"

"Whoa, wait just one moment," Miriam said. "You are not too old for Les. Age has nothing to do with real love. And you and Les love each other, don't you? I think both of you have even said it out loud, haven't you?"

Ricki nodded.

"And as for Les being mean to Muffin, I'm thinking maybe Muffin was mean to him."

"How do you figure that?"

"Well, someone who knows animals really well stopped by the house a week ago all concerned about how mean Muffin was being to Les. Not the other way around."

"Who?"

"I'm sworn to secrecy, but let's just say that he's a real animal lover, and he could see plain as day that Muffin was unhappy and taking it out on Les."

"Oh."

"He told me he'd be on the lookout for another dog for y'all. One that likes both of you. You know dogs are like people. They can be mighty particular."

"I reckon."

"So I think you should give Angel a call, and then you should go find Les and make up."

Pat handed Ricki a tissue, and she blew her nose. "You're sure it's not like I'm just throwing a dog away? Or that Les is mean to animals? Because I don't want to be married to anyone who's mean to animals."

"Honey, folks have seen Les walking Muffin up and down Palmetto Avenue. And believe me, the sight of a man that big being dragged by a dog that small is not pretty. People are laughing at him, but he just keeps on trying, bless his heart. Because that's the way Les is. A more solid man, you'll never find.

"You need to get yourself a bigger dog, and one who doesn't like wearing fancy collars. The kind of dog Les wouldn't look silly trying to walk."

# CHAPTER
## 24

A few days after Simon and Angel left town, Molly looked up from the last bit of welding on the Shelby to find Les standing by the outside exit. He was wearing his coveralls, a Bill's Grease Pit hat, and a happy look in his sky blue eyes.

"Hey," he said.

Molly took off her welding mask. "Hey."

He strolled into her makeshift shop, his gaze trained on the Shelby. "You've been making a lot of progress, haven't you?"

"On the body. But I haven't done crap on the engine. And I'm not really set up for engine work here. I need a proper garage." She refrained from saying that she needed her partner back. With Simon gone, the Coca-Cola building had gotten lonely. The front room was empty. There wasn't any classical music blaring away. There wasn't anyone to heckle.

Or go swimming with.

She looked away, trying to hide the blush that suddenly

ran up her face. It was really funny how her whole body burned whenever she thought of Simon. She wondered how long that would last. She wondered if she would ever forget him. She wondered if this empty feeling in her heart was regret for pushing him away. And she even thought about Miriam Randall's forecast for her. Her great love was going to take his own sweet time arriving. So that could only mean she had a long, long time before real love found her.

And for some reason, she wanted to be found. She'd never really felt that way before. But something had changed.

And she sure hoped that real love wasn't anything like this yearning inside her for Simon. Real love wouldn't be this damn hard or this damn heart-wrenching.

"I've got some news. I thought you'd like to be the first to know," Les said, bringing her thoughts back to the moment at hand.

She lifted her gaze. He was grinning like the Cheshire Cat. He never could keep a secret.

"I hope it's good news."

"Ricki and I went to Georgia last night." He held up his left hand. There was a golden band around his third finger.

"You've gone and got married?"

"Yes," he said, grinning like an imp.

"Married? You and Ricki?"

"I'm afraid so."

"Jeez Louise. You've gone and struck me speechless." She sat cross-legged on the cool concrete floor.

"You speechless? Not ever gonna happen."

"Come here and tell me all about it. "

He strolled into the makeshift garage and sat down beside her. And she was immediately struck by the fact that something had changed in their relationship. Something, maybe, for the good. It felt as if they'd both grown up some in the last couple of months. She reached out and squeezed his hands. "I'm happy for you, Les. Really happy."

He nodded. "Mol, there's something I want to say to you, and then we'll never talk about it again. That night when I asked you to marry me, I didn't do it just because everyone thought Miriam Randall had picked me for you. The fact is that I do love you. I've loved you for a long time. But if I'd waited just a little bit, I would have realized that Ricki was always the one God meant for me. She spins my world. And you will always be my best friend. And I want to apologize for everything that's happened, including the fact that LeRoy fired you. I didn't know he was going to do that to you. But I should have walked away from that job the minute it happened. I didn't because I was angry with you, and being angry never did help any situation."

"Amen to that."

"I've also got some really great news. With a little help from Dash Randall and Simon Wolfe, everything is going to be fixed like it was before."

Molly wasn't sure she wanted things fixed like they were before. But she played it cool. "What are you talking about?"

"Dash Randall has bought Wolfe Ford. He signed the papers yesterday. He called me half an hour ago, and he's offered me my old job back. He wants to get the doors open as fast as possible so customers don't have to drive eighty miles to find warranty service. I talked to LeRoy, and he's willing to give you your job back. And Dash is more than happy to give us space in the dealership's garage to work on the Shelby. He told me that Simon made him promise to do that. He also said he probably would have done it anyway."

Wow. In one or two fell swoops, her life was almost back to normal. Not that normal felt that way anymore.

"If you're okay with it, Dash said we could move the Shelby tonight. Bubba's happy to help, and LeRoy said we could use his flatbed. And that means I can get to work on the engine, and you can get to work painting the thing."

She was happy. Really happy for Les. And for the Ford owners in Allenberg County. And it would be good to have a real job and not to be mooching off Momma and Coach. But it all seemed like kind of a letdown, somehow.

She got up off the floor and looked around at the old loading dock where she'd been working. "I wanted to put our business here," she said, emotions tumbling inside her and making it hard to breathe. Damn it all, her emotions had been on a runaway train for a week at least.

"I'm sorry about that. But there isn't anything we can do about it. I'm sure Lark Chaikin would be happy if she could get in here and start her renovations a little early. And maybe having a bunch of artists and crafters living in Last Chance would be good for the community. We'll find a space for our business. But we need to get the Shelby finished first."

"You still want to be my partner?" she asked.

He stood up and came to stand beside her. "Of course I do. But I would understand if you wanted to boot me to the curb. I've been a real jerk the last couple of months. I'm sorry."

"I forgive you," she said. And then she threw herself into his arms. It was a friendly hug. A brotherly hug. But it was really nice to be hugging on Les once again.


The denizens of the Feather Canyon Retirement Community were in the middle of celebrating July Fourth when Simon pulled Daddy's Taurus up the drive. The place was hung with red, white, and blue bunting while a raucous potato sack race was under way on the lawn.

None of the old folks were actually racing. They evidently had imported a bunch of children for that purpose.

All in all, the place was exactly as it had appeared in the online brochure. The community backed up against a mountain and was set in among tall western pines. It looked clean and tidy and quite patriotic today. It was only a fifteen-minute drive from Simon's mountaintop home, where he and Mother had spent last night after a two-week drive across the country.

The drive had been surprisingly easy, considering the distance and Simon's frame of mind. They'd stopped along the way a few times to take in some sights. But mostly, it had been long stretches of flat farmland with the satellite radio tuned to the classical music station.

Mother had enjoyed that. And she had her knitting to keep her occupied.

Thank God Angel knew something about knitting. He trailed behind them in his Jeep, with his new dog for company, and kept them both on track.

Somewhere in Nebraska, Mother started calling Simon by name, almost as if the farther she got from Last Chance, the harder she clung to the familiar. He didn't know whether to rejoice or feel guilty.

In truth, he didn't know what to feel. He was numb most of the time, confused, and lost in a yearning he had no words for. How could he be missing Last Chance? He'd been running from the place for so long. Or was this ache inside him just for Molly? Either way it didn't matter. The woman and the place were tangled up together.

And he'd been told, in no uncertain terms, that his presence in Last Chance was not welcomed. And clearly, the woman he yearned for was not for him. He needed to move on, as he'd done so effectively in the past.

"Well, Mother, we've made it home," he said as he turned off the engine.

She stared through the windshield at the old folks who seemed to be having one heck of a good time watching the kids race. "The race reminds me of the Watermelon Festival," she said. The longing in her voice matched the one in his heart. "I've never missed a Watermelon Festival. Did you know that?"

"No, I didn't," he said, the guilt spilling through him.

"I remember the time Stone Rhodes ran off with Sharon McKee."

"Mother, everyone remembers that."

She turned toward him, and her dark eyes seemed clear today. "Well, I'm glad I remember it. And I'm surprised you remember it at all."

"Stone was my classmate."

"I know." She looked down at her hands.

"We better get going—"

"Simon, I remember something else."

"What?"

"I remember what I said to you."

He froze, unable to speak.

"I shouldn't have said what I said. I didn't really mean it. I was just upset. I thought you would argue with me instead of just walking away."

"I'm not like Daddy. I don't enjoy arguing. I'd made up my mind, and no amount of yelling at me was going to change things. As for what you said—in my head I knew you didn't mean it. It hurt, though. But I forgave you a long time ago."

She looked up, a frown on her face. "Then why did you stay away for so long? Did you hate me so much for that one ugly thing I said? I remember when you were little and we used to work in the garden together. You didn't hate me then."

He suddenly knew exactly how it felt to have his heart pierced by the sharpest arrow. He stared at his mother. She was still young looking and quite attractive. She held her shoulders straight, as always. She could still manage to keep herself looking well turned out. And on days like this, she seemed herself.

But days like this were rare. Most of the time she seemed confused and cloudy.

This might be the only time to say whatever nasty thing he'd been saving up for all these years.

But it didn't matter. What mattered was telling her the truth. And explaining that his biggest problem with becoming a doctor was his deep-seated fear of death.

"Mother," he said, "do you remember Luke Raintree?"

She nodded.

"Well, I was there when he died. I watched it happen. And it changed me."

"You were there?"

He nodded. And then he told her the rest of the story. By the end of it, tears were tracking down his cheeks.

And Mother's, too.

They sat in the car for another few minutes, saying nothing at all, until finally Mother pulled in a deep breath. "I wish you hadn't kept this a secret. I wish your daddy and I hadn't been arguing that night. I wish..." She paused for a long moment, looking down at her hands, toying with the wedding ring she still wore. "I know you won't believe this, but I loved your daddy with all my heart. We just liked to argue, is all. I miss arguing with him. Some people are like that. And I think maybe you might have been a happier child if you'd had a brother or sister. But I could only have you. I'm sorry."

He didn't feel as if he had to say anything in response. He'd gotten all the forgiveness he would get. He had to be satisfied with it or spend the rest of his life feeling resentful.

And he didn't want to live like that.

"Come on, let's get you moved in." He unbuckled his seat belt.

"I miss home," she said casting her gaze at the bunting-draped buildings. "This is a nice place. I can see that. But it will never be my home."

"It will if I'm here with you, Mother." He said the words, but somehow even he didn't fully believe them.


Dash Randall was holding the be-all and end-all of July Fourth celebrations under a tent out at his stables. He'd invited everyone from Randall Ford and was treating the crowd to beer and barbecue from the Red Hot Pig Place.

But Molly was having trouble eating it. Which was strange because she'd been eating barbecue from the Pig Place all her life.

She looked down at her plate and had to fight her gag reflex. The smell of it was enough to send her stomach into serious knots.

She furtively glanced at Les and Ricki, who were sitting at her table. Thank God they were too busy feeding each other hush puppies to pay her any attention. Beau and Allen were sitting beside her. Allen was scarfing down food like it was the end of the world.

Beau, who was bald and thin, looked at his plate and played with his food. Sort of like Molly. She was beginning to think that she ought to go see Doc Cooper. It was one thing to show solidarity with her little brother by cutting her hair and working on Chemo Caps. But it was quite another to be feeling nauseated all the time. She felt sorry for Beau, but really, did she need to go all the way and share his symptoms?

Especially on the Fourth of July?

In addition to the employees of Randall Ford, Dash had also invited the board of Angel Development; all the volunteers who helped out at Coach's summer camp; the members of the book club, who were Savannah's friends; and all the members of the Christ Church Ladies' Auxiliary.

So it was a big crowd. And Dash had promised fireworks and dancing.

Not that Molly felt like dancing.

In fact, she felt like crap. She'd been feeling like crap for days. And not just the fact that she missed Simon Wolfe. This was a physical thing.

Why should she feel this way when her life had returned to normal? She even had reason to be optimistic about Beau's chances for recovery. In September, he was going to have a bone marrow transplant.

So everything was fine. Except her stomach.

And her heart. Which was sort of broken. But that was her own fault. She should have known better.

Momma sat down at the table. "Aren't you going to eat anything?" she asked, eyeing Molly's plate. The fact that Momma had singled her out, and not Beau, was deeply distressing.

"I'm not that hungry."

Momma's gaze intensified, as if she were on the scent of something serious. When Momma got that look in her eye, it usually meant trouble. Molly didn't like being on the receiving end of a look like that.

"Did you eat any breakfast?"

She forced herself not to shrug or roll her eyes. Doing that would only make Momma mad. "I had some Cheerios."

"Uh-huh. Did you have milk on them?"

"No." She thought about lying, but lying wasn't her strong suit. Milk was another food that just didn't sit very well. Cheerios, on the other hand, were suddenly delicious. Along with peaches and plums, both abundant this time of year. It was kind of too bad that Dash didn't have any peaches or plums on the menu. She could eat a dozen of them.

Momma was really giving her the evil eye now.

"What?" Molly said.

"You and I need to have a talk," Momma said in her parental-command voice.

"Right now?"

"Right now." Momma stood up. And Molly knew there was no escape.

Shoot, she was in trouble, but she was having a hard time figuring out how. She decided not to cause a scene. She stood up. Momma took her by the arm and steered her all the way down to the corral.

When they got there, Momma turned, her gaze kind of somber. "Molly Ann Canaday, are you pregnant?"

Wow. That question was almost like being struck by lightning. So naturally she was utterly unable to think of a reasonable reply.

"Are you?" Momma had the funniest look in her eyes, all soft and dewy. She didn't seem angry about it.

"Uh," Molly said.

"You don't even know, do you?"

Well that was kind of pitiful. Really. How could she be pregnant and not know?

Crap. She and Simon had used condoms. How could she be pregnant *at all*?


"I'm going to get my shotgun and kill that man," Coach bellowed. A big, ugly, red vein had kind of popped out on his forehead. This was a warning sign that Coach's temper had reached a boiling point. Molly had seen Coach angry at game officials, and sometimes even at players, but she'd never had his full wrath aimed at her.

She was sitting at the kitchen table with Coach and Momma. It was two days after July Fourth, and her trip to Doc Cooper's this morning had confirmed what Momma had suspected.

Coach continued to glower.

"You can't take a shotgun on an airplane," Molly said. Right now sassing him seemed like the right thing to do. Because she was not going to have Coach hauling Simon back here. She was not going to be the victim of a shotgun wedding.

No way. No how. Not ever.

And also, she would be very sad if Coach killed Simon.

"Then I'll drive," Coach raged. "I'm not letting that no-account, sissy artist get off scot-free. He has an obligation to you."

"Daddy, you are not going to say one word to Simon Wolfe about anything. Do you understand me?"

"But—"

"I won't have it. If anything is said, I'll do the saying. And before you go off half cocked, stop and think for a minute. Simon refuses to live here in Last Chance, so if I marry him, I will have to live in California. Is that what you want?"

That stopped Coach dead in his tracks. His face began to pale. "I told him to get out of town."

"Of course you did. So did his father and mother. Why would he want to stay in a place where so many people were so disappointed in him?" Not to mention the guilt he was carrying about Luke Raintree, which Molly didn't raise because some secrets were worth keeping.

"She's got a point, doesn't she?" Momma said. She was sitting beside Molly knitting away on a baby sweater. She was embracing the whole grandmother thing with such equanimity, it was reassuring. She was so glad Momma had come home. Because even though Molly enjoyed playing with little Pete Rhodes, that was not the same as becoming someone's mother.

She was going to need lessons, and Momma would make a pretty good teacher.

Coach got up and started pacing. He was not taking this news well. And why would he? He'd gone way out of his way for years to scare away every eligible man except Les. And now Les was married to Ricki, who was an older, more experienced woman. And the father of Coach's grandchild had turned out not to be gay and was obviously not too old to become Molly's husband. It had always been hard for Daddy to admit when he'd made a mistake.

An awkward silence welled up in the kitchen as Momma knitted and Coach paced.

"Listen," Molly said into the silence. "Simon and I are not in love. And therefore we would not be happy together as husband and wife. I don't want to be in an unhappy marriage. So there aren't going to be any shotguns.

"And besides, if you make me marry him, then what's to become of the forecast that Miriam Randall gave me. She told me that one day my prince would arrive. I'd just have to wait for him. So I'm not going to do anything foolish. Is that clear?"

Coach stood there blinking at her as if this had also not occurred to him before this moment. He was a brilliant football coach, but when it came to stuff like this he was kind of slow on the uptake.

Momma looked up from her knitting. "Honey, are you sure you don't care for Simon at all?"

Momma had her X-ray-vision look on her face. But Molly wasn't going to give in on this. She missed Simon every day. But it would be worse to marry him, knowing that he didn't share her feelings. And she wasn't about to delude herself into believing that Simon wanted any part of this situation.

"I'm certain. I have no feelings for him," she lied.

"This has nothing to do with love," Coach said. "The father of that baby has a responsibility to support you."

"I can support myself. And after I sell the Shelby, I'll have a nice nest egg."

"Your father has a point, you know," Momma said.

Molly crossed her arms over her sore boobs and glared at her parents. "I can support myself," she repeated. Maybe they would believe it one day.

"Well, honey, not at the moment since you can't work at Bill's," Momma said, her needles clacking away.

"But Les is working on the Shelby's engine, and the body work is almost done. When we sell it in September, we're going to make a pile of money. And then the baby will be born, and I can get back to work starting my business. I'll be fine."

"What about Simon? Don't you think he deserves to know?" Momma didn't even look up from her knitting.

Crap. Momma had a point there. But then once she told him, he would get all noble on her and do something he didn't want to do. Like marry her and break her heart. And she didn't want to raise her kid in an unhappy marriage. Hadn't Simon been scarred by having his parents argue all the time?

All in all, it was best to keep him in the dark.

She pushed up from the table. "Here's the deal, the baby is certainly unexpected but I just can't think about him as being a mistake."

"I don't think the baby is a mistake," Momma said. "I just wish you weren't so set on doing this all by yourself."

"I'll manage. I'm a little scared, I guess. But I've been meditating about this, and I keep thinking about the baby being like little Pete. And, I don't know . . . I like Pete."

And that, right there, was one hell of a confession.

"But your mother is right. You shouldn't have to do this alone." Coach looked distraught.

"But I *want* to do it alone," she said, steel in her voice. "And I am completely capable of doing this on my own. I'm much stronger than either of you thinks."

# CHAPTER
## 25

Rory Harrison was a big man with a full bushy beard, a red face, and an Ernest Hemingway look to him. When he walked into a room, he filled it up.

Simon's Paradise studio wasn't all that large—certainly not as big as the Coca-Cola building on Palmetto Avenue in Last Chance. Up until recently, his studio, with its redwood tongue-and-groove ceiling and its big windows overlooking the garden, had seemed perfect to Simon.

But not for the last six weeks.

And now, with Harrison standing in the middle of it, his gaze riveted to the painting leaning up against the wall, it seemed about the size of a shoe box.

Simon knew better than to say a thing. He was vaguely aware of Angel standing to one side radiating uncertainty and disquiet like a sonar boom.

Harrison continued to stare at the painting. After about five excruciating minutes, he finally asked, "Who's the girl?"

"A friend from home," Simon said. Of course it wasn't nearly enough of an explanation. But Harrison didn't need to know the details of Simon's broken heart.

Simon pulled in a big breath. "Rory, I know Gillian told you I would paint you a—"

Harrison held up his hand. "Where is this place?"

"It's a public boat landing on the Edisto River in South Carolina." Simon crossed the room and picked up Lark Chaikin's coffee table book, *Rural Scenes*. He flipped through several pages until he found Lark's photographic interpretation of the same locale.

He handed it to Harrison, who glanced down at the photograph for a moment and then back at the painting.

"My God," Harrison said, "it's incredible."

"You like it?" Angel asked, and Simon wanted to drop-kick him like he'd kicked punts all those years ago.

Harrison laughed. He had a big, booming laugh. He walked forward and started flipping through a group of smaller canvases leaning against the wall. It was typical of him. He owned every space he occupied. He respected no one's privacy.

He regarded each painting until he got to the middle of the stack. He stopped and pulled out another, much smaller painting. He regarded it while more tense and silent minutes passed.

"She's beautiful," he finally said. "And this one is the masterpiece." He gazed at the larger canvas. "I like that one, too. But this one..."

Harrison held the small canvas out at arm's length.

The piece had been started in South Carolina. In fact, it was the piece he'd been working on the day Coach had told him that he needed to leave Last Chance and never come back again. He'd followed orders, the way he always had when Coach barked them at him. He'd done the same thing with Daddy. And with Mother, too.

And then he'd come all these miles and painted Last Chance into every canvas he'd worked on. He was homesick. After eighteen damn years of running away from that place, he was never, ever going to get it out of his heart.

And he was never going to get Molly out of it either.

But he hadn't realized the truth of it all. Not until he finished that piece. Not until he'd painted so many others. Not until he'd finally finished Harrison's commission—on his own terms, not the ones Gillian had negotiated.

Harrison looked up from the painting. His smile was as big as he was. "I know this is too small for the space in my great room. But I want it. In my bedroom, I think."

"That one isn't for sale," Simon said.

Harrison tipped back his head and laughed like a man who knew how to laugh. "I'm not surprised. You say this woman is a friend from home?"

Simon turned his gaze toward the little garden outside his window. "Yes."

"Simon, your cityscapes were fabulous, but these are amazing. I guess getting back to the South unlocked something."

"I guess it did," Simon replied, looking back, meeting Rory's gaze. "So you're not disappointed that I haven't painted you a desert?"

"No, I'm not disappointed. In fact, I look at that scene and I want to take off my shoes and go fishing." He chuckled. "Or better yet, maybe shuck my clothes altogether and go skinny-dipping. With that girl."

"Yeah." Simon had trouble breathing. He'd done nothing but think about that day down at the river when they had gone swimming together. When they'd told each other a big passel of lies. He'd painted that moment so he could return to it. So maybe he could, at least in his mind, get a second chance to say something altogether different.

Harrison handed Simon the smaller canvas. "If you change your mind about this one, let me know. You could probably name your price." He turned and looked at the other canvases, the result of a six-week painting frenzy that had seized him.

"I want to do a show," Rory said. "We'll make the big one the centerpiece. And then I'll have it installed at my house. These are fabulous. People are going to want these."

He turned toward Angel. "I'll have Rudy at the gallery get in touch with you, and we'll work out the arrangements." Harrison sailed out the door like a man who owned the world.

"*Gracias a Dios*," Angel said, sagging against the wall. "I have been losing sleep all week. They are good paintings, Simon, but I did not know whether Mr. Harrison would see the truth in them."

"Well, I think we're about to celebrate a big payday."

"And just in time, because the rent is due at the retirement community."

Simon turned and put the smaller canvas up on his easel. He'd been doing that a lot lately. The composition hadn't been painted from life. But from memory and fantasy mixed together.

"Why are you doing this to yourself?" Angel asked.

"Doing what?"

"Torturing yourself. And your mama. Simon, you need to go home."

He didn't even bother to tell Angel that this was his home. Because every time he looked at these canvases or Lark Chaikin's book, he knew damn well it was a lie.

Molly had changed him. Or maybe she'd just scraped away the crap that had settled into his head and his heart—all that stuff that had made him miss the important things.

"Boss?"

"Yeah."

"If you go back, can I come with you?"

Simon turned from the painting. "You want to go live in South Carolina?"

Angel shrugged. "I liked it there."

"But it's not the most tolerant place in the world."

"I know. But I am very fond of your mama. And I liked the Purly Girls. And now that I've gotten rid of Rodrigo it makes me sad to be living here. Too many bad memories. And Muffin would like to go home, too, I think."

"So you want to run away?"

"I do.

"And you think I should go home?"

"I do."

Simon stared at the painting. "I want to go. But what happens if I return and she won't have me? I'm too old for her. She's so young. And she may say that she doesn't want a family, but I think that's bravado. I'm too old to be anyone's father. Can you imagine me teaching a kid how to kick a football?"

"No, but I can see you working in the garden with one." He grinned.

"I can't give her what she deserves. Not to mention the fact that her daddy promised to run me out of town if I ever returned."

"Simon, when are you going to stand up to that anger?"

"What anger?"

"The anger you still feel toward your father. I think you and your mama have made a lot of progress. But I think it was your father who hurt you the most. He wanted you to be something you weren't. He yelled at you when you failed. And all that anger did something to you inside."

"How do you know this?"

"I am your mama's friend. She does not remember things from day to day, but she talks about you, as she remembers you, all the time. She has many regrets. She thinks she should have fought harder for you when your father started screaming or insisting that you should play sports."

"Well, she's conveniently forgotten that she wanted me to be a doctor. And I followed her wishes for years. Until I realized that I couldn't do it. And when I defied her, she was just as angry as my father. I told them what I wanted in my life, and they pushed me away."

"So is this why you are so afraid to tell Molly what you want?"

Simon glanced at the portrait on his easel. Angel was talking sense. Nothing would be right if he couldn't have Molly in his life. The truth was, he was scared to death that she'd say no. But running away was never a good option. Hadn't he told Pat that?

He needed to take charge of his heart and his feelings.

"How do I do this, Angel?"

"Why don't you send her the painting? Or better yet, take it to her. I think she will realize that your heart has changed once she sees what you have done. And then you tell her that you've fallen in love with her and let nature do the rest."

Molly finished packing up the last afghan. Tomorrow morning, Momma, Ricki, and she would haul all these knitted items down to the Knit & Stitch's booth at the annual Allenberg County Watermelon Festival. Most of the items had been knitted by members of the Purly Girls. There were prayer blankets, hats, scarves, and a few pairs of gloves. All the proceeds from the sale would be going to St. Jude Children's Hospital. Along with a big shipment of Chemo Caps that had been knitted by virtually every knitter in Last Chance.

Those hats had come to symbolize the reason she loved living here, even if everyone was all up in her business, especially now that she was an unwed mother. People cared about each other in Last Chance.

She taped up the box and sat down at the kitchen table. The nausea was still bad sometimes, but the nagging fatigue of pregnancy annoyed her more. Doc Cooper promised she'd start feeling better in a month or two— about the time she started to swell up. How that was possible remained a mystery.

She rested her head in her hands and fought against the sudden lonesomeness that stole over her. She figured her confused hormones were to blame for these blue moments and for the times she sometimes cried herself to sleep.

Quietly.

Of course she didn't have a tissue. She never did. So she ran the back of her hand over her suddenly damp cheeks. And that triggered the memory of Simon handing her his handkerchief. Oddly, the memory didn't bring more tears to her eyes.

She sat there for a long time, alone, thinking of Simon. Momma was up in Columbia with Beau and Allen today for a consultation with Beau's doctors. Coach was at summer camp.

So she was free to indulge herself while a long, slow roll of thunder sounded beyond the kitchen window. The sky had gone black and blue with dark clouds. It was late afternoon—prime time for summer thunderstorms.

The rain was just starting when there came a sudden, sharp knock at the front door.

She hurried from the kitchen and opened the door only to find no one there, just a flat parcel wrapped in brown paper and tied in twine. Her name was written on the paper in block letters. Her heart started to pound as she picked up the object. She knew immediately that it was a canvas, even without unwrapping it.

The twine was so tightly tied that she had to carry the painting into the kitchen and cut away the wrappings.

What she found took her breath away. It was a painting only Simon would have painted. He had captured that moment just after she'd dived into the freezing water of the Edisto. It showed her with her long hair slicked back, water droplets on her eyelashes, her eyes a strange reflection of the verdant background and the iced-tea-colored water. He captured a sultry smile and the freckles on her shoulders that she hated.

Good God, he'd made her look beautiful. And womanly.

It wasn't really her. It was some extra-special, pumped-up, idealized version. But she couldn't tear her gaze away from it.

More stupid tears filled up her eyes until the image blurred. And then it occurred to her that someone had delivered this painting. It didn't just spontaneously arrive at her front door.

She flew to the closet and grabbed Coach's big gold and white Georgia Tech golf umbrella. Then she headed out into the thunderstorm like a complete fool.

She would have jumped in her Charger, but Momma had taken it up to Columbia, and Beau's car was in for a tune-up. So she was carless, which she hated.

She had no choice but to run up the street toward the intersection with Dogwood Avenue. If Simon had come from his mother's house, then he would have walked from Cypress to Calhoun to Dogwood to James.

She hit the corner at a dead run, the skies opening up. Her sneakers were drowned in the runoff, a stitch was starting to burn in her side, and a wild sense of elation, mixed with complete fear, had taken hold of her.

She turned the corner and saw him.

Like a true Californian, Simon had neglected to bring an umbrella. He trudged up the street with his hands jammed in the pockets of his dark pants, the collar of his gray sports jacket turned up against his neck. His water-logged hair clung to the back of his head, and he was look-ing down at the pavement, his shoulders hunched against the downpour.

"Simon," she called, her thin voice battling with the roll of thunder. She sprinted toward him. "Simon."

He turned and stood stock-still as she raced toward him, her heart taking flight.

She wanted to throw herself into his arms, but there was something cool and reserved about his stance.

She slowed her pace as she reached him, fighting the urge to wrap him in her arms and blurt out her news.

Instead she angled the umbrella so that it sheltered them both.

"Simon," she said, investing his name with all the feelings she'd been hoarding the last few weeks. "The painting...It's beautiful. Thank you for not even showing my big butt."

Predictably, the corners of his mouth curled, just so, like a pair of apostrophes. But his cool reserve remained, while the rain beat against the shelter of their umbrella.

"You made me look beautiful. Prettier than I am."

"Oh, no," he finally said. "No, Molly, that's the way you look. At least it's the way you look to my heart."

A good kind of dizziness assailed her. The kind of dizziness they talked about in love songs. "It's so good to see you. Why are you here? Why did you leave the painting and not stay until I opened the door?"

There was a world of emotion in his eyes. "I...Well, I was at the hardware store, getting the twine, and Clay Rhodes told me your incredible news. A baby? Well, that's surprising. I guess you and Les finally figured it out, huh?"

"Oh, no. No. Les is with Ricki. He married her, actually. They ran off to Georgia and surprised us all. No, Les is not about to become anyone's daddy."

The funniest look stole over Simon's features. "Molly." Her name seemed to be all he was able to say.

"Why did you come back?" she asked, hoping the question would prod him into saying something. Anything. Because talking about being pregnant was the last thing she wanted to do. Especially after he'd given her that hopelessly romantic painting.

Her worst fears were materializing right in front of her.

"I... Well, I thought if I gave you the painting you'd..." He paused, seemingly unable to go on. His eyes looked sad and confused. He'd always worn his feelings right there for the world to read.

"That I'd what?" she asked.

"Molly, I know this is going to sound very strange coming from me. After all the nonsense I spouted that afternoon down by the river. But, well, the truth is Miriam Randall is a very wise woman. She told me that someone would change my mind. She also told me that it's the stuff you don't do that you regret the most. And she was right about that. I should have come home a long time ago."

"Home?"

"Here." He reached and put his beautiful artist hands over her heart. "Home."

Molly didn't know whether to laugh or cry. She wanted to throw herself into his arms. But of course she couldn't. He wasn't going to stay once he figured it all out.

"You want to stay?" she asked, letting all her fear show through.

"If you'll have me."

"Oh, crap." She was really feeling dizzy now.

The corner of his mouth curled. "That wasn't exactly the response I was looking for."

"No, I mean yes. Yes, yes, yes, yes. I'll have you. Forever, please. Oh God, this is terrible."

"Terrible?"

Her throat started to close, but she forced it to open. "The thing is, that stuff you heard in town? About the baby. It's not a mistake. I mean it was a mistake but it's not. I mean..."

"It's my baby, isn't it?" he asked. He seemed so incredibly calm about the news.

She started to really babble then. "I know I should have called you weeks ago. I know that. But...I..." She took a deep, deep breath. "Simon, I don't want you to feel like you have to marry me. I'm perfectly capable of managing all on my own. And I know you don't want to—"

He put his fingers over her lips. "Being a parent scares me to death. But if you think for one minute that I'm running away from you because of this, you're crazy. And don't get any ideas that I would want to be with you only because of this situation. That's not true either.

"Molly, I love you. And I guess the unexpected is about to happen, and I'm going to become someone's parent. But if you don't want me in your life. If you..."

He sounded so uncertain. And that astounded her until she realized that she had never told him how she felt about him. She'd gone to great lengths to hide those feelings.

"Oh, my God, don't you know? I fell in love with you the minute I danced with you at Dash and Savannah's wedding. But of course, I wasn't about to admit that to you. I thought you would run away if I told you."

"Well, I'm not running now." He reached out and caressed her cheek. His hand was warm despite the cold deluge that was threatening to wash them away. "Molly."

The sound of her name on his lips was like a blessing. "Will you have me?"

"Yes," she whispered back.

And then he kissed her, while the rain beat down on Coach's Georgia Tech umbrella.

# SIMPLE RIBBED STOCKING CAP

This pattern makes a simple ribbed stocking cap with a circumference of 21 inches. As shown it's a short hat, for a variation you can knit the cap an extra 3 inches in length and have a turned up edge.

## MATERIALS

Yarn: Red Heart acrylic wool, worsted weight.
Needles: 16-inch size US8 circular needles; size US8 double-pointed needles

## GAUGE

16 sts x 24 rows = 4 inches in stockinet stitch on size US8 needles

## ABBREVIATIONS

K—knit the stitch
P—purl the stitch
K2tog—knit two stitches together

## PATTERN

Ribbed pattern: *K1, P1* repeat from * to * to the end of the round.

## Instructions

Cast on 84 stitches onto circular needles.

Join the round and place a marker.

Start knitting rounds using the ribbed pattern. Work even until the piece measures 6.5 inches. (For a longer hat, knit to your desired size.)

## Shaping the crown

You can start shaping the crown on the circular needles, but at some point the work will become too small for the circulars and you'll need to switch to the double-pointed needles.

**Round 1:** *K1, P1, K1, P1, K2tog*. Repeat from * to * to the end of the round.

**Round 2:** K1, P1, K1, P1, *K2, P1, K1, P1*. Repeat from * to * until the last stitch in the round, K1.

**Round 3:** *K1, P1, K1, K2tog*. Repeat from * to * to the end of the round.

**Round 4:** K1, P1, *K3, P1*. Repeat from * to * until the last 2 stitches in the round. K2.

**Round 5:** *K1, P1, K2tog*. Repeat from * to * to the end of the round.

**Round 6:** K1, P1, *K2, P* Repeat from * to * until the last stitch in the round. K1.

**Round 7:** *K1, K2tog*. Repeat from * to * until the end of the round.

**Round 8:** Knit for the entire round.

**Round 9:** K2tog for the entire round.

**Round 10:** Knit for the entire round.

**Round 11:** K2tog for the entire round.

You should have 6 stitches remaining on the needles.

Cut your yarn, leaving a six inch tail. Using a tapestry needle thread the end of the yarn back through the loops of the remaining stitches and draw tight to close the top of the hat. Weave in the yarn ends.

# READING GROUP GUIDE

## Discussion Questions for
## *Last Chance Knit & Stitch*

1. *Last Chance Knit & Stitch* shares some important themes with *Little Women*, especially with respect to a woman's role in society. How do the books compare in their portrayal of the conflict women feel between familial duty and personal growth? How do the books compare in their treatment of gender stereotypes?

2. Both *Last Chance Knit & Stitch* and *Little Women* end with the hero and heroine under an umbrella. In one book, the hero is holding the umbrella and in the other the heroine does the honors. Do you think that matters? Which book, in your opinion, has the more satisfying ending? Why do you feel that way?

3. Both Simon's and Molly's parents had expectations of them that were not realistic. Discuss how Simon and Molly handled their parents' expectations. Do you

think their strategies were good ones? Did your own parents have expectations of you that you couldn't fulfill? Do you have expectations of your own children that may not be realistic? What about the parents in *Little Women*? How did Mr. and Mrs. March handle the conflict between what they wanted for their children and their children's personal fulfillment?

4. Learning to deal with anger is an important theme in the book. How is anger a destructive force in Simon's life? Is there any time in the book when Simon uses his anger as a positive force? Do you think he would be as good at harnessing the positive aspects of anger, if he had not also experienced anger's darker side? Do you think Molly's anger was a positive or negative force for her?

5. Scattered throughout the novel are several scenes that mirror *Little Women*. Can you find them? Email your answers to hope@hoperamsay.com for prizes and swag.

6. How is Leslie Hayes similar to Theodore Laurence? How are they different? Are there times in *Last Chance Knit & Stitch* when Simon is more like Laurie? How is Simon similar to Professor Bhaer?

7. At one point in the book Miz Miriam postulates that dogs are closer to God than human beings. Do you agree with this idea? If so, why? And if you don't, why not?

8. Muffin doesn't like Les, but the book is silent about why. Do you have any theories? Do you think Ricki

was right when she made Les work so hard to make friends with the dog? Has a pet ever come between you and your significant other? How did that situation work out?

9. Both Ricki and Les and Molly and Simon were couples dealing with age differences. Do you think age should be a disqualifying factor in seeking someone to love? Why do you think modern society frowns on romances between couples of different ages, while it was often the case that younger women married much older men in the 1800s, when *Little Women* was written? Do you think there are gender stereotypes when it comes to May-December romance?

Jenny Carpenter believes that the way
to a man's heart is through his stomach.

Will famous author Gabe Raintree find
her award-winning pies delectable?

Please turn this page for a preview of

*Inn at Last Chance.*

# CHAPTER 1

The bitter January wind had blown in a cold front. The clouds hung heavy and somber over the swamp. There would be rain. Possibly ice.

Jenny Carpenter wrapped a hand-knit shawl around her shoulders and gazed through the window above the kitchen sink of the house she'd bought last August. The tops of the Carolina pines bent in the wind. The weatherman said it was going to be quite a storm, and Allenberg County had already had one ice storm this year—on Christmas Eve. It was just four days past New Year's Day.

She turned away from the window toward the heart of her almost-restored house. Her kitchen restoration was almost finished. Yellow subway tiles marched up the backsplash behind the Vulcan stove, an antique pie safe occupied the far wall. The curtains were gingham. Eveything about this room was bright and cheerful, in sharp contrast to the weather outside.

She closed her eyes and imagined the smell of apple pie cooking in her professional baker's oven. This kitchen would rival the one Savannah Randall had installed at the old movie theater in town. She smiled. Savannah's strudel was good, but Jenny's apple pie had still won the blue ribbon at the Watermelon Festival last summer.

She could almost hear Mother sermonizing about pride, and her smile faded. She turned back toward the window.

Jenny hated the winter. She hated the cold. And despite her excitement about the kitchen, winter was getting the best of her.

The crew she'd hired to cut back the overgrowth on either side of the driveway had called to say that they wouldn't be out today, and probably not tomorrow. The movers weren't going to show up today either, which meant Mother's antique furniture would spend yet another night in the commercial storage space where it had been sitting for five years. And Gladys Smith, the leader of the Methodist Women's Sewing Club, had called five minutes ago all a-twitter because there was ice in the forecast.

The Sewing Club had graciously volunteered to help Jenny sew curtains for the bedrooms and sitting room. The fabric bolts—all traditional low country floral designs—were stacked in the room that would soon be the dining room. But, as Gladys pointed out, the gals were not coming all the way out to the swamp on an icy day in January. So tomorrow Jenny might be the only one sitting out here sewing.

It wasn't just the weather. She knew that she'd taken a huge risk buying the Jonquil House. The old place wasn't anywhere near downtown. If she'd been able to buy Charlotte Wolfe's house, her bed and breakfast would have been located near the middle of things. And she would probably already be in business, since Charlotte's house was in perfect condition.

But Charlotte had changed her mind about selling.

So Jenny had bought the Jonquil House. Even if it wasn't downtown.

The house was near the public boat launch on the Edisto River. There were some really good fishing and hunting spots right outside the front door. And you couldn't beat the view from the porch on a summer's day. She hoped to attract business from hunters and fishermen and eco tourists anxious to canoe the Edisto or bird watch in the swamp.

The Jonquil House had the additional benefit of being dirt cheap, since it had been abandoned for years. But Jenny had to spend a lot of cash to shore up the foundation, replace the roof, and update the plumbing and electrical. Not to mention installing her state-of-the-art kitchen. Still, the purchase price had been so ridiculously low that on balance, Jenny was financially ahead of where she would have been if she'd bought Charlotte's house.

If all went well, the Jonquil House would be open for business by March first, just in time for the jonquils to be in full bloom. There were hundreds of jonquils naturalized in the woods surrounding the house. No doubt they had been planted by the Raintree family, who had built the house more than a hundred years ago as a hunting camp and summer getaway.

Those jonquils were the reason she'd chosen yellow for her kitchen walls. She couldn't wait to take pictures of her beautiful white house against the backdrop of the dark Carolina woods, gray Spanish moss, and bright yellow daffodils. That photo would be posted right on the home page of the inn's website, which was still under construction too.

She was thinking about her breakfast menu when there came a sudden pounding at her front door. Her new brass knocker had yet to be installed, but that didn't seem to bother whoever had come to call.

In fact it sounded like someone was trying to knock the darn door down.

She hurried down the center hall, enjoying the rich patina of the restored wood floors and the simple country feeling of the white lath walls. Maybe the movers had changed their minds and she'd be able to get Mother's furniture set up in the bedrooms, after all. Then she'd know what additional pieces she needed. A shopping trip to Charleston had already been scheduled for early February.

She pulled open the door.

"It's about damn time; it's freezing out here." A man wearing a rain-spattered, leather jacket, a soggy gray wool hat, and a steely scowl attempted to walk into her hallway. Jenny wasn't about to let this biker dude intimidate her even if he was a head taller than she was.

His features were stern, his nose just a tad broad, as if it had been broken once. Several days' growth shadowed his cheeks, and his eyebrows glowered just above eyes so dark they might have been black. If he'd been handsome or heroic-looking, she might have been afraid of him or lost her nerve. Handsome men always made Jenny nervous. But big guys with leather jackets and attitudes had never bothered her in the least. She always assumed that men like that were hiding a few deep insecurities.

"Can I help you?" she said in her most polite future-innkeeper voice.

"You damn well can. I want a room."

"Um, I'm sorry but the Inn isn't open."

"Of course it's open. You're here. The lights are on. There's heat."

"We're not open for business."

He leaned into the door frame. Jenny held her ground. "Do you have any idea who I am?"

She was tempted to tell him he was an ass, but she didn't use language like that. Mother had beaten that tendency out of her. It didn't stop her from thinking it though.

When she didn't reply, he said. "I'm the man who sold you this house. I would like, very much, to come in out of the rain."

"The man who—"

"The name's Gabriel Raintree. My family built this house. Now let me in."

She studied his face. Gabriel Raintree was a *New York Times* bestselling author of at least twenty books, several of which had been made into blockbuster horror films. His books were not on her reading list. And she wasn't much of a movie-goer.

She'd never met Mr. Raintree. The sale of the Jonquil House had been undertaken by his business manager and attorney. So she had no idea if this guy was the real Gabriel Raintree or just some poser. Either way she wasn't going to let him come in. Besides, the house was not ready for guests. The furniture had not even arrived.

"I'm sorry, the Inn isn't open."

His black eyebrows lowered even further, and his mouth kind of curled up at the corner in something like a sneer. He looked angry, and it occurred to Jenny that maybe she needed to bend a little. The minute that thought crossed her mind, she rejected it. She had inherited a steel backbone from Mother, and this was a good time to employ it. She wouldn't get very far as an innkeeper if she allowed herself to be a doormat.

"I need a place to stay," he said, "for at least three months. I'm behind on my deadline."

Three months. Good lord, she wasn't running a boarding house. But then, she supposed that if anyone could afford three months lodging at a B and B it would be someone like Gabriel Raintree.

The income would be nice. But she wasn't ready for any guests yet. And this guy, if he was Gabriel Raintree, would be a pain in the neck.

"I'm very sorry the Inn won't be open until March. If you need to stay in Last Chance, there's always the Peach Blossom Motor Court. Or you could see if Miriam Randall will take you in. She sometimes takes in boarders."

"Damnit all, woman, this is my house." He pushed against the door, and Jenny pushed back.

"Not anymore," she said.

Thankfully, he stopped pushing and stepped back from the threshold, a surprised frown folding down between his eyes. She didn't wait around to punctuate her point. She slammed the door on him. Then she twisted the bolt lock and took a couple of steps back from it, her heart hammering in her chest.

Gabe stood on the porch breathing hard. It seemed surreal to be back in Allenberg County. Decades had passed since he'd walked down the long driveway to the house. But not much had changed. He'd expected Zeph to be waiting on the porch with a rifle across his knees. He'd expected Violet to open the door and invite him in for a piece of her cornbread.

Instead, he'd come face-to-face with a tiny, birdlike woman who hadn't been very impressed by his name dropping. She'd stood there, framed in the doorway, and given him an intractable look that was as bewitching as it was grave.

His heart twisted in his chest. He was an idiot to come back here. There was a good reason the family had abandoned this place.

But then again, he needed to disappear for a while. He needed to get away from the crazy fans who haunted him wherever he went in Charleston.

So he'd come here to the middle of nowhere, knowing that the old family hunting lodge was being turned into a bed and breakfast. Coming out here to the middle of the swamp was a brilliant idea. It was peaceful here.

He stepped down off the porch, frustration tensing the muscles of his neck and shoulders. If the inn wasn't going to open until March he'd have to come up with another plan. The rain was picking up, and sleet was beginning to mix with it. The roads were going to get bad before too much longer.

He'd have to book a room at the Peach Blossom Motel. But tomorrow, when the storm had passed, he'd come back out here and negotiate. The little innkeeper had her price. Everyone did.

Tomorrow he'd buy the Jonquil House back.

# THE DISH

## Where Authors Give You the Inside Scoop

♥ ♥ ♥ ♥ ♥ ♥ ♥ ♥ ♥ ♥ ♥ ♥ ♥ ♥ ♥ ♥ ♥ ♥

*From the desk of Jennifer Haymore*

Dear Reader,

When Mrs. Emma Curtis, the heroine of THE ROGUE'S PROPOSAL, came to see me, I'd just finished writing *The Duchess Hunt*, the story of the Duke of Trent and his new wife, Sarah, who'd crossed the deep chasm from maid to duchess, and I was feeling very satisfied in their happily ever after.

Mrs. Curtis, however, had no interest in romance.

"I need you to write my story," she told me. "It's urgent."

I encouraged her to sit down and tell me more.

"I'm on a mission of vengeance," she began. "You see, I need to find my husband's murderer—"

I lifted my hand right away to stop her. "Mrs. Curtis, I don't think this is going to work out. You see, I don't write thrillers or mysteries. I am a romance writer."

"I know, but I think you can help me. I really do."

"How's that?"

"You've met the Duke of Trent, haven't you? And his brother, Lord Lukas?" She leaned forward, dark eyes serious and intent. "You see, I'm searching for the same man they are."

My brows rose. "Really? You're looking for Roger Morton?"

"Yes! Roger Morton is the man who murdered my husband. Please—Lord Lukas is here in Bristol. If you could only arrange an introduction . . . I know his lordship could help me to find him."

She was right—I did know Lord Lukas. In fact . . .

I looked over the dark-haired woman sitting in front of me. Mrs. Curtis was a young, beautiful widow. She seemed intelligent and focused.

My mind started working furiously.

Mrs. Curtis and Lord Luke? Could it work?

Maybe . . .

Luke would require a *lot* of effort. He was a rake of the first order, brash, undisciplined, prone to all manner of excess. But something told me that maybe, just maybe, Mrs. Curtis would be a good influence on him . . . If I could join them on the mission to find Roger Morton, it just might work out.

(I am a *romance* writer, after all.)

"Are you *sure* you want to meet Lord Lukas?" I asked her. "Have you heard the rumors about him?"

Her lips firmed. "I have heard he is a rake." Her eyes met mine, steady and serious. "I can manage rakes."

There was a steel behind her voice. A steel I approved of. *Yes.* This could work.

My lips curved into a smile. "All right, Mrs. Curtis. I might be able to manage an introduction . . ."

And that was how I arranged the first meeting between Emma Curtis and Lord Lukas Hawkins, the second brother of the House of Trent. Their relationship proved to be a rocky one—I wasn't joking when I said Luke was a rake, and in fact, "rake" might be too mild a term. But Emma proved to be a worthy adversary for him, and they ended up traveling a dangerous and emotional but ultimately sweetly satisfying path in THE ROGUE'S PROPOSAL.

Come visit me at my website, www.jenniferhaymore .com, where you can share your thoughts about my books, sign up for some fun freebies and contests, and read more about THE ROGUE'S PROPOSAL and the House of Trent Series. I'd also love to see you on Twitter (@ jenniferhaymore) or on Facebook (www.facebook.com/ jenniferhaymore-author).

Sincerely,

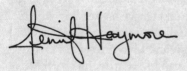

♥ ♥ ♥ ♥ ♥ ♥ ♥ ♥ ♥ ♥ ♥ ♥ ♥ ♥ ♥ ♥

*From the desk of Hope Ramsay*

Dear Reader,

My mother was a prodigious knitter. If she was watching TV or traveling in the car or just relaxing, she would always have a pair of knitting needles in her hand. So, of course, she needed a steady supply of yarn.

We lived in a medium-sized town on Long Island. It had a downtown area not too far from the train station, and tucked in between an interior design place and a quick lunch stand was a yarn shop.

I vividly remember that wonderful place. Floor-to-ceiling shelves occupied the wall space. The cubbies were filled with yarn of amazing hues and cardboard boxes of incredibly beautiful buttons. The place had a few cozy chairs and a table strewn with knitting magazines.

Mom visited that yarn store a lot. She would take her knitting with her sometimes, especially if she was having trouble with a pattern. There was a woman there—I don't remember her name—but I do remember the half-moon glasses that rode her neck on a chain. She was a yarn whiz, and Mom consulted her often. Women gathered there to knit and talk. And little girls tagged along and learned how to knit on big, plastic needles.

I went back in my mind to that old yarn store when I created the Knit & Stitch, and I have to say that writing about it was almost like spending a little time with Mom, even though she's no longer with us. There is something truly wonderful about a circle of women sharing stories while making garments out of luxurious yarn.

I remember some of the yarn Mom bought at that yarn store, too, especially the brown and baby blue tweed alpaca that became a cable knit cardigan. I wore that sweater all through high school until the elbows became threadbare. Wearing it was like being wrapped up in Mom's arms.

There is nothing like the love a knitter puts into a garment. And writing about women who knit proved to be equally joyful for me. I hope you enjoy spending some time with the girls at the Knit & Stitch. They are a great bunch of warm-hearted knitters.

*Hope Ramsay*

♥ ♥ ♥ ♥ ♥ ♥ ♥ ♥ ♥ ♥ ♥ ♥ ♥ ♥

## From the desk of Erin Kern

Dear Reader,

So here we are. Back in Trouble, Wyoming, catching up with those crazy McDermotts. In case you didn't know, these men have a way of sending the ladies of Trouble all into a tizzy by just existing. At the same time there was a collective breaking of hearts when the two older McDermotts, Noah and Chase, surreptitiously removed themselves from the dating scene by getting married.

But what about the other McDermott brother, you ask? Brody is special in many ways, but no less harrowing on those predictable female hormones. And, even though Brody has sworn off dating for good, that doesn't mean he doesn't have it coming. The love bug, I mean. And he gets bitten, big time. Sorry, ladies. But this dark-haired heartbreaker with the piercing gray eyes is about to fall hard.

Happy Reading!

*Erin Kern*

♥ ♥ ♥ ♥ ♥ ♥ ♥ ♥ ♥ ♥ ♥ ♥ ♥ ♥

## From the desk of Mimi Jean Pamfiloff

Dear Reader,

"If you love her, set her free. If she comes back, she's yours. If she doesn't…Christ! Stubborn woman! Hunt her down, and bring her the hell back; she's still yours according to vampire law."

Niccolo DiConti, General of the
Vampire Queen's Army

I always like to believe that the universe has an all-knowing, all-seeing heart filled with the wisdom to grant us not what we want, but that which we need most. Does that mean the universe will simply pop that special something into a box and leave it on your doorstep? Hell no. And if you're Niccolo DiConti, the universe might be planning a very, very long, excruciating obstacle course before handing out any prizes. That is, if he and his over-bloated, vampire ego survive.

Meet Helena Strauss, the obstacle course. According to the infamous prophet and Goddess of the Underworld, Cimil, Niccolo need only to seduce this mortal into being his willing, eternal bride and Niccolo's every wish will be granted. Thank the gods he's the most legendary warrior known to vampire, with equally legendary looks. Seducing a female is hardly a challenge worthy of such greatness.

Famous last words. Because Helena Strauss has no interest in giving up long, sunny days at the beach or exchanging her happy life to be with this dark, arrogant, deadly male.

Mimi

## From the desk of Jessica Lemmon

Dear Reader,

Imagine you're heartbroken. Crying. Literally *into* your drink at a noisy nightclub your best friend has dragged you to. Just as you are lamenting your very bad decision to come out tonight, someone approaches. A tall, handsome someone with a tumble of dark hair, expressive amber eyes, and perfectly contoured lips. Oh, *and* he's rich. Not just plain old rich, but rich of the *filthy, stinking* variety. This is exactly the situation Crickitt Day, the heroine of TEMPTING THE BILLIONAIRE, finds herself in one not-so-fine evening. Oh, to be so lucky!

I may have given the characters of TEMPTING THE BILLIONAIRE a fairy-tale/fantasy set-up, but I still wanted them rooted and realistic. Particularly my hero. It's why you'll find Shane August a bit of a departure from your typical literary billionaire. Shane visits clients personally, does his own dishes, makes his own coffee. And—get ready for it—bakes his own cookies.

*Hero tip: Want to win over a woman? Bake her cookies.*

The recipe for these mysterious and amazing bits of heavenly goodness can be traced back to a cookbook by Erin McKenna, creator of the NYC-based bakery Babycakes. What makes the recipes so special, you ask? They use *coconut oil* instead of vegetable oil or butter. The result is an amazingly moist, melt-in-your-mouth, can't-stop-at-just-one chocolate chip cookie you will happily burn your tongue on when the tray comes out of the oven. Bonus: Coconut oil is rumored to help speed up your metabolism. I'm not saying these cookies are healthy...but I'm not *not* saying it, either.

Attempting this recipe required a step outside my comfort zone. I tracked down unique ingredients. I diligently measured. I spent time and energy getting it right. That's when I knew just the hobby for the down-to-earth billionaire who can't keep himself from showing others how much he cares. And if a hero is going to bake you cookies, what better place to be served *said cookies* than by a picturesque waterfall? None, I say. (Well, okay, I can think of another location or two, but admit it, a waterfall is a pretty dang good choice.)

As you can imagine, Crickitt is beyond impressed. And when a rogue smear of chocolate lands on her lips, Shane is every bit the gentleman by—*ahem*—helping her remove the incriminating splotch. Alas, that's a story for another day. (Or, for chapter nineteen...)

I hope you enjoy losing yourself in the very real fantasy world of Shane and Crickitt. It was a world I happily immersed myself in while writing; a world I *still* imagine myself in whenever a certain rich, nutty, warm, homemade chocolate chip cookie is melting on my tongue.

Happy Reading!
www.jessicalemmon.com

*Jessica Lemmon*